CROWNING SOUL

CROWNING

SOUL

SAHIRA JAVAID

To receive special offers, bonus content,
and info on new releases
sign up to the author's newsletter
http://www.essentuatelife.com

To you. And to the you, who you will slowly reveal to yourself, being true to who you are.

What an achievement a book is, a magic box simultaneously holding the presence of the author and the wonders of the world. – Ivan Doic

Resurrect the dance
of life inside my heart
breathe love through the part
of me that wants to unravel,
let it spool out like sunlight
make the threads glow bright
for I will endure the fight
I wage against my very soul
for this compass needs a role

CHAPTER 1—UNINVITED GUEST

Nezha's gaze pierced through the crowd, the people and their conversations a thousand wings caught in a gale.

"Nuzha." Her aunt Lamis always called her that. A name meaning a promenade, as if Nezha were destined to leave Azzam Morocco on a path far greater and never miss the way. A place filled with flowers and sweets would be ideal to Nezha Zaman. "Ki Dayra?"

"I'm okay." Nezha tilted her head down with a reassuring smile. But her smile was a weapon, a tool, a bandage, spreading across her face with versatility. She could hardly breathe, but being around Aunt Lamis with her warm smile and fun nature, made it more tolerable. "The crowd's getting bigger…"

"Those prices would bring anyone in, even the world of the ghayb," Lamis said as she winked and passed Nezha with a pot of yellow flowers in her hands.

Unseen or not, Nezha wanted to make it through the day without having to force herself to breathe. She'd make it. She would. She always did.

A floral blend of roses and smoke filled Nezha's head as Lamis crossed to the front table. The scent had become a sense of comfort. It was Lamis's scent. Whenever Lamis was present, her cheery nature never failed to ease Nezha's tensed body if the crowds grew, or she had to force herself to breathe.

After a chocolate, she'd make it for sure. Nezha scooped her hand into a glass bowl. She unwrapped the red packaging of one of her childhood favorites, merendina: a sponge cake sandwiched between chocolate ganache and coated in dark chocolate. Soft, sweet and so good!

Okay, back to work again.

Nezha's heart hammered as she interacted with the people. Brothers and husbands made up most of the crowd. So many flowers passed her fingers she was sure they would soon sell out.

Lamis handed a bouquet of red, pink and yellow roses to a customer and bounced over to a watering can. "Could you get one of the lilies from outside?" Lamis's animation reminded Nezha of the white-winged wasp eater birds that roosted over the ancient ruins in the East.

"Yeah. Just don't over water the lilies, Lamis. I wouldn't want the leaves browned by tip burn." Nezha headed for the door. Lamis chuckled behind her.

Nezha's family owned the flower shop, Rhoda's Flowers. The anniversary and forty percent discount attracted crowds. Her father had left in the early morning to take their inventory to a botanical garden where they would hold the party. Her family was well-known to the neighborhood. At their shop, the fragrances of sugar, chocolate and spice would lift her lips into a smile and hush any intruding thought before it stole her peace.

Nezha stepped out to the display in front of the shop, where rows of rich-toned pots of browns and oranges topped with flowers. Atop one, a bumblebee sat, its legs decorated with fuzzy yellow balls of pollen. She watched as it hovered around another flower and then took to the sky. There, something caught her eye.

Her eyebrows raised at the way the darkness rolled, alive and breathing. Nezha's eyes fixed to the morning sky, where smoke whispered through the trees. Billowing in the wind like a satin dress, the smoke took the form of a dark figure among the branches.

Nezha's eyes narrowed. "What is that?" Could the branches or the sun's glare be obscuring her sight? She grabbed the pot and darted into the shop.

Just a shadow.

"Just in time, Nuzha!" Lamis reached for the pot.

Nezha handed it to her and swiftly turned to go behind their front desk. She couldn't waste time thinking about that shadow, even if it undulated in the breeze like a living thing.

A customer walked up to Nezha. "Do you have another fireweed plant?"

Nezha parted her lips. She handed the customer a flyer with a picture of the fireweed plant and its location. "Excuse me," she said, then rushed for Lamis and tapped her shoulder. She heard a "shukran" from the customer as she moved to the back of the shop.

Lamis took over. "How may I help you?"

***

She'd just take a minute. She couldn't leave her aunt out there alone, but Nezha needed a moment just to breathe. Whatever that thing was… she couldn't let the thought stop her from working. It must have been her eyes tricking her.

She'd been diligent all day, so it had to be the exhaustion making her see things.

Nezha turned to one of the flowers, the rose of Venezuela, and cupped her hand around its crimson, tubular petals. It had been watered earlier and still held drops that made it appear like plump fruit. Nezha held her face close and breathed in. Although they didn't have a scent, it quelled the bubble of anxiety in her chest. Somehow, it relaxed her tense shoulders. Warmth flooded her chest and the very tips of her fingers. A curl of fire grew in her palm. Nezha breathed out. She couldn't let the fire run free. Not when crowds of people were right outside the room. She inhaled and pressed her face to the petals and watched as the small flame flickered and vanished.

When she was a child, she had carried boxes of blooming flowers to their shop and sunk her fingers into the coolness of the soil. Every plant taught her how to withstand and make her path. Through the chill of fear, or the burning of anger, damp days filled with tears or dry days of a barren mind, they taught her never to give up. That even in the most inhospitable land, life found a way to fight its way in.

"Nuzha… What happened?" Lamis appeared behind her.

"I just needed to breathe for a moment. I'm okay now."
Nezha gave Lamis's arm a gentle squeeze and her aunt
returned it.

"That's my Nuzha, determined and capable." Lamis's
eyes held concern even though she smiled.

"It's my birthday tomorrow, so I should be getting
wiser," Nezha said with a grin.

"My Nuzha is truly a young woman now." Lamis looked
at Nezha with unfocused eyes, as if she were lost in
thoughts of Nezha when she was a child. She shook her
head. "Let's work."

Nezha readjusted her apron. "Yeah."

***

The door closed behind the last customer with a click.
Nezha placed her hands on her hips and blew out a sigh.

"Nezha, you looked overwhelmed earlier," Lamis said.

"Oh no, you said my actual name." Nezha grinned.

"Come on Nuzha, I know you." Lamis touched the top
of Nezha's head. "You've been keeping your distance from
people."

"I have my two best friends and *we* spend time
together." Nezha shrugged.

"Emotionally, not physically." Lamis took her apron off and hung it up. "If you promise to talk to me about it later, I'll make you an extra treat."

"That's not fair, you know my weakness." Nezha looked out the window. Three girls linked arms with each other and had big smiles on their faces. Their laughter was muffled through the glass. Nezha's gaze dropped, as did her heart. "Let's pack up." She turned to one of the boxes and closed the lid.

They packed up the rest of their inventory and hopped into the car.

The streets bustled with people. Saturday became alive with movement. Downtown was an artist's delight where colors and patterns embroidered buildings in geometric designs. Lined by palm trees, the road met with the heart of her city where the market square reigned. They tailed a car.

Most who strolled through the market wore embroidered kaftans and hooded djellabas. The traditional ways met the modern day.

They passed by stalls of food. Sweets were her weakness, like the creamy, flaky goodness of milk bastilla that melted in her mouth, and the warm softness of freshly baked pastries. She spotted three women with blue, white and green veils over their heads that draped down to their navels, drying their henna-adorned hands in the sun.

The market was its own story, the atmosphere rife with vendors crying their wares and folksingers pulling people in like sirens. Magicians, artists and snake charmers made them second-guess reality.

Tanneries lay out their dried leather to soak in the sun on the pavement. The color and vitality were a living pulse of their own.

Nezha lowered the car's window. The warm and spiced scent of the air wafted into the car. She closed her eyes for a moment as a smile curled over her face. Colorful ceramic bowls, artisanal lamps and handcrafted trinkets graced Nezha's eyes.

They turned the car into the parking lot of Jardine Rababi, the famous garden in the city of Azzam. When they got out of the car, Lamis opened her arms to Nezha's mother.

"As Salaamu Alaikum. How was the shop?" She embraced Lamis. Her mother wore a long red hijab over her dark brown hair. Part of the cloth tumbled forward as she hugged Lamis. Her umber eyes harbored a hint of concern as her gaze lingered on Nezha.

"Wa Alaikum as Salaam. It was good, dear." Aunt Lamis returned the greeting and smiled.

Nezha's father, Wasi, stood beside Lamis. "Sister, you look well." He patted the top of her head, ruffling her turquoise hijab and releasing strands of chestnut hair from underneath. He smiled at her. Even in forty years, the creases along his mouth revealed just how much he'd smiled. He never laughed too loudly. His walk was gentle like the sweeping sands to the South, as was his voice.

Lamis grinned and tucked her hair back in. "Have you been eating better, little brother?" She poked his side. "Looks like not enough."

Nezha's father gave a hearty smile.

"Nuzha, help me unload the car." Lamis walked to the back of their vehicle.

Nezha stood beside her as Lamis opened the trunk. On the right, boxes of yellow star fruits, strawberries, blueberries and melons were arranged to look like baskets of flowers.

On the left were two medium boxes of flowers. Nezha lifted the top box which held one of her favorites, the jade vine flower. Her fingers slipped over its waxy, turquoise flowers held by purple stems. It looked like a pendant, with the cluster flowing down. Nezha had been helping these flowers grow. These were high maintenance, needing full sun, copious amounts of water and fertile soil. She wanted the endangered flower to grow and thrive.

Her parents and aunt approached the building and entered the garden. She followed behind, clutching the box to her chest.

Above her, a cusped arch spilled with golden yellow. Calligraphy in red engraved the columns, showcasing the Moorish charm. Further down the bright orange-tiled lane followed another arch, whose blue and green melted into one another. To her right, a clear stream burbled by and the air carried a sugary fragrance. Cushioned with trees and flowing with ponds, this harmonious place was a retreat from the bustling city.

When Nezha reached the open door, something flickered in the corner of her eye. She snapped her head to the side. The shadow elongated into a figure, thin and inhuman. Nezha's pulse drummed in her neck. The form rolled over the leaves of the trees and disappeared, but Nezha continued to stare.

Something whispered, *fire elemental.*

She almost dropped the box.

How could it have known she was one? It had to be a shadow. Maybe the people and their voices were contorted by the mischievous wind. Her fingers shook over the woven wood. Not again. Just a shadow. It had to be. Nezha walked over the black flooring crisscrossed with taupe diamonds.

She placed the box on one of the long white tables and blew out a sigh. *By the Most High!* She let the view of the grand room sink in. The decorations in shades of blue and green made the room pop with life. Beside her a medium-sized pond gurgled with a stone waterfall. Koi fish swam within. The skylight above their heads welcomed the sun's splendid light.

"What do you think, Nezha?" Her mother asked her.

"It's great." Nezha's voice cracked. She turned to her father just as he brought in more boxes. Another man assisted him in laying the boxes on the tables to the left of the room. "Aunt Lamis, I'm so excited!"

"For the milk bastilla?"

"Oh yes."

Milk bastilla was always sweeter when she got to eat it with Aunt Lamis. Only with her.

Nezha's gaze glided over the walls and decoration. On the ceiling was a dome light with smaller lights circling it, winking like scattered stars. Lamis placed a box on the dining table and opened it. Nezha walked over to the different dishes. All those scents! She couldn't wait to eat. The marriage of sweet and warm smells carried a familiar comfort. "Your homemade milk bastilla?"

There was nearly nothing in the world that made Nezha happy like her aunt's homemade treats, except maybe a trip to her favorite garden, La Jardine Juniper. Not much could match the glow of the sunset when it lit the mountain range.

"Yes, always, Nuzha. Is that all you see?" Lamis hugged Nezha with one arm.

The other unsealed box consisted of roasted lamb shoulders and vegetables, couscous with vegetables, chicken with preserved lemons and a chickpea and carrot tagine. Her mother brought even more food. Thanks to her mother's Pakistani heritage, there were samosas, and biryani with chicken and beef curry.

Pakistani sweets—mithai—were as heavenly as her beloved milk bastilla. Bright pink chum chum dripping with sugar syrup, gulab jamun, sat next to them; golden-brown balls of fluffy, rose goodness. And they couldn't celebrate without ladoos! She couldn't forget those soft squares of barfi, or the orange, swirly wreaths of jalebis, crunchy on the outside and chewy on the inside.

Her gaze shifted to the windows. Was the shadow still there?

By the late morning, guests filled the building.

Nezha could finally eat. The thought of that strange shadow couldn't erase her hunger. She grabbed one of each treat and placed them on her plate, balancing them over a foam container full of savory dishes. Soda, orange juice and mint chai filled decorative stained glasses. Nezha could probably eat half of everything.

She picked up the milk bastilla. Her taste buds welcomed the crunchy layer of warqa sheets and savored the light and creamy orange blossom filling. She grabbed a napkin and nudged Lamis with her elbow, walking with her to the dining area. "Aunt Lamis."

Lamis smiled. "Coming, Nuzha darling."

Nezha consumed her treats, thankful no cream or sticky syrup stained her kaftan. The fluid belted tunic ran down to her ankles and was only worn during special occasions. This one in particular was given to her by Lamis herself. Golden embroidery spotted the cream-yellow fabric and gilded it with lace. Nezha wore a deep orange hijab wrapped around her head which fell over her chest and covered her hair.

She stood to welcome the guests. To the right of the room was a small stage. One man was positioning a podium in the front and another was behind the scene, inspecting the wiring. As Nezha walked past them, a shadow hovered over her. She jerked her head up, only to see a brown bird land on the glass. It jumped for a few seconds before fluttering off, casting a shadow over her. Another shadow followed, slower and fluid, it hovered over the glass. The top of it formed inky blots like a head and shoulders. There was no bird connected to it this time. Nezha's heart leapt into her throat. Could it be a jinni? They were made of smokeless fire. People who swore they saw the beings, said the jinn were humanoid shadows.

Jinn were beings which were known to her people. They existed. Humans prohibited interacting with the jinn. Why was she seeing them now? Seeing them was a sign of having darkness inside you. They tended to inhabit desolate and rundown places. The building wasn't abandoned. There was no bleeding ache of sorrow or stench of corruption.

"Nezha, we're heading to the stage soon. Bring your plant," Her mother said as she approached her.

"Yeah, ma. I'll be there in a minute." Nezha's gaze returned to the glass, but there was nothing there now.

"See you soon." Nezha's mother pursed her lips and headed to the stage, accompanied by her husband.

Nezha and her parents welcomed everyone on the stage. She held the jade vine flower, a smile on her face. People cheered as her father thanked the people and said, "Shukran for attending our anniversary for our shop, Rhoda's Flowers. We are grateful to serve you with our edible arrangements and beautiful flowers. Welcome this new plant, the jade vine flower, to the garden. I hope we enjoy more years to come."

***

It was almost time for the picnic. Guests congratulated her parents. Nezha became drawn to a large skylight near the ceiling. Her eyes searched for the shadow but only took in the birds collecting around a fountain.

Nezha smiled as three women walked over to congratulate her. That's when she saw it. A flower blooming inside a maze garden. Its magenta petals and yellow center caught the sun's rays so vividly; she knew she had to get a closer look. "Baba, I want to explore a bit. I'll be right back."

"Oh. Have fun," her father said with a smile.

Her mother gave her a small wave.

Nezha pushed through the crowd to reach the back door to the gardens. A colonnade of five marble and steel trellises invited her into the main garden. There were flower beds of roses and lilies, some of which she recognized from her family's shop. She ambled along the rows, the scents clinging to her every movement.

She entered the maze. No one else was around. Myriad flowers braided the hedges of the maze. Nezha could peek over them to see the entrance if she balanced on her tiptoes. She bent over to touch the petals of the magenta flower. A dark haze slid by the corner of her eye, and cold rushed all over her.

Nezha's breath hitched.

That low voice entered her mind. *Fire elemental.* A tendril of flames curled from her palm.

Someone was watching her.

CHAPTER 2—THE MENACING SHADOW

Nezha stared as the shadowy figure made its appearance a few feet away. It stared back at her. Its hand rose, blurring like mist to brush the hood of its draping cloak aside. It looked human, but its skin was tinged in gray.

Her feet were glued to where she stood.

Could it be a shaitan or jinni? If this thing harmed her, it could be a shaitan: an evil jinni. Nezha met his intense gaze.

Before today, she'd never seen him or anything like it before. The way he looked at her with so much hatred made her feel sick.

No. Not the fire.

She didn't want the fire to burn. Her nerves sparked and heat radiated through her chest. Adrenaline coursed through her body, and it was the fire that surged through her arms.

The conjured flames grew and fire danced around her trembling hands, the very flames she'd been trying her hardest to smother all day. To keep them dormant.

The figure grinned and his head leaned back to look down on her.

In the blink of an eye, the figure now stood closer to her. Nezha flinched and clenched her hands into fists.

The figure greeted her with a tip of his head and a touch of his brow. "Even your eyes are lit embers. Rimmed in kohl, I see. I'd delight in turning them all black." The being's red piercing eyes bore into hers. "Such heavy footfalls, and a raging fire... I assumed you were going to attack me."

He chuckled. He looked like a young man. He had an oval face and sharp jawline. His golden blond hair reminded Nezha of sand dunes. He wore two light emerald cuff bracelets around his wrists, as if he were some brilliantly colored poisonous animal. Attractive but deadly.

Nezha couldn't move. She breathed heavily and her brow furrowed. "Who are you? What are you?"

The shadow rippled and disappeared.

Flames entwined her fingers, leaving Nezha's nerves on edge.

"Hey." The voice came from behind her and was loud but with a softer, breathier tone.

Nezha spun. A lopsided grin pulled up one side of his face, revealing sharp teeth.

She fled. Her eyes stung, and her chest tightened. Every corner she turned, the figure appeared. Her heart stuck to her ribs, and her muscles burned. She needed to get out of here. *Jinn. He's a jinni. What do the jinn want from me?* Nezha took in a quivering breath and was up on her tiptoes. She ran. Her gaze fell to the fire, coiling about her arms and slipping over her palms. A hissing snake.

She was not afraid of its fangs, the heat which never affected her, but the squeeze of anger—the sinuous coil which would grip her heart. The rage in her would spill over like poison. That was one thing Nezha never accepted about herself. When threatened, she owned the cruelty of a puncturing voice, the devouring blow.

Caught between two worlds, how unfortunate. The being's voice echoed.

Two worlds? I am, aren't I? Having powers in a world where people would fear her. She had to hide them.

Nezha pressed her arms to her body, fearing that she would ignite the maze. It was not an easy task. Unsteady, her hands were like the tail of a rattlesnake warning others to stay away.

Fire essence. Fire jawhar. Run wild... let the fire feed. Faster and faster.

His voice came from either side of her. His growl grew louder behind her as she neared the entrance.

Careful of the shadows your light casts. We are waiting behind them.

The figure vanished just as Nezha turned around. She slumped her shoulders. The fire about her disappeared.

"Nezha?"

Nezha turned, her heart thudding. It was her mother who stood at the entrance of the maze.

She had made it.

"Are you okay?" Her mother scanned Nezha's wide eyes and then to her whole face.

"Y- yeah, I got lost in the maze. Forget it." That was half true. A mixture of relief and worry weighed in her mother's eyes. Nezha could feel the sting of tears in her own.

"Well, you're with me now." She gave Nezha's hand a gentle squeeze, her face softening.

"Tusi fikr na karo—" Don't worry. Nezha forced a smile. Her fingers curled around her mother's arm as if she were a sturdy gate in the garden.

She couldn't involve her parents. Seeing jinn was no laughing matter. Rumors said it was a sign of being corrupted, a warning of the jinn wanting to harm you.

"Everyone's getting ready for the picnic in the gazebo. Let's go and enjoy the company," her mother said.

Nezha glanced back at the maze. She couldn't shake the experience from her mind and body. The fire's display played through her. Wherever she looked, the shadows would be there, the jinn's piercing gaze a threat.

***

By noon, they drove beside the souks—the winding alleyways. With the windows down, Nezha leaned into the wind. The satisfaction of tailoring an item with your own hands owned its own kind of magic. Vibrant blues, oranges and reds, the sounds of conversation, the rumbling of motorbikes and the squeaking wheels of mobile stalls filled in the orchestra of men and women. They imbued their care and passion into their handcrafted charms and dishware which hung over the walls of shops like shining gems.

Nezha had arrived home. She watched the flower petals from the orange trees swirl by their door, slipping off the bronze-plated number seventeen. Their car turned to their lot on Rue Khairan Bani Faiz. As she stepped out of the car, something up in the trees caught her attention. Orange light peeked through the branches, glowing over a shadow which floated above the leaves, taking the shape of a human. The same jinni in the maze. The image of the hooded figure was now ingrained in her mind.

No. No. No. Her eyes widened. She turned her face away and rushed toward the door. A chill prickled along the back of her neck.

"Nezha?" Her mother was at the door, keys jingling in her hand.

Nezha strode past her mother and hung up her hijab on a hook. She slipped her shoes off, shoved them to the side with her foot and went inside. Her chest was tight. As she ran up the stairs, a flicker of flames danced around her fingers as she gripped the railing.

It had followed her.

Shadows plunged into crevices and corners and a wavering light dabbed at the concrete outside her window.

Nezha slammed her bedroom door. Her head reclined back, falling against the door. She heaved a sigh and imagined the fire dying out. She held her breath, a technique she'd taught herself, and watched as the fire around her hand died. Nezha took a breath. Her back slid down the door.

She was holding her breath in again. She couldn't risk a fire inside. Not ever again.

When she was overemotional, Nezha made things burn or light up. It was always her emotions. She wanted to be more collected, like…

Lamis whisked by her mind. *Aunt Lamis. Maybe I should talk to her.*

A knock tore her from her thoughts.

Nezha moved from in front of the door and sat on her bed. "Come in."

Her mother opened the door.

"Nezha, did you enjoy the party?"

"It was fine," Nezha sat down on her bed.

"I noticed you weren't yourself this afternoon."

She took her place beside her daughter. "Is there anything you want to talk about?"

"Well…" Nezha turned her head away. How could she even explain how she was feeling? She couldn't tell her mother what happened. Whenever her parents found anything burned, they would hide her away.

"Nothing really." Nezha looked up at her.

Her mother's eyes gleamed with tears.

"Wait..."

"Nezha, beti," Najwa said in a hushed tone. "Your father and I want you to know we're here for you. If anything is bothering you, I'll listen. We want to protect you. Tanu Khush dekh ne vate"—to see you happy.

Najwa closed her eyes and frowned.

She knew her mother meant it when she slipped into Punjabi. He parents listened to her, but they never helped her with the flames. Nezha pursed her lips, and her breath quickened. "Kadi madat?" What help? "Show me if you mean it!" She stood from her bed and formed fists.

Her mother's eyes widened. A part of Nezha heated up in shame. Her mother said, "From... anything that bothers you, Nezha. You know we're here—"

"Just, please, good night." Nezha turned to her bed and bit the inside of her lip.

Her mother stood. "Goodnight." She left the room.

Nezha sighed. She closed her eyes. It happened again. This time as her anger melted, she regretted what she had said. Her irritation had blinded her. She crossed to her door, and before she could close it, Lamis had her hand on the side.

"Knock, knock." Lamis grinned at Nezha's widened expression.

"Ah, Aunt Lamis, what the hell?" Nezha's hand grabbed at her chest.

Lamis laughed. "Sorry, didn't think you'd be against the door. I just wanted to say goodnight."

"Oh... I want to talk to you about something." Nezha gestured for her to come in and sit down.

"Is this to do with why you were so distant this morning?" Lamis glanced around the room as she took a seat on the bed. She placed a silver box beside her.

"Looking for someone?"

Nezha raised her arched eyebrows and then took her place beside her aunt. In Lamis's company, Nezha could speak louder and be herself.

"Yes, where is the little firecracker?" Lamis put her hand in a bag and pulled out a box.

"She should be somewhere around here." Nezha peeked under the bed and made a clicking sound with her tongue.

A blur of nutmeg spots slunk by Nezha's feet and jumped up on Lamis's lap.

"Comet!" Nezha said in alarm and placed her hands on her small hips. That cat was like an apparition. Countless times, Comet had startled her until flames would burst from Nezha's head. She was thankful the cat was never injured.

"Hey there, feisty one." Lamis scratched the Bengal behind her milk chocolate ears. Comet's vibrant blue eyes closed as she nuzzled into Lamis's palm.

"Looks like she's happy to see you too." Nezha's fingers glided over the thick velvety fur and glittering rosettes as Comet arched her back and meowed.

Nezha lowered herself beside Lamis.

"So..."

Lamis tilted her head. "It's the fire again, isn't it?"

Nezha nodded. Aunt Lamis always masked her abilities with perfume so no one could tell she smelled like smoke and char. "You helped me hide my fire when I was little, and you're good at hiding yours. But recently, I've been getting more stressed."

"What's bothering you, Nuzha?" Lamis touched Nezha's shoulder.

"I think I need to vent."

When Nezha was a little girl, it was a weekly occurrence for her flames to burn different places in their home. Her parents would clean the smudges of soot on the walls and the char in the carpet. She got angry when they told her to stay inside when she wanted to go out and play. She wanted them just once to tell her not to do it again. Anything to make her believe they understood her. Anything to make her think she was not a secret to keep. Lamis was the one who told her to be careful, who tried to teach her to control the flames.

"Is it fear? Or is it the fact that you have to hide it?" Lamis kept her eyes on Nezha's as she lifted her hand and flames bloomed from her palms. The light made her short brown hair glow with strands of red. She shrugged, a playful smile on her face. "Fire isn't just a wild force bent on destruction. It's a source of light too, Nuzha." Lamis added with a wink.

"Yeah... I know."

"We could set the sky on fire and wear the light like a crown."

"Yeah, that's what you used to tell me," Nezha sighed. "Aunt Lamis, I'm sick of hiding this part of me. My parents know I'm a fire jawhar, but they won't accept it. Who am I? Where do I belong?"

Lamis wrapped her arms around Nezha's shoulders and held her close. "They love you as you are, Nuzha. Sometimes, we break, only to see the pieces we were blind to. The pieces we needed to lose and the ones we need to keep. You belong, Nezha. There is a place for you." In a hushed voice, she said, "There's a world where you'll feel like you belong. One day, you'll find it. You'll enter that place and find yourself accepted as a fire jawhar. You'll never need to hide."

Nezha cracked a smile. She wasn't sure what Lamis meant by the last part and, frankly, she was too exhausted to work it out. "Thank you." But how was she supposed to tell her the rest? The jinni. That jinni was after her. Nezha's fingers tightened around Lamis's shoulders. She couldn't let it hurt them. She couldn't tell her aunt and endanger her whole family. They didn't even have powers, and she couldn't control hers to protect them.

"Of course. And I think you poked one of my kidneys," Lamis said.

"Sorry." Nezha reached her arm out to pet Comet's arching back. The cat's head rubbed against Nezha's arm. Comet knew just when Nezha needed comfort.

"I haven't given you your gift yet, Nuzha." Lamis handed her a box.

Nezha took the small box and stripped the silver wrapping paper away. Inside the box was a hair clip. The exquisite etched rose design was marred by tiny scratches.

"It's to tame your long hair." Lamis smiled. "This is an heirloom that belonged to your great grandmother."

"It's beautiful, Aunt Lamis." Nezha ran a finger over the rose design. "Was she a fire jawhar too?" Her eyes softened.

"Yes." A shine gleamed in Lamis's eyes. "As powerful as she was compassionate. Now it's yours, so don't let anyone else touch it."

"Don't worry, I won't."

Nezha twisted her golden-brown locks into a bun and clicked the clip into place.

"I like how you do that without a mirror," Aunt Lamis teased and then picked up a crinkly toy from the ground and placed it in front of Comet, who began swatting it.

"It looks beautiful on you, my sweet girl. Like a crown." Lamis's face lit up in an admiring smile.

Nezha winked and tickled Comet's belly.

"Tesbah ala kheyr, Nuzha." Lamis kissed Nezha's forehead and switched off the lights.

"Goodnight." Nezha turned to her side in bed.

Comet sniffed at Nezha's forehead before slinking down to Nezha's legs to knead them with her paws.

"You sweetie." Her voice was lax, just as her mind was. That talk with Lamis gave Nezha much-needed peace of mind. She relaxed into her warm blankets. "Only you, God and Lamis understand me." She closed her eyes.

The next day, pastel shades of pinks and purples painted the evening sky. Wasi and Najwa stood by their front door. They had said their goodbyes to Lamis. Although Lamis lived a few blocks away, it always felt like years to Nezha.

"I'm going to miss you." Nezha's voice was hushed.

"Nuzha darling, I'll be back tomorrow." Lamis embraced her. Her hold was tight and warm.

Nezha held on tightly and breathed deeply. "I know. But..."

"Don't stuff yourself with too much milk bastilla, all right?" Lamis's lips lifted into a cheeky smile.

"I can't help it." Nezha nudged her. "I love you, Aunt Lamis."

"I love you too, Nuzha." She swept her fingers through Nezha's hair one last time, then slipped into her car where her husband was waiting. He waved to Nezha, and they drove off.

***

The shadowy figure stood behind the car as it drove off, his blond hair turned bronze by the dying light. Motionless as a statue, the demonic being's eyes glowed red as he suppressed his laugh. The sun lowered in the sky as if it, too, did not want to witness the frightening shadows gaping behind its light.

The Zaman family had been under surveillance. *Foolish humans. Shadows accompany the light.* He would continue stalking his prey. Placing the plans of his lady into motion, beyond the veil of the worlds. To the world where fire jawhars had prodded the anger within him to roil and gasp to life.

"My lady is eager to curse their fate." The shadow oozed like ink. "Fire jawhar... we shall be waiting."

Its lips stitched into a grim smile. Content, it shrunk into the night.

CHAPTER 3—SLUMBER IS DEATH'S PREREQUISITE

The ringing phone echoed through the house.

"Wasi dear, could you get that? I'm fixing Nezha's tunic." Nezha's mother was in the living room working with a needle and thread.

"Okay, I'll get it." Nezha's father dried his hands on the towel in the kitchen and headed for the phone. "Ahlan, Wasi speaking." Then silence won again as he listened. This silence was broken by the phone slamming on its receiver.

"Wasi? What happened? I—" Nezha's mother turned to him.

Wasi's eyes widened, and his lips formed a trembling frown as he bent over the kitchen table. "It was the hospital…"

As Wasi explained the situation, Najwa's face paled. She dropped her sewing supplies and rushed to the back door, where Nezha was out back gardening.

"Nezha, we need to go!" her mother called her from the back door.

"Ma? What happened?" She tossed her watering can aside and rushed inside to pull on a hijab.

***

At the hospital, the bright lights and the heavy scent of iodoform assaulted Nezha's eyes and nose. Her parents still hadn't told her what happened. Bile rose in her throat. The nurse led them to a hallway. There by the doors at the end of the hallway, her uncle paced. He had a gauze wrapped around his arm and a bandage on his forehead.

Her mother held Nezha's shoulder and pushed her to the bench.

"Your uncle and Lamis were in an accident." Her mother closed her eyes, pain straining her features. "Their car crashed into a tree."

Nezha jolted upwards and rushed over to the nurse.

"Please sir, you need to rest," the nurse said as she neared Nezha's uncle.

"I just need to see her," he pleaded through his tears.

Nezha's head ached as they stood at the open door. *Oh God, please let her be okay.*

"You can see her now." The nurse gestured to the door. When Nezha walked into the room, a shiver surged down her back.

Her aunt lay there, a snowy blanket over her. She looked like she was sleeping. Her familiar cheeky smile was still gently present on her lips.

"Aunt Lamis." Nezha's voice quaked with desperation. She and her father rushed to the bedside.

"Nuzha..." Lamis spoke, and her hand clasped around Nezha's.

"Aunt Lamis..." Nezha leaned in. Feeling her warm touch was good.

"Don't forget. Set the sky on fire. Wear the light like a crown." She pointed to her head with a shaky finger.

"I won't forget. Aunt Lamis... you'll be okay."

"Be a light. The other dimension needs you, Nuzha."

Lamis closed her eyes and brought her hand to her chest.

Just then, the machine's alarm went off. Nezha stood up and gaped at the machines next to her. She didn't let go of Lamis's hand.

"What's that sound?" Her mother asked.

The nurse rushed to the machines and took hold of Lamis's wrist. For a moment, the room stilled—a slow hum occupying the space. The nurse pursed her pink lips, and her fingers slipped from Lamis's arm. The nurse hit the emergency button and pushed everyone out of the room.

"Wait! What—" Nezha turned to Lamis, but her mother put an arm around her shoulders to stop her.

The doctor and nurse rushed past with a crash cart in tow.

Nezha's breath quickened. She held onto her mother's arm and placed her head on her father's shoulder. No. No, they had to save her. Maybe they were injecting something into her or giving her oxygen. Nezha needed Lamis.

Lamis would wake up. She had to.

***

They'd been there for only God knew how long. Nezha paced.

The door opened and the doctor came out, sweat glistening on his forehead. He pulled his mask down and shook his head. The electrocardiograph machine had flatlined.

They couldn't save her.

He spoke to the nurse and left.

"I'm sorry," the nurse said. "Please take your time to say goodbye," she said, solemnly.

Nezha's father rushed into the room. He took his sister's limp hand in his.

"Lamis? Lamis? Sister, please. Lamis!" His cries tore through the room. He slumped to his knees.

"Nezha, Wasi…" Her mother pressed her hand to her mouth, tears spilling over her jawline. She rushed to her husband's side and put a hand on his shoulder. Wasi entwined his fingers with hers, his gaze glued to Lamis, and continued his cries.

Her uncle stood beside her and Wasi. He brushed back a piece of Lamis's hair and kissed her forehead. His movements were mechanical as he sobbed.

"Aunt Lamis?" The hand Nezha held was cold. "No, she's sleeping," Nezha's voice trembled, nervous laughter escaping her breath. "She can't be gone." Nezha jostled Lamis's shoulder. Hollow emptiness grew in her stomach. Lamis was gone. Lamis was gone? She let go of her aunt's hand and broke into sobs. Her body collapsed over her aunt's chest.

Smoke. The familiar smell of char comforted her. She touched Lamis's hand again and saw it. Char on her fingertips. Had Lamis used her fire? Had something attacked her? Did she fight someone? Something?

Her father's fingers gently gripped Nezha's shoulder.

"No dear, don't hurt... more." His voice was raw and husky. He could hardly form a sentence.

Nezha's stomach wrenched. She put a hand to her mouth, ran to the bathroom adjacent to the bed and retched.

When she came out of the bathroom, her arms were limp at her sides. She stood by Lamis's bed once more and lowered her eyes. The sides of Nezha's eyes were red, and her gut was icy cold. It was as if the fire inside her was reduced to coal.

All she could think of was the time she'd never get to spend with her aunt. She'd never again help her make treats or sit together in the garden. Never laugh with her. Never get annoyed at her pranks. She would never call her Nuzha again. It wasn't just sadness that she felt. *How could this have happened?* Her breath was unsteady and her hands formed fists. The coal became a glowing cinder ready to ignite once again.

The machines in the room began to beep, then fizz and spark.

It's not the machines... it's me. Nezha looked down at her hands. Heat radiated through her body. Sparks danced about the wires. A flame erupted from the monitor.

"Fire!"

A nurse rushed to Lamis's bed. Everyone pushed out the door, but Nezha remained inside. The nurses scrambled to push Lamis's bed out the room, but Nezha stood in their way.

"You can't take her!" Nezha fell across Lamis's chest and shook her head. "Please. Don't take the only person that truly believes in me!"

The nurses both frowned at her as her mother held her shoulders.

"Nezha, please don't hurt yourself." Najwa's voice trembled.

"No! They can't take her! Lamis..." The hallway was spinning, and whatever was in it looked like it was rippling. The muffled voices of the nurses' soothing words fell upon her ears as they pulled her off Lamis. Alarms blared repeatedly until they just seemed like a distant hum.

"You can't. No! Lamis! Lamis..." Nezha fell to her knees and hid her face in her hands.

It was all a blur to Nezha as the doctor spoke to Wasi, his voice a hush, his eyes swollen. One nurse brought in a fire extinguisher, flooding the side of the room with a sea of white foam. A whispered verse reached her ears. "Inna lillahi wa inna ilayhi raji uun." *Indeed, to God we belong, and truly, to Him, we shall return.* She whispered it under her breath. Whenever anyone suffered a loss, the verse passed their lips.

Nezha could hardly stand when she lifted herself off the ground. She dropped onto the bench by the door. Her uncle was beside her. "What happened, uncle?" Nezha wasn't asking. It was more of an order.

Her uncle swallowed and faced her, his head low, his round face pale. "I... a man appeared in the middle of the road. I swerved, and before I could gain control, we were off the road and smashed into a tree."

He started to sob again.

"What did he look like?" Nezha rubbed his shoulder.

"I don't know. I can't..."

"I'm sorry uncle. Please, try to remember."

"Blond hair. I remember blond hair."

Nezha froze. *Blond? That shadow had blond hair. But that thing, it was threatening me. It wanted Aunt Lamis all this time. What if I'm next?* Nezha couldn't be sure who it was. All she knew was that the shadow, the shaitan, had blond hair.

"What did he look like?"

Her uncle sniffled. "Just darkness, blond hair."

Nezha's head fell to his shoulder, and she gritted her teeth. The words Lamis had said burned into her soul. She'd never forget them. She'd set the whole world on fire and wear the damn thing like a crown to light the way if it meant she'd find the one responsible for Lamis's death.

***

Nezha was up early in the morning, her cream blanket wrapped around her waist. The small kink on the left side of her mattress pressed against her thigh. Her half-eaten breakfast consisting of a baguette, olive oil to dip and mint chai lay on the small wooden table to her right. Her laptop was open in front of her. On the screen, a video played. Nezha was about five years old in it. She was walking in a mall, a vanilla ice cream cone in one hand, licking the sweet creamy coldness.

Lamis grinned at her, pulled out a napkin and had wiped her nose. "You're so messy."

Nezha giggled as Lamis patted her head and kissed her forehead.

The screen buffered and another video played. They were in the park. Her parents were holding six-year-old Nezha's hands, walking up to Lamis, who was sitting on a

40

bench. They sat beside her. Lamis revealed a tin with milk bastilla from her maroon handbag.

"Auntie, is that the bastilla we made today?" Nezha chirped.

Lamis chuckled. "Yes, and we need to share it with everyone. We can't keep it for ourselves, my little Nuzha. Sweet things are meant to be shared."

Nezha clicked out of the video and closed her laptop. She'd been watching them all morning, replaying the memories until they hurt. Her eyes became blurry, glossed by her tears. She wiped them away and stood.

Nezha headed to the kitchen, her chest heavy; her jaw clenched. She opened the fridge and took a piece of chocolate cake and milk bastilla and swiped a spoon. Nezha closed the door and exhaled a shaky breath. Her back slid down the fridge. She sat on the floor and spooned the milk bastilla into her mouth. The creamy, crispy comfort was a warm embrace, the sweetness filling in the void of loss. Bastilla could not match the warm hugs from Lamis, her cheerful energy, her vibrant laugh or her kind and comforting smile. *Aunt Lamis, I miss you.*

She hated that she couldn't resist eating so much bastilla. This was the last one in the fridge. Her parents wanted to stop literally feeding her addiction. They wanted her to do the things she enjoyed. Planting and tending flowers, working at the shop, painting the sunset, even learning martial arts. But drowning in memories of Lamis was all she could do. It had been three weeks since Lamis's funeral. Her parents were right, she still had the memories and her love for Lamis.

"Nezha?" Her mother walked into the kitchen. "Nezha meri jaan—my love."

Nezha stood. Her mother placed her plates on the counter.

Najwa pulled Nezha into a hug.

"Ma, I miss her." Nezha's throat closed up, tears gleaming in her eyes. She tightened her arms around her mother.

"Me too, jaan. Me too."

"I want to make more prayers for her, with you and baba." Nezha looked into her mother's eyes, finding them shining with tears too. While Lamis could not hear Nezha anymore, all Nezha could do was pray for her. Pray for mercy and happiness. Pray, even if the emptiness would not fill in with Lamis's warm cheeky smiles or the bastilla she lovingly baked with Nezha.

"Of course." Her mother's voice cracked.

Nezha swallowed, willing the tears and emotions down. To make sure the flames would not unfurl as she embraced her mother.

"Your grandfather will be here soon. How about we get some mithai?" Her mother pressed a hand to Nezha's cheeks, wiping away her tears.

Nezha smiled faintly. "Sure."

She grabbed her cardigan and headed for the door. Ever since Aunt Lamis died, family members had been visiting them to pay their respects. She was done crying and moping around the house. It didn't mean she had stopped hurting, though. But she adored her grandfather, too. She wouldn't let him see her so depressed.

Eisen Ibn Hariz's eyes reflected in a shard of metal. His blood had stained his purple jalabiya. It had speckled the word embellished in Arabic on the front of his garment from right to left, fastened with silver buttons. Hadid. The word for iron. The element he could manipulate. His own element had betrayed him and the Fire Kingdom mansion, now strewn across the field like a shattered vase.

The Fire court had been called the jewel of Noorenia. The country of Wadi Alma was known as the Fire Kingdom.

It was far from the more urban city of Equus, where the hustle and bustle of the gem transportation vehicles and the noise of people juxtaposed the serenity of the meadow neighboring the kingdom.

The doors had had a cinquefoil arch, painted in a red so vivid it glittered in the sun's light. It had marked the household as royalty. Patterns of lattice and ogee had bordered the doors in gold and white.

The ruling kingdom had played a vital role in the War of Jahalia, bringing peace back to their nation and sending aid to the other countries across the world.

All that remained of the manor now was the iron spikes protruding from the earth and the foundation of the mansion like the teeth of a creature belonging to the jinn.

The dark clouds above him cloaked the sun from the tragedy.

His beloved, Sanari, lay beside him. His jalabiya had been tattered by the iron as he'd protected her with his own body.

Parts of her body were encased with iron. A splash of iron coated her jawline, stark against the tinge of pink under her fawn skin. Her long fuchsia tunic looked like armor that Sanari would wear whenever she'd defended her kingdom from mischievous jinn.

Eisen raised his hand and tried to pull the iron from her. It wouldn't budge. Not one ripple. "No..." Tears rolled down his cheeks. "Please, iron. Please, Creator, help me!"

He punched the ground. "Please, Creator, don't take her from me. She's all I have."

Eisen's heart thudded. His mind went numb to the pain aching in his body. "I don't want this life! Sanari. Sanari!" Anger and agony twisted in his voice. A heaviness pulled at Eisen's chest. *All I wanted was to be with Sanari. How did this happen?*

"Prince Eisen, are you lost?" a feminine voice called out.

He spun around. A jinni appeared behind him.

Eisen stumbled back. Darkness like smoke bloomed around her body.

"Why are you here, jinni?" His voice was raw and hushed. *Why did it happen?* A shiver coursed down his spine, casting a sea of cold into his belly. He frowned and sat where he was. His muscles denied him any function.

"I smelled the heady scent of loss and followed it to you. Do you want to change. To be stronger?" the jinni inquired. *That's right. I'm all alone.* Stars sparkled and popped in Eisen's vision. For a split-second, he wished he were lost in the vastness of this space, falling into dreams. He'd be safe there. "I… I was weak. I can't protect Sanari like this. I can't be anything without her." His mind was clouded with all the thoughts repeating in his head. The thoughts of

Sanari who smiled at him so warmly, and her laying beside him, his iron trying to consume her.

*****

The jinni with blond hair peeked from behind a jagged marble wall. Going through the dimensions was as simple as parting a curtain. The palpitating agony of the jawhars from both worlds filled the earth beneath him. The whine of energy a muffled cry. It filled his heart with anticipation. Soon. Soon it would be his next move. To play the game of vengeance. The prince, a knight. All that was left was the next pawn. The jinni lifted a brow and grinned.

*****

"I see. I can lead you whichever way, either aright or astray." The female jinni snickered. "With a new life, you must have a new name. You will no longer be Eisen. You are… you are Zul. Zul Sharr. Possessor of evil. Demonic energy will course through your blood, unless you have a change of heart. I'm Lexa of the shadow jinn. Do you accept your new name?"

She licked her lips, eager to take hold of his heart.

"La'a." Eisen breathed out, but the look on her face showed him she didn't believe his refusal. Eisen gulped.

"Your tongue may lie, but your eyes certainly speak volumes." The jinni tipped her head.

47

"I… accept." Eisen shivered. This was wrong, but he had no choice. He never did. "I don't want to live that life anymore. It's too much pain." Memories of his mother's grimace, her nails scratching his neck, her callous words cutting like daggers in his heart. "I want to become a strong king, not a weak prince. Princess Sanari is my only peace."

Lexa grinned. "Prince, your heart is as strong as iron, your hatred and yearning in a dance for power." Her red hair bounced as she met his gaze. Curls like fire lapped at the rounds of her shoulders. Her round vibrant green eyes mocked him.

"So, you're certain you want this? Young prince, I need your confirmation once more." She placed a hand to her hip. Her long georgette kameez touched the ground. It was enhanced with patch border work, embroidery of resham, zari and sequins, all shimmering in brown. Her shoulders peeked through elbow-length sleeves, her fair skin tinged with gray.

Eisen gulped. "Yes."

He had to. He couldn't break the curse on Sanari like this, especially as he had no idea how his iron became wild and destroyed Sanari's mansion. He'd get power, break the curse and be the king Sanari deserved.

The jinni's lips parted and a small grin curled up her face as she held him up and embraced him. She became translucent.

His eyes widened, every cell in his body sent into animation. His veins pulsed, the vibration racing through his body in a dance. An icy touch bloomed from where she held him, slowly fading into euphoria. He sighed and she let him go. With a soft sound, he fell to his knees. His brown eyes lit up in orange and a hunger clenched his heart.

"Welcome to your new life, Zul Sharr." Lexa looked down at him, biting her finger. The demonic aura was perfumed by his hatred and longing.

Zul covered his face with his hands. The scent of saffron and vanilla filled his head. His black hair fell upon his forehead like a raven's wing. A sudden fiery passion grew in his heart. He sat up, raised his head and smirked. "I think 'sire' is more befitting." His eyes glowed as if they mirrored the birth of the pyre lit in his heart.

He craned his neck. A burning sensation crept over his skin. He struggled to tug at his collar and revealed his neck and chest. Between rasps, he spoke,

"What... happened?"

He touched his skin, but he didn't feel anything there.

Lexa snapped her fingers. A dark mirror appeared in her hand. Zul Sharr turned his face upward to reveal his neck. Black lines ran across his skin like raised veins.

"Ghadab?" The Arabic word for anger in cursive stretched out to form the image of a scorpion on his skin.

"You give and take. So I've marked you. Anger connects us." Lexa sneered.

The tip of the scorpion's stinger was above his heart and its claws stretched over his neck, the thick black lines running over his jugular vein.

Zul Sharr exhaled through his nose. His shoulders slumped.

"The one who carries mercy will only get in your way." Lexa sat on her knees and leaned in, her face a few inches from his cheek. Her kameez pooled around her legs like shadows kissed by the coral sky at dawn.

"I know that if the Angel of Mercy stays, I can't have my Sanari. He didn't even do anything when... when my iron destroyed the mansion." Zul grimaced.

"He won't let you. He will forsake you, withholding mercy from you for what you've done." The sultry taste of her voice grew louder as she spoke, entrancing him deeper and deeper.

"You hate him, don't you? For making you feel so guilty." Lexa's breath feathered across his cheek. Her garnet lips curled.

Hate. Zul wasn't sure if it was the right word. He felt betrayed and angry. "He won't get to decide how deserving I am of mercy." Zul Sharr narrowed his eyes. His breath was shallow. A sneer pulled at his lips, a laugh about to surface.

"You know what to do. We'll cross paths again, sire." She grinned viciously. Lexa winked and melted into the shadows.

A harsh breath escaped his lips. Zul Sharr stood. He'd become strong. He'd undo what happened to his beloved Sanari. There was no hesitation as he unpinned a feather from the girl's hair. "I'm sorry, Sanari."

He held the feather to his lips and blew it. It sounded a musical trill like a bird and echoed throughout the valley behind him.

The Angel of Mercy, Mirkhas, ascended above Zul Sharr.

Gems and pearls adorned the angel's wings. Their span took over the whole sky. Golden light shimmered through clouds.

"I greet you with peace. Was it you who wanted my company, Eisen ibn Hariz, or rather, Zul Sharr? By the will of God, I will grant His mercy upon you so long as He wills."

"Yes, I did." Zul's voice was monotonous.

"I am not an intercessor nor a guide without the will of my creator. I am mercy materialized. If it is willed, I shall spread His mercy to you." Mirkhas stood still. The sun's life-giving glow threaded his clothing, as was befitting such a being. The angel was responsible for the pouring of rain, the winds, the crops, the ordering of the seasons, the management of the supplications of the created beings. All with the power of the Divine and his order.

Lexa's voice swam into his thoughts. She wanted him to curse the angel. *Curse him for not helping you.*

Lexa whispered a spell into his head. *Say it.*

A part of him didn't want to. He didn't want to hurt anyone. But he'd already accepted the jinni energy into his veins. The magic that would give him power. Then he could surely break the iron over Sanari.

Zul inhaled sharply and a wicked incantation spilled from his lips. "I command you to be sealed within the cluch of darkness, in an cold icy chamber!"

He lifted his arm and a purple light poured through his palm.

The light pushed through Sanari, who ran into the purple light. It surged its way to the angel. The angel's wings enveloped his chest where the light had forced entry. The light struck the angel's chest, sending white orbs scattering across the sky like a flock of panicked birds. Just as the angel disappeared, Sanari fell back.

Zul Sharr's eyes widened.

"No!" Zul's hand stretched out in front of him. He fell beside her. "Sanari. Why?" He scooped her into his arms.

"I heard the angel. He said to keep the light safe." Sanari's breath was shallow.

"I'm so sorry." His vision blurred as tears rolled over his face.

"The soul fragmented. The orbs are the pieces." The iron crept over her body, encasing more of her.

"I'm calling an Aylaalmashi. You'll be fine." Zul struggled to take out his Tome, a communication device made of crystal. He unrolled it from his wrist. His hands trembled as he dialed the number.

"You need to take the angel's light." Sanari placed her trembling hands to her heart, the light appeared, and she lifted her hand to Zul.

53

The light stung him. He leaned away from it. His Tome slipped from his hands and fell into his lap. "I'm sorry, Sanari. The iron, it won't stop. I'm sorry. I'm so sorry."

"Don't worry, Eisen. Protect the light."

"I…" His voice cracked as tears streamed down his face.

"Smile for me, please. That beautiful smile." Sanari lifted her hand.

Eisen forced a smile, as bright and as warm as he could manage. Anything for her.

"There it is, my sweet prince." Sanari smiled and her arm fell as the iron took over her whole body.

The light gleamed and disappeared into her chest.

"Sanari." His voice low and breathy, Eisen placed his ear to her chest. Her heart was beating. She was still alive. His arms covered her like a blanket and his tears flooded his vision. He shook with his sobs, rocking her like an infant.

***

Zul Sharr took a trembling breath through parched lips as he carried Sanari. Her whole body was now encased in a bandage of iron. His arms tensed and his knees buckled under him. With a thud, he crashed under the weight of her body.

He never imagined he'd have her in his arms like this. At least not before marriage. He winced and yelped as pain shot up his spine. He stood, her slow heart beating against his shoulder.

He leaned over the bed and lay the girl as gently as he could onto the white sheets.

The room he entered was washed in midnight blue. It may have very well been a sea, and he was truly drowning. His fingers brushed aside the curtains that draped about the bed. For a moment, he shivered, his skin brushing the silken, white fabric. He wanted the feelings of warmth from her smile and kindness. Not the sadness. Not the hollowness. Not the numbness that held him back, pressing a hand over his mouth, anchoring an arm around his neck, when he wanted to scream and writhe.

He couldn't tear his eyes from her silver-masked face.

Sanari didn't open her eyes or move her body. Only her chest rose and fell. She'd been cursed into a slumber. This had been meant for the angel. To be hidden away in a dark cold place. Now, the cold iron was Sanari's blanket.

Zul placed a hand to his back and stretched muscles that were taught only to strain and never rest. He wished she would wake up. That maybe all she needed was someone to whisper to her. He parted his lips yearning to speak. How strange it was. There was the memory of her smile, warm like the sunrise. He gulped and his brow furrowed. If only this were just a nightmare.

He gave her one final look, a long look, and fled the mansion.

***

Zul Sharr stood between Unicorn Valley and the meadow behind the ruins of the Fire Kingdom mansion.

The blood in his veins pulsed through his body. He needed to fill the void inside.

He found himself on his knees, sobbing. The realization of what happened now came crashing down on him. The images of Sanari flashed through his mind, his beloved who stood in the way of his curse. The purple light of the curse he cast on the angel and her iron-encased body. He hugged his own, feeling cold inside. His shoulders shook with the strength of each cry. "Why! Why? Sanari... Sanari," he repeated as he smashed his fist to the ground. His emotions urged the metal to seep from his body like blood. The iron crackled as it headed toward the valley like a long vein and stopped at a tree.

Zul Sharr gasped for air and raised his head to the valley. The iron glinting from the mournful sun encased everything in its path like ice.

Unicorns lived in the valley. They were powerful, noble creatures. Two, in particular, were known for their abilities. "I'll do whatever it takes to be strong, sweet Sanari. I'll break the iron's curse on you. Wait for me." The demonic aura in him grasped his heart. He smiled, wiping away his tears and slammed his palms to the ground. Iron rippled towards Unicorn Valley, engulfing everything in metal and preying upon the grazing unicorns in the distance. He approached the winding river. He watched as the iron moved across the ground. The coldness left him, and in its place, a burning sensation seeped into his heart.

CHAPTER 5–UNICORN VALLEY

Thunderbolt wanted nothing more than to stretch his wings and take flight, the cool breeze whistling past his horn and through his honey-blond mane. Not standing around in the meadow, the blue and purple trees shaking their dense branches in anticipation around him. He dragged his hoof through the thick grass, dew still clutching the blades.

Everywhere was movement. Feathered seeds carried by the wind, pirouetting past his muzzle, tickling his nostrils. The batches of pink primrose swaying, the petals taunting him. They could brush through the grass, while all he could do was have it for a snack.

Here he was, that hum under his hooves seeping under his skin, coursing through his veins. The energy of the land itself, beating like a heart, coaxing him to run in rhythm with it. The very energy a life force for all of Noorenia. The bright colors of the plants, the thoughts, the conscious mind of all living things were connected to this vibration running through the ground. That was why it was called the heartbeat of the land. A spiritual power that fed on their intentions.

Being idle ached his bones. Unicorns were made to move.

"Do we have t' stand around?" He flapped his wings and sparks of lightning popped around his head.

"The Elder said to guard the valley and stay in the meadow." His sister Sapphire stood tall. Not a feather out of place from her wings.

Thunderbolt wasn't sure how she stayed so still, her violet legs straight as the stalks of grain in the far distance.

"We're always guarding the valley. How come he didn't tell me?"

"If I recall, you were climbing the trees." Sapphire's mouth quirked, a small smile.

Thunderbolt shook his head and bristled. "Yeah, I'm a monkey... Okay so what was so important that he didn't want us with him?"

Sapphire turned, wisps of her wavy mane of blue sticking to her neck. "The presence of darkness."

"And he went alone." Thunderbolt's lips curled and he kicked the ground. Of course their Elder did. They were the only two unicorns with wings. The two who gave their vow to protect all of Wadi Alma and Unicorn Valley.

Sapphire opened her mouth.

"I know what you're gonna say." Thunderbolt met her gaze. "Duty before Desire," he breathed out.

A high-pitched whine surrounded them. Thunderbolt raised his head. White orbs scattered in every direction across the sky like a meteor shower.

"Seven hells... What is that?"

Sapphire raised one hoof, then pressed her muzzle to the ground. "Noorenia's heartbeat..." She stuttered.

Thunderbolt's legs stiffened. The energy under his hooves faltered, skipping heart beats. The hum was slower. Sharp panic raced in his chest. This wasn't the kind of action he wanted.

Dense clouds like ink swallowed the sky, the wind ripped through the grass, tearing through the trees.

"Sapphire!" Thunderbolt wrapped his wing around his sister's body. Their hooves dragged across the ground. The smell of saffron imbued the wind, until the air stilled, a held breath.

Thunderbolt blinked at the glare from the distance, the ground glistened in silver, the coating running over the ground.

"The Elder, we..." Thunderbolt craned his neck, trying to glimpse the city. The Elder was still in the city and who knew what this silver thing was, or if the Elder was safe.

"We must go to the valley." Sapphire tugged at the maroon collar at his neck with her teeth.

"Noor's sake!" Thunderbolt took to the sky beside his sister. His heart racing, he panted as they reached closer to their home. Unicorn Valley.

Below, the deep blue river in the valley ran between walls of sloping mountains cradled by peaks dusted in snow. With darkness painting across the land, the hills and mountains sharpened, belonging in the maw of a terrible creature.

Torn between finding the Elder and protecting the valley, he had to go back to the unicorns. Too many lives were there. The Elder could take care of himself, but his friends and family were unaware of the hunter coming for them, and they couldn't flee into the sky from the danger.

As soon as their hooves touched the ground, Thunderbolt and his sister turned to the nearest unicorn. "There's something coming this way!"

"Salaam, Thunderbolt!" one unicorn called out.

"What is?" Another unicorn greeted him with a press of his head.

The other unicorn followed Thunderbolt's gaze and his ears pricked up.

Thunderbolt spun around. The silver slinked ever closer. There was no more time. He pointed his horn to the ground. A ball of light crackling and popping, grew around his horn and pulsed. He launched it at the silver and it exploded. For a moment the silver bubbled, revealing gaps of trampled grass and a small ant. The silver poured over the ant like living liquid and continued its path.

It should have stopped.

His lightning should have cracked it or done something to it to stop.

Thunderbolt huffed and panted. "Run!" Behind him the others' ears flicked, but they fled, their hooves striking the ground and whinnies echoing out through the walls of the mountains.

Sapphire waved her head beside him, light bursts and lines of hardened flares struck the silver, but even her powers did nothing. It only pooled back into the gaps.

"Keep going!" Thunderbolt continued his attack with his sister.

Light, electricity, both popped and crackled. The silver sizzled and cracked, only stopping for moments. It was like trying to hold water in one fist. Impossible.

Thunderbolt and Sapphire hovered over the ground. No matter the barrage of attacks, the silver crept closer and closer, nearly gluing to their hooves.

In the distance, a form appeared like a mirage over the pool of silver. A young man dressed in purple followed behind it. His orange eyes glowed bright as he neared them.

"The symbol on his clothing... isn't that the Iron Prince?" Sapphire stared into the distance.

Thunderbolt gritted his teeth. "What? Is he doing this? Then... this is iron?" He gaped at the man. It was no mistaking it. The word for iron was on his chest. It was the prince. But, Thunderbolt couldn't let it distract him from stopping the iron from taking the lives of his friends and family.

The liquid silver passed under them, moving faster, leaving behind it grass, flowers and insects preserved in metal. It sped toward a fleeing unicorn, pressing its kiss like ice around its hoof and up its legs, and then finally encasing the whole creature.

"No..." Sapphire gasped.

Thunderbolt kept shocking the ground, sending bursts upon bursts, but nothing. The iron kept going, the attacks no longer containing it.

His muscles spasmed, his throat burned. Thunderbolt's legs buzzed from the exertion, but he wouldn't stop.

"Damn you!"

More unicorns fell prey, turning into glistening statues.

He whinnied loudly, his voice like thunder, clapping across the valley.

Their hooves collided with the ground like bullets as the crackling iron followed right behind them. Thunderbolt and his sister zig zagged as if they were prey and the metal were a snake. When they were far enough from the valley, they took to the sky again. Their wings beat at the air, just as their hearts—their muscles frantic in the panic—fizzed with their emotions.

The iron finally stopped when it reached a tall tree. It was Thunderbolt who looked down every now and again. His heart clawed in his chest through his skin. His large white wings flapped once and then glided as he found a place to land by a small clearing, just ahead of a tree.

The river which flowed through their valley was snaking its way into the meadow, running beside it to meet up with a pond.

They had found their elder, Halim.

"The Fire Kingdom mansion is in ruin..." Halim coughed. The remnants of debris were still caught in his lungs.

Sapphire's eyes widened. "The Fire Kingdom? I fear for those who were inside. Could they have lost their lives?"

Thunderbolt snorted. *Lost their lives?*

Sapphire had brought her horn beside the old unicorn's chest. A white rippling light encased his body. "This should heal you, elder," Her voice had been faint.

"Thank you... I am thankful I managed to escape the Fire Kingdom mansion. There is a terror in the air. I can feel the Angel of Mercy's presence has faded. Something has happened to Mirkhas's soul."

Halim told them to wait at the pond. The door to the barrier between their dimension and the other.

They made sure to keep themselves in stride with Halim as they made their way to the pond.

With every hoof, it sent them farther from the valley caught in suspended animation. The sun peeked through leaves, spotting them in its light.

Thunderbolt swallowed. His throat burned from his breathing.

"This is the pond." Halim's choppy reflection stared back at him. His gray dappled skin and mane swirled in

66

slate and white and his snout and legs were dipped in charcoal.

"The barrier between the two dimensions." Thunderbolt said it more to himself.

A silence pierced the air. The beating hooves across the ground, the violent breaths and panicked whinnies were all behind him. His chest clenched.

"Brother?"

Thunderbolt swung around just as his olive green eyes met his sister's. Her eyes had been misty. "Hey, we're all in this together. So, I won't even try to break down." A grin had appeared over his mouth.

Sapphire nodded.

"You two... It warms my heart to see hope reside in you." Halim's ears twitched as he spoke. "I have a feeling the pond could manifest something."

Halim lowered his shoulders. "As angels who were sent down to Noorenia, do not forget your main role is to be guardians of the Valley and the country of Wadi Alma."

Thunderbolt exhaled deeply. "I haven't forgotten our responsibility, elder Halim. Sorry. I know... duty before desire." How could he? The iron still flashed before his eyes.

"Don't worry." Halim pressed his head against Thunderbolt's. His silken coat like a gentle pat. One given to a child.

Once the elder left them, they stood at the pond.

Thunderbolt focused his eyes on the water's surface. Tall grasses, weeds and roots lined the pond. "There's something the elder wasn't telling us."

"Brother, how could you say that? You don't doubt his sincerity, do you?" Sapphire narrowed her eyes.

"Nah, that's not it. I mean, there's a reason he had us stay at the pond. There's something only he trusted us to handle and it's not just about whatever might surface from the depths."

Sapphire softened her eyes. "Guardians are accustomed to being entrusted with the safety of others, brother. I am willing to wait. Our priority now is to revive the Angel of Mercy."

"Right, Saph." Electricity zipped about Thunderbolt's body.

The pond rippled as if there were a group of fish feeding under its surface.

As soon as it began it stilled.

Thunderbolt snorted and shook his head. "What in the name of the Divine was that?"

"Our intruder." Sapphire lowered her head to the pond.

Nezha dreamed. The lick of fire surrounded her.

Sweat beaded on her forehead, and she was surrounded by a misty white sky, as if she were above the clouds.

Fire crackled and danced about her. An image of a human formed from within the flames. All she could make out was a glowing head, then shoulders. Flames cleared a path, revealing curly brown hair and vivid green eyes that blinked back at her. A young woman stood before her.

"Who… who are you?"

The young woman searched Nezha's eyes for several moments. *"Your cousin."*

The way she said it, it seemed even she was unsure.

"What?" Nezha had never seen her before. The young woman carried herself with a head held high and the elegant gait of a gazelle. Her long fuchsia dress undulated along the flames as if they were one. Her eyes on the other hand were fierce. The gaze of a lioness protecting her cubs.

"Are you Nezha?"

Nezha's lips parted. She gulped and nodded her head. How did this woman know her name?

"I don't blame you for not remembering me. You were a child the last time I saw you. I'm Sanari. Your father Wasi is my uncle." A gentle smile warmed her skin.

So she knew her after all.

"It seems our souls have connected," Sanari said.

Nezha wasn't sure if this was real or a dream. She had heard about stories, that dreams were more than strange visions. They could be premonitions, or meetings of two souls both asleep, thinking of the other. In her culture, sleeping was likened to a form of death. A part of your spirit taken as your body rested, and if not returned, the angel of death would seize it.

"Is it the fire?" There was no scent, only warmth and a gentle breeze playing through Nezha's hair. Maybe the flames connected them, if Sanari was a fire jawhar like her.

"Nezha, listen carefully. Take this light and restore peace." Sanari lifted her hand to her chest. There, a round glowing light appeared. She carried the light in her palms and held it in front of Nezha.

"What is it?" The warmth and whirr from the light touched Nezha's skin, her heart, enrobing her mind in a velvet calm.

"We don't have much time. Take the angel's light and mend its soul. Noorenia needs it." Sanari's eyes were filled with emotion. The light from the fire trembled in her eyes.

The light grew, the warmth stronger. It pushed against Nezha's chest growing smaller until it melted inside her heart.

"The angel? What angel?"

"The Angel of Mercy's light." As Sanari's voice faded, the flames tumbled over her, consuming her form.

Embers crackled past Nezha's face.

***

"Fire!" Nezha woke, panting.

Comet meowed. Her brilliant blue eyes slowly opened. She rushed to Nezha's side and rubbed her cheek against Nezha's belly. Comet's plush fur stood up like freshly cut grass.

That dream. Warmth pressed against her heart. Nezha lifted her hands to her chest. Was it all just a dream or did she really have an angel's light inside her? No. It was a dream. It couldn't be real. The panic, that was the warm buzzing she felt in her heart. That's all. But she remembered everything. An angel's light. First jinn, now her dreams were about an angel.

***

Nezha was sitting in her backyard on the blue patio swing, facing the pond. Bordered in mosaic tiles in blues, oranges and yellow, white lotus flowers drifted across the surface. Since her father was a botanist, an array of plants made their home along the sidelines, their leaves dipping into the cool water.

Comet purred beside her on the swing, pressing her silky nose to Nezha's fingers. The swing rocked back and forth, obeying the agitated wind. The rustling of leaves from the trees had Nezha lost in images of flames.

"There are no jinn here. There can't be. We're safe here, Comet." Nezha smiled down at her, and scratched Comet's chin. Comet gave a hushed meow. Her eyes were half-closed. She nestled closer to Nezha as they enjoyed the lullaby of the swing.

"Nezha, my dear, how are you?" her grandfather, Basim, called as he walked to the swing.

"Grandfather." She smiled.

He ruffled her hair. "Ma Sha Allah. You look like you're in good health."

"How are you?" Nezha ran her fingers through her hair. She didn't wear her hijab around close male family members.

"I'm well," He said.

"Oh, good. I was getting pretty sleepy out here. I think I dozed off," Nezha said.

"It must be all that karate. Of course you're exhausted." Her grandfather chuckled.

"I quit a while ago, actually. We'd been busy with the shop."

"Oh yes. Well, I enjoy taking care of the aloe plant you gave me. Such a good plant too. I get to use its gel for scrapes. Always taking care of two things at once."

"Well, of course. Have you still been fixing old cars? How's two-seat Muna?" Nezha nudged him.

"Ah, her windows still need fixing, but I can do it."

"Try to take it easy. You've been working too hard on them." With a great smile, Nezha gestured to her grandfather to sit on the swing.

Basim grasped the swing and sat down, careful not to swing them violently backwards. "We should talk, Nezha."

Nezha reclined in the swing, rocking it into a lulling rhythm. She sighed a little. "Well, I still haven't been able to control my fire."

"Hmm… I hope you don't mean to smother your power." A gentle smile crossed his face. "Fire is warmth, dear."

"I know. But, when I get emotional, I can't keep the fire from spreading out of my control." The jinni crossed her mind. "Grandfather, can you tell me about our family's powers?" Lamis and her grandfather had tried to tell her all about her family. She had never wanted to listen. Until now. Until she realized she couldn't protect her family.

She needed to learn more.

Basim raised his eyebrows and took a breath. "Our family is a bloodline of fire jawhars. This is a gift from the Creator, young girl. I do hope you don't consider it a burden."

"No, I don't think that." Nezha gave a bitter laugh. "I just wanted to know, since ma and baba never discussed this with me. When I was a kid, they'd clean up the char, the burned furniture, everything. Then they went on as though nothing happened, telling me to stay inside and to say my prayers to protect myself from evil. They made me feel like I was trouble for them. I didn't think they understood."

"You have every right to know. The thing is, fear can control a person. Your parents have been trying to protect

you. It's a long story. A lot of people say that, don't they?"
Basim smiled.

"Yeah." Nezha turned to Basim.

"A decade ago, a war broke out against the jinn, the angels and the humans. The War of Jahalia, they called it." *The War of the Wild.* "Some jinn wanted to teach magic to humans, to condemn humankind to evil. The royal family—*our* family—found out. The aftermath of the war left our family on Earth on the jinn's radar. They have been keeping their eye on us. When your parents noticed, they tried their best to keep them away from you."

Goosebumps rippled across her skin. "I'm royalty... What?" That explained how they had such a large house or how Nezha never heard her parents worry about money problems.

Nezha scanned his eyes.

Her grandfather winked. "Yes. Why do you think I can afford to wear such nice things when my tunics get dirty from the garage?"

"Wow, so no one thought they should tell me I'm a princess?" Nezha grinned back at him.

"Maybe we didn't want you to be a spoiled one."

"Okay, that was a good one. So, where's our palace then? Do we own one?"

"Well, another world."

"You're kidding."

"No, I'm quite serious."

Nezha shook her head. She could tell by the look in his eyes he wasn't lying, but a part of her couldn't believe it.

"Okay, so we're royalty and the jinn had a war with us. To protect me, my parents tried to hide me?" Once the words left her lips, the rims of her eyes welled up with tears. Her parents always reminded her to say her invocations, to keep the jinn out of the house.

Basim put his hand on Nezha's head. "Fear is the oppressor and truth is light. Fear might dress as a leader, but love is a mightier guide."

She opened her eyes and lifted her head, and they both shared a warm smile. "I know they love me..."

"They always will. Nezha, I still have a gift for you. We should head back inside."

"Sure. I hope it's a chest of jewelry and gold. You said I was a princess." Nezha stood, her back to the pond.

The pond's surface rippled, then formed rolls of water.

Comet pounced at a string by her feet.

Strips of water from the pond rose up and lashed out at Nezha from behind. They were like translucent snakes, wrapping themselves about her limbs and her waist. Nezha screamed. Her eyes widened as the water wrapped tighter around her arms. Nezha pulled and twisted, but they would not loosen their hold. Warmth flooded her chest, a hum prickling her skin. Her grandfather called out to her, but the water kept him back.

The watery arms coiled tighter, constricting her chest. Then, with one mighty tug, Nezha and Comet were plunged into the murky pond.

Her lungs burned. Her arms and legs writhed against the pull of the living water. She felt like she was holding her breath forever, but it was probably only a minute. Then, when her strength finally gave out, she succumbed. Pond water hadn't flooded her lungs.

She wasn't drowning.

CHAPTER 8—DESTINATION

Bubbles danced about Nezha as Comet waved her paws frantically in her arms. Nezha writhed within the water's tight grip. The water rippled, then the waves calmed and it stilled. She sank to the bottom. The water turned blue, and sunlight poured over them from above. She kicked towards the surface, holding Comet tight under one arm. She pulled herself out with her left elbow, placing Comet on the ground.

"Comet. Comet, are you okay?" Nezha pulled her into her arms. Comet looked up at her and mewed loudly and purred. She was okay. *Thank the Creator.*

When she looked up, her eyes met with two unicorns. Both staring at her.

I'm seeing unicorns now? Okay, what was in the water?

"Comet, I think we're not in Morocco anymore." Nezha stood with Comet in her arms. When her fingers ran across Comet's fur, they were dry. The water hadn't soaked them.

The violet-coated unicorn was face to face with Nezha, its blue horn spiraled into a sharp tip, nearly pricking Nezha's forehead.

The unicorn was speaking another language she couldn't understand. In a way, it seemed familiar. Like a taste she craved.

"Shno?" *What?* Nezha said. Nezha glanced at the tall tree, and at the river that bordered the meadow. Small round yellow and taller blue wildflowers popped up from the weaves of tall grass.

"She appears to be speaking Darija," the unicorn said to its companion. It turned back to Nezha. "This is Noorenia." The unicorn spoke in Darija this time.

Noorenia?

"You can understand me?" Nezha raised her brows.

"Yes. We speak quite a few languages here, including Darija. We are in another dimension veiled from you," the creature explained.

The other said something in their language in a gruffer voice as if it was angry. It snorted and backed away from

Nezha. A puff of air tangled in electricity escaped its nostrils.

The violet unicorn replied back, its voice gentler.

"This can't be…" Nezha stared at them in awe.

The light gave their hair a glow, a soft aura that Nezha could not tear her eyes from. Above their shoulders sprouted long, white wings. The violet unicorn had a gentle look in its eyes and soft featured face.

Unlike the gentle, ethereal unicorns she heard of in fairy tales, the other—with its head lowered—made Nezha's heart pound and her body light from fear. It had a strong jaw, giving it an intense look. Its muscled body was a pale gold, as was its horn. A sparkling mane of golden blond shook furiously as it swayed its head up, meeting her gaze. Nezha flinched at the scrutiny in its eyes and turned back to its companion.

"I sense an energy inside you. It is similar to the Angel of Mercy's aura. We need your help to find the Angel of Mercy's soul," the violet unicorn continued.

Angel? The woman in my dream said something. What was it? "Angel's soul?" When they mentioned the angel, a comforting warmth bloomed inside her.

"Yeah, kid," the gold unicorn said.

"Please, tell me, did you get any message or sign?" The violet unicorn's eyes held a look of desperation.

"Hey, I am not a kid. A woman told me to protect the light and... to restore peace."

"You must be the one," the violet one said.

"How is this happening?" Nezha said.

"Please, we need you. This is what our elder must have meant."

"Sapphire, don't beg her. She seems weak anyways. If she doesn't want t' help us, you don't need t' worry yourself." The gold unicorn snorted.

Sapphire stared at him.

"How do I know you aren't the bad guys? I mean, sure you're unicorns, but, are you *all* good?" Nezha resisted a grin.

The fiercer one's eyes narrowed and its nostrils flared. "Nah, you didn't just—"

"Brother, control yourself," Sapphire rebuked.

Nezha walked forward, now inches from Sapphire. "What did you expect? I was pulled into another world and now I'm talking to unicorns. I still think I hit my head on something and I'm in a coma."

"You know what? I think I'm goin' t' like her. She's got a sense of humor." The golden unicorn raised his head and closed in towards Nezha. She reached out a hand as it brushed against his silken mane. She wanted to make sure he was real. Not another dream.

"So, what's your name, kid?"

"Again, with the kid," Nezha muttered. "I'm Nezha and my cat is called Comet."

Comet twitched her ears, rubbing her head against Sapphire's leg.

"I am Sapphire Almasi and this is my brother Thunderbolt Almasi." Sapphire gently pressed her snout to Nezha's cheek. Nezha placed her hand across Sapphire's head. The softness was a welcomed sensation. It reminded her of Lamis's strong warm hugs.

"We're goin' t' have t' get you all caught up with the situation," Thunderbolt said.

"I can sense a light within you. You must have the angel's light. That may mean the angel's soul is broken."

It all came back to Nezha. The young woman telling her about the angel.

Lamis's death had been devastating, of course, and yet Nezha could not deny the light easiness that had settled in her heart. Could it be the angel's light the unicorns were talking about?

Nezha recounted her dream to them.

"Why do I have it? What happened to the angel who owned this light?"

"Good question, kid. We're not sure what happened to the Angel of Mercy."

"Mirkhas. May the Divine smile upon him," Sapphire said.

"Mirkhas?" Nezha repeated.

"Yes, that is his name."

"What is the light?" Nezha asked.

"It is the angel's life force. The energy and purity it was created from. I fear for the soul. Without this light, the soul may be corrupted," Sapphire said.

Comet leapt out of Nezha's arms and ran her paw across a silver coating over the ground, gleaming like ice.

"What about the ice over there?" Nezha asked.

"That ice is metal," Sapphire said.

Nezha's gaze fell upon the iron in the distance, folding over the thick protruding roots of a tall tree.

"Does this mean you will help us?" Sapphire asked.

"But why are you looking for that soul?"

"The angel was our connection t' the life force of Noorenia," Thunderbolt said, kicking his hoof at the metal.

"Without him, there is an imbalance to Noorenia's electromagnetic energy. The very energy that is like a heartbeat within the ground. If the energy dies, the veil between our worlds will completely shatter. It will bring chaos to both."

Nezha imagined it to be like someone's body. Their heart was the life force. If their heart was beating they were alive, but if it stopped, they would lose their life.

Inside her heart, Nezha felt a tug. It would affect her world too? "I... I have to find the soul."

"That settles it. We'll be doin' some treasure hunting," Thunderbolt said.

"Before I forget, our elder Halim gave me a device called an Atlas. It has Noorenia's map and will allow us to locate where the soul is. It is in the holster by my left hip," Sapphire said.

Nezha pulled out a square shape from the unicorn's pouch. The Atlas was about the shape and size of a tablet but was gleaming with pinks and blues. It was made from a translucent material, flexing as Nezha pressed her fingers in the middle.

"Wait, it has a button. Is this thing electronic?"

"What did you expect? Villages and no electricity?" Thunderbolt huffed at her.

"The Atlas is made of a special crystal. Beco crystals," Sapphire explained.

The crystals could be made into glass and were attracted to the heartbeat of the land, creating pressure against the crystals to form electricity. The Fire Kingdom, Wadi Alma, was the number one producer of the gems. The crystals powered nearly all of their devices.

"It will not be as strong as it used to be. That is one reason why we need the angel Mirkhas, may the Divine smile upon him, or the heartbeat will fade."

Nezha pressed the button on the top of the device and it emitted a soft glow. It worked just as a tablet back home. The map appeared, depicting the regions of Noorenia. They were in the Western Beyond. It showed their position, a blue arrow pointed to the meadow they were currently in.

"There are two energies in this world. One beats within the heart of the land and the other is magic, a jinni's play thing, acquired by blood ritual and unlawful incantations. When it picks up the energy the soul emits, I can simply program the device to detect them," continued Sapphire.

Wait, did they say jinni?

There were jinn here. That meant she could find a way to avenge Lamis. But she had to control her powers first. Power here was depleting, unlike hers. The energy tingled over her feet, running under her skin as soon as she'd stood on the grass.

"I know, she's amazingly smart like that. Geek."
Thunderbolt nudged Sapphire.

"Thank you for that enlightening statement." Sapphire huffed.

The group visited the nearby city and stocked up on supplies and food.

***

The group walked on a rocky path. "In the meantime, you should be able t' sense the orbs. Follow it and lead the way." Thunderbolt walked with Nezha on his back and a large backpack filled with their food and supplies.

A force inside Nezha pushed her to go east toward the soul. A warm sensation washed over her heart and a sensation lifted around her head, an energy she couldn't explain.

"We should go this way." Nezha pointed. She wrapped her other hand in Thunderbolt's golden mane. *My head's still spinning.*

The rocky path was met with grassy plains. The breeze carried the strong scent of dirt and smoke, making Nezha scrunch her nose. Comet pranced beside Thunderbolt, occasionally chasing an insect through the blades of grass. The fragments of light peeking through the tall skinny trees slid across Nezha's hands and face.

There were two paths ahead with signs. One read Moth Territory and the other read Troll Terror. "So, now we're at a dead end," Nezha said, grimacing at the signs.

Thunderbolt snapped his head up. "We've never left the Valley or city before." He stomped his hooves, dragging them over the dirt.

"What should we do then? Go through the moth path?" The paths were each covered by dusty gravel and brown sand, moist from a trail of water curling over from a puddle nearby. A flock of birds flew by overhead, shrieking as they passed, their voices a haunting alarm.

Out of the corner of her eye, a dark blur passed. Nezha whipped around. She caught a black paw on a branch. Something moved in the trees, the branches shaking. *Was that a tail?*

"There's no more time t' stand around!" Thunderbolt galloped toward the moth path.

"Try to warn me next time!" Nezha tightened her fingers around his hair and threw her arms around his neck. *Whatever it was, we'll be far from it now. Hopefully.*

Sapphire gently held Comet's collar between her teeth and dropped Comet into her pouch. She followed her brother, the cat meowing loudly.

To their right, green slime oozed from a small purple bush. "Gross. Maybe we should have gone another way." Nezha curled her lips in disgust.

"We'll be fine," Thunderbolt murmured. Among the dark purple and ivy green bushes, creatures hissed.

"I think you spoke too soon." Nezha sighed.

A strong gust of wind tugged at their bodies and did not relent. Three moths about four feet tall loomed over them. They opened their wings and revealed sepia tips and two blue eyes. the lines of black, yellow and pink in their eyes were vivid. They headed straight for Nezha.

Thunderbolt swung his head. His horn cutting through the incoming moths and they dropped to the ground. Another swarm came out of nowhere. "There's too many!"

He struck again, electricity bursting into the air which burned many of the beasts.

Just as they fell, more flew in to attack, unaffected by the strange onset of wind. One of the moths tugged at Nezha in its clutches. "Let go!" She struggled against the legs wrapping around her torso. Nezha tightened her hold on Thunderbolt's hair.

"Ow, don't pull so hard!" Thunderbolt craned his neck back and struck the creatures with lightning. Nezha flinched at the loud boom. Her muscles numbed, the feeling in her legs gone, her heart thudding.

Comet yowled in distress.

"Nezha!" Sapphire's hooves dragged over the ground, the wind tugging the unicorns' bodies. Two other moths held Nezha's arms as they carried her off.

"Let go of me! Sapphire!" Nezha screamed into the distance.

***

"Great, they took the girl? We just found her." Thunderbolt threw his head up, his mane shaking, electricity popping around his horn.

Sapphire formed a bubble of light around Comet. "You will be safe in there." She couldn't risk the cat falling out.

Thunderbolt and Sapphire unfurled their wings and took to the sky, racing after the moths carrying Nezha.

Fog pressed over them, a shroud of green.

Thunderbolt flapped his wings and veered toward Sapphire.

A black-stoned castle pierced the sky. It was more of a dragon's claw than a structure. Here, the wind died and the moths soared over and disappeared through its rectangular windows. Vines constricted the castle like snakes coiling their prey. The castle was inlaid with cracked gray bricks jutting through the thick fog. As they staggered closer to the castle grounds, four moths guarded the door.

"More of them." Thunderbolt raised his front legs and a burst of electricity danced toward the moths. The beasts shook their antennae and a sparkling powder wafted over the unicorns.

Sapphire flapped her wings repeatedly, fanning away most of the strange dust, but most of it setteled over their bodies.

Thunderbolt fanned his wings and shook his head. "It burns so bad!"

Sapphire gasped in pain. The particles had speckled her too.

The moths dove down, curling their legs around the unicorn's bodies and attached themselves.

Lightning cracked and burst around the moths. Thunderbolt kicked at them as hard as he could and rolled around in the dirt, desperate to get the powder off of him. "Roll... around, Sapphire!"

Sapphire did as he told.

Comet ducked her head into the pouch, the bubble around her keeping her safe.

The pinching pain over him was soothed by the dirt. Thunderbolt sat on his knees and pointed his horn to the sky. The dark clouds overhead would be perfect for his attack. Electricity flashed from his horn and popped around his whole body. The moths on him and Sapphire singed and disintegrated into ash. Now was his chance to get them before more attacked.

Thunderbolt stood. The lightning flared in the clouds, shaped like twisting veins, it struck the moths. Thunder groaned, fracturing the silence. The impact hummed in the air long after it had died.

"Lightning rarely strikes a place twice," Sapphire joked.

"Strange for you t' be this funny, Saphy."

A huff escaped Sapphire's lips.

Inside, the castle's stone walls collected spots of moisture. Their hooves echoed with each step as they reached the walls where a long staircase winded up. That was when Nezha screamed.

"Let's go." Sapphire lifted up her large white wings and took off.

"Right behind ya."

They turned left and right through the gray bricked stairs. A door appeared, and they crashed through it with their diamond-hard hooves.

They found themselves in a room. In it, Nezha was on her back in the middle of a red circle, her bound wrists were resting over her chest. A blue cloth was tied over Nezha's mouth. She turned her head, her hijab ruffled around her neck. She tried to speak, but her voice was muffled. In front of her a tall man with pointed ears, fair skin and long blond hair turned to them.

"Guests? How uncordial of you."

"Let the innocent soul go." Sapphire requested.

His blue eyes met Sapphire's. "A unicorn? A noble adversary."

"A jinni." Thunderbolt narrowed his eyes.

"This human has great power within her. It beats like the heartbeat of the land." He lifted his hand and a green light shot out at Sapphire, but she inclined her head and the surge of power reflected off her horn and hit the back shelf, toppling books and breaking it to pieces. The jinni smirked. Another surge of energy zipped from his hand and blasted the siblings back into the wall. A crack formed behind them.

"I have been searching for months for a power this great. I must have it, to break the curse over my body. How would you know how it feels to live in isolation, unable to leave this place? Surrounded by these moths as my servants. Fated to live here until another with a pure heart frees you. Nonsense… But, with this girl's power, I will be free!"

"Stop your blabbering. Give us the girl now!"

Thunderbolt stood.

"Oh? I'm not surprised you didn't die. After all, unicorns are powerful. Not as strong as the jinn."

Thunderbolt charged at the creature.

***

While the jinni and Thunderbolt were tangled in their fight, Nezha formed flames in her hands. The fire's disposition was perfect for her situation. *There's no way I'm going to be kept like a damsel. I'm supposed to be fire. This is probably the only time I want it to be unruly.* The fire lapped hungrily at the cloth and soon enough it had eaten away her bindings. The fabric withered away to ash. With her freed hands, she tore the cloth off her mouth, it too singed. She gasped. *"That jerk!"* The fire licked away, until Nezha held her breath for a few seconds until it vanished in a curl of smoke.

The jinni caught sight of Nezha as he whirled around, dodging the burst of Thunderbolt's lightning. He chanted something under his breath. His lips curled into a toothy grin.

Nezha fell, and her wrists and feet fell to her sides. Her body numbed, feeling heavy. She tried to open her mouth, but only her lips parted. She wanted to tell the unicorns that she could feel the angel's soul from him. He must have had a fragment of it.

The jinni grew two orange antennae from his temples.

Light from Sapphire's horn stretched out and flared across the room nearly cutting through the jinni's arm.

"That's your best effort?" He scoffed.

He opened his mouth and strands like silk fanned out, wrapping around the unicorns, encasing them both in a cocoon. *No!* Nezha could only stare in open horror.

CHAPTER 9—ANGEL'S LIGHT

The jinni raised his hand, a barrier of energy formed like a bubble of oily film around Nezha. Her chest warmed.

"Be a dear and give me that energy. I need my freedom."

Nezha's eyes paled. Her skin tingled, her body feeling heavier. Light grew from her chest. Round and beating like a pulse. *The angel's li*—Nezha's eyes began to glow.

"Now… her name." The jinni stood over Nezha.

Don't say it. Don't say my name.

***

Sapphire pressed her body on Thunderbolt's making sure they didn't touch the coccoon around them. The silk had singed Thunderbolt's wing and nearly melted it to the bone.

Sapphire's horn pulsed out a frequency, constantly jabbing at the cocoon. The muscles in her neck pinched, but she kept her head up. Beside her, Thunderbolt's horn emitted a loud boom, pounding like a drum.

"Thunderbolt... keep the sound going."

"Are you okay, Saphy?"

"Yes." The sound rang in her ears. She could no longer hear the jinni on the other side or Nezha. Only the sensation of the sound rumbling in her stomach and vibrating under her hooves.

***

Sapphire... Thunderbolt. Nezha willed herself to move. To break through the jinni's spell over her. The muscles in her arms ticked. She breathed, the surrounding flames flared and hissed.

Cracks formed around the cocoon and shattered, the pieces flying out, and sound blasting through the jinni. He crashed into the beige wall next to the castle's window.

They did it. Relief settled in Nezha's mind. The barrier around her faded, a drop of water turning to steam.

"Now, how about some lightning!" The bolt sparked down on the jinni. The creature sneered and shot out a green light, but it was pushed back by the sparking bolt, the energies racing to consume the other.

Thunderbolt dug his hooves into the floor, being pushed back. The jinni's shot nearly swallowed his.

Light from Sapphire joined the blast from Thunderbolt's horn.

The bolt finally devoured the jinni's powers.

"I... I suppose...this is freedom." Its body spiderwebbed with cracks. With a shriek it shattered and was reduced to ashes on the ground.

Thunder pealed off the walls, carrying a whine long after it had died.

Within the ashes, a ball twinkled. It was an orb.

Nezha gasped as the weight from her arms lifted and the light in her chest faded. She sat up and Sapphire rushed to her side.

Her muzzle poked Nezha's cheek. "Are you okay?"

"I think so," Nezha said. She pressed her palm to the bubble around Comet, who pressed her head in return and whimpered. "You'll be okay, Comet."

"Noor's sake. Look at that." Thunderbolt walked over to the orb.

Nezha's shoulders slumped. Her nose crinkled when she took in a breath of air mixed with the metallic taste of blood and burnt flesh.

"That is an orb," Sapphire said, uncertainty in her voice. "I was correct. It truly has fragmented into pieces. Our fears were true."

"By the Most High. Who could'a broke it though?" Thunderbolt said.

Nezha walked over to it, with one hand on Sapphire's neck. She held it in her hands. "So, this is what's inside of me too? That light was what you said, right? From its soul."

"Yes. You have the light of the soul. We're fortunate that jinni couldn't take it from you."

"Is that why my pond pulled me in?"

Sapphire nodded. "The land wanted the soul back. Noorenia was trying to restore its heartbeat, mistaking the angel's light for its life force."

"So, the orbs want the light?" Nezha asked.

"Divine will wants you to piece the soul back together again."

Divine will. It forced her to this place. And now, her fate was tied to the angel Mirkhas too, not just the shadow jinni.

A part of the wall collapsed, the whole place began to rumble under them.

Thunderbolt turned to Sapphire. "We need t' get outta here!"

Sapphire nudged Nezha to climb on to her back. Her feathers brushed up against Nezha's thighs, and when they flew out the damaged window, the air swept up by Sapphire's wings undulated her sleeves. Nezha twined her fingers through the unicorn's mane and pressed her face into her neck.

***

They flew until they reached a patch of soft grass, far from the crumbling castle and moths. "Ow. Horseback riding hurts." Nezha dismounted. She pressed a hand to her thigh. She'd have to get used to it.

"Technically it's unicorn-back riding."

Nezha rolled her eyes at Thunderbolt. The white orb was the size of a pearl, a white crystallized energy. A strong pulse radiated off it, singing over her skin.

"Where do I keep it?" Nezha asked hesitantly, the orb pressed between her fingers.

"You may have to house it inside you. Before you do, let me program the map to locate their energy," Sapphire said.

"Sure." Nezha took the map in her hands and the orb. "Wait, you don't have fingers…"

"You will have to be my hands." Sapphire instructed Nezha as she pressed buttons and tapped the map, until they had configured it.

"Perfect. Now you can keep the orb."

Nezha held it in her finger tips and slowly brought it to her heart, where it melted into her. Her expression turned placid. "I know you need me, so I'll do my best, all right?"

"Kid, you'll have t' be strong and full of faith. You up for the challenge?" Thunderbolt nudged her shoulder.

Nezha pulled Comet out of the pouch and clutched her tight to her body. "Challenge accepted."

Sapphire smiled.

Lamis told me there's another dimension. She was talking about Noorenia. Her aunt's death wasn't just an accident. That shadow had something to do with it. *Jinn were here and I might find her murderer.*

They set up a fire and slept in the forest. The setting sun cast crimson lights across the clouds, filling the sky with a glowing fire.

CHAPTER 10—THE FEATHER

The Atlas illuminated as Nezha tapped on the letters,
entering in the word 'feather.' She had her back to a tall
tree shedding blue petals, thumbprints of color scattering
across the soil. Comet pawed at one petal, eyeing another
that drifted toward her, until she pounced and caught it with
her teeth.

"The feather belonged to the Fire Kingdom. Your
family," Sapphire nibbled on the stray grass that shot up
around the tree's thick winding roots.

"Chnahiya?"—Are you serious? "So I really am
royalty." Nezha's eyes widened. "By the Most High!" Her
grandfather hadn't been joking. Being in Noorenia had
proved it.

Thunderbolt ignored her outburst. "The feather was treasured by Princess Sanari. She used t' play it for the birds."

"That is right Nezha. You are a part of the royal family of Wadi Alma," Sapphire said.

"My grandfather said we were. I just couldn't believe it." Nezha shook her head. "Where did Sanari get the feather?"

"It was from the Angel of Mercy."

"What was Sanari like?" Nezha twisted a petal between her fingertips.

"She was known to be strong-willed and did not take no for an answer. She was brave and had a part to play in the War of Jahalia. Princess Sanari was truly a great young woman. Unfortunately, when the Fire Kingdom mansion was destroyed, she also disappeared. I fear the worst, I'm afraid. She was so young." Sapphire explained, frowning.

"I think I met her in a dream."

Thunderbolt tilted his head at her. "What?"

Nezha recounted her dream to them and how Sanari had given her the angel's light to protect.

"Perhaps, she is still alive..." Sapphire said, a shine in her eyes.

Hope warmed Nezha's heart. If Sanari was, she would want to meet her in person one day. If they could find her.

Nezha pulled out the Atlas directing them to an island to a place called The Angel Cave. For now, she'd have to move forward, searching for more orbs of the angel's soul.

***

Nezha sat atop Sapphire's back, and they took to the sky, flying over a series of hills, like small bumps on a crocodile's back. The air swept up by the unicorn's beating wings tousled Nezha's long sleeves.

Nezha kept her fingers curled tightly around Sapphire's neck. Being in the sky like this made her heart flutter. The wind breathed past her ears, sharing the scent of soil and the chatter of birds with her.

She closed her eyes and all she could think of was Lamis. The time she'd dared Lamis to go on a roller coaster and how she'd given her a hesitant laugh, shaking her head as Nezha had dragged her toward the ride. Once they'd been buckled into their seats, and it had started, Lamis had clenched her arm. When the coaster clanked up to a higher part and dove, Lamis screamed and laughed, letting go of her hand, a wide smile on her face.

Now, it was Nezha who wanted to scream. To scream in pain. Uncertainty gnawed at her mind. Going on this search for the pieces of a soul, finding items. All she'd wanted was to find who was responsible for Lamis's death. Who was responsible for breaking her heart into tiny pieces, and sweeping them into her mind. Her thoughts weren't a refuge. Only battlegrounds rife with despair.

She needed to focus on the mission she'd accepted. To keep busy on the motions. To keep moving forward.

The unicorns lowered toward the approaching ground. Nezha inhaled sharply as their hooves touched land at Bickering Barrens. The terrain of textured brown sand and small hills lived up to its name.

Sapphire stared with a contemplative expression at the gurgling river.

Over them loomed a large thick and mangled tree just across the river.

"Can't we fly over the river?" Thunderbolt suggested as he flapped his wings.

"Unfortunately, there is a barrier surrounding the outside of the river." Sapphire flew up to the sky and kicked the barrier with her right front hoof, which bounced off the invisible barrier like rubber.

"Would you mind if we swam through it?" Thunderbolt asked Nezha.

"I wouldn't mind," Nezha said, caught off guard. She parsed the water with her hand. Comet dipped a paw in and shook it. "Come on." Nezha lifted her up.

A tiny bubble grew from the tip of Sapphire's horn. Gradually, it grew larger, until the bubble was bigger than all of them. It slid from her horn and landed softly to the ground.

"Step in." Sapphire smiled.

"In there?" Nezha looked the bubble up and down. "Are we going to float in the water?"

"Yes."

Nezha stepped into the big bubble after the siblings. "Can I touch it?" She was unsure if it would pop the moment her shoulder smacked into it.

"It will not pop, I can assure you." Sapphire's lips formed a small smile.

The bubble sealed them in, like honey rolling across a spoon. It bobbed and slid over the skin of the river, smaller bubbles trailed past them as they picked up speed. Large purple-leaved trees zipped by them, blurring into streaks of color.

Sapphire kept her eyes ahead, calm across her face, until they would near land. Nezha looked down at the map. "We are close, but we will have to walk from here." Sapphire peered over Nezha's shoulder, seeing that a meadow was still to be reached.

The bubble rose up and landed over the ground without a sound. They all stepped out.

Sapphire pricked the bubble with her horn, and it blinked out of existence.

They wandered across the dry land of Bickering Barrens where scraggly rocks littered the ground. Nezha passed by a few trees with sunken branches. Brown hills rolled between them, bites of chocolate and nuts.

Nezha's stomach groaned. She placed Comet in Sapphire's pouch and rummaged through their bags, finding a bar with dates, studded in chewy cranberries, chopped nuts and drizzled with chocolate. This would have to be enough to satisfy her hunger.

"This place is sacred ground, so if any transgress, for them is an awful chastisement," Sapphire explained.

Nezha's eyebrows shot up. "It's so dry here." She took a bite of her bar.

"This is a pathway to the Angel Cave. The path was fondly named The Mirage. What you see here is different from the Angel Cave."

"What's this Angel Cave like?" Nezha asked. She finished her treat and carried Comet in her arms again.

"You will see when we get there. The cave is a place where those from Wadi Alma, where my brother and I are from, visit to pray and contemplate their lives. It is a serene place that emits a calming energy. Most pray at home. But, for those who seek solitude in their most grievous of times, they trek to the cave. To find true *khushu*. Concentration and contentment, in their hearts."

"That sounds poetic," Nezha said as she eyed an ant carrying a leaf.

"Such is the intention. To find what we own, but cannot see," Sapphire said and then her head whipped to the side.

"Wait."

"What?" Nezha followed Sapphire's line of sight to the rocks ahead of them. Rings of toothed metal dotted the boulders, opening and shutting meticulously.

"Should we fly over them?" Thunderbolt asked.

"You really want to fly, don't you?" Nezha said.

Thunderbolt turned to her, flapping his wings in place and winked. He rose up into the air but was caught by his sister. She grabbed him with her teeth by the collar around his muscular neck. "Eh? What's wrong now Sapphire? Another barrier?" He landed by her side, looking flustered.

Sapphire and Thunderbolt both yawned. Their movements slowed and they blinked heavily.

Nezha turned to Thunderbolt who closed his eyes. He nodded his head and jerked up. "This is..."

He fell asleep on all four hooves.

Sapphire's eyes closed as she joined her brother in slumber.

I don't feel so good. Comet was next to fall asleep, going limp in Nezha's arms. "Oh no, you too? What's going on?"

Mist like rumpled cotton sheets suffocated the area.

Something didn't feel right. Nezha's thoughts came slow and thick like molasses, but the warning bells rang fast and true as Nezha fell to the ground, joining her companions in their enchanted slumber.

***

"Where am I?" Nezha walked in her garden, the familiar scent of roses tickling her nose. The pond shimmered like diamonds. She was pulled through the pond by the blue ribbons of water, bubbles braided around her head.

"No! I want to go home. I can't do this!" She was on the ground now, thrown in front of the unicorns.

"You are the one to save us," Sapphire spoke gently.

"Me?"

"She's right you know. You're the one. You have the fire. Don't you want peace? Your world might suffer." Thunderbolt's velvet snout brushed her cheek.

"I want to go home."

The angel Mirkhas rose up from behind her, sending her flying forward and hitting the ground. An orb rose in front of her. Its light casting a glow around her face. "You are blessed with fire. Do you not feel it within you?"

The orb beckoned her, whirring over her skin. It glided to her chest and melted against her.

"No. What is this? The warmth, It's. . . It's hot now." Her eyes widened. She shook her head from side to side trying her best to move, but she froze in place.

"This is my light. Safeguard my light within your heart. You must learn the truth of yourself." The angel glided over to her. Its white feathers and blond hair were bathed in light. The radiance danced and eddied like an unrelenting breeze.

Nezha's hair kindled with red flames. Her body temperature rose as she sat up and struggled to her feet. "My truth?" Her voice strained.

"You are blessed," the angel's voice echoed.

Nezha looked around her. A whirlwind of fire and warm air mingled. It spun around her. "What am I? Am I a wildfire?"

"You are a burning will. A light."

The wind then dispersed rapidly to the ground, rippling over her feet. "I . . . am light!"

***

Nezha stirred, her eyes wide as she sat up. She was on the rocks of Bickering Barrens. The realization of the mist jabbed at her mind.

"Sapphire? Thunderbolt?" Her desperate voice echoed back to her. A low hum accompanied her as Comet sat beside her. Nezha picked up the cat and hugged her against her chest. She wandered the grounds, hoping she would find them. *I have to find my truth, huh? All I want to know is who or what killed Aunt Lamis.*

***

Sapphire's throat dried, her tongue glued to the roof of her mouth. Thunderbolt lay, other unicorns surrounding him over an inky pool. All of them were on their backs, legs sprawled.

There was something odd about Thunderbolt's forehead. Where his horn should have been, there was a small lump. It was gone. His horn was gone.

A dark purple sky embroidered with flocks of birds, screeching as if to cry of death.

"No!" Her eyes widened. Her heart was a searing wound. She walked, then half ran, stumbling down upon her knees. She nudged Thunderbolt but he did not move. "I had to protect them..."

Her sole purpose in life was to be a guardian. Even when she wanted to play as a youngling. Even when she would tinker with Beco crystals, finding ways to form energy. The other unicorns told her it was unlike her. That she should simply protect the valley and the city. To be a good guardian. They'd embedded words she and Thunderbolt were told to follow and live by. "Duty before desire." Behind her, the valley's river was a flow of blood.

***

Thunderbolt galloped at a fierce pace. His muscles burning, protesting, yet he wasn't going to stop. Fear clawed at his heart and mind. He shook his head side to side. In dark woods, the trees loomed over him. Sticks cracked under his hooves.

Finally, he entered a clearing of grass. Shadows were his audience, following him as he kept moving forward. He was trying to escape something. He wasn't sure what that something was, but he didn't want to stop and find out.

"Why?" The Iron Prince appeared before him and frowned.

The side of Thunderbolt's head ached. "I... I need to do what's right."

The prince's gaze shifted to his scythe. "Are you following the law or your heart?"

Thunderbolt took in a sharp breath. "What? I can't break the law."

The boy, with his crown tilted on his head smiled sadly. "I see."

The Iron Prince faced him, the metal at his fingertips morphed into a scythe. The silver blade twinkled like the veiled stars of the night sky. Prince Eisen's eyes and smile were bright while he speared the blade into his left leg. Thunderbolt tripped over his own hooves and fell. His mane swished up like wisps of smoke, and then he screeched in pain.

***

"Where are you?" Nezha called out, hoping the unicorns may have awakened from their slumber. The mist had thickened, persuading her mind to surrender to the strange sleep. She tightened her grip around Comet's soft fur as the animal let out a loud mew from her touch. "You're awake." Nezha's relieved voice quivered. "I'm so sorry girl. We're in a huge mess. Please, we have to be brave." She tripped and gasped.

Comet jumped out of her hands and impulsively pushed her right arm, twisting Nezha to fall onto her back and on to what seemed to her a large soft boulder. Nezha turned to Comet shocked, as her feline companion purred loudly and rubbed her cheek against Nezha's leg, before doing the same to the soft boulder and repeatedly head butting it... the soft boulder, the color of violet.

"Sapphire!" Nezha slipped off the unicorn's side. "Sapphire, wake up."

Sapphire's eyes fluttered open as she lifted her head.

"Nezha?"

"Yeah, it's me. I'm fine. Are you okay?" Nezha sighed.

"Yes. Where is Thariq?" Sapphire said, disoriented.

"Who?"

"Oh. Brother's name. Thunderbolt is his nickname. I am the only one who ever calls him by his name," Sapphire said.

"Let's go find him." Nezha urged. She stood as Sapphire followed suit.

Together they walked into the mist, enveloping them in its cool embrace. "I wonder how we separated if we were together when the mist fell around us."

"It's the land, Nezha. We are in sacred land so anything is possible." Sapphire's eyes searched the girl's. "It is testing us."

Nezha faced the mist as it thinned, their surroundings becoming clearer. Her heart was humming like a bee in her chest. The wind brushed across her skin.

"Thunderbolt might be over there." Sapphire trotted over to a shape.

"I hope it's him!" Nezha called out as she followed.

Sapphire stopped in front of the shape and bent her head down. It *was* Thunderbolt. "Brother, please wake up," Sapphire urged.

Thunderbolt lay on his side on top of the scraggly rocks. He suddenly opened his eyes and gave out a loud yell.

"Thunderbolt, it's us." Nezha knelt beside him and brushed the side of his head.

"Sapphire… kid, you two. I'm glad you're both here." He breathed out and lifted himself off the ground with the help of his wings.

"We're here." Sapphire turned her head forward. A smile rolled her lips.

The mist vanished and revealed the Angel Cave. The gray and blue rock protruded. Over it hung a canopy of lush trees. To its right, a waterfall surged into a small river. The exposed river bank revealed multi-colored parrots that were consuming clay from the clay licks. They were like hidden gems and splashes of colors Nezha never knew possible.

The parrots broke out into a furor of squawks and wing beats.

Nezha's jaw dropped as her shoulders slumped, and she rose. "Now this is more like an illusion."

"I assure you it is real." Sapphire walked ahead of her.

"I knew you'd make it." A young man' s head was held low. A smile of certainty appeared over his pink lips. He spoke with a deep buoyant voice. His hands were stuffed into his coffee brown trouser pockets and his periwinkle tunic was stark against the glinting blue of the cave wall he leaned on. The man's light blond fringes kinked to the right side of his forehead like a crown. He turned his head to them and stood straight. His fingers loosened his dark brown high collar. It was gilded in gold as were his sleeves, catching the sun's glare.

"Ansam?" Thunderbolt called out, a look of reminiscence softening in his eyes.

Ansam walked toward them with his open arms. "By the Most High." He breathed out. Happiness shone in his translucent ochre eyes. He placed his hands around their manes. "Thunderbolt! Lady Sapphire! I had a feeling you two would arrive." He turned to Nezha and gave her a polite smile. His face was an oval with arched brows. "I'm the guardian Ansam, protecting the sacred land of

116

Bickering Barrens and the Angel Cave. Who is this young lady that has graced our presence?"

"Nice to meet you, Ansam. My name is Nezha." She lowered her head and smiled.

Thunderbolt related the details about the angel's soul to Ansam. "Speaking of the angel, what're you doing here, Ansam? Were you in Wadi Alma? Usually, there's no guardian here."

"Well, I know something happened regarding Mirkhas, but not everything. I was at the Iron Kingdom when the Fire Kingdom mansion collapsed. When I arrived, there were ruins and the Iron Prince Eisen ibn Hariz had the feather in his hands. We had a heated discussion and told me the feather was useless to him, and so he handed it over to me."

"Ah zaan," Thunderbolt said.

"Zaan?" Nezha raised a brow. Thunderbolt told her it meant person or man in Noorenian.

"The princess, Lady Sanari, adored the feather. I knew that someone had to keep it safe. That's why I brought it to the Angel Cave. I'm just surprised he relinquished the feather to me so easily." Ansam's voice hushed as he turned to Sapphire.

"Was Eisen with Sanari?" Nezha asked.

Ansam shook his head. "She wasn't with him."

Nezha frowned. What could have made the prince destroy the Fire Mansion and encase the unicorns of the valley in iron? Was it pain?

"Ansam, you have been bearing so much responsibility. Today we can relieve you of one," Sapphire said.

"What do you mean, Lady Sapphire?" Ansam's lips parted.

Thunderbolt craned his neck to Nezha. "Nezha here is the princess's cousin. Since she has the angel's light, we can keep the feather with her."

"It would be an honor if she did." Ansam's face brightened, and his cheeks flushed. "I'm sorry you had to go through those dreams. It was Illusory Heart. The land tests anyone who enters for the first time. No matter who it is, angel or other being. Whatever you dreamed of was your inner fears."

"Ansam, I never thought we would see you again," Sapphire chortled cheerfully.

Ansam's smile remained delicate yet sad as he spoke. "Lady Sapphire I am glad to see you both. When I saw ruin in place of the Fire Kingdom mansion and the state of the late prince, then and there I promised myself I would protect the feather."

"And you're doing well." Nezha smiled warmly and pet both the unicorns on their muzzles.

"That's right." Thunderbolt nodded his head.

"Ansam, I know the princess is proud of you. No matter what it takes, we must be resilient in our efforts today and find the orbs." Sapphire nudged Ansam.

"Speaking of the feather, it is inside waiting for you Lady Nezha," Ansam said. "Are you ready?"

"Yes." Nezha's voice had a confident boldness as she followed Ansam inside the cave.

A silver feather, as if fossilized within white rock peeked through, catching and reflecting the light. Nezha couldn't break her gaze from the wall. Her lips parted.

"It's a beauty, isn't it?" Ansam gestured with one hand at the feather.

"It's as ethereal as I remember it," Sapphire whispered.

Nezha walked over to the wall. Her fingers caressed the cracks around where the feather merged into the rock. It was not completely absorbed by the wall.

"I think she's speechless," mused Ansam, laughing warmly.

"That's a first. She kept asking questions up until now."

***

Thunderbolt stepped over to Nezha and huffed meekly. The feather let memories of the princess flood his mind.

He could picture her with her curly brown hair, morphing to a flutter of flames from her enjoyment as she played the feather like a flute. All the while, the Angel of Mercy Mirkhas would fan his wings and bless the land with new crops, beautiful flora and healthy livestock.

Thunderbolt's jaw clenched. He remembered times when the princess would shower light every weekend. Just before sunset, a glittering show would evoke cheers and smiles from those around her. She was a light and all she ever did was make others happy.

***

"How do I use the feather?" Nezha's eyes were overwhelmed with anticipation.

"Well," Ansam managed, caught off guard. "I only guard the feather. My take is, you inherently know what to do. After all, it's imbued with the beating heart of the land."

"That's how it has been all this time. Trust your heart and let your intuition guide you," Sapphire said.

A gentle smile grew over Nezha's lips. "You're right. It's worked before anyways," she agreed, laughing. At that moment, she turned to the feather again, her heart thudding.

The back of her head tingled and the same sensation cascaded down to her shoulders.

The walls of the cave shook.

Nezha grabbed the wall for support as the unicorns spread their wings and held them against Nezha's back. Before anyone could utter a word, the shaking halted, replaced by silver blurs dashing in front of her eyes. The feather released from the rock and was poised in mid-air, mere inches from Nezha's face.

"I think the feather is answering your anticipation." Ansam closed his gaping mouth.

Nezha gulped. It glided closer, as if it too were quivering from its awakening.

Her trembling hand rose slowly, until a power within her as strong as a magnet guided her actions, overpowering her fear. Her fingers gripped the feather, and she held it to her lips and blew softly. A palpitating melody resembling a bird call, emanated from the feather. Flames erupted over it. Nezha's eyes flashed crimson and a sword formed among the licking fire. She held the sword, moving her arm like a flapping wing, easing the blade into blue flames. As her red eyes turned amber once again, she gazed at the sword, her eyes wide and breath unsteady.

"I told you it's inherent." Ansam grinned.

121

"Nezha, you truly are of Sanari's family." Sapphire huffed happily.

Nezha brought the sword to her face, eyeing the sword from the pommel, shaped like a silver wing, to the diamond patterned hilt. The quillon block was a silver wing, fanned out and pointing downward, toward the blade of living blue fire. The quillon was a gold crown pointing over the hilt.

Ansam explained, "The blue fire gives no pain when it pierces human flesh, nor can it harm anyone who is not to die, until at their appointed time. It only kills evil jinn."

"I knew something from an angel couldn't cause pain." Thunderbolt stood by Ansam.

"Who knew a feather could become something like this?" Nezha waved the sword as it returned to its former being.

"Here is where the journey begins." Sapphire locked eyes with the girl.

"So, Nezha." Thunderbolt's horn sparked. "If there were any doubts, they must be all gone by now..."

"Here, I'll make it easier for you to carry it." Ansam formed a cuff out of the feather. The feather curled with a layer of gold behind it, forming a bracelet. "The golden lining will act as a sheath."

"That's right. I knew this is my journey," Nezha wore the cuff over her hand. She continued, her voice filled with a new-found determination and faced the unicorns and Ansam. "The moment I felt the feather call out to me like a lost beloved. The Most High bless our journey."

CHAPTER 11—SUSPENDED ANIMATION

Upon landing at Unicorn Valley, the siblings led Nezha to the meadow which was in a state of suspended animation.

"So, the prince caused that to happen?" Nezha asked.

The siblings' canter seemed slower than usual. Nezha didn't blame them for being that way. Trauma was never easy, especially not when they were going back to the root cause of it.

Nezha massaged Sapphire's back, trying to comfort her as she sat atop her.

"Don't worry yourself. I am fine," Sapphire said.

"I just want you to know I'm here for you." With a gentle and kind smile Nezha placed her cheek against Sapphire's mane and wrapped her arms around Sapphire's neck.

Sapphire neighed softly. "I know, Nezha, I don't doubt your support for us. Thank you."

The smile slipped off Nezha's face. Her arms tightened around Sapphire's neck. She didn't want the warmth and softness to leave her. It reminded her of the warmth of home. Her parents weren't here for her. Would she ever see them again? Sure, she was probably trouble for them. Maybe they didn't entirely accept her as a fire jawhar, but they were still family.

"We wanted t' show you the meadow so you can see for yourself what he did." Thunderbolt was ahead of the two. His fawn tail swished back and forth, nearly swatting a dragonfly as it flew past.

Sapphire lowered her head.

Moments passed in silence. The evening wind went still. Comet took this time to take a nap in the gap between Nezha's stomach and Sapphire's neck. Even the movement of Sapphire's canter didn't wake her.

They passed by tall trees, their shadows falling over them.

Nezha sat tall, surveying the area as they passed. There were statues not too far from where they were. For a few moments, all she could do was stare. "I see forms from far away." She pointed toward the field.

Sapphire and Thunderbolt slowed down and let Nezha off. She carried Comet in her arms, cradling her like a newborn.

The unicorns legs became arms, their hooves changed into fingers, their snouts into human faces. They looked like angels.

"Wait, you're alicorns?" Nezha stared at them.

"Uh... no. We're angels. We take the form of unicorns. There's a *big* difference, kid. Surprise." Thunderbolt winked. "We'll be blessed if we don't see jinn unicorns..." He ran his fingers through his thick hair. His short blond hair feathered over his forehead where it was much thicker, as if he still had a mane. His skin was as golden as when he was a unicorn. He wore a deep cerulean tunic with layers of gold and maroon fabric around his chest and a thin sienna belt. The teal elbow-length sleeves were tight and accentuated his muscles. The diamond shaped high collar around his neck was open and gold and maroon. Under his right forearm he had a spiraled and curved blade hidden under his maroon arm gauntlet.

He walked toward his sister, in knee-high bronze boots. "Looks like she's going t' swoon over our good looks."

Sapphire gave him a gentle nudge. She turned her head to Nezha with her blue-violet eyes. Her fair skin contrasted her bright blue hair, curling into loose waves. She pulled at her long-sleeved tunic, the purple such a bold color, Nezha pictured one flower prized for its rich color.

She had visited markets where they would dye fabrics with the flower rightfully named the purple-kissed thread.

Sapphire's tunic was buttoned halfway down with a square collar. The front tucked in and the rest reaching her thighs. Her blue necklace was her own horn but had been curled around her neck. She was wearing loose charcoal pants with a blue belt and black wedges.

There was a mischievous grin on Thunderbolt's face.

Nezha's mouth opened. "Why did you keep this from me until now?"

"It is our duty that held us back, Nezha. The prince is aware that we are angels. If we were to transform before, it would have been easier for the prince to find us." Sapphire said.

"We had t' hide. It was easier in our unicorn forms," Thunderbolt said.

"Still, you could have told me who you were."

"Nezha, we did not want to risk your life. When we realized you had the angel's light, and we needed to search for the orbs, it gave us our hope. We can show you now, because we know you are Sanari's cousin. We will not hide," Sapphire said.

"You need t' understand. We need t' abide our duty, all right?"

Nezha sighed. "Okay. But, if I find any reason to not trust you, you have to bring me to humans."

Sapphire and Thunderbolt nodded. "We will," They said in unison.

***

Thunderbolt winced at the glistening shapes of unicorns in the distance.

"Nezha, we're close to the valley now." Sapphire gently lifted Nezha as they took flight.

The crunch of their feet against metal sent his mind back in time, tearing his heart.

Sapphire's eyebrows furrowed. Her eyes softened in sadness. She walked over to a familiar unicorn. It was her mother. She stretched her hand, until her palm met the coldness of metal. Her parents were side by side, their heads pressed against one another. She closed her eyes. "Mother's skin... it is so cold."

Thunderbolt walked up to his sister and patted her shoulder. Seeing the unicorns encased in iron, he relived the moment after the iron had grasped their valley.

"Thunderbolt, Sapphire, you must run!" Their mother had warned.

"But, mother, we have t' protect the valley!" Thunderbolt had tried to plead.

"You need to go now!" Their father nudged them both. It was futile to do anything. Unlike Thunderbolt and his sister, the other unicorns didn't have wings.

"You need to survive." Their mother looked back toward the metal that rapidly crept closer.

"Go and don't look back!" Pain and haste mingled in his father's voice.

Sapphire and Thunderbolt galloped. He had hesitated for a split-second, looking back, and then with anger and sadness in his eyes, he joined his sister.

Thunderbolt gasped. His eyes filled with tears at the memories. Sapphire's forehead fell to his shoulder.

He sobbed uncontrollably and held her.

***

Surrounding them were unicorns in different positions. Some stood on their hind legs, caught in the lapse of time trying to escape. Others were on all fours, trapped before they could even react.

Nezha stood motionless. Her eyes filled with her own tears. How long had they been smothering those tears? She couldn't imagine. Seeing them like this made most of her frustration with them ebb.

She embraced Sapphire and Thunderbolt. Nezha yearned to be with her own family and friends. To be held by Lamis again. To shop and laugh with Jessenia. To learn calligraphy and pray beside Aisha. To find her reason to truly smile again.

The sudden touch brought the two siblings out of their sadness, as they looked down toward Nezha. She looked up to them both and swept her fingers at her eyes, whisking away a stray tear. "I know it hurts right now, and I don't know exactly how you feel, but I will do my best. So please don't ever feel like you're alone."

Sapphire smiled at Nezha's words. She hugged her tight. "Thank you. We are here for you too," she whispered.

Thunderbolt looked at Nezha with a gentle expression and gave a light pat on her head. He wiped his eyes with the back of his hand. "I know, Nezha. You're stronger than you think."

The siblings took one more look at the frozen statues of their kin and then bid them farewell.

"Flowers may wither," Thunderbolt started softly.

"Roots will be the anchor," Sapphire said demurely in response.

"What does that mean?" Nezha asked, although she had her own interpretation.

"It is a reminder to keep hope and not forget who you are." Sapphire explained. "Nezha, you don't feel the presence of any orbs, do you? I do not see your device detecting anything."

Nezha pulled it out of her pocket. She tapped through its screen and then shoved it back into her pocket, shaking her head. "Nothing. Even I don't sense any—" Stars popped in her vision.

Her head buzzed, her knees unable to take her weight. The siblings' voices fell on her ears and her eyes rolled back, everything going dark.

***

"Is she going t' be okay?" Nezha heard Thunderbolt saying. She had regained consciousness.

"Yes, her body needs rest. After a good night's sleep, she should be ready to go," An unfamiliar voice replied.

Nezha opened her eyes and directed her attention to the girl who was speaking. "Where am I?"

"We are in Equus City," Sapphire brushed back Nezha's hijab, fixing up the tangled hair that peeked through.

That's right. The city beyond Unicorn Valley. Thank the Creator that they'd been close to a city and not in some forest infested with malicious jinn.

"I'm Tasa. It's nice to meet you, zwina." Tasa smiled, brushing aside her long blonde hair. She wore a long green dress with silver details, similar to the traditional kaftan Nezha would wear.

"I'm Nezha. Thank you for taking care of me." *She's speaking Darija.*

"Oh, don't you worry." Tasa helped Nezha sit up in the bed and handed her a bowl of soup. "You need to rest cousin, or your body's going to give out on you again." Her dark oval blue eyes were warm and inviting.

Nezha pushed her hand into the bed and tried to get up. "But I need to find the orbs... and jinn are after us."

"Yes, but you must take care of your health," Sapphire said and placed a firm hand on Nezha's shoulder.

Nezha relaxed her shoulders and sighed. She wanted to keep going. But what good would she be if she was going to faint again? She had no choice but to sleep. It was late anyway. Still, being alone would only make her worries gnaw at her mind. She'd rather fall into dreams.

***

"Sbah lkhayr—Good morning cuz'!" The next morning, Tasa went over to hug Nezha. "I hope you slept well. Hmm? You didn't want to eat in bed?"

"I didn't want to eat alone."

"So sweet. Go freshen up and join us." Tasa guided Nezha, halfway to the bathroom.

Nezha brushed her teeth and washed her face with fancy face wash. There was also a rosy floral spray. *Wow, they have nice things here.* She spritzed her face twice with it and exhaled in joy.

Nezha sat beside Tasa and joined them for breakfast. "That was so good. Thank you so much Tasa. I can't thank you enough for your hospitality."

Comet brushed against Nezha's legs and then leaped into her lap.

"Oh, you're welcome hon. What's family for, right?"

"Are you my cousin on my baba's side?"

"Yep. He has two brothers who both live here."

Nezha's feet touched the soft blue carpet. It was woven with diamond shapes and triangles. It was a kilim, a rug the Amazigh people would weave with their own hands.

"So, Tasa, how did you heal me?"

"I'm a herbalist. I've been studying medicine since I was a teenager." Tasa glanced at the potted plants on her windowsill. "I've helped all kinds of wounds and illnesses." Her voice became quieter, her lips a straight pink line against her fair skin. The morning light accentuated the yellow tinge in her cheeks. Her eyes held a sadness Nezha couldn't understand.

Nezha placed a hand on her shoulder. "You're talented."

Tasa smiled.

After breakfast, Nezha and the siblings stood outside Tasa's home.

"I'll be leaving you for now, "Nezha said. "I have to head home for a while."

"Wait! Take this bag of medicine. There are different herbs, elixirs, flower essences and various compresses," Tasa said.

"Thank you." Nezha embraced her and then took the bag.

"Farewell, Tasa," Sapphire said.

Thunderbolt placed a hand to his heart. "We'll see you."

Chapter 12—WHERE THE HEART IS

"I have something to talk to you about," Nezha said.

"Yes?" Sapphire said.

"I wanted to head back home to let my parents know I'm safe. I'm hoping you know how I can, or even if I can." She shrugged her bag onto her shoulders.

"Yes, you can," Sapphire said.

Nezha smiled. "I've been longing to go home for so long. You've both made me feel like this is home, so you're not lacking in the care you gave me, but I know you understand."

"Of course we do." Thunderbolt assured.

"Nezha, water reacts to the vibrations and the intent of those around it," Sapphire explained. "You need to speak your intention as you stand in the pond. You should be able to reopen the way back to your home."

Nezha walked toward the pond with Comet in her arms. "Let's go." Nezha whispered to her cat, seeing Comet's half open gaze.

Water rippled as she walked within it, and stood facing the others. Nezha pushed her hands through the water as she was now shoulder deep in. She looked toward Sapphire and then Thunderbolt.

They smiled back at her. She returned their smiles and then said softly, "I want to go back home to Morocco. I want to see my parents again." *Please Creator, please help me get back home.* For a while nothing happened.

Then, the water started to ripple more intensely.

Nezha waved to the others. "Bye, I'll see you later. Don't worry about me." The water undulated and then enveloped her into its depth.

She held out her arms to Comet in the water, gesturing to follow her. They both swam up to the surface.

Her face lit up from what she saw. It was home. The smell of their garden mingled with the warmth of spice and cooked food.

"Nezha? Nezha." Her mother bolted from the porch swing and rushed towards her.

"Nezha! I knew you would be back!" She pulled Nezha out of the water and into a tight hug.

"Ma!" Nezha cried in joy.

"Meri jaan, I'm so happy to see you again," Hearing her mother use those words of endearment melted her heart.

She was home. She was really home.

Her mother held her tight.

Comet followed them inside. Najwa picked Comet up, her fingers sliding through her silky fur. Comet brushed her cheek with her own. Najwa placed Comet in her round plush bed.

An hour later, Nezha finished praying *Zhur Salah*, the noon prayer.

She then slipped into a long off-white kurti with tribal print in shades of gold and maroon. All her casual clothing reached just shy of her knees. It was only the traditional kaftans which feathered to the floor. It had a white chiffon underlay that peeked out under it as if it were a trim of lace. Her fingers caught a small dried up rose in her pocket. She had wanted to keep it in a book. Next, she checked the other pocket of her churidar pajama.

It was so good to be clean again. No layer of dirt or sweat over her body, just the smell of her citrus lotion and the argan oil in her hair.

She felt the Atlas at her fingertips. It was still there. A reminder that she'd really been in another world. It hadn't been a dream.

She tousled her hair and placed it into a ponytail and then headed out of her room, gliding down the stairs and into the kitchen. Her parents sat beside each other.

"Ma, how did you know I'd be in the pond?" Nezha took a seat at the rectangular dining table. "I thought you would file me as a missing person."

"Well," her father said, as her parents exchanged glances. "Your grandfather told us what happened. You were pulled into Noorenia."

"Ma, baba, I want to know. Why didn't you ever discuss my powers with me? Grandfather told me about the shadow jinn from Noorenia. Even when I was a kid, you would clean up the mess and made me stay inside." Nezha searched their eyes. It felt like a weight had lifted off her heart even as her cheeks heated. She'd wanted to say this for so long.

"I guess it's time we tell you. We can't escape it anyway." Wasi's lips were a thin line, and his eyebrows knitted. "They knew of our lineage, that we were part of the Fire Kingdom in Noorenia. Because of a war involving the angels, they sought out whoever was allied. We wanted to protect you Nezha. We were afraid they would get their hands on you or use your fire jawhar powers, that they'd..." His hands cupped his face, his breathing shallow.

"Baba." Nezha rose her hand.

Wasi lifted his head. "We were only thinking of protecting you, keeping your powers away from those creatures... that we... we forgot about acknowledging your feelings. I'm so sorry." His voice shook with emotion.

"Your father's right. If they took control of you, we were afraid of what they would do to you. We didn't want to lose you." Najwa closed her arms around Nezha's shoulders. "My girl, can we be forgiven? Is there any way we can make it up to you?" Her eyes pooled with tears. She adjusted her purple embroidered dupatta over her shoulders.

"I… just knowing that you believe me. I'm so relieved. I want you to believe in me too." Her voice cracked, and her mother's embrace tightened.

Her father stood from his seat and kneeled by his daughter. "We've believed you all this time. We were just so blinded by fear. It'll be different now. Lamis would be so proud of you." Wasi put a hand on Nezha's head.

Nezha smiled as tears streamed down her face. Her mother wiped them away with her thumb, and they had a moment of silence.

Nezha explained to them what the situation was in Noorenia.

"I knew one of my brothers was blessed with powers and that he could control fire. When you were born, I never expected my offspring would inherit it. Not until you were ten. Then we made sure Lamis helped you with your powers, and we tried to keep you close to us, made sure you protected yourself with invocations against the jinn." Wasi sighed and his eyes were now full of emotion. "I was worried about your safety, but you mentioned there were others with you."

"Yes."

"How are Sanari and Tasa? They must be young women by now." Najwa smiled.

"They're good..." Sanari? That was the late princess. She didn't want to mention her. Nezha didn't even know what exactly happened to her. She couldn't risk hurting them.

"I'm glad to hear that. This is quite a responsibility you have to uphold. But my daughter, I know you are stronger than I think, especially when you've been gifted with such an ability." Wasi looked toward his wife.

Najwa smiled and kissed Nezha's forehead.

"We could never stop you from your journey. Just promise me, that you'll keep in contact with us," Wasi said.

"In Sha Allah," Nezha said. "My phone won't work there, but I know Sapphire can help me."

"Remember, jinni magic is forbidden in Noorenia. Only that which was blessed to you is accepted, so be careful of jinn,"

"I will baba," she said, relieved they could talk so openly now. "I should probably head back soon."

Najwa held Nezha's hand. "You just got here, beti. Are you up for a picnic this afternoon?" Najwa said.

Nezha saw the desperation in their eyes. To hold on to their daughter. Noorenia still needed her, and she had the angel's light inside her heart. How long could she stay away from the other world? But, she wanted to be with ma and baba. Lamis wasn't here, but her parent's love was.

"That's a good idea, hon. We should spend time together." Her father held her hand and smiled at her warmly.

"Okay... just a little while longer."

***

When Nezha and her parents got back from the picnic, the evening rolled in. It was time for her to go.

"Dear, you looked so happy today. It really gave me relief, seeing you like that," Wasi squeezed her shoulder and smiled.

"Yes, you were simply glowing." Her mother chuckled.

"Yeah." As her parents conversed, their smiles were brighter. She hadn't seen them both smile in so long. She hadn't seen them so warm, so open.

Wasi's eyes were full of concern as he stood beside his wife. They were in front of their backyard pond.

Nezha twirled a part of her purple hijab around one finger. The lace detailed under-scarf crossed over her forehead, accentuating the rich blue and gold embroidery of her long kurta.

Najwa hugged her. "Be safe, sweetheart. Remember what we say when we leave home?"

Nezha nodded. "Bismillahi tawakkaltu al Allah la hawla wala quwwata illa billah." In the name of God, I put my trust in God, there is no might or power except with him. She kissed her mother on the cheek. "Don't worry ma. I love you." With Comet in one arm, she waved to her

142

parents and jumped into the pond. Her heart was airy, no more pain building up, like when she'd hold her breath. Speaking to them, sharing her thoughts, all of it shoved the anger away, making space for a more open heart.

In a way, she could breathe easier. "I want to go back to Noorenia to see Sapphire and Thunderbolt." The water brightened, then rippled and engulfed them.

CHAPTER 13—THE MARID

The sun peered from behind the mountains. Sapphire flew through the yellow and lilac petals which danced through the nearby trees. Her mane was still beaded with drops of water from the drizzle.

They landed and from there, they broke into a gallop. A field with sculpted mountains grew with blue lilies, dotting the grass like small footsteps. A shallow pond blurred past them, with a turtle slipping in.

Nezha hugged Sapphire's neck. She sensed the orbs, the energy radiating deep in her chest, reminding them which way to turn.

"We heading the right way?" Thunderbolt asked, momentarily turning his head to Nezha.

"Yes. My instinct tells me to go this way." Nezha sat straight, her hands entwined in Sapphire's blue mane. Her heart fluttered. Thoughts of Lamis jeered her, but she kept her heart filled with hope, that she'd have Lamis in her heart. Always.

She looked over to the pouch at Sapphire's side where Comet was curled up. She purred with contentment. Nezha turned to face the way again. With a deep breath Nezha steadied her mind, letting the beat of Sapphire's steps erode her discomfort.

Sapphire's head jerked back.

"What's wrong?" Nezha leaned in.

"Forgive me. I taste strong winds in the air."

Without another word, the wind swept in and lifted the unicorns off the ground, sending them spiraling toward a large tree stump. Impulsively, both Sapphire and Thunderbolt summoned their powers of light and lightning which morphed together, forming a net, as if it was tailored by a spider. The net stretched out to form a dome above their bodies, its ends latched to the grass anchoring to the soil like thirsting roots. With no means of gripping the stump, the unicorns' bodies pressed against the net.

Nezha tried to dismount, but Sapphire raised her wing.

"Sapphire, you're already strained, if I keep sitting on you—"

"It is fine, Nezha. I don't intend to risk any harm to you." Her voice gave no strain.

Nezha's brows furrowed. She looked over to Thunderbolt who seemed to hold his ground well. He was either nonchalant about it or a very good actor. To assure herself, she called out to him. "Thunderbolt are you okay?"

He strained his neck back. "Hey, stop worrying, I'm fine. Good thing Saphy and I used our powers together. This net is strong."

Once the wind stopped tugging them, the unicorns' horns moved like needles through the thread to untangle it. The shaken feeling passed as they stood and continued further into the field.

Floral scents permeated the area, teasing her sense of smell. The white light emanating from the Atlas caught Nezha off guard.

"Marid Island." Sapphire's eyes widened.

Nezha took note of Sapphire's expression. "What's wrong?"

Sapphire shifted to Nezha. "Marid Island is a dangerous place. I am worried about your safety."

"Don't worry so much sis. We need t' find the orb no matter what we have to face." Thunderbolt gave her a reassuring huff.

Nezha managed a soft smile and brushed Sapphire's nose. "I knew there would be danger, when I realized you needed me. I can't just give up now."

Sapphire let out a deep sigh. "Then please try to be careful. At least give me that much."

"I will," Nezha said softly.

***

They slipped above the trees, the red blossoms shuddering over the branches. Nezha inhaled the sweetness. The flowers, their scent, it reminded her of her shop. All the good times spent there. She missed being lost in picking the right soil for the plants to thrive in, the sun pouring through the windows. She missed Lamis making faces with the fruits they'd make edible gifts from. Even when baba joined along, picking a grape that was meant to look like a nose and Lamis elbowing him. She missed those carefree times.

Sapphire landed, her hooves pressing prints into the wet green soil. The wind rushing past her, drew Nezha out of her thoughts.

They found themselves staring into a lush forest. As if it were an artist's canvas, greens in every shade painted the trees. In the center a small wild dog lapped at the lake. The dog turned to them and then retreated deep into the forest, disappearing among the blue-leaved bushes.

Nezha was near the edge of the lake and backed away. "The water's awfully deep."

Something glinted by a tree. Thunderbolt walked over to it, and between two roots, an orb winked back at him in the sunlight. "Look at this."

He bent down, yanked roughly at the roots repeatedly until they tore. He held the orb between his teeth as Nezha walked over to him.

"You found one. Great job, Thunderbolt." Nezha's arms roped around his neck as she squeezed him.

"Kid, come on. No need t' get so excited," Thunderbolt said.

"Let's get out of here." She climbed onto Sapphire's back.

A head appeared from the shimmering water, splashing as it dove back under.

Taken aback, Sapphire raised her front hooves. A tumultuous neigh escaped her throat.

Nezha impulsively coiled her fingers in Sapphire's mane and embraced her neck.

"Forgive me Nezha," Sapphire whispered as she regained her composure.

The orb slipped from Nezha's fingers.

"No!" Nezha stretched her arm, her fingers brushing the orb. It dropped into the lake and sank into its depth. She knelt beside it and frowned.

The water rippled as fish surfaced to snatch insects for their meal. "What scared you?"

"I may have seen a marid's head rise from the water," Sapphire said.

Nezha's eyes widened. "What? Another kind of jinni?"

Thunderbolt snorted.

"Yes. The marid are a type of jinni, and around these parts, they take the form of what you may call a mermaid. I have read about them singing to lost humans or those who have great sadness inside their hearts. They lure them to the water and drag them beneath. It is said they play with your mind and make you lose your memories. They are one of the most powerful of jinn," Sapphire said.

Nezha gulped. "Oh. So marids... are like sirens? Then how are we going to get the orb back?"

A splash sounded from the water. A shimmering green tail surfaced, the scales catching the light of the sun and disappearing again.

"Nezha, you must stay behind with Thunderbolt. I will go in," Sapphire said.

"What? You said they lure those who are sad? Hello. We're both suffering from a loss! Not sure about the kid though." Thunderbolt muttered.

A loss.

There wasn't any time to think. The water rippled, and a song rang in Nezha's ears.

"Oh aching heart, you have become broken by your past,"

The unicorns froze, the song taking its effect.

Sapphire's front leg twitched. "N—Nezha."

Nezha walked toward the lake. She'd lost control of her body.

The marid continued singing.

"Have you yearned for the release? To immerse your soul in peace?

Nezha came closer to the edge.

"Come, let the tears become the tides, wipe all your fears and pain."

"May you be at ease, oh dear soul, let the waves wash you away,"

Nezha walked into the water, the ripples lacing around her chest, pulsing at her legs as she continued to walk toward the middle.

"Oh yearning one, you want to forget the past?

Do you want to start anew?"

She was neck deep. The only sound was the marid's melodious voice. She couldn't see anything but the blue water lulling back and forth in front of her, ready to embrace her.

"We will forget it all and begin again.
Beloved, we will learn to live."

Nezha was completely underwater. Bubbles danced about her body and a marid appeared, reaching out and clasped her hands. A tight-lipped smile curled over her blue face.

"You and I will be free." The marid sang her final line, her face inching toward Nezha and her eyes beginning to glow white. Nezha's eyes mirrored hers.

Was this peace? What was this emptiness starting to fill her heart in? Was the water rushing in? There was still something there. A prick, a warmth?

Nezha Zaman... The angel Mirkhas's voice. It was there. It was pulling her back from the marid. *Do not forget. Do not sink. You are a burning will.*

Everything hurt though. Losing Lamis was too much. She didn't want to live through that. Aunt Lamis had been there for her. She had believed in her abilities. That Nezha could be more than the destruction her fire spread. That she was a human being with a heart.

Your heart must remain a light. Mirkhas's voice rang again.

Was that right? Ma... baba... Who were they again? People that cared for her. Her parents. They were waiting for her.

Do not let the marid take you into the darkness. It is not time to sleep.

Sleep? Nezha's eyes grew heavier. She wanted to hide away from the pain. To wake up and be someone else, but...

She had to find the orbs. She had to find her aunt's killer. She had to... She had to do what?

You must burn. Your will is a burning crown.

The marid blinked, the light fading from her eyes. Even the light from Nezha's began to diminish and then an orange glow emitted from her body. Nezha could move again.

"*I can't stay here,*" Nezha's fingers curled.

"*How sad. Young girl, would you not rather live here in peace?*" The marid spoke to her through her mind.

"*It's not peace when you're lonely. I'd rather be alone with love inside me, than lonely with you.*"

Other marids had gathered, green and blue tails swaying, arms reaching out.

Hands clasped her arms and Nezha struggled. She kicked them, tried to push back at their arms. Pressure had begun building in her chest.

She'd drown. She'd drown and never find her aunt's killer.

Or be a botanist.

Or live.

Never have any firsts.

She was a fire jawhar. There was still so much more she wanted to be. So much more to the fire burning inside her. She couldn't be destruction, or the burning pain that had settled inside her.

No.

No, she had to live. She had to.

The marid who tried to switch with Nezha gasped. Nezha struggled to raise her arm and once it was close enough to her face, she pressed the feather to her lips. She couldn't cut them down with the sword. Nezha didn't want to kill. Instead, she played a lovely yet ear-splitting tune. She just wasn't brought up like that.

"Stop this," one cried.

"Agh, it hurts," said another.

"What's happening!" The marids pressed their hands to their ears.

The same marid who had tried to steal Nezha's memories turned to the others as they surrounded her.

She is not ours. The marid's palm held the orb, bright and shining.

The other marids gathered around their companion, tilting their heads at the orb and turned to Nezha.

Are you sure?

Yes. She cannot be ours. One of them said.

Nezha's eyes widened.

The marid rushed to her and pulled her up from the water and swam up. Before she could break the surface, Thunderbolt dropped in beside them, moving clumsily with his four legs. He nudged Nezha up with his snout, the marid helping him.

Nezha was now on the ground, with Sapphire right beside her.

In a few moments Nezha opened her eyes, coughing out water.

"By The Most High. The Divine smiles upon us." Sapphire sighed.

"You're one resilient kid." Thunderbolt patted her shoulder with his nose.

"It was my fault," Sapphire said. "We should have taken you far away. We could have come back for the orb another day."

"No. We had to," Nezha said.

"This orb is yours?" The marid held it in her webbed fingers. She watched Sapphire as she gave it to Nezha.

"We lost it," Nezha replied. "You were trying to kill me."

"No. Although erasing your memories seems like it, doesn't it? This orb fell on me. It gives off incredible energy. It must belong to an ethereal being." The marid smiled, revealing sharp teeth. She pushed her hair back, the orange locks swaying on the water's surface like a goldfish's fins. She propped her elbow onto the shore. The wet pebbles slid against her skin.

Thunderbolt glared at the marid. "You still tried t' take her. Why'd you change your mind, marid?"

The marid's deep blue eyes softened. "Her will. I felt her love and her will. It's very strong. Most people we encounter feel like they have nothing to live for." The marid turned in the water. "And the orb… Noorenia is plagued by a growing darkness, a depleting heartbeat. This orb must be given back to its owner." The marid swam to the middle of the water. "Young girl, be cautious. You will meet other jinn who will not be as considerate as I. Do not cross us again, or we will take your life."

She ducked into the water and disappeared.

***

As Nezha and the unicorns flew over the island, she cried in silence. Before the tears fell, she'd pressed her fingers to her eyes and wiped them away. A part of her had wanted to forget everything.

CHAPTER 14—FULL OF SPRITE

The sharp tang of brine tingled Nezha's nose. The taste of salt coated her throat. The group soared over the ocean, waves lapping at the limestone by the shoreline. The siblings had transformed into unicorns once more, until they reached land.

Nezha pointed at a part in the map where her senses beckoned her toward an orb.

"Sprite Sanity Island huh?" Thunderbolt rose his brows when he read the map.

"Those creatures are quite notorious." Sapphire's wings caught the wind as they glided over Marid Ocean. She flew low, the waves cradled back and forth as the foam sent droplets skipping over her feathers.

"I get the feeling every creature is a dangerous jinni around here." The orbs were located on an island north-east of the ocean. Sprite Sanity Island's name was inspired by the mind games that the creatures who dwelt there delighted to play.

When they landed, the unicorn's hooves pressed into the wet sand, like thick clay made for pottery.

Into the forested area, Nezha passed a tree oozing with green slime from the small holes in its gray trunk. The dark trees bunched together as they rose over them. There was only the rolling crash of the ocean against stone. No birds, no chatter of insects.

Just ahead of them was a cave wearing a coating of purple moss.

"The orb's in there," Nezha said.

The Atlas picked up the orb's energy, revealing its location was toward the cave. She pocketed the device.

The back of her neck prickled as she clung to Comet and entered through the mouth of the cave. "It's so dark, I can barely see." She was about to light a flame in her hands, when Sapphire's horn lit up.

Guided by the light, they made their way through the damp cave, their feet crushing sticks and kicking pebbles. Nezha's skin was cold as the very stone the damp cave was fashioned from.

"Whoa." Nezha's head turned up to the stalactites above their heads, the spikes of minerals dripping from the walls like icicles.

Sapphire's ear twitched. She took quick steps to the other side of the cave with her brother and Nezha not too far from her.

An energy pressed around Nezha's head, tingling over her skin. "I feel it... There's an orb somewhere around here."

Thunderbolt's ears pricked up. "Yeah?"

The energy summoned Nezha to the rock of the cave as they moved farther away from the formations overhead. Her hand dragged over the walls of the cave until she found the spot.

"It's here." Nezha's voice was like a breeze. Her fingertips pressed into the wall as if she were absorbing every sensation. The orb was within the rock. The other parts of the soul within her beckoned it, and it replied to the call. Light streamed through her fingers, as she clasped her fingers around the orb, now holding it in the palm of her hand, warmth flowing into her veins.

"Nice work, kid!" Thunderbolt patted her shoulder.

"Thanks." With a light hand, she pushed the orb to her chest and it melted through, into her heart.

"Nezha, do you sense more?" Sapphire asked as she glanced around.

"Yeah, but further away, somewhere off this Island."

Light from the outside cast shadows in the cave, fingers reaching out to them.

Sapphire narrowed her eyes and spun around. "There may be a malevolent creature nearby."

Nezha held a flame in one hand. Electricity skipped by Thunderbolt's shoulders and spun upon his fingertips. Comet leaped from Nezha's arms and her tail thrashed against the cave's floor.

A young girl peeked out from behind a cavern, her cheeks flushed in mauve. She chuckled. "I'm lost. Can you help me?" The girl held a closed hand to her chest, her eyes downcast as she walked out into view.

Nezha's eyebrows slanted. A twitch of fear poked her heart before she could take a step. "It's a girl."

"No, Nezha. This is a sprite. That's not its true form." Sapphire hadn't taken her eyes off the seemingly harmless girl as she spoke.

"Please? I don't know how to get out." The girl kept her distance, her voice tinged in sadness.

"It's a girl. It's probably her fear you're sensing." Nezha walked forward. "I want to help her. Poor girl." Nezha's voice became monotonous, her mind taken over by the sprite's suggestive powers. *No, they said she's not what she seems.* Nezha took a shaky step back, but the voice tumbled around in her mind. Her foot slid forward against her will.

Closer. Closer. Listen. It repeated in her head.

"Please, miss, help me. You need to help me." The girl's voice grew tense, a growl escaping her breath as if she were a hungry wolf.

Nezha was being drawn to the girl. After she took one step, Thunderbolt stood in her path and poked her, sending a small shock through her arm.

"Ow." Nezha blinked back at him.

"Sorry, kid. I'm not letting a brat destroy you while I'm around. It's the sprite and I think it knows we have a you-know-what." Thunderbolt stood by Nezha and scowled at the girl.

"Please help me. Help me already." The girl's voice became a high-pitched groan. She looked up at them, her eyes jade. Two dark stares clawed at their soul. Her back cracked, giving birth to two glimmering purple wings dripping in green as her skin turned purple.

Nezha let out a strangled scream and then clasped her hand to her mouth.

"Stay away, jinni." Sapphire's horn lit up, but the sprite did not relent.

She chuckled, the sound echoing off the cave walls, and before they knew it they were drawn to her again.

"Damn it!" Thunderbolt snarled. He shoved his hand forward and a tangle of electricity surged from his palm toward the sprite. The sprite screeched and then giggled again.

After some moments, the earth under them cracked and tore apart. A strange sound escaped the sprite's lips. Then, all was a blur as they fell through.

The sprite slumped and looked down at them at the mouth of the hole, a wide sneer across her face.

Nezha's arms trembled. She'd held on to Comet, who yowled as she kicked her legs, trying to scramble out of her arms. She scratched Nezha, but her claws dug into the bracelet, save for one which met with her skin and dragged across her arm.

Nezha blinked out of her trance and hissed from the stinging heat of the scratch. Thunderbolt lay beside her. Nezha had fallen on Sapphire.

With a still struggling cat in her arms, Nezha stood and pressed against Comet's neck, making sure she didn't apply too much pressure. She cooed at her. "It's okay. You're okay." It worked. Comet mewed up at her and licked at Nezha's arm.

"Sapphire… Thunderbolt! Hey! Are you two okay?"

Neither responded. They simply stared at the sprite.

The sprite tilted her head. "Give me the orbs girl, or I will bury you all alive!"

Nezha glared up at her.

"I see you've trapped them," another voice, more masculine sounding echoed back. It was another sprite. He stood beside his companion.

They both had orbs inside them. Nezha could sense them. Two—no, three each.

The male sprite jumped down into the hole. All Nezha could see were his bright purple eyes and skin as pale as snow. Flames erupted around Nezha's body, whipping around the sprite's chest.

"That actually tickles." The sprite tilted his head.

Nezha screamed when his fingers sank into her shoulders. With his other hand, he pointed two fingers to her chest. A small ball of green light formed at his fingertips.

He was going to rip the orbs from her heart.

"Th…under…bolt! Sapphire!" Nezha couldn't reach them. Not her voice. Not her screams. They simply stood still. If she couldn't bring them back to their senses, this would be it. Her chest tightened and she gasped as three orbs appeared from her. "N—no!" A steady pulse pricked at her chest.

She needed to do something, and quick.

"Thunderbolt, I admire... how you push us into action," She blurted, as two orbs popped out, landing with a clink to the ground. The last one was half visible. "Sapphire, you are wise... you both... need to heal Unicorn Valley! I believe in you!" Nezha screamed again as lightning flared over the sprite and light beams created burn lines at his legs.

She collapsed, grabbing her chest, but the last orb fell and rolled away. Her vision blurred. In front of her lightning climbed about Thunderbolt's arms and the sprite as it stunned the demonic creature. Two swords of light formed in Sapphire's palms.

"Kid. Hey, you okay?" Thunderbolt placed a hand on Nezha's shoulder.

"Y—yeah I am now."

The other sprite jumped down when she saw the orbs.

"Don't you dare." Nezha lifted her hand and gritted her teeth. Flames swathed around the sprite, but the creature shook, as if she'd shaken water droplets off her body. The sprite reached out, her fingers skimming over one of the three orbs, when the ground rumbled. Her male companion laughed as Sapphire's light weapons did nothing to him. His muscles bulged and his eyes glowed bright.

"The orbs," Nezha said.

"Get those orbs. We will hold them off," Sapphire said.

"Hurry." Thunderbolt kicked the sprite, missing the jinni's head by an inch.

Nezha ran for the orbs, but she stumbled as the ground shook and rippled underneath her. The sprites caused a windstorm of pebbles and dirt. Their laughter echoed across the walls, the sound vibrating in her chest.

Nezha squinted. Her fingers wrapped around two orbs when the rocks began piling up underneath her. The last one was so close. She stretched her hand, the rocks pricking her sides, jabbing her ribs as she lay atop them. She grabbed the last one, but the sprite placed her hand around Nezha's and yanked.

"Give them to me," The sprite said.

"Never." Nezha's skin heated up. Her heart burned. Her hand trembled. Her desperation, her fear, her anger, all of it fueled the fire inside her. She wouldn't let it take them from her. Not anything.

The demonic creature yelped and let Nezha's hand go.

Nezha waded through the rocks back to the angels, who were on their knees. Behind her, a wall of rocks separated them and the two jinn. On the other side, the sprites hands pounded the wall.

Nezha opened her palm, revealing the three orbs.

"Raise your hands," Sapphire said.

Nezha did so.

"Make dua."

"Dua?" That's right. She had to supplicate, asking the Divine for help. In any situation, whether of need or thankfulness, asking the Divine and remembering him was devotion. It was an act of worship.

"Since the orbs do not have their own light, we will imbue them with our own."

"The orbs'll have purity," Thunderbolt said.

Nezha and the angels held their hands up, the orbs in her right palm facing heavenwards, touching together. In a softer voice she said, "Oh Creator, you are worthy of praise, peace upon the messenger. Oh Creator, you are the one who sees everything."

With every word the light grew around them and the orbs.

"You are light. You are love. You are the sublime, the supreme. Please protect us from these evil creatures. Help us." Behind them the wall of stone crumbled to powder and the sprites broke through. Their arms reaching, one of their fingers nearly touching Nezha's shoulder.

"Ameen," the angels said in unison.

As the light touched the sprites' skin they screamed and fell back.

Nezha looked down at her palm. The three orbs had become one.

She stood. The fire burned bright in her hand, opening like a lotus. She made a pushing motion with the hand that held the orb. The flames crackled toward the sprites. "You're finished!"

Nezha and the angels shielded their eyes. The sprites screamed. The white light dissipated, leaving particles of diminishing energy and the single orb falling to the ground. The air held a piercing whine long after they'd perished.

Nezha picked up the orb and blew out a sigh. She pushed the orb to her heart, returning it to her body once more. That force, that power had surged through Nezha's veins. Something she'd never felt before. It had heightened all her senses, the energy singing to her heart and spirit.

Her attack left a massive hole beside the cave they'd fallen from. At least now they had a way out.

Sapphire and Thunderbolt held Nezha's arms and glided away from the cave.

The three stared at the edge. Pebbles loosened and skipped down into the chasm.

"Well..." Nezha said.

"We will have to camp somewhere tonight," Sapphire said. It would have been too long for them to fly. And it would be foolish to pass the waters of the marid in the darkness.

The angels took Nezha and flew over a lake to the nearby forest, off of the Island. Far from any other sprite wanting to prey on them next. There, they spent the night.

CHAPTER 15—K'AMI CITY

The air fumed with the smell of freshly burnt bark. This
open land was meant for logging and a gateway to the city
ahead. In the distance rectangular homes made of tuff stone
balanced over the mountains, gliding like glaciers in shades
of blues and grays.

The gateway was met by a canyon to its left and a
stairwell that curved over the ravine and passed through the
ruddy textured walls.

Nezha and company walked a path of deep red sand,
heading to the arched stairwell that was adjacent to the
canyon. "Whoa, what is this place?" Nezha craned her
neck, gazing at the engraved walls of the canyon, as unique
as the ridges of her fingertips. Her eyes widened.

Sapphire walked alongside Nezha. She and her brother
had morphed into their angel forms.

"This is Dev Open. It is connected to K'ami City."

"Welcome t' the country Mahluka," Thunderbolt said as he grinned.

"Another country? Wow, we traveled far. What was that other country called anyways? The rhythm of Nezha's heart steadily increased and her senses heightened. "I feel another orb ahead."

"We are from Wadi Alma. You appeared outside Equus City," Sapphire explained.

Thunderbolt folded his arms.

The group stepped onto the stairwell. Below, the silky ravine rippled by the gentle breeze.

Nezha peered over the edge, gripping the white rock that served as the railing. The waterfall fell to the end of the caverns, the aquamarine water foaming up as droplets scattered like dust.

Water sprinkled over her head as they continued over the stairs. The closer they reached the city, the more her chest warmed.

Panic shot through her when she made the mistake of looking down. The stairs stretched up, to the city in the sky.

Sapphire squeezed her shoulder, a gentle smile on her lips.

Nezha wasn't alone. She had the angels with her. She kept her gaze ahead, not looking down again. She had to keep going.

Once they reached the end of the stairs, they were welcomed by the quiet and bright city. In the distance a mountain range appeared, like chipped ice and lapis lazuli gems.

"Are you both looking forward to lunch now?" Nezha said, pressing a hand to her groaning stomach.

Comet leapt from Sapphire's arms and pawed at Nezha's leg.

Thunderbolt raised a brow. "Sounds good to me."

"We would do best to increase our supplies too," Sapphire offered.

***

This was the only time Kayan Zogby had for himself. Here inside the cathedral, he would hand his worries over to the merciful Divine. He sat on his knees at the chancel before the alter, his head low. He clasped his hands together. The wax melted from the seven candles, their flames swaying from his breath.

Worshippers had long gone, leaving only him here, his heart set on pouring out his thoughts. The monks would come by on nights when he'd stayed too long, fallen asleep, candle light trembling over his face and revealing tears. They'd leave him wrapped in a blanket and a plate of dolma to wake up to.

It was that love, just as was inscribed over the alter, "Asdvadz Ser Eh." God is love. That made him savor the moments here. To stay under that love.

The silence, the air by the open door, it embraced his heart with a gentle kiss. "Oh Divine, please help me find a cure for father." The only prayer that left his lips and ached in his heart. To find a cure for his father's ailment.

He raised his head to rustling behind him.

There was no one there. No human. Just the tip of a black tail twitching by the door's edge and vanishing out of view. It might have been a cat. But it was far too long to belong to a small cat.

Kayan stood and left the building.

Outside, he couldn't find the animal. Whatever it was. Maybe it had been after this, the strange crystal he'd found in the beak of one of the birds he'd been feeding.

He looked down at the round crystal. A strange energy whirred over his palm, and coursed through his veins. He pocketed the gem and sighed. Was it attracting malevolent creatures like the jinn?

He never wanted to see them ever again.

A giant paw ripped the air, its nails digging into his side.

Kayan gasped out a groan and held his side. He had no time to register the form that blurred past him. Simply warmth pouring over his hip.

He whipped his head back.

Before him was a jaguar, black fur with ghostly dark spots, teeth bared. Its wide eyes filled with hunger. Its paw was sticky with Kayan's blood.

"Surrender the orb." A woman stepped out of a tumble of ink, shadows that swung open like a door.

Kayan's body buzzed, his hand trembled as he pulled his bloody fingers away and pulled out the sword over his hips. The blade unraveled, a sharp ribbon ready to shred his attackers.

He breathed. This was the time to fight. He'd said he'd never fight the jinn again. He'd never want to even think of them. Now, he was forced into it. Forced to summon the wind and taint it with blood. His brown hair twirled, his fringe like petals caught in the wind.

The wind coiled over the blade and up his arms. Ali. His sword Ali had been by his side all these years. Even Ali tasted the adrenaline in Kayan's veins.

"You're a wind jawhar? Interesting. Foolish choice."
The woman licked her red lips, as bright as her short copper
hair.

"You have no idea who you're dealing with, jinni."

"Do you? Threatening Lexa of the shadow jinn. How
courageous," She scoffed. "Don't you listen?" The jinni
opened her palm and revealed the small gem, round and
glowing that sat upon it. The same one he had in his pocket.

"Give me the orb. If not, my pets will have to pry it from
your cold hands." She winked. With a flick of her wrist,
two more jaguars formed from the clouds of smoke.

Kayan whipped his blade, but shadows feathered out
around her and she vanished.

His blade sung through the air.

"Divine's sake." Blood poured down his legs. He
couldn't let anyone see the creatures.

He fled to the fields. Blood trailed behind him even as
he pushed his fingers over it. The wind laced around his
palms. *Please body, don't give up on me. Just a little
longer.*

Kayan looked over his shoulder. Both jaguars pounced
at him. He twisted his torso, a loud yelp tearing from his
lips. It burned so bad, the pain biting into his skin. The

blade of his sword coiled, then flattened. One beast chomped on the blade and the other struck his leg.

Kayan's leg gave out and he fell to his knees. His eyelids were heavy, his sight blurring. *No. I have to fight it. Have to live for father.*

The jaguars snarled and leapt into the air.

He had to live for father.

Kayan roared, spinning his arm in circles, the wind winding and hissing past his ears. He had to fight through the dizziness. His sword tore through the beasts, their bodies shredding into ribbons and dissipating into the air, lit wicks dying into streams of smoke.

Kayan panted, his side ached, sharp pain struck through him in pinpricks. He struggled to his feet and took out the orb. His fingers trembled. "All for this gem?" Its energy coursed under his skin.

He was curious. He held it close to his side. Maybe it could heal him. It must have been powerful if jinn were after it. But his wound didn't heal. Only the blood stopped, drying over the claw marks.

He stumbled all the way back to the monastery, nearly at the entrance.

I'll have to ask Monk Ara what this is.

When the monk found him in the state he was, dizzy and barely conscious, he took him inside the building and tended to his wound.

Kayan refused to be bed ridden. Despite the monk begging him to rest, he let him go.

He'd asked the monk about the gem, but even he didn't know. All he told him was that there was a strange energy and nothing good would come from it.

Kayan still had to get dinner for his family. This injury was nothing. Nothing compared to the aches and terrible pain of seeing someone he loved suffer before his eyes. His pain would stop, but he couldn't make his father's.

***

Kayan walked into the bazaar. He looked over the roasted ducks, packaged in fresh mint leaves. "Hey butcher, how much for a pack of two ducks?"

"Ah, Kayan. For you, not much. Won't cost you an arm or a leg, that's for sure." The butcher chuckled.

Kayan gave a hearty smile. "Hand me two packs." He would smile. Smile as much as he could, pretending that he hadn't nearly been killed.

No one needed to know what had happened to him.

***

Most people lay blankets over the green grass, enjoying a meal with their loved ones. Others passed shop keepers laying their wares.

"Could we get more clothes? I'd need a new hijab too." Nezha only had one hijab that they'd bought from Wadi Alma. This one was torn and dark with dirt, blood and sweat. Nezha crinkled her nose. She needed a shower too.

"Of course," said Sapphire. "We *are* in the middle of a bazaar."

"Don't worry. Let big bro handle any fools who try t' mess with you." Thunderbolt grinned.

"He has that sinister look to him again," Nezha murmured.

Stalls of pomegranates, shawarama and kunafeh vendors, baskets of flowers and jewelry shaped like honeycomb, with shades of orange and red passed the companions by, as they walked through the bazaar. A few stalls back Nezha had even found a few books. She'd even bought toys for Comet.

Nezha eyed a stall of scarves. She found a maroon hijab where the fabric crisscrossed at the forehead. On the right of it, a long fold hung down with three orange stripes on the end. It went well with the gray textured blouse she was wearing. She fell in love with it in an instant. "This one. It just slips on and doesn't need pins."

"Beautiful, nearly matches my beauty." Thunderbolt held it to the side of her head.

Nezha nudged him and pulled it over her head. There was a mirror on the vendor's table in which she adjusted it.

"That's four riatas or two drepatas," The seller said.

Sapphire handed the coins to the seller and examined the fabric. "It's very light and breathable material."

"Yeah." She wouldn't have to worry about anyone stealing the pin Lamis had given her either. It would be safe.

***

Kayan walked past the stalls, the sweetness of fruit and the strong scent of flowers swept through the lane. As he made his way toward the field, he noticed a group of girls staring at him from afar. When he met eyes with one she smiled widely at him, followed by the others waving and squealing in glee. "Kayan jan! Kayan jan!" They spoke the word of endearment. Everyone here would be heard addressing those they cared about as jan. Even visitors who were drawn to the simplistic styled chapels and temples and mountainous ranges were dealt with kindness.

Kayan smiled back and gave a single wave. Girls tended to follow him in the bazaar from across the white stone monastery, ever since he'd decided to train in the field at night thinking no one would bother him. It took one girl stumbling on his training to gather most of the girls in the small city. Everyone knew each other. There wasn't anywhere to hide.

He picked up on their voices as he turned back around.

"He's so darn gorgeous!"

"Ugh! He's so amazing!"

"Why can't he be mine?"

"He won't..." One girl said. "You know what happened months ago. It's been tough on him."

"Yeah, I can't imagine how it was like being a well-known jinni slayer and then losing his mother..."

Some girls shushed the other girl speaking and then just like that, the tense conversation switched to another of sighs and laughter.

Kayan walked away. He couldn't let anyone into his heart. Not when he had responsibilities, dividing the love he only knew how to share.

***

"Let's go buy food." Sapphire walked with Nezha, who linked an arm with hers.

"Sounds good to me." Nezha picked up a basket of honey tangerines and two pomegranates. "Wow, I didn't expect you to have these here."

"This is after all another dimension," Sapphire said.

"You'd be surprised." Thunderbolt grinned.

They'd placed four blue plums, a rollable bread called lavash, pilaf, various vegetables, manakeesh which was fresh flat bread topped with cheese, meat and zaatar. They paired it with tomatoes, olives, cucumbers and fresh mint. Nezha picked up a package of butter and a small container of salt.

"I think we have enough food." Sapphire turned to Nezha.

"There is no *enough*," Nezha whispered. "I mean, yeah." She bit into the plum, ravenously eating it in just a few bites. She flushed. "I'm so hungry."

"That is fine, I know how you feel." Sapphire took bites of the juicy plum.

Nezha bit her lip and grabbed another plum.

They found a picnic table situated close to the bazaar, finished their meal and turned to a path far from the bazaar and its raucous. A field with a temple on the other side popped into view.

Following Nezha's reactions to the orbs, they walked. Comet pranced alongside Nezha.

The boy from the market, Kayan, crossed their path. Their heads were mere inches from each other. Kayan's heart pulsed and their eyes widened.

Air swirled about his sword, Ali. Fire blossomed from Nezha's palms, and she gasped.

In unison, both Nezha and the boy turned around, where their gazes locked.

Kayan's lips parted. "Fire from her palms?" He mumbled.

Who is he? Why is my fire getting stronger? Nezha clenched her hand.

Sapphire and Thunderbolt halted. They silently stared at the boy, who was now focused on the flames around Nezha's hands.

He must have an orb.

As if magnetized, Nezha walked toward him.

His topaz eyes glowed lime. A wind swirled about him.

Nezha raised her palm, and the flames swayed like a cobra's head.

The boy's almond-shaped eyes now had a wild look to him, his face turning tense. It was opposite to the languid and jovial expressions of before. He looked like a tree being ravished by stormy winds.

Without moving an inch, a gust of air brushed at Nezha's flame, increasing the flame's size. She clenched her hand, then reopened it. "Who are you?"

The boy's expression softened. "The wind?"

He tilted his head to the right, his face bright and full of youth. A hint of coral flushed his cheeks across beige-toned skin. The wind and fire disappeared, and they averted their gazes.

"Boy, how could you have the audacity t' stare at her?" Thunderbolt approached the boy.

"Thunderbolt, it's fine." Nezha wanted to avoid any conflict, but had a feeling it wouldn't happen.

Kayan returned his attention to Nezha, his face placid and his eyes still cast down. He combed his fingers through his hair. "If I was being inappropriate, I'm sorry."

"Are you a jawhar?" Nezha gave him a tentative gaze.

"The wind submits to my call," he said with a calm smile. He threw his arm back, in one swift circular move, the surrounding wind twisted and formed an updraft, which he glided on in midair. Kayan stepped down from the mass of air.

"Like prophet Suleiman, peace be upon him. He could control the wind," Nezha said in awe. There were more jawhars in various regions. She'd heard of The Iron Prince and now this boy.

"You're not one of her subordinates, are you?" Kayan's eyes narrowed.

"What? Who are you talking about?" Thunderbolt stood in a protective stance in front of Nezha.

"Don't be foolish. As if I'd fall for your tricks." Kayan gritted his teeth as he painfully shouted, "I won't hand it over to you or your demonic master."

Before Thunderbolt could react, Nezha formed a barrier of flames around him just as a harsh gust of air slammed against it.

Kayan's voice was edgy. "You won't get anything from me."

"You misunderstand us." Sapphire trapped him in a bubble. "Forgive me, but please listen. We are here to—"

He burst through the bubble. "You can't capture me," he said. "Look, I don't want to hurt anyone, so stop now. I've warned you."

The wind pulsated and slashed at Thunderbolt, who shielded himself repeatedly from the blows, squinting from the buffeting gusts.

"Please, at least listen to us. We're not here to harm you." Nezha pleaded.

"You won't deceive me with your human form." He glanced at her.

"The wind formed a scar on the ground." Her eyes widened at the deep gashes across the ground. Her chest clenched. This was all wrong. She needed him to understand they meant no harm.

"This is the last time I warn you. Just turn back now."

Their feet slid across the ground, the wind tugging and shoving them.

He formed a fist of icy wind, the crystals building over his skin like crawling ants.

Nezha called out to him. "Please stop this. We don't want to hurt you!"

"You give me no choice but to freeze you where you stand." He advanced toward Nezha. With his fist poised in the air, he spun his body, opened his hand and gestured his palm at Nezha's feet.

Thunderbolt's hands and head effervesced with sparks to strike the boy with lightning. Nezha lowered her head. Her arms trembled as she formed a shield of fire over herself. The flames pooling into a rectangle, a glass made of flame.

This time the fire obeyed. Few tendrils of flame coiled over her feet and like snakes into the air above her head. The wind recoiled and forced Kayan's arms back.

Shock engraved his face.

Lightning strikes danced about his feet, sputtering over the ground.

The shield of fire loosened and puffed into a cloud of smoke around Nezha.

They were both frozen in place. Warmth flooded Nezha's chest.

Kayan fell to his knees. Tears threatened to spill over his face as his adam's apple bobbed in his throat. He locked gazes with Nezha, and she stared back at him, and then his head fell into his palms as he breathed hard. "I'm sorry. It's… it's just so strange. The wind held me back. It's never done that before."

Sapphire and Thunderbolt rushed over to Nezha.

"I'm fine," she said in a soft tone, as Sapphire helped her up.

"You! How dare you?" Thunderbolt charged toward him.

"No, Thunderbolt. I think he and I have a connection. Didn't you see it? The wind held him back and the fire disintegrated. The elements God gave us power over, that would submit to our will, they disobeyed us. It's a sign for something." Nezha looked toward Kayan, who struggled to stand.

"I'm ashamed," he said. "I don't know if you'll forgive me for attacking you, but I only did so, because I thought you were Lexa's pawns."

"Lexa?" Thunderbolt said.

"The jinn she controlled attacked me a few hours ago and left me wounded." Kayan unwrapped the thick pink-and-green sash that lay loosely above his hips and then pulled back his cobalt blue dress shirt revealing a gauze wrapped around his waist.

Nezha gasped at his bandages. "He was injured this whole time, yet he was fighting us with all his might."

"So, despite your injury, you still fought us. I like your nerve kid," Thunderbolt said.

"So why are all these jinn after the orbs, when they're from an angel?" Nezha said.

"The orbs have no light, so they're corruptible. Whatever power they have can be manipulated by anyone, human or jinni," Sapphire said.

"When my wind reacted to you, I only thought it meant you were my enemies, and so I showed my hostility toward you." Kayan's eyes fixated on Nezha's expression. "I felt something, like we had a connection."

Nezha's lips parted in awe as she gave a cheeky grin. "Are you flirting?"

He played with his hair and flushed. "I didn't mean—I mean, that we both control an element."

"So, what's your name, boy? Maybe if you help us fight the prince we'll tackle this Lexa woman and forgive you." Thunderbolt patted the boy's back.

"It's Kayan. Kayan Zogby," he said quietly, his gaze shifting to Nezha.

Nezha introduced herself and the others.

"You're planning on fighting a prince?" Kayan said.

"This girl is a relative of the late princess. We're looking for the orbs. It was the Iron Prince from Qadam who caused these orbs," Sapphire said.

"That means I froze royalty?" Kayan nearly choked on his words. "She belongs to the Fire Kingdom?"

"Well, you didn't intend to kill me, remember?" Nezha reminded.

"Yeah. I still feel horrible about it. But, I guess if I join you in fighting, I'd feel a little better." He rubbed the back of his neck.

"Why did Lexa attack you?" Thunderbolt asked, now standing next to Kayan.

"I have an orb. I knew it was powerful when I felt its energy. It's from an angel of mercy?" Kayan put a hand in the pocket of his black trousers.

"It is true," Sapphire answered.

Kayan looked over at Nezha coyly, frowning.

So, he did have an orb. Nezha had sensed the energy around him. "You'll have to show us how you're the wind. We can't see it, yet it carries the clouds in the sky, cools us on a hot day. Be the effect, and we'll understand your cause." Her eyes glimmered as her lips held a content smile.

"Looks like Sheikh Sapphire's rubbing off on you," Thunderbolt murmured to Nezha.

Nezha shrugged and raised a brow.

Kayan smiled as thankfulness filled his eyes. "That'll be a breeze."

"And... don't you dare try that again. Unless you want to burn." Nezha narrowed her eyes and leaned toward him.

"Whoa… I won't." Kayan waved his hands in front of him in defense.

"Good." Nezha grinned.

"She's snarky sometimes. Watch out for that."
Thunderbolt nudged Kayan. "So, you wanted its power huh? You look so young. How old are you?" he blurted. "You're strong as it is."

"I'm seventeen." Kayan clicked his tongue. "Not for me. For my father. He's critically ill with a rare disease. A few months ago he suddenly had a fever. After that, he became weak and was bed ridden, unable to walk. The most painful thing about it is that he keeps falling in and out of consciousness."

Sapphire gasped. "The lawaya disease. It translates to not conscious. It can be healed by a certain flower."

"Which is it?" Kayan's eyes lit up.

"The Alstroemeria flower can cure him. I have studied about it in one of our books. I am not sure where to find it, but our journey will take us to many places. We are bound to find one for you." Sapphire assured.

"So you would really help me?" Kayan said, lowering his head.

"Yeah. You seem to care about your family a lot." Nezha smiled at him.

He looked at her in astonishment. "Thank you."

"In the meantime, I can help your father recover," Sapphire said.

Kayan's heart pounded in joy. "You can... heal my father?" He took a deep breath in.

"Well, I can help him. Here, let me show you." Sapphire hovered her hand over his injury.

Kayan's lips parted in shock as a warmth embraced him. His skin tingled, like there were small fingers working to regenerate every tissue.

"Remove your bandages. You will find that there is no scar," Sapphire said gently.

He slowly unraveled the bandages and found Sapphire to be correct. The wound was completely gone. Only smooth skin remained.

"Oh wow," Nezha breathed out, lifting her hand to her lips.

"Thanks. You and Thunderbolt are angels, aren't you?" Sapphire nodded.

"So, do you always have hordes of girls stalking you?" Thunderbolt gestured to the building behind them.

Kayan turned back, five girls ducked out of the way, but one remained. She waved at him energetically. "Only Tuesdays and Fridays." Kayan grinned.

Thunderbolt kept his left hand over his heart and held out the other in greeting. "Nice t' meet you."

Kayan emulated his actions and patted Thunderbolt on the back with a smile. "Marhaba friends, to Mahluka."

***

He led them further inside the city, where the ground was more elevated from the bridge they had passed, touching the sky. The winding roads of compacted gray sand, the tall blue-leaved trees that stood over grassy trails and lakes and the brown baked earth sidewalks all pointed to a city that was more in tune with nature. To her right, Nezha could spot a few cemented roads that led through a hill where taller buildings in white towered above.

Kayan stood before a tall home, the walls inlaid with tuff stone and lapis lazuli. He passed a key card through a small circular slot and turned a key into the knob of the door.

"May we come in?" Sapphire said.

"Yeah." Kayan nodded and turned as they followed him into the living room. He headed to the kitchen and took out the ducks he had bought earlier from his pack, then gestured for them to sit.

"Take a seat in the living room. I'll lead you to my father in a minute."

The plush sofas contoured to their body's shapes. The dark hardwood flooring matched the taupe silk curtains.

Next to the table in the living room was a vine-detailed fountain with marble at its base. Clay bars of soaps in earthy tones lay on the sink.

Kayan yelped.

"What happened?" Nezha called out as they rushed into the kitchen.

"I guess you can say... my duck is ready." Kayan laughed.

"Oh no! I think it's my fault," Nezha said.

"No problem, it saved me time! Smoked duck anyone?" Kayan smiled heartily.

After he was done with the kitchen, he led them to the room on his left and knocked the door. "Father, it's Kayan, I'm coming in." He slowly pushed the door open.

His father was on a bed with blue sheets and a mahogany bed frame. At his right side was a gray wood night table. On it was a pitcher of water and a plate where food had previously been. His father opened his eyes.

"Welcome back, my son."

"Father, I have people with me who can help you." Kayan sat beside him on the bed and held his hand. His eyes were full of emotion.

His father's gaze moved to Sapphire and Thunderbolt and then to Nezha.

"Sir, relax your body, and I will heal you as much I can," Sapphire said in her soothing voice. She whispered a prayer and kept a hand over the man's chest. A light glimmered across his body.

"Who are you?" The man closed his eyes momentarily.

"Sapphire. I used a prayer to help heal you. You will feel its effects soon, Creator willing."

Mr. Zogby opened his eyes slowly.

Kayan felt his father's forehead for the fever and was taken aback, his body leaning away.

"His fever is…gone," Kayan said in pleasant astonishment, his arms going limp by his sides.

Nezha smiled and kept her hand to her mouth.

"He may still fall unconscious, but at least he will no longer have painful fevers or weakness." Sapphire smiled at the man.

"Thank you. You are very kind. You are not human, are you? There is something distinguished about you," Mr. Zogby said.

Sapphire smiled. "Yes, I am an angel."

"By the Most High. The power of prayer is astounding," Nezha said.

"Kayan." His father put a hand to his son's cheek and sat up to kiss his forehead. Kayan's eyes filled with tears, and he cried in joy.

"It's been months. I was so worried about you father. I thought I would—" Kayan smothered his words and wiped his eyes as his father put his hands on his son's head.

"Kayan, you and Kimmy have both endured so much for me. I am grateful the Divine blessed me with such wonderful children."

Kayan met his father's green eyes. "The Divine smiles upon us."

"This is so heartwarming. I think I'm going t' cry." Thunderbolt said, tears pooling in his eyes.

"How may I thank you, angel?" Mr. Zogby said.

Sapphire simply smiled. "Your recovery will be enough. There is a flower that can completely cure you."

"Father, I'll go give Kimmy a call and let her know the great news."

As Kayan stood up, his father spoke again.

"The angel mentioned a flower. Do you have it with you?"

Sapphire explained. "Sir, we do not have the flower with us, but your son says he would like to find it for you."

"That's right. I want to find the flower for you. These three are traveling to fight and bring peace back to Noorenia and I want to join them. If you give me permission, I'll tell Kimmy to stay home to help you. I know she's been working hard, but we have enough money for the both of you. It should last for a few months. Besides, even if we run out, I'll take up jobs as we travel and send you money."

"Why would I stop you? Of course, I give you permission." His father smiled. "Do not worry about me so much, son. You have your Tome with you, and I am but a dial away. We can chat over video call."

Kayan smiled at his father. He stood up to call his sister.

When he returned he said, "Dad, I brought some ducks for tonight's dinner too,"

"Thank you. Now, go on son, and don't worry about me." Mr. Zogby embraced his son.

Kayan squeezed his father's shoulder.

"Kayan, Mr. Zogby, we'll do our best." Nezha reassured.

The angel siblings smiled at Kayan's father and said their farewell. As they all walked toward the bedroom door, Mr. Zogby gestured to Nezha. She stepped over to him.

"Take care of my son," he whispered.

"We will," Nezha whispered back.

Kayan insisted they eat at his house, and half an hour later they left with bread, vegetables, leftover bozbash, a soup made from lamb fillet, potatoes, peas, beans and fruit, kibbeh which was bites of fried bulgur wheat on the outside and stuffed with mince meats and pine nuts with a side of tahini sauce, tabbouleh and Fattoush salad. Kayan had recommended hummus too. As they were walking out, the Atlas illuminated.

"Huh? What's sketchin', sis?" Thunderbolt said.

Sapphire pulled the Atlas out. "It has detected an orb."

"Hey, Nezha, remember how I told you I have an orb?" Kayan turned to face her.

"I can sense it. I could feel it around you." Nezha squared her shoulders and faced him. "I didn't say anything because you were talking about your father and I didn't want to be rude."

They were now beside a park where a river was flowing. The light gleamed as it danced across the water. Birds perched on trees and warbled their melodies as the companions were bathed in the sun's light. Around them the laughter of children mingled with the sounds of running.

Kayan reached into his pocket. A pearl-sized orb was in the middle of his palm. A white light glowed bright at Nezha's touch.

"Thank you, Kayan." She lifted it close to her chest as it melted inside her.

"Whoa." Kayan raised his eyebrows.

"Nezha has the light of the soul, so this is natural," Sapphire said.

They walked past a few people. Among them were a pair throwing a ball to each other and two girls skipping rope.

Nezha stopped in her tracks. The Atlas beeped again. Her senses pulsed. "An orb is nearby."

Her companions were at attention. A rope whirled toward Nezha, but she jumped out of the way. She gasped and stumbled into Sapphire's arms.

Thunderbolt instinctively stood closer to Nezha. "Damn, we have a troublemaker."

The rope was a vivid blue, undulating like a ribbon. It recoiled back to the one who whipped it.

A young girl.

Black hair with plum highlights fell to her shoulders. She held the rope out as if she were going to skip.

"Are you up for a skipping match?" A devious smile twisted her lips.

CHAPTER 17—BRAVERY

"It's not a human girl, is it?" Nezha took a step back.

"No. She's a corrupted jinni. I can sense the evil emanating from her," Sapphire said.

Nezha stared at the creature in disbelief. It was supposed to be a harmless little girl. "Not again..."

"What's wrong? Afraid you'll be beaten by a little girl? How about I be frank with you? Give me the orbs and I promise I won't squeeze the life out of you."

Nezha sent a wave of fire cascading toward her. It burned the ribbon, but the ashes started to peel and rubberize into ropes once more.

Sapphire zapped a light from the necklace, which momentarily blinded the girl.

"We're taking this t' the field." Thunderbolt nodded to the others. They followed him away from the other kids, who ran to their parents.

The jinni rubbed at her eyes. "You can't escape."

She rushed to them. They headed further from the park and close to the canyon they had passed earlier.

The rope ricocheted off Thunderbolt's blade as he dodged her advance. "You're bound by Noorenian law not to harm humans."

The girl skipped with the ropes and then attacked once more. "Oh? When your precious Fire Kingdom collapsed, so did the world's protection. We do not fear you. Now, I need your energy and the orbs. Give them to me." Her face formed a sickening expression as she repeatedly whipped at them. Her skin became blue and her canine teeth extended over her lips.

Thunderbolt's eyes widened. "Wretched creature."

Kayan spun his arms in a circle and twirled the wind toward her. She struggled to control her rope as the wind clasped it like a fist.

"Damn you," she snarled. Her arms trembled, trying to force her rope against the wind.

As she struggled, Nezha's fire didn't affect the creature.

"We have to help him." Nezha called out. *Think of heat. Think of waves, like a sea and the movement of the... wind.*

Thunderbolt went onward. "Leave it to me."

He snickered as he was face to face with the jinni girl.

She grinned.

Another side of the rope latched onto his arm.

Sapphire reached a hand out.

Thunderbolt grunted as the rope took his energy, but a whiplash of electricity rippled over the jinni's body.

"Not today." Thunderbolt turned his head, his arms and body moving in isolated circular rolls as if he had no bones. Electricity speared the ground around the jinni in the same rhythm as Thunderbolt's movements. Sapphire's hands cupped, forming balls of light. She fired them at the jinni as the ropes whipped to burst them. It was a shower of electricity and light blasts among the lashing ropes.

Kayan raised his hands. "I'm not sure how long I can take this."

Desperation wrenched Nezha's gut. "My sword. I'll have to fight her head on."

Nezha raised her arm with the feather bracelet. She neared the feather to her lips and closed her eyes, blowing on it as it sounded its beautiful bird call. The girl twitched.

Both the jinni and Thunderbolt spun into battle as wind and electricity danced.

The feather transformed into the sword. The bracelet acted as a sheath as Nezha released the sword from it. Blue fire licked away. Nezha charged toward the girl. *If I don't do anything... How can I help?*

"Nezha, no," Sapphire called out to her. It was too late to stop Nezha. Sapphire directed her light toward the jinni's eyes again.

The jinni girl screamed. The electricity hadn't fazed her, but the light had blinded her.

"I want you t' shake in fear of your stupidity. You messed with the wrong people." Thunderbolt's fists collided with each other and sent lightning shooting out in a vicious tangle toward her. She screamed, and fell to the ground, convulsing. Before anyone got close, the ropes vibrated, alive again. The jinni stood, clutching at her chest and fled. Thunderbolt rolled his head. With Sapphire by his side, they followed Kayan and Nezha.

"Give up the orbs." Kayan spun his legs in a three-sixty kick. Once he landed, a strong surge of wind held the jinni down to the ground.

"Noor's sake!" Thunderbolt yelled as he caught up to Kayan.

The jinni's body contorted as she dug her fingers into the ground, pulling herself up. The wind's assault continued, howling and slashing the ground. She got to her knees. Her toothy snicker sent chills down Nezha's back.

"I'll try to keep her down," Kayan screamed over the howling wind.

Nezha turned around to Sapphire.

"Nezha, we're by your side. Your sword is our last option. Do what you must," Sapphire said desperately.

Nezha took in a deep breath.

"She's trying to get away!" Kayan's fingers shook, eddies of wind wrestled with the rope and their clothing.

The jinni was on her feet now. "You think you can overcome me?" The ropes wove a sinuous path through the air. Kayan's hands were being forced back, the pressure gathering small folds of skin over his palms. He circled her.

Sapphire emerged behind Nezha, freeing two arrows of light that pierced the jinni's flesh and pinned her to the ground. Sapphire patted Nezha's shoulder and stood back.

It was Nezha's turn now. To deliver the final blow.

Kayan's feet slipped and he fell to his knees. He breathed out a deep sigh.

Nezha walked toward the jinni with the sword swaying over her head. Her fingers trembled over the hilt. Her feet were heavy, But she willed herself to move.

Nezha was the one with a sword that could kill jinn. She had to.

Just do it. Just move the sword. Now!

Nezha slashed the sword toward the girl as Sapphire's arrows of light fizzled away from the jinni's body and the jinni sat up. The jinni's ropes wrapped around her arm and became a spear.

Warmth, pain, both shot through Nezha's shoulder. Her shoulder birthed its own burning pulse.

Just as the sword's glowing blue fire cut into the jinni's skull, the jinni's head lifted up, and she choked. She disintegrated into flecks of ash within the soft light.

As Nezha collapsed, light from two orbs streaked by her widened eyes blurring into streaks of sunshine. Blood dribbled out from her wound and pooled around her arm. When she fell, a bubble, something light slipped under her, lessening the impact of her fall. The sword clattered to her side, the flames still blazing.

"Hey!" Kayan ran up to her.

Sapphire and Thunderbolt ran toward them. Sapphire quickly turned Nezha over. "Nezha, you are going to be all right."

Faint voices fell upon Nezha's ears. Her vision blurred, and everything quieted, fading into nothing.

***

"How is she?" Nezha heard Kayan ask as she regained consciousness.

Sapphire answered, "The wound has healed, but she lost a lot of blood. I applied herbs to her shoulder to ease any pain. When she wakes up, I'll give her warm tea and iron supplements."

When Nezha's eyes opened, Sapphire and Thunderbolt came into view.

Sapphire embraced her.

Kayan turned to the bedside. "You might be as brave as my sister."

"Where are we?"

"At Kayan's home," Sapphire brushed back Nezha's hijab, fixing up the tangled hair that peeked through.

"You need to rest up after your bravery."

"Right, the orbs. Did we get them? And the feather. Is it okay?" Nezha took a sip of the tea and sat up.

"Kid, don't try to sit up. We don't want you t' strain yourself," Thunderbolt said calmly.

Comet's ears flicked, she raised her head and meowed at Nezha. She pawed at Nezha's arm and rubbed her head against Nezha's shoulder.

"Comet... I'm okay, sweetheart." Nezha brushed her fingers through silky fur. Comet was always by her side. Whenever Nezha felt ill, or her heart ached, Comet would be there, curled beside her, pressed up against her. Always there, her soft fur, her soothing purr. She didn't feel that alone with her around.

"We recovered them after you defeated the jinni. Sapphire fitted the feather back on the bracelet again." Kayan handed the two orbs to Thunderbolt, who moved them close to Nezha.

Their warm energy melted into her.

"Go to sleep, and we'll see you in the morning. I'm in the next room, so if you need me I will be close by."

Sapphire smiled at her tenderly and walked out of the room.

"Hey, kid, I'm here for you too. Consider me your guard tonight. Not sure what Kayan is though." Thunderbolt winked at her.

"Hey, I heard that," Kayan said, annoyed.

Thunderbolt stood outside the door.

"Kayan?" Nezha looked up at him.

"Yeah? Is something wrong?"

"No. I felt the wind when I fell. You cushioned my fall, didn't you?"

"Mm-hmm. Goodnight." Kayan smiled, averting his gaze and walked out the door.

"Goodnight."

Nezha looked up at the ceiling. There was no pressure or pain in her body anymore, but she could still remember the sting and throbbing when she had collapsed by the jinni. Jinni... The thought of Lamis crept into her mind. She still needed to know who the jinni was who'd killed her aunt.

Comet slipped to her side, purring. "Comet, my sweet girl."

Nezha stroked the cat's head. The cat stood up and plopped herself beside Nezha's head. Soon, they were both pulled into slumber.

The next morning sunlight cascaded over the table beside Nezha's bed. She woke up and swung her feet over, her toes touching cold blue hardwood. She looked around the bed to see if there were slippers and slipped her feet into a white pair. She fitted her hijab over her head and headed to the hallway, the wood floors shone, recently polished.

"Good morning," Kayan sang. He carried a plate full of breakfast. There was a tall glass of mint tea. Beside it was khobz—a round bread with melted butter over it. Fried eggs with golden yolks seasoned with cumin, had green olives on the side, and three glistening dates. A small ramekin held strawberry jam.

She looked up at him as he greeted her with a hesitant smile.

"Good morning." Nezha's mouth salivated upon seeing food.

"Sapphire and Thunderbolt are visiting the market for supplies." Kayan hesitantly looked at her.

Nezha smiled. "Thank you Kayan. It looks so good. Have you eaten yet?"

"Nope." He started walking toward the kitchen.

"Let's all eat together." Nezha walked with him to the dining table in the kitchen. "I appreciate your concern, Kayan. Thank you."

Kayan looked over to her and smiled. "You're welcome, Nezha jan."

Nezha narrowed her eyes at him. *What had he just said?* Maybe she heard him wrong, but whatever he'd said it made her think of her ma, when she would say. "Meri jaan," the endearment she used for her.

Both anger and sadness bubbled up from inside her. She continued to look at him.

"Huh?" Kayan raised his brows.

***

After breakfast Kayan walked outside and stretched his arms. The freedom of the wind playing through his hair, the coolness a caress across his skin. The way the wind was so light, buoyant, without restraint, it all soothed his spirit. To be carefree was something he could never afford.

He found Nezha sitting by a small pond, a paintbrush in one hand. "Hey there... Nezha."

He sat beside her with a bit of distance.

"Hey, Kayan." Nezha tipped her head up, but soon returned her focus on her painting.

"So, how are you feeling?"

"Oh, I'm good. Peaceful, even." Comet was by her side, nuzzling Nezha's arm with her head. She was belly up, her paws together, as Nezha petted and tickled her furry stomach.

Kayan lit up with a smile. "Ah, that's good. So earlier, you looked mad. Were you upset?"

Nezha glanced at him. "Oh, I wasn't mad. Well, you called me jaan. I didn't think you knew Punjabi."

"Oh, that?" Kayan's cheeks heated. "It's not. It's something my people say when we want to be friendly and on good terms with someone."

She turned to him. "It's just that, *jaan* in my language is a word only used when someone cares a lot about you. Kind of like sweet words."

Kayan flushed deeper. "Oh. Oh! Well, I uh…"

Nezha chuckled and turned back to her painting. "It's okay."

He gulped and took a breath in. This would be the right time to change the subject. "You know, Thunderbolt looked grumpy before he left." Kayan grinned at Nezha and before he knew it, he was leaning in, being pulled in by her.

"That's how he is," she said. You know, he and Sapphire have been my friends since I first got here. The pond outside Equus city is where it all began. It was the pond that brought me to Noorenia." She dipped her brush and glanced at the flowers beside the pond. The wide yellow petals had a tapered edge.

"So, it's Divine will."

"Yes." A forlorn smile crossed Nezha's face.

"Hey, your painting's really nice." He leaned to take a better look. She'd captured the light glinting off them and the delicate lines across the petals.

"Thank you. Aren't they just beautiful?" She tipped her head back, a bright smile on her face. There was this sparkle in her eye.

"Yeah. Yellow is a happy color." Kayan chewed his lower lip. He wanted to get along with her. The warmth on her face, the sunlight and the yellow flowers all made the amber in her skin glow over her face. She was bright and that bright cheer tugged at his heart.

"Huh? I was talking about my paintings." Nezha grinned and motioned her head to two other canvases.

Kayan widened his eyes. Oh, zaan. She had pride in her work that was for sure.

"So, what do you think of our group?"

"Well, I still need time to adjust." His shoulders were facing her as he leaned in.

Nezha and his gaze lingered. The wind carried her aura, that combination of her spunk and gentleness. He didn't want to look away, but the reality that he was staring at her made him avert his gaze and direct it toward the water.

His breath caught and he had the sudden urge to hide. Maybe he would have to be as brave as Nezha was. Facing his fear of someone seeing who he was on the inside, just as Nezha captured beauty on her canvas.

CHAPTER 18—THE DARK DAY

"The sky is pretty dark now." Kayan noticed, staring up at the rivulets of black clouds in the sky. "Some kind of storm?" They were outside in a field by K'ami city. Kayan's home.

"I sense something sinister." Sapphire looked up into the dark sky as the wind roiled, dragging the branches of trees.

Nezha's eyebrows furrowed in concern. "Just as we all got a chance to relax."

Kayan stared at the sky. "There's something coming this way. I can feel the wind's pressure! Hold your breath."

Nezha and the others looked up. A mass of dark clouds swirled above them. From the mass, fumes plummeted to the ground.

It was too late. Nezha inhaled the thick vapors, filling her throat and lungs. Her face turned pale before she brought her hijab to her lips and held her breath.

The siblings followed suit.

Kayan covered his mouth with one hand and spun the other, quickly dispersing the dark gas and sent it up, siphoning it toward the sky.

Nezha gasped.

"That was slick, Kayan," Thunderbolt said.

Kayan grinned.

Nezha glanced at Kayan. "What was that stuff I inhaled?"

"It's that aura that worries me. Something about it is demonic. I just pray that it wasn't poison," Sapphire said.

Terror clasped Nezha's heart.

"I hope it wasn't either. You don't feel any pain, do you?" Thunderbolt faced Nezha and searched her eyes.

"No, I feel fine," Nezha said, but anxiety wrenched her gut.

"I'll prepare a herbal tea for you." Sapphire rushed back into the house as the rest followed.

The evening sky bruised into pinks and purples. Nezha sipped her tea, the warmth coating her throat, soothing some of the knots in her stomach.

An ache embedded into Nezha's head, and a sudden urge shook over her.

Kill them, a voice echoed in her head.

Her vision blurred. *What's happening? I*—Her hands fell limply to her sides, and she took a knife from the kitchen, the dying light gleaming off the blade's edge. She lunged at Sapphire, but she moved and Nezha missed.

She tucked the knife into the belt loop of her pants and walked out toward the tree.

Kayan was on his knees beside the tree, his face in his palms. He stood up and turned.

Kayan raised his brows. His lips parted and eyes widened.

Nezha was internally shaking, so much that even her hands started to tremble. Her voice turned ominous. "You tried to hurt me when we first met."

No, that's not me saying this! Try as she might, she couldn't say the words aloud.

His eyes widened. "I thought you were Lexa's pawn. That icy hand was never meant to hurt you."

Nezha was mere inches from him. "You jerk."

Kayan gasped. "You hold grudges, huh?" He grimaced.

"What do you think?" Nezha lunged at him as she pulled the knife out. Her eyes stung with tears.

216

Kayan backed up into the tree. He twisted the wind, which held her arm in its grasp.

"Are you going to kill me?"

"K… Kayan, r-run." It was truly Nezha who struggled to speak.

"Wait… what's going on?" Kayan winced as the knife's point pricked his chest. The blade shook, and dragged on his shirt, leaving tiny scratches.

Tears sprang from her eyes. She was doing her best to resist. The muscles in her arms were taut, and with each spasm, she fought back harder against whatever tried to pull her strings like a marionette.

"You really are possessed." The wind rippled around Kayan as he held Nezha back. He took a step forward.

Nezha regained control over her body again. Every muscle relaxing, her skin becoming warm instead of hot. A strong light engulfed her.

Kayan shaded his eyes from the light as she gasped and fell to her knees.

"Nezha? Nezha. Hey!"

She smiled weakly. "Do you still think I wanted to hurt you?"

He regarded her in silence, his lips a straight line. It was the first time he hardly smiled. "No." Kayan's shoulders slumped.

"I'm so—"

"Hey, you don't need to be sorry. It wasn't you. You were being controlled. Now, we need to head back inside. I feel that sickening fume again."

In the house, they discussed the mysterious fumes and Nezha's condition.

"I almost injured Kayan," Nezha cried.

"Ever since you inhaled those fumes, I had a bad feeling something like this would happen," Kayan said, clenching his fist.

Nezha turned to Sapphire. "Are we going to have to keep fighting jinn and live in anxiety?"

"It is the power of the orbs that draws them. It won't be like this forever," Sapphire said.

Kayan stood at the window, looking up at the sky.

"Where's Thunderbolt?" Nezha asked.

"Oh, he was also worried about those fumes. He wanted to keep an eye on things and alert us if anything happened," Sapphire explained.

"Nezha, you believe you are being controlled by someone?" Sapphire asked.

"Most definitely. Someone was speaking through me. I couldn't control my body at all. Although, I finally regained some control right before a white light glowed from me, and I was able to break the hold."

"Hmm, it must have been the angel's light that helped you," Sapphire said.

"I believe that too." Nezha turned to Kayan. He was looking out the window. "Thank the Creator, I feel much better now."

Thunderbolt rushed in. "The fumes are back and there's a jinni!" Thunderbolt rummaged through a bag. "I bought these gas masks. We won't be able t' inhale the fumes."

"Wait, how did you know?" Nezha asked.

"Saphy called me. It was her idea."

"It was a good idea."

Thunderbolt handed a mask to each of them. They fitted them to their mouths as everyone followed him out of the house.

They found a dark, angry cloud above their heads. A woman descended from the heavens as her laughter rang in their ears.

The Atlas glowed from within Nezha's pocket, and the orbs beckoned her, chills ran down the back of her head. "She must have an orb," she whispered to Sapphire.

The fume grew darker and expanded.

"Oh, how ghastly you look. Those masks don't suit you," the jinni mused. She sat atop dark fumes. Her one leg hanging over the other. She had her forefinger to the side of her brown face, her head titled and a snarky grin at her lips. She brushed her short brown hair aside. "Give me your orbs, lest I suffocate you to shades of blue. The last thing you'll remember is Kharqa slaughtered you."

"No one cares what your name is." Thunderbolt exhaled harshly.

"Prepare yourselves." Kharqa released more fumes toward the companions, but Kayan swiftly thwarted her attack. He spun his hands, lulling the wind into a sphere of air that sucked in the fumes.

"You weren't prepared for this." He raised one eyebrow and grinned. The ball of fumes spun at his finger.

Silently, Kharqa stood from her cloud of fumes. "No matter."

Nezha's heart throbbed, and she fell to her knees. The angels and Kayan fell with her. Her skin tingled, her muscles tautening and a pressure shoving her toward the ground.

"The fumes seep through skin. It's a shame really. I thought I would have more fun with you."

How will we get out of this? My heart is burning. Nezha struggled to stand, but she merely flinched.

"Now, let me see. Who will I torture to tell me of the orbs? You, boy." The jinni pulled Kayan's head up by his hair. "It will be a delight."

Kayan grimaced at the pain. He spoke through gritted teeth. "I won't tell you."

"Oh, but you must." Kharqa took off his mask. "Lest your hands are sullied by the blood of your companions."

His eyes widened and his face paled.

Nezha's eyes widened, her heart slamming against her chest. The jinni couldn't sense the orbs? "Don't hurt him."

"Now, who has them? Kharqa ignored Nezha, her face mere inches from Kayan.

Her icy blue eyes gazed deep into his.

He craned his neck away from her face.

She threw him to the ground. Kayan gasped and coughed.

Kharqa sat on her knees. "Stop being such a brat. Young wind jawhar, my winds are poisoned by darkness." She leaned in to his face again. "You stupid humans."

"Noor's sake..." Thunderbolt gritted his teeth.

Despite having her gas mask, Nezha found it difficult to breathe, her chest tightening. Her hands shook. *I have to help Kayan.*

Kayan held his breath.

"Boy, holding your breath won't help you. I won't let you die like this." She trailed a finger on his arm and then abruptly punched him.

Kayan choked and coughed. He couldn't help but breathe in. His lungs took in the poisoned air.

She's hurting him. The pain was too much to bear for Nezha. If only she could move and use her feather, she could get rid of the jinni. Her tears soaked through her hijab and into her hair.

"Let me suck up your energy, or I'll kill you." Kharqa opened her mouth and her tongue protruded.

Tears pooled in Kayan's eyes.

The wind smacked Kharqa, and she flew into the air and hit the ground. He stood up shakily and walked toward her. "Don't you dare even lay as much as a finger on me, or anyone, you revolting jinni. You won't take anyone from me!"

Kayan spun in an arch and repeatedly slashed her with the wind. She screeched in pain.

Nezha couldn't believe it. Kayan, normally a gentle lulling breeze, turned to a tumultuous cyclone bent on destruction. In his eyes there was more than just anger, sadness ran deep.

The pressure, the tingling, it all disappeared from Nezha's skin. They stood. Nezha managed to regain her composure.

"Kayan, please." Her feet slipped as the wind caused turbulence. "I'll use my sword." But her voice did not reach him. Nezha fashioned a wall of fire in front of Kayan, her hands raised.

He was taken aback, as if he had been jolted out of a nightmare.

"N-Nezha." Kayan breathed in deeply.

She waved the fire away with one hand, wisps of the smoke lifted into the air. "Kayan, it's fine. We're all fine now." Nezha smiled at him, grateful to him for what he'd done.

Kayan breathed in. "She won't take me from my family. I need to help find a cure for my father."

Sapphire and Thunderbolt both stood in front of them.

"You're not in pain, are you?" Sapphire placed her hands over Nezha's shoulders.

"I'm all right," Nezha replied.

"I'm relieved kid," Thunderbolt said. "Kayan? That jinni was throwin' you around like a rag doll. The nerve of that thing." He put a hand on Kayan's shoulder. Concern took over his expression.

"I'm fine now. She's fortunate, I would have torn her apart if it wasn't for Nezha." Kayan glanced at Nezha, who had transformed the feather into a sword and stood over Kharqa. As soon as Nezha took a step, Comet jumped out from the bushes, hissing, her claws digging into Kharqa's face. The jinni shrieked and backed away. Comet jumped to Nezha's side.

"Whoa. Thanks, Comet." Nezha was taken aback by the ferocity. "The pure light will now seal your fate." Nezha spoke almost as if she were chanting. She brought the blade down, their eyes meeting as the blue flames cut into the jinni's shoulder. The jinni screamed and faded into specks of ash.

Nezha's eyes remained without any joy, except for the relief that now settled in her heart. Where the jinni once lay, four orbs sparkled under the light of the moon.

"Seven hells," Thunderbolt said.

"Divine's sake." Kayan's eyes widened.

Nezha bent down to pick them up, and they melted within her heart. "This was too much for one day." She sighed.

Comet brushed into her leg. Her soft fur was a much-needed comfort. She scooped up the feline into her arms. Comet head-butted her, and her purring rumbled against Nezha's neck.

Inside Kayan's kitchen, they sipped tea that Sapphire brewed in haste.

"I'll be fine everyone, don't worry." Kayan smiled.

"You say that Kayan, but you're the one who worries so much," Thunderbolt stated.

Sapphire helped heal Kayan, giving him a hot and cold compress mixed with herbs and powerful flower essences.

Nezha focused her attention on Kayan. How he beamed as Thunderbolt teased him. She sipped the last drops of her herbal tea.

***

On the way to their beds, Kayan walked close behind Nezha.

"Nezha?" His voice was a low and gentle breeze.

Nezha turned and met his gaze. "Kayan."

Kayan's eyes were full of emotion and longing. "I'm sorry." His voice cracked halfway.

"You're talking about when we met and the icy fist."

Kayan nodded.

"Don't look so guilty. I was definitely shocked and angry, but not anymore. You're showing us you're a good person." With sincerity, she lifted her hands, palms open toward Kayan.

"I just hate when someone is mad at me." He looked up at her.

"I'm not mad at you." Nezha smiled.

Kayan's eyes filled with gratitude, and he smiled warmly at her. Their gaze lingered for a few seconds.

Nezha noticed the flecks of green, blue and gold in Kayan's eyes, before he looked away.

"Good night," Nezha said, breaking their silence.

"Goodnight."

The house was silent except for the white noise of the crickets, serenading them under the moonlight.

CHAPTER 19—MAGMA'S ENCASEMENT

The warm spices and sweet smells of breakfast lured Nezha out of bed. Comet was by her side, weaving in and out of her legs, marking Nezha with her own scent. Nezha washed up in the bathroom and dressed. She walked down the white marble stairs and turned into the kitchen.

"Good morning," Nezha said.

"Morning, kid." Thunderbolt grinned.

He set a plate on the table. Both scrambled and sunny side eggs took their place with the rest of the food. Soft rolled breads, glistening bowls of vegetable stock, with various vegetables and a lamb shoulder marinated in pomegranate molasses on a decorative blue plate. All kinds of spices and sweetness melted into the dishes.

Nezha's mouth watered.

Nezha gave him a look of confusion and adjusted her hijab. He'd really outdone himself this time.

"What?"

"I didn't think of you as a five-star chef type."

The way Thunderbolt's lips tautened, Nezha felt as if she'd wounded him.

"I learned it from the Fire Kingdom. Cooking's a way for me t' give something back t' others. If they ever smelled or tasted something like what I gave them, maybe they'd think of me. So, it wasn't like I wasn't around. Ah, I'm just blabbering on though, huh? I'll stop."

"No, that's really thoughtful of you. I get it. Even for me, food is memories. Enjoying their company." Nezha noticed the way Thunderbolt's expression shifted as he turned to her.

"Anyways, take a seat since you're here. I'll go wake up everyone else. Don't forget t' compliment the chef." At that, he ambled past Nezha.

After breakfast, they flew for an hour over the sea, heading Southeast.

***

Upon landing, they walked across a green field where the grass was so thick it reminded Nezha of Comet's fur. She tapped on the Atlas and located the direction where another orb was detected. "It's a place called Molten Magma Trench." She surveyed the area, catching a glimpse of large mineral spikes in the distance, which Sapphire told her was a place called Silver Spikes. "Are we ever going to go there?"

"No, it's barren land," Sapphire said.

A murder of crows flew above their heads. They found the trench with a wooden bridge over it. It was rickety, like it would fall if a breeze happened to pass by. Lava had formed layers of crust in red and black. Underneath the trench was an active volcano. A pool of lava lay just to their right as they approached the trench. A bubble rose up and popped, wafting over the companions. Its scent was sickeningly sweet.

"It's so hot around here." Kayan tugged at his collar and inhaled the scent. His breathing was shallow. Then he sneezed.

"Should I leave?" Thunderbolt winked.

Nezha inhaled the scent and furrowed her brows. "It's all about you, isn't it?" Nezha snapped.

Nezha's eyebrows twitched. A part of her didn't want to argue with him. There was pain deep in his eyes. But another part of her was pressed on being angry. An inexplicable pull.

"About me? Look, I took care of my dad. I'm not always thinking of myself," Kayan said.

"Stop acting like you're so righteous. I'm an angel and so much more powerful than you are," Thunderbolt said.

"Brother, don't be so rude. Why are you all behaving like this? It's getting on my nerves." Sapphire formed fists.

"Took care of your dad? What about when you nearly hurt me when we just met? Did you care then?" Nezha leaned in, close to Kayan's face.

"I thought you got over that. I didn't want to hurt you."

"I did, but I'm reminding you not to make assumptions of people. And you, Thunderbolt, calling me kid all the time. I'm a teen, okay?"

Flames erupted around Nezha's arms, coiling around them like a serpent.

"Assumptions? Do you know how it feels to become a fighter at a young age? To see people you care about disappear around you? To see what the jinn have done to people here, first-hand?"

"Well, I'm fighting now. I didn't want to." Nezha threw her hands up.

"I didn't want to either. When my mother d—" Kayan stared at her and turned around.

Kayan groaned. "I wanted to be free. I didn't want to fight anymore... And then dad got sick. Those months were torture."

Nezha's gaze shifted to the ground. "It's not easy. I didn't want to live without..." A part of her anger seemed to subside.

"You *are* a kid! I'm so much older than you. Relax with the fire already. I don't want you burning my golden hair." Thunderbolt lifted his palms up and swiped his fingers through his hair. "Don't get me started on miss I-know-everything..."

"I am not a-know-it-all. I may be wiser than you, but that is only because I try to learn whatever I can."

"You try too much t' be perfect! There is no perfect, okay?"

"But one must use their logic! Emotions alone are not enough for survival!" Sapphire leaned toward Thunderbolt and her necklace began glowing.

"So, stop hurting yourself all the time!"

"Hurting... How do you know if I am hurting?" Sapphire yelled so loud that even Kayan and Nezha quieted their argument.

"I *don't* know! You're always being all, I'm wise, we should be patient, we should do this and the books say that." Thunderbolt mocked. "You never frown, you hardly tell me how you feel! You were becoming distant and cold. I was glad t' see you angry now!" Thunderbolt's voice softened. "Don't push me away, sis. You're all I have left."

Thunderbolt had the last words as they stepped on the bridge.

Water rained down on them as a large dragon awoke from the magma and its head rose above them and yawned. The hot liquid did not seem to bother him one bit.

"Forgive me." Sapphire pressed her head to Thunderbolt's shoulder.

He sighed. "Nah. It's all right now, sis." He messed up her hair.

"Well, at least we got that out of our systems." Nezha raised her hands up, the water dripping from her sleeves. Comet stood by her feet and shook her body. She meowed in protest as the bridge shook.

"Kayan... was that all true?" Nezha's eyebrows furrowed.

"Yeah. I don't think I can talk about it yet. But, I've had to fight for a long time." He unwrapped the flexible blade, curled around his hips. "You see this sword? Ali. My mother gave me Ali. An urumi sword. He's all I have left of her."

Before Nezha could say anything, the dragon yawned.

"DAMB dragon." Thunderbolt's voice was more in awe than accusatory.

"Well, damn's right." Nezha said, just as Kayan spun his hands, evoking the air to dry their clothes.

"Thanks," she muttered and gave an apologetic smile to Kayan.

Kayan gave a slight nod as he blinked and smiled.

"No, I mean it," Thunderbolt said. "Dragon accorded magma's breath. D. A. M. B."

"You know this dragon?" Nezha hung onto the bridge as it swayed back and forth.

"We learned about him through the Fire Kingdom. A dragon who was created from magma itself. He is peaceful unless threatened, or if you wake him from his slumber." Sapphire explained.

"Sounds like someone I know." Thunderbolt glanced at Nezha.

Nezha ignored the comment as the dragon lowered its head. His smooth body had burgundy scales. Sharper black scales ran down his back.

The dragon yawned again, exhibiting his clean bright teeth. His breath fumed over them. It was sweet with a hint of smoke. "What is the meaning of this?" the dragon bellowed and narrowed his blood-red eyes at them.

"We—" Nezha rubbed the feather bracelet.

Before anyone else could dare to speak, the dragon's eyes pooled over in lava, and to their horror, it rushed toward them. They broke out into a run, as Nezha scooped Comet into her arms. It ran over the bridge like half-baked cake batter.

Nezha stopped just as they were about halfway there. "I sense the orb. It's somewhere with the dragon. We need it, remember?"

"How are we going t' tell him that?" Thunderbolt side-stepped Kayan, who made a pushing motion with his hands, the wind shoving the lava back into the trench like waves returning to the sea.

"I wonder why the lava didn't disintegrate the bridge?" Sapphire said it more to herself.

"Yeah, that is really strange," Nezha said. The lava rolled over the bridge as if it were velvet forming pleats.

"I have a bottle of fire spider silk," Kayan blurted just as the dragon turned to them again. He slumped down into the magma, only his head and shoulders visible.

"What?" Nezha gaped at him.

Kayan grinned as he brought out a pouch from his side and pulled out a metal spray bottle. "I always keep a few things with me."

"Well, what are you waiting for? Spray us already." Thunderbolt looked back at the dragon and sighed, seeing the beast's eyes close.

Kayan sprayed everyone down with the clear liquid. "You know it's not exactly silk. It's pretty much spider spit. It repels fire and magma." He grinned.

"Eww... and cool!" Nezha's eyes scanned her body. She touched her cheeks. "Oh my goodness! My face is so silky smooth!"

"Yup." Kayan held one hand out to the bottle. "Fire Spider silk, keeps your skin smooth and soft and stops you from burning to a crisp!" He beamed and then quickly said, "Spider not included, may cause itching."

"Interesting." Sapphire's fingers slipped over her arm and in curiosity she softly touched Nezha's face. "You're right."

"Yeah. Plus, who would buy fire spider spit?" Kayan laughed a little. "Try saying that fast."

"The dragon is currently sleeping. Can you tell where the orb is?" Sapphire turned to Nezha.

Nezha walked backwards, stepping over the magma where it had crusted over. She approached the dragon, staying a safe distance from him. The orb was definitely with him. She kept walking to different places back and forth, until she felt it stronger. "It's somewhere around his head."

"I think if you tell him who you are and show him the feather, he should believe you. Since he knows the Fire Kingdom, he would know about the feather."

"Good idea." Kayan gripped the ropes of the bridge.

"So, you are still here." The dragon opened his eyes as he regarded them and stood up from the magma once more. The magma rolled off his back. His eyes again dripped with lava. He was readying himself to attack. It oozed over them.

Nezha cringed, but the fire spider's silk truly kept them from burning. No heat, no flesh burning off of her.

Before they could recover from the shock, the dragon roared.

"Wait." Nezha unleashed the fire, her control over it once again faltering. Waves of flame were sent toward the dragon as she raised her hand.

The dragon widened its eyes and blew water across the flames, sending it raining down upon the companions.

Thunderbolt spit out water and said unamused, "Thanks... I needed another shower."

Sapphire wrung out her hair, drops falling onto the bridge.

"A fire jawhar?" The dragon's features softened as his breath misted within the heat.

"Yes. I have the feather belonging to Princess Sanari." Nezha lifted up her left arm, where the feather glistened around her wrist.

"Her feather? How?" The dragon lowered to Nezha's eye level.

"It was given to me by the angel Ansam."

The dragon looked over at the others. "Hmm. The Fire Kingdom mansion has been destroyed. Why do you have it, young flame jawhar? Do you belong to her lineage?"

"Yeah, she's my cousin. You have one of the Angel of Mercy's soul orbs, right? I can feel it. I know it's somewhere near your head."

"Ah. You truly are her relative. I indeed have one. It lodged into my scale when it fell from the sky. Why are you looking for the orbs?"

Nezha sighed. "Well, I have the angel's light within me."

The dragon smiled. "I do feel a familiar warmth from you. It would be my pleasure to hand it over in your protection. My name is Rahil."

"I'm Nezha." She introduced the others.

The dragon's claws picked out the orb from the scale on his head and placed into Nezha's hands.

"Thank you so much." The orb melted against Nezha's chest and disappeared.

"I hope you forgive me. I don't like my sleep being disrupted, Lady Nezha." Rahil placed his hand to his large chest.

"By the way, why do you blow water? And, why did we all suddenly start fighting?" Kayan said.

"Ah, the heat from the pool of magma near the bridge enhances a person's innate negativity. As for the water, everything needs balance. When one is angry, it is like fire eating away at them. They need to cool their mind and sometimes need water itself to pull the heat of anger away. Here, if you need my services, you can contact me with this." Rahil dipped his clawed finger into the magma. A curled horn formed as he drew his palm to Nezha's face.

"I can fashion barriers out of magma. If you are ever in need of one built or destroyed, blow it three times, and I will come."

Nezha took the horn. "Thank you."

CHAPTER 20—FEATHERS OF FIXATION

The companions arrived in Mellow Meadow. It was beside K'ami City where Kayan resided. The soft grass stretched into the horizon, dotted with daises, their plump yellow center and white petals feathering out. They were neighbors to the patches of echinacea, the bright purple flowers bobbing in the gentle breeze.

"This meadow is beautiful." Sapphire bent down to smell one of the flowers.

"Yeah, I love it. I just hope I don't see any bees." Nezha grimaced and tightened her shoulders. If even one bee got close, she knew she'd scream.

"Oh, now that's a sight I'd pay t' see." Thunderbolt teased.

"I'll be your swatter. One whoosh of air, and they'll be gone," Kayan said as he gestured with his hands as if he were striking a baseball. He placed his palm to his mouth, trying to hide his smile at her reaction. Nezha seemed exasperated.

"Are you teasing me too?" Nezha blushed and placed her hand to her heart.

"The Atlas was glowing toward here in K'ami City." Nezha grasped the device in her palms looking at the arrow on the screen point toward the meadow.

Thunderbolt eyed Nezha. "Last night was a pain."

"Yeah. At least we found another orb. I'm just anxious to find them all." Nezha rubbed her shoulder.

Nezha nodded slowly as she spoke. "I was thinking about what we had to go through. We've had to deal with so many problems. Now we're beside a calm meadow and need to keep moving." She sighed.

Sapphire looked at her sympathetically and placed a hand on her shoulder. "The road to harmony is paved with deceptions and troubles, Nezha. How else would we savor the happiness and peace we seek?"

"Tell me more, oh wise sheikh." Thunderbolt grinned, and Sapphire nudged him. "She's right though."

"Yeah Nezha, Sapphire's right. I know we need rest, but others in Noorenia don't get time to relax or have any peace. If it wasn't for me fighting off those jinn that attacked me, I would have died and my family..." Kayan trailed off.

"I'm sorry... I probably sound like I'm complaining," Nezha said. " I just want things done so badly."

Kayan smiled at her. "Don't worry. I know it's overwhelming, but we can get through it all."

"I know how you feel, kid. Believe me. I'm as anxious as you are. It's been a month since you got here. All of this is a major responsibility for you. We're here for you," Thunderbolt said.

Nezha regarded the three. Comet brushed against her legs. "Thanks, everyone. I needed it."

Sapphire smiled and held Nezha in an embrace. "In time, you'll learn more about yourself, Nezha. There's always room for progression."

"The glowing is stronger here," Nezha said. They had walked further into the meadow.

Sapphire experienced a pang of fear inside her heart. Her eyes widened.

Nezha noticed the look on Sapphire's face and turned to her. "Sapphire?"

With a flap of wings and a blur, a jinni materialized before them. Her voice was smooth and clear. Her tight black lace dress revealed her plump figure. "I have another uninvited guest." She turned and behind her was someone who looked exactly like Sapphire, except her wings were black, and she had a sinister grin on her face. "Welcome, Doppelganger... Sapphire D," the jinni crowed. Her gaze settled on Sapphire.

Thunderbolt impulsively shot lightning at the jinni. She raised a feather and shook her head.

"I'm not the one you should be concerned about." The jinni fiddled with the three crow feathers in her long black hair.

He grunted in disgust and sped up right in front of her, shooting a spike of lightning by her head.

Kayan had his hand on his sword, his fingers tapping on the hilt.

"I won't be wasting my time." The jinni disappeared into plumes of smoke before Thunderbolt could make another move.

Nezha's mouth was agape as she walked over to him.

Sapphire was immobile, aside from her shaking hands at her sides. Her lips pressed into a frown.

Sapphire D ran toward them. A black light emanated from her necklace and shot toward Sapphire.

Kayan jumped in front and unsheathed his sword. The blade danced like a ribbon and straightened as the wind circled it, slicing through the black light and twirled around Sapphire D. She formed bubbles that obscured his view, but he whipped the sword and caught her legs.

"Hey, Sapphire. We can't just stand around," Thunderbolt called to her.

***

Her appearance is like mine, but I feel darkness within her. Sapphire flinched at Thunderbolt's booming voice. She breathed out. "I know. Forgive me."

"Sis, she might look like you, but we won't let her get away."

Sapphire D ran to Nezha, who formed a shield of flames.

From behind, Sapphire shot a white light at Sapphire D. Her doppelganger fell to her knees and glared back at her. Her skin stitched up as she waved her hand over it. She showed off a grim smirk.

"I won't allow you to hurt them. You will fight *me.*" Sapphire held up her hand, the light was a pinprick, then it grew, pulsing and shooting out.

"You are not aware of your own strength, are you?" Sapphire D said as she pivoted and dodged.

Nezha sent flames toward Sapphire D, who twirled a sword of hard light between her fingers, the fire spraying in either direction.

"Nezha, please, I will handle her," Sapphire said, fear in her eyes. This look-alike was hers. She would fight and no one else. Sapphire couldn't bear anyone getting hurt because of her.

"Okay." Nezha conceded and stood back.

The look-alike punched Sapphire, who grabbed her fist and glided over her, flipping into the air and casting her light. The duplicate kicked her from behind. Sapphire landed with a thud but twisted her body and slid her right leg to trip Sapphire D.

Sapphire grabbed the doppelganger by the feet and swung her like an ax, but the doppelganger flew back to her in midair, and they collided.

"How much more will you handle?" Sapphire D said, lifting herself. She placed a hand to her necklace, which was just like the one Sapphire owned. "You'll see how my Sapphire horn necklace will come in handy."

The pain throbbed in Sapphire's hands as she stood. Her fingers pressed into the necklace around her neck.

Sapphire?

Sapphire D stepped with her right foot, her left sliding to meet the other. Lasers from her palms shot out, missing Sapphire each time. Sapphire D slid to her and smacked Sapphire, sending her stumbling back and hitting the ground.

"You're too stiff. Do you think you'll accomplish anything with logic alone?"

"Sapphire!" Nezha started over to her, but Thunderbolt stopped her.

"Nezha, don't you see it? She doesn't want anyone t' get hurt. She's been like this since she was little. Sapphire's the strongest unicorn I knew. She let others' burdens carry her over. Even with the pain, she just wanted t' be an example t' others. She's like a shield. She refuses t' show her pain even if she cracks." Thunderbolt's eyes were soft.

Nezha relaxed her shoulders and looked over at Sapphire. "She's been hiding it so well. She really is selfless."

"I want to help her too, but it's her fight. We need to respect that," Kayan said.

"I just won't tolerate it if her life is endangered. No one can stop me then." Fire bloomed around Nezha's body.

"Come on, I want you to feel the bubbling of pressure Sapphire. Feel something." Sapphire D lowered her head, and her eyes rose up with a piercing stare.

Sapphire stood and faced Sapphire D. She brushed at her jaw. *I must use it.* Sapphire reached for the holster on her leg and pulled up a small Beco crystal, colors flashing in the sunlight. Light washed over the gem from Sapphire's palms and it grew, becoming a boomerang the length of her wrist to her elbow. Her arm reeled back, and she pivoted to the right and swung it with full force. "My boomerang is made from Beco crystals. Add pressure, and it will emit a charge. That's the piezoelectric effect." The boomerang met with the doppelganger's stomach, sending Sapphire D flying back.

"Really, sis? This isn't time for a science lesson." Thunderbolt threw his hands up.

"Oh, that buzz of power. That's more like it." Sapphire D stood up slowly, her hand to her stomach. She tilted her head. "I'll break you."

They were in a heated battle. Sword and boomerang collided and whooshed through the air.

Sapphire D dodged.

Both turned right or left, forward and back, never swaying as if they were straight lines in motion.

"Whoa. I've never seen her fight like this before. She doesn't even look like the blows faze her," Nezha said.

"Sis, just what're you thinking?" Thunderbolt whispered.

Eventually, Sapphire D crashed into a boulder. She let out a scream and her breath turned shallow. While she rose, her skin rippled and resembled black glass.

Sapphire's eyebrows furrowed. *Someone wants us to battle to the death.*

"This is our peak. Why do you think you were named Sapphire?" Sapphire D snickered as she walked up to her. Her fingers slipped across her horn necklace. She then took a piece of the Beco crystal in her possession and had her own boomerang.

Sapphire slid to the side as she avoided the spinning weapon. When the boomerang collided with her own, she pushed it up, throwing it backward.

Sapphire D slid forward and flipped backward, her legs rising up, sharply kicking Sapphire in the stomach and sending her flying behind her doppelganger. With a sharp intake of breath, Sapphire met the ground and tumbled to a stop. Her hair lit up, like she was bathed in the glowing sun. Her skin crackled. She stood up gracefully, her skin purple and shining.

Her skin became made of Sapphire.

This is why I was named Sapphire? She tugged her boomerang from the ground, light surrounded it from her hand and it shrunk. She placed it back into her holster. There was a look of determination in her eyes as light glistened on her lips. Light. She had powers of light. Being a sapphire, with the power of light. The frequency worked in combination with the crystal.

"Ah, the rare purple Sapphire. This is what you're made of." Sapphire D exclaimed.

"Stop speaking. Fight!" Sapphire shot bursts of sapphire. Flipping back and rolling to her left, Sapphire D avoided her aim. Sapphire continued the bursts that collided with her doppelganger. A crack snaked up the doppelganger's arm.

Sapphire rushed toward her like a bull. That was when they were in the middle of throwing a punch. If she hit a facet at a certain angle, she'd be victorious. At that moment, Sapphire pierced one of the facets across the duplicate's knuckles. A loud shattering clapped through the meadow. The faintest crackling appeared over Sapphire D's hands and twisted up her arm.

"You felt it?" Her doppelgänger shattered into countless pieces. A dark mist formed from where she once stood and in her place, was a black feather. It singed and turned to dust.

I won't allow my heart to. Sapphire closed her eyes. Her head fell back as she lost consciousness. She reverted to her former appearance.

***

Nezha and the others ran up to her. Thunderbolt gently placed her on the ground. "You were amazing, Saphy. You deserve the rest."

Nezha's eyes widened in astonishment. "It's just like real gems. The intense pressure forms energy. So, Sapphire was only getting stronger with each blow."

"It's amazing. I never knew this form of her." Thunderbolt looked down at Sapphire in awe.

***

Zul Sharr arrived in the meadow where Rana had contacted him. His glowing gaze fell to the feather on Nezha's bracelet and widened. His heart hammered within his chest. *She has Sanari's feather. Who is she? Now this is a problem.*

"Fire jawhar, it's a pleasure to meet you. I can feel the sparks fly already!" Zul appeared behind them and tossed

250

iron powder into the air, whilst doing a flip. Yellow sparks flew up and as they fell, they turned black.

CHAPTER 21—GUNS RICOCHET

"You finally reveal yourself, prince." Thunderbolt's fingers tensed and relaxed as balls of lightning formed in his palms. He moved his arms in a fluid motion. But Zul simply raised his arm and brought it down in a swift motion and contained them within iron.

Thunderbolt managed to strike Zul, but Zul anchored his scythe and jumped into the air, landing upon the ground.

"Oh, is that how you treat a prince? You have better etiquette than that, surely." He smiled.

"Cut the trash. You're no more than a delinquent now."

Zul chained Kayan's hands in iron, but Kayan's high speed wind ripped through them. Wind and ice encircled his fist. He jabbed at Zul, who formed a shield of iron, but Kayan kept at it, until he struck Zul's shoulder.

Zul held his shoulder. "Damn, I get the hint to cool it, but this is ridiculous. Did you like the sparks? I wanted to introduce myself in a more celebratory way."

"Why did you freeze the valley, Eisen?" Thunderbolt's hands spun with electricity.

"Huh. I haven't heard that name in a while. I'm not Eisen anymore."

"What in the seven hells are you talking about?" Thunderbolt snarled.

"Oh, you don't know? I guess you have the honor of hearing it from me. I cursed the Angel of Mercy. Unfortunately, its soul shattered. Oops." Zul Sharr shrugged.

"You did it?"

Zul Sharr raised a brow. "It's Zul Sharr, by the way. Jinni aura runs in my blood now."

"Jinni aura? So that jinni Lexa who attacked me works with you?" Kayan widened his eyes.

"How could you forsake Noorenian law? You knew that jinni magic's forbidden." Thunderbolt's fists tightened.

"You're just full of pain, Zul. I know you're hiding it behind your smile." Nezha blurted out. She placed a hand over her mouth momentarily and then wrung her hands.

"Let's properly introduce ourselves. Even enemies are close, Nezha. You seem to be related to Sanari. There are no other fire jawhars in these parts besides her lineage," Zul said and looked at Nezha with a sympathetic expression.

"You knew my name?"

"Oh, I was here when you were fighting. I knew the others, but you were the newcomer," Zul said conversationally.

"Are we seriously going t' chat with him?" Thunderbolt tossed a bomb of electricity at Zul, who let it explode within a block of iron.

"Look, that's getting old," Zul said, irritated.

"I'm Sanari's cousin. Losing someone dear to you creates a void. I know how it feels to love someone and lose them." Nezha said, her eyes welled up with emotion. *I still feel like I might hit a nerve. It's not bad to try, is it? Besides, it's true. Losing Aunt Lamis still hurts.*

Zul's eyebrows knitted. "Her cousin?"

If she'd blinked, Nezha would have missed the way he'd winced, as if she'd pricked his heart.

"Lose? You don't know how I feel about Sanari. I don't want to kill anyone, but if you don't get out of my way, you'll be testing my patience."

He doesn't want to kill anyone? Did he love Sanari?
Was the good inside him still there? Nezha gave him a long
stare, taking in his sad oval eyes flecked with orange, the
small birthmark on the left side of the bridge of his nose,
his strong jaw line and round cheeks. The way his fuller
bottom lip quirked.

Zul Sharr tore his gaze from hers.

"Are you scared of our interference?" Kayan said and
smiled impishly.

"Not the slightest."

"Don't make me laugh. You froze Unicorn Valley, and
you need t' pay for it!" Thunderbolt grunted as he struck his
sword against Zul, who brought up his scythe.

"Did I hit a few circuits?" Zul said, as their blades
clashed, his face reflected in Thunderbolt's sword.

Thunderbolt drove a strike of lightning toward Zul, but
the sparks skipped across Zul's scythe. He jumped out of
the way. A small crater formed in the ground.

"As if I wanted to," Zul murmured.

Thunderbolt opened his mouth like he intended to say
something but kept quiet.

Sapphire was still on the ground, surrounded by a ball of
swirling wind made by Kayan, with Comet inside with her.

Zul stood up. "So, is Sapphire still passed out?" His eyes held a discernible emotion.

"You keep her out of this," Thunderbolt said, his anger getting the best of him.

Kayan spun his blade for him, wrapping it around his scythe and aiming the tip of his sword at his chest.

"You're really trying your best to injure me, huh?" Zul's scythe became liquid metal and sculpted into a shield. "What did Lexa do to you?"

"Don't talk about that jinni!" Kayan gritted his teeth.

Zul spun and his kick landed against Kayan's shoulder, and Kayan fell back. In a split-second, Kayan was able to manipulate the wind into circulating discs, planting his hands over them, stopping his fall. He spun the wind again and threw Zul farther into the grass.

Zul grinned and stood up again.

Kayan ran toward Zul and leapt into the air. He spun and smacked his leg against the shield Zul fashioned for himself. It dented but protected Zul from the blow. Zul lifted himself up with his legs and sent a shower of iron spikes toward Kayan.

Thunderbolt magnetized the spikes and sent them back to their caster with sparks circling about. Nezha ignited the sparks and Zul raised his hand, metal clinking through the air and falling at his feet.

He threw his scythe and it spun like a wheel toward them. Thunderbolt raised his hands, his magnetism swatting it away.

"The angels have a reason to think I'm a threat." Zul scowled at Thunderbolt. His scythe liquified and returned to his hands. "But you, fire jawhar, why do you fight me?"

"You froze Unicorn Valley and cursed the Angel of Mercy," Nezha's hair ignited within her hijab. "Either we destroy you or save you."

"I'm doing this to save Sanari." Zul Sharr's eyes softened. He ran his fingers through his short black hair.

A foreign type of heat rose in her body. She drew her arms back and a bow and five arrows made of fire formed. She flung the arrows toward Zul and one struck his shoulder. The arrow disintegrated, but it tore the fabric of his jalabiya, revealing the scorpion mark on his neck.

***

Zul hissed, holding his bare shoulder as the cloth around it singed, and he fell to his knees. The ashes flew past his head. The heat was pulsating through his veins. Another surge of heat pushed back the pure fire Nezha had

257

unleashed on his body. The jinni aura was coursing through his veins.

Zul Sharr thought of the jinni Lexa who had found him broken. She had made a deal with him. He could still remember her voice echoing in his mind.

Prince, use your anger and pain as fuel. Curse the Angel of Mercy. The Divine will not be merciful to you for what you've done. The angel will never let his mercy touch you. If you do so, I will give you the power of the shadow jinn. You can awaken your beloved Sanari from her slumber. You will break the iron's curse on her.

He'd practically sold his soul. He wouldn't let it go to waste.

***

"Whoa. He has a scorpion tattoo." Nezha stared at him. The black lines seemed raised across his brown skin. The stinger was over his heart, with the pincers climbing up his neck, the tips over his jugular vein. *Why do I feel so bad for him?* He had lost Sanari. She knew loss all too well.

Zul Sharr chuckled. It was laced with pain as he stood up.

Thunderbolt took another chance to attack Zul with electricity, but the particles of iron only created sparks and a small explosion. As the cloud of smoke cleared,

Thunderbolt saw the scorpion mark and his lip curled in disgust.

Zul twirled his scythe, interchanging it between hands as he attacked Nezha. Nezha formed her flame arrows again as they blazed toward him. Zul diverted them toward Kayan, who did nothing to avoid them. They simply faded as they touched the wind dancing around him.

Kayan stood without even flinching, and Zul lowered his scythe.

***

Why did they think he wanted to do this? That day he'd gone to the Fire Kingdom mansion to speak with Sanari's parents, Eisen had been beaten by his mother. His mother had told him to die. She always did. His mother had screamed at him, swore at him for missing his fighting lessons. That wasn't even the excuse. Whenever she was around, all she did was abuse. All he could feel was pain that day. Instead of finding joy, his iron betrayed him. It destroyed the mansion and encased Sanari. He wanted to be stronger. Not be a weak prince, but one day, he'd be a strong king. One who deserved her.

The demonic aura pulsed inside Zul again. Pain and cold consumed him. It urged him to fall to the poison, and he obeyed. Taking control of his desires for power. He had to get stronger. That was the only way he could save her. No one would get it in his way.

***

Kayan's blade wrapped around Zul's legs and launched him toward Reflecto River. Zul's scythe helped with his fall, as he anchored it to the ground, stood on its hilt and flipped. His eyes glowed a burnt orange and a smirk curled up his lips. "Come at me."

Reflecto river was situated beside the meadow. It wasn't very deep, but it had unknown properties and was considered highly unstable. Most people wouldn't dare to look into the water let alone go for a swim in it.

Kayan ran toward Zul but Zul jumped into the water.

"Are you trying t' escape us?" Thunderbolt flew over him, sending down sparks, dancing across the surface. "Wrong move, Zul. You're a fool for jumping into water, when you know I use electricity."

Zul grinned. The electricity danced about in the water, but Zul seemed unharmed. Nezha and Kayan joined Thunderbolt.

Zul threw a dagger from afar, aiming it at Sapphire. Nezha leapt between the two and summoned flames to halt its advance. "You won't harm anyone." Her eyes glowed a piercing yellow. She stepped at the edge of the river, her fingers on the arrows. She aimed her fire arrows and took a shot at Zul. One arrow struck his chest while the others zipped into the water. Zul's form cracked and then shattered.

"Amazing. You are so naive." Zul was not in the water. He stood on the other side of the river. "Over here." He titled his head.

"Damn you," Thunderbolt whispered.

Nezha's head whipped to Zul.

Steam drifted up from the strange water. Zul held a fist of iron and dropped it. The steam reacted, causing it to create hydrogen.

"You should have done your homework before you dared to face me!"

Zul's scythe melted, dropping into the water. Zul stuck his hand in and pulled out a gun made of iron. He loaded his gun with the hydrogen energy and along with magic, he formed a weapon that rarely ever needed to refuel. His newly formed weapon glinted in the sun.

***

The demonic aura pulsed again in his veins. The voice spoke in his mind. The voice of the jinn energy. *Fight. Fight for your love. Do it no matter what the cost.*

I don't want to hurt them! Eisen thought. The part of him that still remained as a witness in his heart. His hands trembled.

Oh prince, you want Sanari awakened? You want to be stronger? Then fight.

His fingers shook and tightened around the gun. His muscle ticked at his temple. Zul gulped and raised the gun at them. Energy blasts tore through the air.

***

Kayan pushed his hands side to side, forming pockets of air that redirected the shots. He darted and avoided the blasts.

Nezha formed another shield from flames, as Zul approached her with the gun. Her hands moved in waves as she turned the energy masses into smoke.

From behind, Kayan plowed his icy fists through the air, but Zul turned around and thwarted him with more blasts.

A round beating light formed around Nezha.

Zul's balance faltered, and he seemed to weaken as she became bright. "What is this?"

A tornado of fire formed in front of her as she spun her hands and sent it toward him. Zul stumbled back.

"I'd love to see you flop around, but it's time I depart. It was a pleasure to meet you. Salaam, Nezha." He smiled, and a shadow clouded Zul's form, and he was gone.

"He got away." Nezha's shoulders slumped. The fire tornado slowly unraveled and faded into tufts of smoke. She was left breathing hard and fell to her knees.

"Don't worry." Kayan bent down to give her a reassuring smile. "By the way, that tornado was awesome."

"Thank you." Nezha stood up and gave Kayan a slight smile. She looked toward Sapphire. Worry etched between her brows.

Thunderbolt grumbled. He flew down to Nezha and Kayan. "I can't believe he fooled me like that."

"Don't be hard on yourself. We didn't know what we were up against. He's using magic." Nezha's eyes narrowed.

"It's strange, when Nezha became brighter, he looked like he was swooning with weakness," Kayan said.

"Yeah, I have an inclination that the angel's light is the reason. He has jinni energy in him, so light weakens him," Nezha said.

"Hey, how's my sister?" Thunderbolt walked up to her. She was still unconscious.

Kayan tilted Sapphire's head back and leaned in to listen for her breathing. He then placed two fingers to her neck, checking for a pulse. "She's breathing. Don't worry, I'll help revive her." He placed her in a recovery position, placing her left arm over her right shoulder and then gently turning her onto her side.

"Hey zaan, please tell me she'll be okay," Thunderbolt said.

"We need to be calm." Kayan took off his light jacket and placed it over Sapphire.

Thunderbolt placed his hands on his head and blew out a breath. "Yeah. Okay. Okay. Just... help her."

After nearly a minute, Sapphire opened her eyes and coughed.

"Sis," Thunderbolt said, smiling and gasping in happiness.

"Sapphire, you're okay. We're all here with you." Nezha brushed aside a lock of hair from Sapphire's face.

"Hey, Kayan?" Thunderbolt placed a hand on his shoulder.

"Yeah?"

"Thank you."

Kayan smiled.

Sapphire slowly sat up. "What happened?"

"Zul was here, but he escaped. It's more important for us to head back to K'ami City and rest up. Especially you."

"Nezha, I am well. Really," Sapphire said and smiled. "I am an angel, remember? We are different from mortal beings."

"I know, but I still want you to rest." There was agitation in Nezha's voice as she started walking toward the city.

***

"You have all been freed from your slumber. Set out to find your other self and aim to replace them," the crow jinni Rana said.

"We are much obliged," A male figure said, as he and three others smirked.

"You are a sign of disease and death for your other halves. If you succeed in eliminating them, you can have their lives," Rana told them.

"Sounds very promising." A female figure laughed.

A boy who looked like Kayan walked nonchalantly toward the city as the others followed him. "Prepare yourself, Kayan. We will have our sweet freedom."

CHAPTER 22—DOPPELGANGERS

"Sapphire, I was worried about you." Nezha sat on the edge of one of the sofas and sighed.

The early evening had rolled in. She and Sapphire had settled in Kayan's living room as he and his sister had gone out to buy supplies and food for tonight. Comet jumped into her lap, closed her eyes and purred loudly.

"I know, Nezha." Sapphire rubbed her back. She smiled with a warmth in her eyes. "I am well."

Nezha gripped her for a few more seconds until they both sat back again. "I know. It's just that you've always been so gentle and grounded. Seeing you enraged, almost wild, was a shock."

"Everyone has their limits. Today mine were broken. There's a difference between fighting *for* something and fighting something. One only makes you, and the other breaks you."

Nezha listened attentively and shifted in her seat.

"Hey, we should discuss that crow jinni. That doppelgänger of you must have been her doing," Thunderbolt said as he walked into the living room. He brought out mint chai and handed it to both Nezha and Sapphire.

"Thank you. There was a feather in the place of Sapphire D, as she called herself." Nezha took a sip.

"If so, I doubt if she stopped at only me," Sapphire said and also took a sip, seeing her brother sit down and lean in.

"I agree with you," he started. "We'll have t' be on the alert. It looks like another distasteful way for Zul t' buy time t' gain more power. If you guys would agree with me, we should leave K'ami City as soon as possible and look for the rest of the orbs, maybe even lead those doppelgängers toward uninhabited land."

"It will be difficult. If there are more, they may attack us wherever we go," Sapphire said.

Thunderbolt frowned. "I want t' drag Zul t' his knees and for him to undo the damage he did t' the valley and our family. Knowing that they're still in that state sickens me. They're still alive. They have t' be."

"I'm sorry. I know you've gone through that pain, but we have to look at it this way. We can't blame him for everything. We need to become stronger. He has a weakness, the light that shone around me. Concentrate on doing what you can." Nezha smiled at Thunderbolt.

"Kid," Thunderbolt began, "That's a good way t' look at it. I know what we need t' do right now. As angels, we need t' uphold the peace. I'm going t' stay outside and check the city for any mischief."

Sapphire nodded. She stood up and patted his shoulder. "Don't be too hard on yourself. Call me if you see anything and don't be late for dinner."

Thunderbolt grinned. "All right. See you two later! Oh, hey, kid."

Nezha stood up and walked toward him.

"When Kayan gets back, tell him I'm on guard duty and he too is t' be by your side."

"I can take care of myself," Nezha grinned.

"I know. That's why Saphy's with you. Someone has t' protect Kayan from you." Thunderbolt winked and headed out the door.

"Is Thunderbolt going to be all right? He was really upset. We reassured him, but was he only being calm for our sake?" Nezha said.

"He's always been emotional Nezha. Ever since our parents were encased in metal, he's been trying much harder to not show his sadness. He's eager to be by their side and anxious to find the cure to break that curse. I believe even Zul Sharr wants to find a way to fix it," Sapphire said.

"How can you tell?"

"He was once Eisen, Nezha. There is deep sadness in his eyes. We do not even know the full truth about princess Sanari. Is she dead, or is she alive? Is she enshrouded in iron like my parents and friends?"

Nezha raised her eyebrows. "He never said he lost her, just that he wants her back."

Sapphire stood up and took the empty glass from Nezha's hand. "I will check on Kayan's father." She walked toward the kitchen.

Nezha looked through the window. It was getting darker. *It'll be night soon. I hope Thunderbolt is doing well.*

Kayan walked in from the door, holding bags. "Hey, I'm home everyone.

Nezha smiled back at him.

"Uh, hey, where are the angels?"

"Sapphire is checking on your father. Thunderbolt said he's going to keep guard over the city."

"Keep guard? Did something come up?" Kayan asked as he and Nezha went to the kitchen. He unpacked his bags, and Nezha helped him put the items in their place.

"Well, we all think Sapphire D wasn't the only doppelganger we'll see."

"Oh, well, we'll have to be ready," Kayan said.

"Where's your sister?"

"She went to the backyard."

Nezha nodded.

When they were done, they both sat on the couch. Kayan sat in front of her on the couch on the other side.

"Hey, Nezha?"

"Yes?"

"I don't mean to pry, but you mentioned you lost someone? Only if you want to talk about it." Kayan was blushing now.

"Oh." Her eyes softened. "It was my aunt. She passed away two months ago. We were really close." Her voice was barely above a whisper.

"I'm sorry. My condolences." Kayan's voice softened, his head lowered and his eyes cast to the ground.

"Hello Kayan," Sapphire said as she came to stand beside him.

"Hey. How is my father doing?" He turned his head to Sapphire, his shoulders still toward Nezha.

"He is well. Your sister is by his side."

"Good. We'll make dinner as soon as Thunderbolt gets back. I just need something from my room." He rolled up his sleeves and stood up.

"Okay," Sapphire replied.

"Uh, Kayan, mind if I follow?" Nezha got to her feet.

"No problem." His eyebrows raised.

Kayan entered his room, as Nezha stood near the door. "Wow, a big shelf of books." Nezha said, amazed. There was a poster with the words *Dance to the beat of your heart.*

"Yeah. You wouldn't be able to tell, but since taking care of my father, I've been researching different things. Medicine, food... about everything. I want to take better care of him and those around me. It lead me to want to be a doctor... I even had time to read for fun too. There's this epic story about devs and a prince. Oh, zaan, when they battled, it was so amazing." Kayan's hands were animated and his voice rose. He turned to her. "Uh... I guess I'm getting too excited."

She smiled. "Nope. I read too. I get what it means to be excited about them."

"Yeah? What kinds?"

"Mostly fantasy. But, I love mystery and adventure books too. There's this manga called InuYasha by Rumiko Takahashi. It was my first and it has a special place in my heart."

"Maybe you could share some of your dimension's books with me sometime?"

"Yeah. That sounds good. I'm glad I found this side of you."

Kayan looked at her, his eyes wide.

It was then that Sapphire called them downstairs.

They rushed down the stairs and were met by Sapphire partway. She gripped her Tome in one hand.

"It's Thunderbolt... I called him, and he suddenly hung up. We need to head out and find him." She brushed her hand through her hair, and her fingers slipped by her lips.

"Don't worry. Stay calm. We'll find him," Kayan said.

"Let's go," Nezha said and squeezed Sapphire's hand in reassurance.

Sapphire nodded. "Let's go."

They walked the street, the mist of the mountains clustering in faint clouds around them. Sapphire redialed on her Tome, the brightest source of light in the darkness.

"I feel his presence, but it is far from here. The direction is from the outskirts of the city."

"We'll have to be faster than this." Kayan formed an updraft. "Get on, you two. It's faster this way."

Sapphire stood on the draft behind him, Nezha right behind her.

"You lead us. Hold on." Kayan said as the updraft moved swiftly.

Nezha grasped Sapphire's shoulders. Sapphire formed a bubble around them, keeping them from falling off.

"Good thinking." Nezha was breathing rapidly. The streets blurred past them, the sounds of people walking, their conversations, all of it drowned out by the whistling wind.

"Turn left," Sapphire's fingers gripped at her necklace, tightening around the bumps.

***

Thunderbolt was on the outskirts of K'ami city, near Mellow Meadow. As he walked closer to the meadow, he spotted two people.

Is that Nezha?

On closer inspection, he realized Nezha was with his doppelganger.

No, it's Nezha D. I was right after all. Thunderbolt hid behind a tree. *I don't even mind if they sense me. I'd rather get rid of them sooner, than later.* He approached them slowly, their voices getting louder as they conversed. He took out his Tome to call Sapphire until his doppelganger faced him. Thunderbolt jumped back.

"What a surprise. You saved us the trouble of finding you, at least... one of you that is." Thunderbolt D flashed him a grin. "Hey, my less handsome twin."

"What disrespect." Thunderbolt sent a bolt of lightning and lightning bombs his way, but they crashed toward the earth. In the crash and the clap of thunder, Thunderbolt threw his fist into the air. "I'll keep you occupied."

***

They drifted down to the meadow, where blue and yellow sparks spurted up into the air like a fountain. "I found him." Kayan swerved, lowering the updraft.

Thunderbolt and his doppelganger were in battle. Nezha saw her own, who was now looking up at the sky.

They were whisked into the air, flying upward. Nezha flailed her arms, her mouth open in a silent scream. Kayan formed another updraft that caught her. Kayan D was now facing Kayan in the sky. *They look like us.*

"Yo. You know who I am." Kayan D folded his arms and had a crooked smile as he hovered in front of Kayan.

Kayan and Kayan D landed, just as Sapphire and Nezha touched ground.

***

"So, we're going to get caught in the wind, huh?" Kayan blocked with his arm, when Kayan D spun and attempted to cut him.

"Damn, you really are my more inexperienced half," Kayan D retorted and caused a blast of air. It sent Kayan sliding back.

"Is that all?" Kayan said with a distasteful smirk.

"Yeah, you wish." Kayan D snorted.

They unsheathed their swords. Kayan D's blade whipped toward him, but Kayan dodged, until he made a fist of ice, forming a barrage of ice shards. The blades whirled around again, and a thick blinding mist hung over them.

"Where is he?" Kayan was pulled from behind.

"You think you're a great person, Kayan?" Kayan D landed a punch to Kayan's side. He coughed and the wind frantically danced around him, knocking down Kayan D. Kayan held his side.

"What? What are you talking about?"

"Don't act dumb. Be honest. You were sick of taking care of your father. Bathing him, giving him his meals, staying up nights. You were chained. You hated it."

"Stop it! I didn't." Kayan swung his arm up, but his doppelgänger grabbed him by the neck and threw him forward. He landed hard on his side.

"It was a prison and you know it. Nowhere to go. Losing your mother, then no time for the friends you had left. No love or freedom."

"Shut up!" Kayan turned to his back and rolled as soon as Kayan D's sword skimmed the ground.

His doppelganger snickered. "Poor sweet boy, you're more selfish than you thought."

Kayan stood up. "I… I did hate it, but I wanted him to get better. I didn't want him to suffer. Sure, I felt like I couldn't go anywhere, but I learned a lot about myself. I'm stronger now. I'm looking for his cure, and I'm not selfish for wanting to be happy too."

"Too bad you'll die before you can find it."

"I want to be free. I want to love freely. You won't take it away. The wind is the same. You're only from a different direction," Kayan said, his eyes glowing green.

Kayan D acted like he was being throttled by a rope. He was pinned to the ground, though Kayan was being clawed back by the wind Kayan D was manipulating.

"You're still weak." Kayan D grunted and an uneasy laugh escaped through his mouth. The wind swerved and knocked Kayan down.

***

Kayan D ran toward Nezha, who was facing Nezha D. "Nezha..."

"Kayan?" Nezha looked at him carefully, but something seemed off. Before she could react, he took hold of her with the wind and stood behind her.

"Don't try anything," he whispered to her.

Kayan hissed in pain and struggled to his feet.

Nezha gasped and tried to ignite him, but there was a sudden pressure on her hands. The flames enveloped around her arms as the wind streamed around the blaze. Her back curled when her wrists pressed together.

"What a beauty. Don't make me take you for my own," Kayan D said.

She grimaced and her cheeks flushed. "Oh, don't start that with me. Let go and I'll show you. You're definitely a creep, unlike Kayan. He's better than you."

"Leave her!" Kayan snarled. He faced Kayan D.

"Darling, she's no match for me. I'll handle her." Nezha D caressed Kayan D's shoulder as she stepped out from behind him. Her palms twirled with flames. "I think a wave of fire will do nicely for the job."

"Nezha D, remember our plan? Let's stick to it," Kayan D said.

Sapphire walked over. "If you kill her, you die as well." She looked over to Nezha D.

"What? Stop your nonsense." Nezha D's voice let out a strangled sound and sent a wave of flames toward Sapphire, but the fire faded away into a mist with a wave of Sapphire's glowing hand.

"I am telling the truth. You have been set up. If you kill us, you will not survive. You are made from our hair. The darkness within our souls. A part of us."

Nezha D's face contorted into horror.

Kayan D glared at Sapphire.

"Oh Creator, please help me. Give me strength." Nezha's heart thundered. The light within her rippled like waves through her body and started to shine around her. Nezha turned her head toward Kayan D. Her face lit with a soft glow.

"By the turner of hearts, the Divine, surrender yourself to the softening light of purity."

Nezha D's knees shook, and she fell to the ground. Her eyebrows softened. "Be... be quiet."

Kayan D let go of his hold on her. His eyes were unfocused. "We no longer want to be condemned. Return us," he said calmly. "Forgive our transgression."

"You're forgiven. You may return." Nezha pulled out the feather from her bracelet.

She raised her trembling hand and closed her eyes. The tip of the blade pierced his heart, and he took his last breath, fading away. She did the same with Nezha D. They turned back into hair and disappeared for good.

Pressure filled Nezha's heart, as a part of her returned to her soul.

"Well, that was—" Kayan started, but then looked in awe at Nezha. "Are you going to be okay?"

"Yeah," she said softly. She touched her temples. *That was so strange, yet, it felt natural to me.*

"Thank goodness," Sapphire stood over Nezha and looked into the distance. "We still have Thunderbolt D."

Thunderbolt was busy with his doppelganger. "Ugh. I'm stuck with you," Thunderbolt said. Sparks flew about as they were still in combat.

His doppelgänger snickered and drove a beam of electricity toward Thunderbolt from his pointed hands. "What, are you going to run away from me too?"

Thunderbolt shielded himself and magnetized the beams. They were being pulled in until, to their surprise, a black hole appeared therein.

"Whoa." Thunderbolt D backed away.

"Well, it's time we depart, so repel already," Thunderbolt said, and as his doppelgänger was halfway pulled in, Thunderbolt demagnetized and sent a flash of lightning straight into Thunderbolt D, one of such magnitude it sounded a clap of thunder.

Thunderbolt D screamed as he returned to Thunderbolt.

"Tch. I'm way more handsome... and not a coward." Thunderbolt kicked the dirt.

Thunderbolt blew out a breath. "Hey, how's it going? Miss me?"

"At least now we can go back and rest. It's late." Nezha looked up at the night sky, littered with stars. "That was something I'll never forget. I think I'm scarred for life."

"You said it." Kayan yawned. Kayan turned his face away from the others.

They all headed back to the city. There, a soldier's cruiser parked in front of them, and an officer stepped out of the vehicle.

"What now?" Thunderbolt said in frustration.

"By order of the Iron Kingdom, you will abide to their summon."

CHAPTER 23—TESTIFY

The officer showed them his badge. "I am a Mahlukan officer. We received a message from Falaz City in the Iron Kingdom. They want to meet you all. Especially the girl." He gestured for them to take a seat in the cruiser. "Don't be alarmed."

"Okay." Nezha sat down before casting a cautious glance at Sapphire and Thunderbolt.

The siblings and Kayan followed suit.

"Don't worry," Thunderbolt said as the vehicle moved on to the highway. "His badge looks official."

"That's not what I'm worried about. The Iron court will want to know about Eisen, once the prince of the Iron Kingdom. How are we going to explain that he's Zul Sharr now?" Nezha brushed her fingers through Comet's fur.

"Perhaps, they know," Sapphire said.

The cruiser was a highly-advanced transportation vehicle. Built sleek, the cruiser's silver-and-red colored Beco crystals and metal glinted. By the time they arrived outside Dev Open, the vehicle glided over the sea. Another three hours, and they entered Equus City, beside Unicorn Valley. The valley couldn't be seen by those in the city and so as they drove by, a tall brick wall came into view, blocking off the valley.

"That wall. What's it doing there?" Thunderbolt asked and narrowed his eyes.

"The valley has been blocked off for the public. I assume you know what happened there," the officer said.

"All too well," Thunderbolt said, his jaw muscles tensed.

"So, they know something is going on in Noorenia," Nezha said.

She placed her chin in her palm. *I can imagine the pain Sapphire and Thunderbolt must feel, seeing that wall.* She sighed.

"I saw lightning and decided to check out what was going on, when I saw you four at the city's edge," the officer said. "Since you were accompanied by two angels, I knew you had to be the ones the Iron Kingdom ordered for me to bring."

"Well, it'll be an honor to meet them," Nezha said.

The rest of the ride was quiet.

They arrived at the border between Wadi Alma and the Iron Kingdom. The country of Qadam. Nezha's gaze lingered on the long slim river, snaking its way between the countries' borders. Dem River, the longest river in these parts.

"I cannot go further. Your next vehicle awaits you." The Mahlukan officer placed a hand to this heart and nodded.

"Thank you," Nezha said.

Beside the border, across the compact-sand a silver-and-purple cruiser drove up to them. The Beco crystals winked back at them as an officer opened the door, and they got in.

The cruiser transformed and flew over the body of water. It contrasted the dunes, rivulets of sand like copper satin surrounding the city. Forty minutes passed, and they had reached the city, in the heart of this desert country.

The Iron mansion had an iron gate. The mansion itself was slate gray on the outside with large windows. Two security guards unlocked the gate for them as their vehicle approached. Their uniforms were the kingdom's high-collard purple jalabiya with *hadid* emblazoned in iron on their chests.

"Here you are," The officer said as they all got out of the vehicle.

"Thank you for transporting us here," Sapphire said.

"No problem. Salaam." He nodded, saluted them and drove off.

The mansion was surrounded by hedges. A concrete front yard exhibited a large alabaster fountain with calligraphy in Noorenian letters.

Another guard met with them in front of the main door. The massive door was decorated in tiles, in shades of purple and blue like scales of a fish.

"Ah, yes, our visitors, the angels and their companions. The king and queen have been waiting for you," a man said with a gentle smile and opened the door for them.

"May we enter?" Sapphire said, as did the rest.

"Come in. May the Divine smile upon you. Welcome to Falaz. I am King Hariz ibn Massoud and this lovely lady is Queen Laiqa bint Amir Moez." King Hariz had a rectangular jaw line. He wore a dark gray dress shirt and had peach toned skin. His black hair was cut short, the waves barely touching the end of his neck. His dark brown eyes glinted, as his gaze settled on the angels and he gestured to his wife, who stood next to him.

The group paid their respect and introduced themselves.

"Now, you must be wondering why you were called here." Queen Laiqa wore her dark brown hair in a loose bun. She wore a long-textured purple and yellow kaftan that had a transparent upper layer and a bottom dress with a belt around the midriff. Her umber eyes caught the light and showed more of their yellow tinge. The lines around her mouth were starting to show her age.

The Iron Queen and King gestured for them to sit down on the golden sofas.

They sat down, and the Iron Queen sat before Nezha. "Are you Sanari's relative that I've been hearing about?"

"Yes, I'm her cousin." Nezha felt shy in front of the woman, although she was from a family of royalty herself. *So, they know she's gone.*

"Dear girl," Laiqa laughed and patted her shoulder gently, "you don't need to feel so shy. We don't distinguish ourselves higher than the people we rule over. I wasn't sure if you two were related. But, I do see that fiery spirit in your eyes."

Nezha was shocked at her statement. They weren't being snarky or proud.

Comet leaped onto the sofa and sat beside Nezha. The queen raised her hands. "Oh, Nezha, please keep your cat off the sofa. You see, the servants cleaned it and it would need to be cleaned again."

"Oh, uh... sure." Nezha picked up Comet and placed her in her lap. Nezha hadn't liked the look in the queen's eyes, but maybe they were just very strict about their cleaning. Cat hair *did* get everywhere and on anything.

"Today we were informed by the officer who escorted you, that you were outside K'ami City. Halim the unicorn and Vinci are our close allies. They both informed us that you siblings would be accompanied by Princess Sanari's relative." The queen frowned.

Thunderbolt's stomach grumbled loudly. The reaction from those around him was as if there was an avalanche.

"Uh, sorry." Thunderbolt put a hand to his stomach, his gaze darting around.

Kayan and Nezha snickered.

Hariz smiled heartily at Thunderbolt. "How about we have our guests join us for food?"

"Sounds like they agree," Laiqa said.

They sat at a table fashioned from a deep grayish-blue wood. There were many options. A whole roasted lamb with assorted vegetables, bram rice and bowls of koshari. In the middle was a bowl of roz be laban. The rice pudding had a hint of vanilla. Beside each of their plates was a plate of baklava, drenched in honey syrup.

"Queen Laiqa, you mean to say you know what happened to the Fire Kingdom mansion? Nezha asked.

"Not everything. It was two Aylaalmashi— ambulance— healing technicians who told us." Queen Laiqa frowned, and her lips trembled.

Nezha turned to the queen as she dabbed her eyes with her fingers. But there were no tears.

"I'll continue," King Hariz said and rubbed his wife's shoulder. He frowned as he spoke. "Our son had disappeared, so there is no doubt in my mind it was Eisen who was responsible. Unfortunately, or perhaps fortunately, there were no bodies discovered."

"Zul Sharr is your son?" Kayan said, as politely as he could.

"Yes, before this atrocity, he was our son. He wanted to marry Princess Sanari. Now that news of his change reached us, we are distraught to have found he is with a jinni." Queen Laiqa's voice was laced with anger and pain.

"Our son, I can't believe he has forsaken his own land and forged a bond with a jinni." King Hariz said harshly, his eyes unfocused.

"King Hariz, we too are deeply saddened by Zul's transgressions," Sapphire said and told them her concerns about the Angel's light and soul.

"Your highness, we will stop Zul." Thunderbolt squeezed his hands into a fist.

King Hariz looked over at the angels. There was silence as everyone finished their meals.

"What gives me more concern is that now that he is demonic, his abilities will be in the wrong hands."

Nezha looked at the king and queen with sympathy. "We don't know what the future is. But, I think there's hope for Zul, and we should keep that hope alive."

"Thank you Nezha. We appreciate what you are doing for all of Noorenia. If fate will allow it, we will get our son back, Creator willing," Queen Laiqa turned to Nezha.

"Thank you for the dinner," Nezha said, as the others smiled and showed their gratitude.

"Nezha, every country signed a promise with the law of Noorenia, including the Fire Kingdom, since they have influence over Qadam and Mahluka. The jinn were told to uphold the peace, live in their own city and homes, and not to interact with humans. If the boundaries are transgressed, we have no regrets to defend ourselves however needed." Laiqa's hands tightened into fists. "We are leaving

Noorenia's well-being in your hands." The queen smiled, though her voice was strained.

Nezha embraced her and whispered, "Ameen."

Queen Laiqa returned the embrace.

"You must keep this between us for now. If the public knows, it may create hysteria," King Hariz said.

The queen whispered to Sapphire. "You and Thunderbolt protect Nezha, please don't let any harm befall her."

"You have my word, Queen. We have been and will always protect her."

"Yeah, Nezha's like a little sister t' us," Thunderbolt said and smiled.

Nezha and Kayan were at the door, waiting for the angels.

"Nezha, are you okay?" he asked her, as he caught a glimpse of her worried expression.

"Ah, don't worry."

"You can be open with me you know.

"I know you worry Kayan," Nezha smiled. *He's as straight forward as usual.* "It's almost foolish. I feel a bit overwhelmed. I mean, we have a huge responsibility."

"It's not foolish. It's normal to feel overwhelmed by responsibility. I should know. When my father was sick and needed my help, I felt huge responsibility. I tried not to let it get to me. All I could think about was that I can handle it and that my father's well-being is what's important."

Nezha's eyes filled with wonderment at Kayan.

He blushed.

"Hey Kayan, Nezha, let's go," Thunderbolt said as they both jolted and looked at him.

He grinned, with a knowing look.

"We will see you again," Queen Laiqa said.

"Yes, visit whenever you like. You are all welcome here. Consider this your second home," King Hariz patted Thunderbolt's back.

"It was an honor to meet you both," Nezha said.

"The honor is ours." Queen Laiqa guided Nezha with her hand at her back.

"Let our driver escort you," King Hariz said as they opened the door and walked to the gate.

"Oh, you don't need to trouble yourselves," Sapphire said.

"No, it's no trouble. You have a long way to go, unless you are staying at Equus City," Laiqa said.

"Yes, we are staying there," Sapphire said.

"At Tasa's?" Nezha asked.

"Yes."

"All right then, keep contact with us. Farewell," the queen said.

Nezha waved as they walked out the gate.

Kayan yawned. He covered his mouth. "I'm so exhausted."

"Same here," Nezha said.

"We'll carry both of you. We don't tire like you do, at least not as easily as you," Sapphire transformed back into a unicorn and gestured for Nezha to sit on her back as her neck stretched to her side.

"Thank you, Sapphire." Nezha let out a content sigh. She brushed Sapphire's mane gently.

"You're very welcome,"

"You too, Kayan," Thunderbolt said.

"My updraft is faster though. You don't need to waste energy," Kayan said.

"Don't make any excuses. You're exhausted. Just sit on my back, so we can head t' Tasa's already," Thunderbolt said.

Kayan smiled. "All right."

They flew over the city and reached Wadi Alma. When they arrived, Tasa greeted them with a big smile. It was late, so they headed to bed.

***

"Good night dad," Kayan said as he disconnected his call.

"I could hear you from the other room," Nezha said, standing at the doorway.

"Did I disturb you?" he asked as he placed his Tome on the table.

"No, I was just about to lie down, but I wanted to say goodnight. You were the last one," Nezha said shyly.

His lips parted, eyebrows raised. "Aw, well, good night," He drawled.

She turned to leave, but he called her name. "Nezha?"

"Yeah?" She said in a quiet voice.

"You're nice." His voice was pretty quiet and sounded sleepy. Kayan lay on his side and closed his eyes.

Nezha's eyes widened. *My heart's beating louder.* "Uh, you're nice too. I'm going to sleep now."

"Mm-hmm," Kayan said quietly.

CHAPTER 24—WATERFALL

Sapphire, Kayan and Thunderbolt sat in Kayan's living room, huddled around the screen of Kayan's Atlas.

"There's a waterfall outside Volcano Valley. The water there is supposed to be rich in mineral deposits. They have springs from that water surrounding it."

Sapphire spoke to Kayan as he sat with his Atlas in his hands. "It looks like that waterfall is the closest location. I think Nezha would appreciate it."

"Yeah, let's try not t' speak too loud. It's a surprise remember?" Thunderbolt said.

***

Nezha walked down the stairs. It was the evening, and she had just taken a shower and finished her maghrib prayer. Comet walked alongside her. Her ghostly spots blurred as she passed the railing.

"Hey, everyone." Nezha sat down beside Sapphire and stretched her arms.

"Hey, Nezha." Kayan said. "Now that we had some time to think, I was searching for anyone nearby who had the Alstroemeria flower. I found a florist who lives close to Fruit Flora Field."

"That's great news." Joy sparkled in Nezha's eyes. "We can finally cure your father."

"Yes, we should be on our way now," Sapphire said.

Nezha stood and followed them as they walked to the door.

***

The dark sky was clouded like pleats over velvet cloth. They reached an inn beside the waterfall.

"It's late, so we should stay at this inn tonight," Thunderbolt said.

"Yeah, I feel like we're having a vacation," Nezha said.

"Nezha, you and Sapphire have one room, and Kayan and I will be beside yours." Thunderbolt handed their keys to them.

"Thank you," Nezha sang as she walked past him, taking the keys.

***

After breakfast the next morning, Sapphire said. "Nezha, would you mind going with me?"

"Sure."

She led Nezha to the back of the inn. Sapphire stopped at a door.

"I have a surprise for you, so close your eyes."

"Did you find an orb?" Nezha closed her eyes.

Sapphire opened the sky-blue door and led her through. Nezha could hear the bubbling and murmuring of water.

"Open your eyes," Sapphire said.

Nezha gasped. "It's beautiful."

"We all figured you needed a break. We never know when we will get another chance."

"But, won't you all be joining me? You need it," Nezha said.

Sapphire smiled at her. "Well, Thunderbolt and I don't tire easy, but it would be nice. I think Kayan would appreciate it."

"Then your fate is sealed," Nezha laughed. "You three will relax and like it."

Sapphire smiled widely and patted Nezha's back.

"Now, the waterfall has a bridge right there. You can choose to sight-see and even relax at the spring right next to it. There are signs for where to go."

Comet rubbed her back against Sapphire's legs and then looked up as Sapphire lifted her.

"Comet and I will relax at the garden right over there, if you don't mind."

"Aww, I was just about to ask about her. That would be great, though we're inseparable." Nezha looked over at Comet, who was purring and butting her head against Sapphire's.

"I think she knows you need a break. Do not worry about her." Sapphire smiled and then walked off. "I'll let Kayan and my brother know."

"I'll see you later then." Nezha lifted her hand to wave, but dropped it. "Now, I'm just acting like Kayan… getting worried. Pfft. It'll be fine."

She walked over to the springs.

"Well, what's going on here?" Thunderbolt asked, his expression amused.

"We're all going to relax at the waterfall. Even though I want to go to the florist, but it's not open yet either," Kayan said.

"As soon as it opens, we'll all go over there, okay, my zaan?" Thunderbolt asked.

Kayan sighed. "Okay. It's not like I'd break in to the shop."

"Don't get any ideas," Thunderbolt laughed and bumped shoulders with Kayan. Thunderbolt stretched and looked up at the waterfall. "This is going t' be nice!"

* * *

Nezha changed into an orange bathing suit. The water warmed her skin. She looked up at the large beige wall which separated the two springs. She rested her head on the ledge and hid her face in her arms. *I wonder how the others are.*

She sat up and formed a flame in her hand. She gazed within the licking flames. Zul would probably become strong. Zul... He was actually the Iron Prince. She wanted to train and get stronger if they had to face him. Nezha shook her head and let the flame fade. *But now I need peace.* She let her head fall back on the ledge and took a deep breath in and exhaled slowly. The waves of water lulled her body, pressing lightly against her taut muscles.

As Nezha swam toward the middle of the water her leg got lodged between two rocks. She yelped.

Nezha grimaced and let out a painful groan as she tried to move the boulders. *They won't move and my leg's hurting. I can't even set them on fire. It might cause another problem for me. Note to self, give this place a poor review.*

The door to the spring swung open and Kayan walked through. "Nezha, what happened?" Kayan said as he steadily walked through the entryway and into the water.

"Kayan? No! Don't—" Nezha had turned away from him, hugging herself, because he shouldn't see her like this. But when she looked over her shoulder she noticed he had blindfolded himself.

She gasped. *Abs! Uh no. Look away!* She hid her face in her hands.

"I can't... I mean, I'm sorry, Nezha. I heard your voice and you sounded like you were in trouble. So don't worry, okay?" Kayan said speedily, his cheeks florid. He stood motionless. Water rippled around his legs.

Nezha's heart leapt into her throat, as heat rushed over her chest.

"Some boulders pinned my leg. I tried to move them, but they're too heavy." Her voice was hushed.

"Lead me closer. I'll use the wind to break them."

"Okay. Walk slowly."

The water lapped against Kayan's legs and then his torso. His breath became unsteady.

"There," Nezha said, lifting her hand. "Reach your hand out. You'll be able to touch the boulder." Her heart was thundering as her gaze followed his hand.

He nodded. His hand shook as he reached out and was welcomed by the smooth surface of the boulder. "I'll try. Just stay still."

His face was beside hers. His lips parted, and his cheeks remained pink. His breath tickled her cheek.

***

Kayan could feel her presence. His skin became hot as the back of his neck tingled. Since his eyes were closed, his senses were heightened. Nezha's breath shifted. Her scent was intoxicating. Citrus and warm, akin to lemon with notes of smoke, or maybe it was spice. The scent filled his head. The wind was playing with her scent. Her very beating pulse echoed in his ears.

***

"Okay." Nezha gulped and her fingers tightened around her arms. Her skin had become so hot it might have become a body of flames. She didn't doubt it could happen.

He used his hand to twirl the wind around his palm and touched the boulders, sending a pulse of wind into the stone. Instantly, a crack formed and the boulders crumbled.

Nezha was free.

"Did it work?" Kayan asked.

"Yes. I'm okay now." Nezha gasped in delight.

"Thank the Divine." Kayan sighed.

Nezha gasped. A bruise blossomed over her skin.

"What's wrong? It hurt you badly, didn't it?" Kayan leaned in closer.

"Yeah." When Nezha tried to stand up, sharp pain cut through her leg. "I don't think I can walk."

Kayan gulped. "Lean on me..."

"Wha—" Nezha turned to him.

"Lean your shoulder on mine. Then I'll use the wind to keep you up." The redness in his cheeks turned bright.

There was no way out of this. She wasn't supposed to have any kind of physical interaction with men who weren't in her family. Injured, and with no one else here, she had to.

"Okay." Nezha pressed her shoulder against his. Sparks zipped through her, an energy she couldn't understand. Euphoria made her heart pound. The way Kayan's breathing deepened, she wondered if he felt it too. Soft warmth bloomed where their shoulders pressed.

"Nezha..." Kayan breathed out.

"Yes?" Nezha's heart was pounding loud. Deep inside her mind a part of her wanted to stay like this. A strange feeling that wished time would stand still. At least it felt like time had paused for them.

"I'm going to lift you with the wind," Kayan said, the air shifting around him.

It pushed against her thigh, pulling her up as they both made their way slowly out of the water.

"Here, there's a robe over here and a place to lie down." He felt his way around. Kayan lifted her with the wind, placing her gently upon the lounging chair.

"Kayan?"

"Yeah?"

"Thank you, and for being so considerate."

"You're welcome." He slowly walked toward the entrance but bumped into the side with a small thud. "Ow."

"Are you okay?" Nezha placed her hand to her mouth.

"Yeah, I'm okay. Don't worry about me." He rubbed his forehead.

"But..."*Oh my gosh, he sounds so adorable when he's nervous.* "Okay."

"Relax here, and I'll get Sapphire." Kayan walked through the entrance.

***

Kayan pressed his back to the wall and untied the towel from his eyes. He let out several deep breaths. The towel slipped down his face and he grabbed it. *My hands were shaking... and I could feel... smell her... feel her. Anyways, she needs healing.* He headed back to the dressing room, his head still buzzing.

***

"You can hear me in my thoughts, shadow jinni?" Zul said. He was sitting on his couch and turned his head to Lexa.

"Zaroor. Of course. Sire, you have demonic energy coursing through your blood. It's easy for me to hear you when you call." Lexa sat beside him and grinned.

"Jinni, that fire jawhar is a nuisance. The light surrounding her weakened me."

"With respect, I would prefer if you called me Lexa. Yes sire, jinn hate the light. It's something you must be careful of."

Zul huffed with annoyance and looked through the window to the city before him. Zul grimaced as memories of his kingdom life stabbed at his heart. His heart hummed in his chest like a bee. Yearning sweetness, yet the sting always a risk. Who was next to break him? Who else would be hurt? He formed a fist and repeatedly slammed his arm against the window.

"Sire," Lexa grabbed his arm, as he turned around and looked into her green eyes. His expression was cold. "It's not good for you to self-harm. You have power that anyone would envy." Her dark brown chiffon suit draped around her legs like ink in water.

"Lexa, you are under my command, are you not?"

"Aao, sire." Lexa smiled and bowed her head.

"We need more orbs." He wanted his sweet Sanari awakened. He wanted to keep the angel sealed away, so he couldn't meddle with his plans. Zul wanted to be powerful, but he also didn't want to hurt anyone. The demonic aura in his veins had the opposite intention.

"I know how you feel Zul. Don't let the pain be your weight. Don't fear anything. Make your mark, have no mercy." Lexa growled.

Zul Sharr fiddled with the iron ring around his pinky. It held a round white crystal, a large collected orb. "Find more of the soul orbs, Lexa."

"Your desire is my command, sire." Lexa's lips parted.

***

After Sapphire healed Nezha, they walked out together. The angel left to find her brother.

Kayan turned to her, a childish grin over his lips. "I just checked, and the florist's shop is open. I can finally get a lead on the Alstroemeria flower."

"Yes, and we can cure your father." Nezha walked with him, side by side.

"I can't wait," Kayan admitted.

They reached the back door of the inn and met the angels.

The moment Nezha walked into view, Comet jumped out of Sapphire's arms.

"Comet." Nezha bent down, her arms open. Comet lifted her head and pressed it against Nezha's palm. She scooped her up and Comet purred.

"No doubt she missed you." Sapphire smiled.

"Wow, you really are close," Kayan said.

As if to answer, Comet rubbed her head on Nezha's.

"Let's grab our belongings and head out," Thunderbolt said.

"Yes!" Kayan's fist pumped in the air, and his eyes shone with enthusiasm.

It's great to see him so happy. Nezha tickled Comet's ears.

***

A short while later, they were on their way.

"Which direction?" Kayan asked.

Thunderbolt faced him. "Calm your nerves. I know you're excited, but we're almost there."

"How can I be calm? We're finally getting a cure for my father." Kayan nearly ran.

"You are usually composed," Sapphire said.

"Yeah, unless it's something to do with his own feelings, I guess," Nezha said.

Kayan glanced at Nezha and then pulled out his phone. "Fruit Flora Field is due northeast and so is the florist."

"Does she own a shop there?" Nezha asked.

"Yeah, she owns a flower shop and it's pretty popular, judging by the reviews."

"Kayan, how are you feeling?" Nezha asked him. "The wind seems excited for you."

"I just want to run there."

"Look, the Divine's given you the gift of manipulating the wind. Shouldn't you be free like it then?" Thunderbolt said.

Kayan smiled widely and sped off.

"Just imagine, his father's cure is only steps away. I don't blame him for being so impatient," Nezha said. Like whenever Lamis would visit her.

"Yeah, the guy was taking care of his father for so long. He's admirable t' say the least," Thunderbolt said.

"Wow, I thought you'd make fun of him. You really are a teddy bear under that tough guy façade of yours." Nezha laughed.

"Nah, he's a good guy. Besides, I make fun of *you*."

"So are you, Thunderbolt, and hey!"

Thunderbolt grinned.

***

Kayan's breath and the wind were one as the flowers and grass blurred by him. The wind pushed at his back, as if it were playfully nudging him forward. The scent of rose and jasmine enveloped him. As he continued to run, all he could feel was him and the wind. The mischievous wind mirrored his own personality. Just as he wanted to be free, to uplift others, so did the wind. He couldn't feel the ground anymore. He was a bird soaring through the sky, clouds fading as he'd approach, wings beating like a pulse and his body was weightless in flight.

He smiled at the shop ahead of him.

Finally, finally. Kayan repeated in his head. *My father deserves to get better. It's the least I can do for him when he had to rear us when mother passed away.*

***

Kayan reached the florist, put his hand on the door and leaned, his head low. After a few minutes he raised his head and saw Nezha and the angels. They were just a few steps away.

"You made it in time," he said. " I was just about to open the door."

Nezha's lips parted as she took in a big breath. "Sure did."

He opened the door of the shop. As it swung open, a bell rang.

The others all stood outside the shop, excited and impatient.

Unfortunately the shop keeper had run out of Alstroemeria flowers.

"We're always all over the place," Thunderbolt said and rubbed his head.

Fortunately, Kayan always had a positive outlook. "So, Pari Flower Field huh?" Kayan looked at his Tome. "Okay, it's east of Unicorn Valley."

CHAPTER 25—ALSTROEMERIA FLOWER

"We should use your updrafts. Kayan, can you make one for each of us?" Nezha asked.

"I've tried that once. I would need to control them all. But I could make one giant updraft." He raised an eyebrow and grinned as his hand swooped up. It took him only a few seconds of twisting the wind until it formed.

"Hop on board, everyone!"

The wind swung them into the clouds as they hovered across the sky.

The wind crackled with euphoria. It was like electricity coursing through his heart, his mind and his skin. It drove him into giddiness. A wide grin appeared over his face as he waved his hands and guided the wind to their destination.

As they landed, the updraft disappeared. A large sign before them read Pari Flower Field. Right by the sign, there was a poster on a tree.

"Hey, look at this." Nezha pointed to the poster.

Kayan followed her gaze toward the tree.

"There is a festival coming up," Sapphire said as she read the sign.

"I couldn't read that." Nezha narrowed her eyes.

Kayan stood before the poster. The various lines had curves and lines that were in the Noorenian alphabet.

"Yes, although we can speak Darija, there are many languages here. Including Noorenian, our own official language," Sapphire said.

"We need to find the flower," Kayan said, walking into the field as the rest followed him.

"Hey, there," a voice called.

Nezha turned. "Who said that?"

"Oh, up here."

The girl who spoke seemed human, but her ears were pointed. Her bright yellow eyes sparkled as her face lit up with a wide smile. She hovered in the air with two large purple wings that resembled those of a dragonfly. She was around four feet tall.

"You almost gave me a heart attack." Thunderbolt grabbed at his collar.

"I thought you were braver than that," Nezha said amused.

"I'm sorry about that." The pari gave an apologetic smile. The sun cast its light over her brown skin and short wavy brown locks.

"As you might know, we're having a festival tonight. Are you travelers?"

"Yes, we were looking for the Alstroemeria flower," Kayan replied.

"Oh, they bloom at night here. So, you won't be able to pick them yet." The pari explained.

"If you're a pari, are you another type of jinni?" Nezha asked.

"Although paries are a type of jinni, we're not malevolent like some of them."

"So… wait… aren't you supposed to stay away from humans?" Nezha asked.

"We're only entertainers. Wadi Alma signed us into a contract. Who would say no to having fun, right?" The pari winked.

"Yes, I'd heard of those paries who entertain for a living, but never reach out to humans," Sapphire said.

"What's your name?" Nezha asked.

"I'm Layla." The pari landed on the soft grass. "It's my stage name."

"Nice to meet you," Nezha held Comet in her arms.

"It's a pleasure to meet you."

Layla grinned as everyone followed her into the field. There were stalls of various kinds and paries putting out different items for sale.

"As payment for the flowers, you can help us with the festival."

"Yeah, I think we can do that," Kayan said absentmindedly. All Kayan wanted was to find the flower and take it back home to cure his father.

"Of course we can." Nezha gave his shoe a tap with her own.

"Great! I am so excited." Layla twirled and led them to the different stalls.

"Kayan, are you okay with it? "Nezha asked.

"With what?" Kayan asked as he turned to her.

"I mean, with waiting to pick the flowers. You look anxious."

"Yeah, what can we do right? It is annoying, but I have to be patient." Kayan fidgeted with his fingers. Of course he was anxious. A cure he was trying to find for months was nearly in his grasp.

"We get to help out with something fun, and I think you all deserve a break." Nezha walked ahead of him and joined Sapphire as she placed toys at a stall.

The wide-open field was decorated with small kiosks for food like beignets showered with powdered sugar, ice creams and blue sugar floss which glimmered in the light. A twisty roller coaster that was shaped like a green and blue dragon with yellow eyes was still incomplete. To their left was a game where they could fish for real glowing fish. Some would trick people as they began to float in midair and other vehicles and hovering boards had widened Kayan's eyes in astonishment. Most of the rides were powered from other creatures or people with elemental power.

***

It was early evening as Kayan used the wind to help lift up heavier items, as did Thunderbolt with his own strength. One ride was not working properly, so he sent electricity through its wires to help kick start it.

"Amazing." Exclaimed one pari as she started the roller coaster.

"Thank you so much for your help," Layla said.

313

The angels and Kayan turned to her.

"It's no problem," Thunderbolt said.

"You're welcome, Layla, We were happy to assist you," Sapphire said.

The rides, the food stands and toys were all put in their proper place, as the sun set and the sky was now a wash of deep blues.

"It's the evening already." Kayan turned toward Layla. She was busy making a few more adjustments here and there to make sure everything was perfect.

Kayan's lips parted and his eyes furrowed as he looked around.

"Layla," Nezha called out to the pari. In one hand, Nezha held an unfinished beignet, which she would probably devour and replace with another. Beside her, Comet pawed at a glowing fish.

"Yes?" Layla spun around.

"Has the Alstroemeria flower blossomed now?"

"I was about to ask the same thing." Kayan looked at Nezha. She'd probably seen the way he was searching for the flowers.

"It has to be very dark until they do. Here, how about I walk you to them?" Layla clasped her hands behind her back and her wings fluttered as she led them to the flowers.

They followed Layla further into the field where eventually, there were flowers with their petals still clenched like fists.

"Here they are. See, they're still closed. As soon as the sky becomes black they'll open up. It looks like tonight the moon will glow and the light with glisten on their petals." Layla looked up at the sky.

Kayan tapped his foot and spun the wind with one hand.

"Patience is hard for you, isn't it?" Nezha asked and looked at him apologetically. She'd finished her second treat.

"Heh, Yeah, I can't help it." He couldn't keep anything from anyone. The look in eyes always gave away how he felt. He was always in motion. A raise of his brows, a quirk of his lips. His body language gave away how anxious he was. Kayan sighed and looked up at the sky as it darkened. His smile was the only way he could cover up his negative emotions.

***

"Here," Layla and a few other paries brought a plate of assorted chocolates. "These should help with Kayan's nerves, and they'll reenergize you."

Nezha raised an eyebrow at the chocolates and her chest fizzed with heat. *These... I can only think of Lamis now...*

and how it was always better when we ate bastilla with
her... and... how much chocolate I was eating... Her craving
for sweetness and comfort took the wheel.

"Reenergize?" Thunderbolt said.

"Yes, we add herbs and flower parts to them."

"Ah," Sapphire said in delight and took a bite. "They
truly taste amazing."

"Whoa, easy there," A pari said, as Nezha ate four
pieces.

Kayan smiled. "I guess she has a sweet tooth."

"I... uh... I couldn't help myself." Nezha grabbed
another piece, but the pari took the piece from her.

"I'm sorry young lady, but these are herbal after all, you
don't want to eat too many. They are potent. If you take
more than two you can upset your stomach."

Nezha looked ashamed and placed her hand down. "I'm
sorry... I'm—" Nezha backed away. Tears pushed at her
eyes. A few tendrils of fire escaped around her feet.

"Wait, Nezha," Kayan called out to her.

"I'm sorry," the pari said.

"It's no one's fault," Thunderbolt said.

Nezha ran past Sapphire who followed her.

***

"Nezha, what pain are you hiding from us, and keeping hidden within yourself?"

Nezha sighed. "I used to have a problem with my... the way I had to hide my fire abilities. Being told to stay inside. I felt like an outsider. I felt like I didn't belong... I started eating more sweets 'cause they gave me comfort. But my aunt was there for me. She was like me, a fire jawhar. My friends never found out, but they still cared about me. I reached out to others and I started to feel better. But I still eat a ton of chocolate, because just now... I feel sick."

I don't want to keep talking about Lamis. It hurts too much. Nezha's eyebrows furrowed. She looked up and dabbed at her eyes, trying to keep the tears inside.

"Nezha, you belong. You are brave, kind and open-minded. Not to mention a beautiful young woman. I believe you have found your place." Sapphire's eyes softened and she smiled.

Nezha's eyes welled with tears.

"You say you felt that way, but our worries lie to us. All those fears aren't what others see. It is who you are that makes you needed. I know they would agree with me." Sapphire held her. "You reached out and that's what matters. You have a crowning soul, Nezha. A bright will paired with a noble heart."

317

Nezha smiled. She couldn't keep her emotions in any longer. The tears rolled down her cheeks. Her hands trembled as she lifted them to her mouth.

"Nezha." Sapphire wiped away her tears.

Nezha lowered her hands. "You're strong too, Sapphire. Your wisdom and composure help you in everything you do. And I do feel a bit better now."

"I hope so. You know we're all here for each other. So, if anything is bothering you, let us know."

"Yeah." *I don't think I'm ready to talk about Lamis just yet. Someday, I know I'll have to. I just want to find the jinni who's responsible for her death.* Her head was lighter, and her heart regained its tempo.

Sapphire smiled and embraced her.

"Finally, Kayan is going to get the cure for his father," Nezha whispered and tightened her grip for a few moments longer around Sapphire's waist. "I feel much better. You do know how great and wise you are right?" Nezha and Sapphire walked up to the others.

***

"We've been waiting for you two for half an hour." Thunderbolt said, annoyed.

"It's been that long?" Nezha asked, a hint of a grin on her lips.

"He's exaggerating." Kayan shook his head.

Sapphire whispered to Nezha, "I am not wise. I am only seeking to learn. By the way, I like chocolate too." She winked.

They headed to the field of Alstroemeria flowers. Their petals unfurled, inviting the moonlight to caress them.

Thunderbolt looped his fingers in his belt.

Kayan's heart hammered in his chest. This was it. The cure for his father in his reach. He snapped the stem from the flower and held it in his palm. Tears pushed at his eyes. All he could do was stare at the petals. "Finally..."

"Flowers may wither," Nezha said as she met Sapphire's gaze and then looked at Kayan.

"Roots will be the anchor," Kayan said, a soft smile spreading across his face. A joyful sigh escaped Kayan's lips. There was a jump in his step as he went over to the pari. "Thank you very much for helping us find this flower. It was fun helping you out with the festival."

"Ah, yes, thank you everyone." Layla smiled. "Are you staying?"

"I'm afraid these flowers are for someone. It's important we get it to them as soon as possible," Kayan said.

"It *is* nightfall now. We'd have to head back to the Inn for the night," Nezha said.

"Well, no use in stopping you. It's important to you after all," Layla said.

"Thank you for understanding," Kayan said.

***

People and other paries had lined up outside the field. A large glowing blue banner was torn as the people walked in. Children skipped and held onto their parent's hands. Some pointed at various rides as the night was lit by the winking and sweeping lights. Whirring of gears, the song of night birds and the laughter and cheers of the crowds were the heartbeat of the fair as it began.

***

Kayan was in a reverie. He sat on the bed, sinking into the mattress. He turned the flower in his hands, studying the lines on the petals, but mostly he wanted to go home. To make these petals into medicine and spoon them into his father's mouth with his own hands. When his mom died, it was his father who did everything for him. Nights when his body was burning with a fever, his father would stay all night with him. Kayan would drift out of sleep, only to feel the coolness of a soaked cloth over his forehead or a press of his father's fingers against his head. He'd always been by his side, so Kayan would never leave him. He knew no matter how much he cared, how much he did for his father, he'd never be able to repay him. All he could do was love him and care for him. To give back all the gentleness, those smiles, that laughter and embraces with more, tenfold.

"Kayan, you need to sleep," Nezha said.

Kayan turned his head, pressing his back into the headboard. It was Nezha who stood at his room's door, with Thunderbolt right beside her.

"How much longer are you going t' stare at that flower, zaan?" Thunderbolt sounded both worried and amused.

"I'm just so anxious," Kayan said.

"Well, if we don't take care of ourselves, how will we take care of the ones we want to care for?" Nezha said. "I know you understand this well. Just please, don't let your mind get the best of you."

Kayan slumped his shoulders. His eyes must have had that soft look, giving away his emotions. "You're right. Okay, I'll sleep now." He looked at the flower one last time and stretched his arm to the wooden night table, picking up a casing Sapphire had given him. He dropped the flower into the case and sealed it.

Thunderbolt slipped away to his room as he said goodnight to Nezha.

"Good night." Nezha turned back to Kayan again.

"And thank you." Kayan managed with a smile. His heart thudded. "Goodnight." He pulled the table's drawer open and slipped the case inside. His eyelids were getting heavy and pressure tightened around his head.

***

They left early the next morning. The sun bathed Kayan. His topaz eyes sparkled aboard the updraft he formed.

"Isn't this an amazing day?" He said. "The sky is beautiful and the breeze is so energetic."

"Ugh, don't remind me of the breeze. I feel dizzy." Thunderbolt complained. They'd flown as unicorns with Nezha and Kayan on their backs for two hours. For the last hour, they switched to Kayan's updraft.

"Would it be wrong for me to say, zaan up? Or, am I being out of context for you being an angel and all," Kayan said and laughed.

"Not funny." Thunderbolt glared at Kayan.

"Come on, you two, we're almost at Kayan's home." Nezha held Comet close.

***

Kayan wasted no time after he landed. As soon as his feet touched the grass of his lawn, he was jumping and running like a small boy. Nezha and the others followed behind him.

"Father, I'm home." He nearly tripped on the mat as his fingers slipped off the doorknob and made his way up the stairs.

"Kayan!" Nezha called out to him as she followed him swiftly up the stairs.

Kayan reached the door of his father's bedroom and knocked.

"Father, I have amazing news!" As he opened the door, his father gave him a gentle smile.

Nezha gasped as she got to the door and stood inside.

Sapphire and Thunderbolt were soon beside her.

"Could you be any giddier?" Thunderbolt rolled his eyes and smiled.

"Welcome back, Kayan." Mr. Zogby brushed Kayan's hair from his brow.

"Father," Kayan started and brought out the flower. "This is the cure. We've finally found it." He was out of breath. He took a big breath in and couldn't stop from smiling.

His father's eyes lit up.

Quickly, Sapphire and Kayan readied the medicine. The flower petals were crushed up and made into a sweet paste with two drops of honey and a few dates.

Kayan held his breath as he lifted a spoon full of the medicine into his father's mouth and he took it.

At first his father seemed very tired. His eyelids drooped, and his head tilted to the side as if he were soon to fall asleep. This was the time to see how well the cure worked.

Kayan gulped and stared, waiting for any sign of improvements.

"The medicine should show its effects in a few minutes." Sapphire broke the silence.

"All right." Kayan sighed.

Nezha stood by his side. She smiled at him as their gazes met.

Within a few minutes, Kayan's father had changed. His eyes were fully open, and his skin regained color. He shifted in his bed and Kayan turned to him in anticipation. His father stood up.

Kayan automatically lifted his arms, but his father simply smiled and nodded to him.

Everyone's attention was on him as he stood.

"By the Divine. I feel awake." Mr. Zogby looked at his hands.

"Father..." Kayan stood up and embraced him. He felt his father's arms, once which were weak, now strong, as they held each other. "We've waited for this for so long. I wanted to hug you again. The Divine smiles upon us. Thank you. Thank you!"

"It's beautiful. A wonderful recovery." Sapphire smiled wide.

Nezha teared up and laughed between her smiling. "Now you don't need to worry so much anymore. You're both so happy."

Mr. Zogby turned to Sapphire and Nezha. "Thank you. Without the three of you, we wouldn't be so happy right now. My children have been sacrificing their own happiness for me. We are obliged. Thank you so much."

"Sir, it was our pleasure. To see you recover was truly worth the effort." Nezha smiled.

Kayan informed Kimmy, who was out working, about their father's recovery. She was elated as she spoke to him on the phone. When he hung up, they were off again.

"Father, I'll maintain contact with you. I'll send you money every month."

"Son, don't worry so much. I want you to know I love you and I'm so proud of you."

Kayan's eyes teared up and he embraced his father once more. He was okay. His father had finally recovered. This light airy feeling grew in Kayan's heart. A smile curled his lips and he remembered the saying on the alter of the cathedral. Asdvadz Ser Eh. God is love.

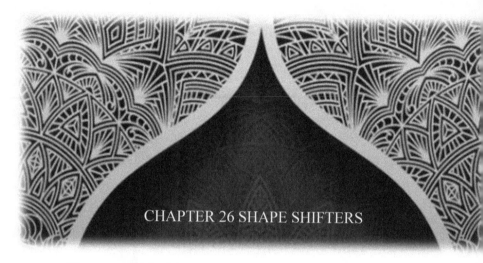

CHAPTER 26 SHAPE SHIFTERS

Kayan smiled wide as the group sat by the water front. His shoulders eased.

"Kayan." Nezha grinned as he turned to her.

"Yes, Nezha jan?"

She searched his eyes and the words left her mind. Something seemed so different about him. He looked so reserved before, barely saying anything about himself, and always smiling. But now there was a softer look in his eyes, his jaw more relaxed. *It's as if after his father's recovery, Kayan is showing his true self.*

He leaned toward her. "So, have you checked the Atlas about the orbs?"

"Yeah, I have. There's one toward a place called Dragon Designation."

Sapphire stretched and turned to Nezha. "That place is peaceful. If we are headed that way, we shouldn't have too much trouble."

"If there is, we know how t' handle it." Thunderbolt grinned as electricity danced in his palms.

"You're just itching to use your powers, huh?" Nezha skipped a rock on the pond's shimmering surface.

"They won't know what hit 'em." Thunderbolt smacked his fist into his palm.

"Let's get going, everyone. We don't want Zul getting high and mighty now, do we?" Kayan stood.

"No, we don't." Nezha joined everyone on the updraft.

"Kayan, it's great to see you so happy."

He tilted his head and responded after a pause. "Ever since my father fell ill, my thoughts were consumed with responsibility. Since he finally recovered, I feel like I can be myself. Like I've always wanted to be able to do my own thing. And now I can. I feel so free."

"I'm glad you feel the freedom to be yourself." Nezha held the Atlas in her hands. Comet lay her head on her arm.

"Kayan, it's great seeing you livelier." Thunderbolt patted Kayan's back.

"Whoa, careful. Don't make me fall." Kayan swayed and then regained his balance.

"You're a wind jawhar, you basically know how to fly," Thunderbolt said and laughed.

"The orb is getting closer." Sapphire peeked over Nezha's shoulder. "That area is familiar."

"Hmm? Do you remember what it is?" Thunderbolt asked, in a knowing tone.

"Yes, I do," Sapphire said calmly.

"Hey, are we missing something? What do you both know that we don't?" Kayan asked.

"There is an old palace there that belonged to the Fire Kingdom family," Sapphire said.

"It's been deserted for a long time. We probably have a jinni who's possessing an orb there," Thunderbolt said.

"A jinni, huh? Not surprised about that one," Nezha said as they approached the area.

When they landed, they stood for a few minutes as they surveyed the area.

"I think we should be on the alert for Zul. This may very well be a trap." Sapphire's expression was stoic as she stared ahead.

Nezha turned to her. "If it is, what do you think we should do? We can't turn back. We need the orb."

"We'll have t' go after it. I'm not backing down because of him. He's full of tricks, but so are we." Thunderbolt gritted his teeth.

"It's now or never. We can do this." Kayan flashed a cheeky smile.

Sapphire turned to the others. "I know that's what you all think. I'm just concerned because we don't know what he is capable of. We have to keep in mind, that the jinn have influence over him."

Nezha stepped forward. "We have to try, but I guess we should plan it out and not go in there blindly."

"That's a good idea." Kayan sat on the grass, cross-legged.

They took turns discussing their ideas and formulated a plan.

***

Within minutes, they were surrounded by jinn. A few of the creatures had flowing manes of smoke, and their lithe bodies shone like polished obsidian. Their limbs would ooze and drip to the floor, melting once more to their dismembered bodies. Other jinn were human-like, their arms extended and fingers elongated into thin claws.

"Oh no, there's…" Thunderbolt gaped. "Jinn unicorns."

"I don't know if I should laugh or run," Nezha said.

One of the jinn unicorns raised its skeletal head. The tip of its curved gray horn reminded Nezha of a knife's point. It snorted, and its eyes bled red so bright it felt as if it were locking onto her very soul. A mane of thick old blood and black hair whirled in the air like smoke. It stepped toward them, showcasing a belly of tendons and blood. Nezha's stomach dropped.

Sapphire shone a light toward the shadow jinn and they disintegrated in a plume of ebony smoke and dust.

"Well, that looked too easy." Nezha looked over at everyone who looked as uneasy as her. *Don't be afraid. They're just made of smokeless fire. They're not the shadow jinn... and I'm not afraid of them.*

"What about the jinni unicorns?" Nezha glanced at the two that roamed the yellow-stoned ruins, vines snaking through the fallen arches. The creatures didn't seem interested in them.

"Unless we provoke them or start to bleed, they won't harm us. They seem occupied with the other jinn," Sapphire said.

One of the jinni unicorns sounded a guttural whinny. It charged at one jinni, stabbing it with its horn. Red gleamed over it and dripped. The sight sent heat into Nezha's chest and a cold tingle down her spine and up her midsection. She kept her eyes on Sapphire as she spoke again.

"We must move forward." Sapphire placed a hand on Nezha's shoulder and started over to her brother. Thunderbolt lead them forward.

"The orb is definitely here," Nezha whispered, as she glanced at the Atlas. It was pointing toward somewhere inside the labyrinthine ruins.

***

It was evening as the companions walked deeper within the walls, guided by Sapphire's light, cascading against the walls.

A jinni approached Nezha and Comet hissed, her fur raised. It backed away as Nezha transformed the feather into a sword. The blue flames licked at the ground. Nezha charged toward it. It faded as her blade ripped through its midsection. She panted, and her heart thundered.

"Whoever has the orb must be protected by either a more powerful jinni or Zul himself." Sapphire assumed.

"Well, whichever it is, I'm not giving up," Nezha said and sighed.

Jinn surrounded them again. They tried their best to stay together, but in the fight of flames, wind, electricity and light bursts, they were separated from each other.

"Damn it!" Thunderbolt yelled as two electricity beams sent three more jinn into a cloud of smoke.

Thunderbolt was alone, among walls.

***

Kayan spun and kicked one jinni in the face, while the other was thwarted with an icy fist and faded. The previous jinni stood up and tried to run, but Kayan caught it by its arm with his blade, slicing through its skin in a jagged line. His eyebrows furrowed, and he pursed his lips in disdain.

The angels and Nezha aren't anywhere near me. I want to be there to help them. He walked over to press his fingers to the cold yellow sandblasted wall. The wind picked up their scent. He could definitely smell them, but they were farther away. The one that was the closest was Thunderbolt's.

"I know they can manage." He saw Nezha in the ruins, running. "Huh? Nezha?" He walked over to her.

"I fought a jinni," she said. But I thought I saw Sapphire and wanted to catch up to her."

The shock that appeared over his face melted as he looked at her carefully and noticed her scent. It wasn't citrus or spice. It was metallic. He frowned as he approached her.

"Heh, not the one," He mumbled and tilted his head, his tongue in his cheek. This person he thought was Nezha was actually a jinni. It lunged toward him and snaked its fingers around his neck.

"It was exciting to see you relieved to see your companion. I'd rather see you scream." The jinni's voice rumbled as he morphed into his original form.

"No. That last line is for you." A mass of air spun in his fist and he twisted in the jinni's grip. He smacked it with his back to the jinni. The creature let go, and instantly, Kayan swerved his sword toward it. The curling blade sent it rising into a puff of smoke.

He collapsed to his knees. When he stood up, he gasped for air and rubbed his neck.

Kayan worked his way through the ruins. Some areas were open overhead to the cold night air, sweeping past the walls, whistling as it ambled through cracks. With all the narrow passages, it was like he was back in the tunnels, the last time he'd been with his mom.

***

His mother had been part of an underground regime. They called themselves Azatuthun. Freedom. They weren't criminals but fought against jinn and humans who would break the law of peace they were supposed to uphold. Laws

334

which had fractured after the War of Jahalia left some vengeful jinn to wreak havoc under the guise of granting their masters great power. He remembered that day five years ago, where he and his mother formed a storm within the facility. Where jinni and human blood had shed. They had rescued his cousin.

It wasn't just his mother's smile he remembered or the way she'd nurtured his cuts and bruises, or even when she'd told him to be strong and never show his weakness. It was when she kissed his hands and told him, "Our intentions are for the good. Those who suffer in silence carry a desert in their hearts. Their hope is depleted. Be the storm to their silence. We can't let them continue to be voiceless."

With his sword Ali by his side, they had infiltrated a facility of human traffickers. It was so long ago. His cousin had moved since, and Kayan's life had truly become a storm.

***

One jinni lashed out at him, tearing him from the flood of memories. He'd believed the past had died along with his mom. Whenever Kayan used his sword gifted by her, he couldn't help but remember his past. His past continued to pursue him.

Kayan turned a corner, the walls here were narrower, tighter, as if they were two snakes about to constrict him. His lungs squeezed. He hadn't been left unscathed by their rescues. The constricted tunnels had left their mark like a bruise over his mind. His breath quickened as panic closed in on him.

I am the wind. I move freely with no shape. Kayan repeated in his mind. These words had kept him grounded years ago. Today, they'd do the same. He tried to inhale deeply and exhale out a slow breath. He had to keep focusing on the present. He had no time for his fears.

I need to find Nezha. The wind carried her scent. I can do this. I am the wind. I move freely with no shape.

***

Nezha and Comet were together. It had been a few minutes since they had been fighting off jinn and running toward where Nezha's heart and the Atlas led them.

"You're doing a good job, Comet." Nezha looked down at her feline and scratched her chin. The cat closed her eyes and meowed softly. Nezha turned around at a crack and a jingle of small bells.

"I'd welcome you, but that would mean I expected you to reach this far." A woman stood against the wall, a wicked smile painted across her face. On her chin were three small black diamonds. Tattoos that marked her as one of the tribe of shadows.

"Zul's accomplice, right?" Nezha's voice came out like a whisper. *She's pale. Just like the other jinni I saw back home. So, she's the one the prince sided with.* Nezha's hands trembled. She was alone with this jinni.

"Impudent girl. You casually name him in such a tone. Prince Zul Sharr would not be amused." She walked toward her. The small coins that fell over her forehead clinked. Lexa's silver headdress had a turquoise tinted glass gem in the center of the pendant. The gold chains ran around her head, with the coins dangling. A domineering expression formed over the jinni's face.

"I'm Lexa. Accomplice? Na, I'm Zul Sharr's lifeblood."

With an irritated look on her face, Nezha raised an eyebrow. "Lifeblood. That's funny." Fire danced around her, sculpting into an arrow. "Your poison is coursing through him." She sent three fire arrows shooting toward the jinni.

Lexa dodged them just as Comet jumped up to scratch at the jinni. She tilted back, allowing Comet to land on all fours. "Foolish girl. Are your own *wants* a poison?"

Nezha flinched and backed away.

"Your kind sickens me. You, of flesh and bone, so mediocre to smokeless fire, and the beauty of shadows. I was born to hate you and those angels. Pitiful creatures, fated to languish within these walls." Her finger trailed over her lower lip, down to her neck and then her arm. Her fingers splayed and she formed knives out of shadows and flung them toward Nezha.

Nezha jumped, but one dagger struck her arm and what swept over her was a dreadful feeling. She stumbled to the ground. Her skin tingled, all her senses high and her breath unsteady. She was nearly in tears when the fear subsided, leaving her heart thudding and her throat aching in its wake.

"I see you tasted fear. You humans assume evil is always hidden and fear the unknown. It's in plain sight. Your blindness is the darkness you find comfort in. You should be careful of the shadows, the past that haunts you. The mistakes you fear to repeat. How ironic." Lexa raised a brow.

So, that's how she wants to play huh?

"Why are you and Zul together? What do you get from him?"

Lexa widened her eyes and combed her fingers through her short copper hair. "Curious thing. The prince was in agony and despair. He desires power and so I gave him exactly that. His corruption perfumes him with an impeccable scent." Her eyes had a look of excitement. She raised her arms.

"Disgusting." Nezha remarked. *Now's my chance.* She formed another flaming arrow and sent it toward Lexa and pushed a crumbling wall toward the jinni.

Lexa gritted her teeth and began to fade between the walls. The arrow grazed her torso, ripping through her chiffon suit, her dark blood staining the aqua fabric. Her eyes widened. "Naïve human. Pain is my servant." Before Lexa disappeared, a surge of shadows shot through the walls and wrapped around Nezha's neck.

Nezha began choking. Her chest tightened and pain cut at her throat. Beside her, Comet meowed loudly in distress.

She raised her left arm, which stiffened, but she managed to bring her wrist and the feather to her lips. Sharp breaths escaped her and fortunately, the bird call sounded from the feather and it transformed into a sword. Nezha's fingers clawed at the dark. Her sight filled with stars and black spots, but she waved the sword wildly at the tumble of darkness. As the blue flames finally met the inky shadows, the dark disintegrated.

Nezha gasped and coughed. She sat up and took in deep shaky breaths. She grazed her fingers over her neck. She could still feel it, the pressure a ghostly reminder of the shadow's grip on her. One thing she couldn't understand was, why the shadows would loosen their grip. It was as if Lexa had only toyed with her.

Comet leaped into Nezha's lap and licked her wrists, sniffed her neck and purred loudly. Her head rubbed firmly against Nezha's chest.

"I'm okay now, Comet."

She'd been so close to death. But death had overlooked her. The Divine was on her side. She still had to avenge her aunt. She still needed to find the orbs.

"Creator help me." Nezha took Comet into her arms and fled. Her gaze bobbed from the Atlas to the paths ahead of her. Her heavy breath and pulsing veins accompanied the song of her frantic heart.

Lexa's been holding back. I'm just lucky she had a reason.

***

Thunderbolt lifted his muscled arms and four pillars of electricity unearthed from the ground, striking the three jinn in a string of lightning. A loud clap of thunder echoed in the destruction's wake. "Damn them t' seven hells."

There were footsteps reaching him. "If it's more jinn, I'm really going t' lose it!"

"Thariq? Thunderbolt!" It was Sapphire's voice that echoed behind him.

"Sapphire?"

He saw her as she turned the corner and faced him. She smiled when they were face to face.

"Lightning rarely strikes a place twice."

Thunderbolt smiled wide. "Saphy. It really is you. Real long code you have."

"Well, I didn't just want one word. I like my sentence." Sapphire smiled.

Thunderbolt and Sapphire started to walk together, keeping close as they turned corners.

***

Zul paced around his mansion's top floor.

"I wonder what's taking them so long. Lexa's usually pretty swift. Hmm?" Zul turned toward the window behind him. He heard a thump. It was Lexa. She was on the ground and looked up at Zul with downward drawn eyebrows and trembling lips.

"Lexa? By the Most High! What happened?" He looked her over. Her blood spilled over her torso.

"Sire. She hit me when I least expected it." *Damn that girl.* Her fingers ran over the scar on her left shoulder. A pink line running horizontally from the round of her shoulder.

"Look, save your breath. You need the energy."

Lexa's eyes widened. Zul's expression was soft as his fingers moved. His iron powers stopped the blood flow and slowly closed the wound's gap.

The prince is helping me? He looks as if he has concern. Lexa grimaced and her heart thudded. *Feeling sympathy for him hurts. Damn it.*

"Well, I tried to close the wound. You *are* a jinni, so you'll live. How you feel?" Zul stood and his expression became indifferent once more.

"I'm good sire. I don't have a human body. My body is more resilient."

Zul smirked and raised his eyebrows. "Lexa, are the angels and the humans scrambling around like bugs in the ruins?"

"Yes, sire, it's pretty funny." Lexa chuckled.

Zul shared her in chuckling. Lexa couldn't believe they were having a lighthearted conversation.

Lexa gently touched her torso. There was warmth. She tugged her lips in a makeshift smile. Her gaze returned to

Zul, who was communicating with a jinni through a Tome. *He tried to heal me. I haven't been like this for so long. It's sickening.*

***

Nezha huffed and placed her hands to her knees. Comet looked up at her and pressed one paw over her hand.

"Comet. We've never been alone like this before. I just want to find the others and get the orb. I hope everyone is okay."

***

Kayan turned a corner. Finally.

He halted, and his expression opened up. Kayan chuckled. "Surfer."

"Kayan. I mean, flamethrower." Nezha smiled.

"I couldn't keep a straight face while saying my word. I hope I didn't give you a mini heart attack and make you think I was a jinni." He rubbed the back of his neck.

"No, I could tell it was you. Have you seen the angels?"

"Nope. I could smell Thunderbolt before with the wind, but I wanted to find you." He looked away.

"Kayan, we need to find the orb."

"So, should I signal to them when we do?" Kayan said as they started walking.

"Yeah, we can't just run around looking for each other. Our best bet is to go for the orb first."

"I agree. Which way does it say?"

"It's to our right. We'll have to turn."

Kayan nodded as they started to run. The Atlas was tracking the orb, and they were getting closer. "We're almost there."

"Yes, I'm just nervous about what we'll encounter." Nezha's eyebrows furrowed.

"We've been through so much. I know we can get that orb. I just know we can."

"I love how optimistic you are. You're never nervous for yourself."

"That's where you're wrong, Nezha." Kayan glanced at her. "I'm so unsure about you. I get anxious and sometimes giddy around you."

She widened her eyes as they stopped at one point. "Kayan. You're so straightforward..."

Kayan faced her. "Nezha... don't hit that wall." He grinned to her and then they ran.

They turned another corner and found Thunderbolt. His hands were full of electricity.

"Surfer," Kayan said and grinned as he saw Thunderbolt's face.

"Heh, flamethrower," Nezha said and cast a worried look at Thunderbolt who seemed like he was about to faint.

"You nearly gave me a heart attack. Saphy, you see this?" Thunderbolt pressed a hand to his chest.

"Sorry, Thunderbolt. I was just excited." Kayan patted Thunderbolt's back.

Nezha embraced Sapphire. "We're getting closer to the orb."

"You didn't even give me a chance to say my line." Sapphire laughed.

"Oh, right. You can if you want to." Nezha stepped back.

Sapphire took a breath in. "Lightning rarely strikes a place twice."

"I think she just says that t' make fun of me," Thunderbolt murmured.

"Let's go. I can't take the suspense any longer," Kayan said.

Thunderbolt marched on as they followed the Atlas's directions.

They turned one corner and were met by Zul, Lexa and a jinni with the orb.

"Glad you made it," Zul said.

The tall jinni stood up and charged.

CHAPTER 27—UNFAZED SHOTGUNS

Kayan smirked. A cyclone spun at his fingertip. "Not a chance." He whipped his sword. The malleable blade slapped the jinni toward the cyclone and it spun him a few feet away as it crashed into the ground.

"Nice reflexes, Kayan," Thunderbolt said.

Zul appeared within the particles of dust and dirt as if a waving curtain had been stretched back.

With a smug smile, Lexa appeared from behind Zul. "This is where the fun begins."

"Wait, who's she?" Thunderbolt glared at Lexa.

"That's the jinni, Lexa. She's the one Zul Sharr made a pact with. I met her in the ruins before," Nezha said, her gaze sliding to the ground.

"Hmm, it seems we are in real trouble now," Sapphire said as Zul took out a revolver.

"Welcome, angels and humans." Zul's voice seemed cheery. As he continued, his voice darkened. "I was waiting for you to get here. You took too long."

He pointed his gun at them.

Nezha readied herself.

She glanced at the jinni, who stood up. The jinni was a large stygian bull, tusks curved up from his upper lip. His skin rippled as he stood.

The Atlas was pointing in its direction as the jinni moved toward them. That familiar hum of energy surged through Nezha's heart. *He's the one who has the orb.*

Zul fired his gun, sending out a hydrogen blast. The explosion sent a pulse of energy toward Nezha and Thunderbolt.

Sapphire formed a large barrier of light around herself and the others. When the hydrogen blast collided with the barrier, it undulated across the wall like molten lava and stretched toward them, nearly touching Sapphire's face.

Nezha flinched as the force shook around her, the sound rumbling in her stomach. She clutched at her chest. A wisp of flames cascaded from her hands and made their way toward Thunderbolt.

"What the—Nezha!" Thunderbolt said, alarmed. The flames nipped around his boots as he stomped at them.

"I'm sorry." Nezha imagined the flames dwindling to nothingness and held her breath momentarily. The flames were gone. She really needed to be careful.

Thunderbolt clapped, sending a shock wave. Zul morphed iron into knives and flung them.

Nezha ducked and showered the knives with fire as they melted.

Sapphire stood in front of everyone. Her hands shot out lasers at the jinni, who had approached Nezha.

"Guh! You need to do better than that." The bull jinni bellowed as the lasers struck his gray arms, cracking like chipped paint. His strong arms lunged toward Nezha but petals of flame danced over him. They barely touched him.

Sapphire charged at the jinni and knocked him over.

"What are you doing?" Nezha asked.

"I can take all the shots and eventually become a sapphire. My pain receptors become dull at that point."

Zul sent another spray of blasts.

Kayan's sword formed a tornado, and the spiraling blade sucked in the blasts and created pops of sound. One nearly hit him as he spun and jumped into the air. Kayan swiftly went on his updraft to spin Zul around in a cyclone, but Lexa was able to grab his feet and swing him to the ground.

"Kayan!" Nezha ran toward Lexa. Her hands fanned out flames, as Lexa jumped and dodged.

"You are determined, aren't you?" Lexa moved swiftly toward Nezha, shadows forming a sword.

Kayan intervened. His icy cold wind eddied about his fists. He stopped Lexa's blows and kicked her leg but was caught by Zul's scythe and flew into the air. Nezha aimed her fire arrows toward Zul, but they only scraped his leg and left shoulder.

"So close," Nezha whispered.

Zul brushed his hand over the cuts and winced from the singes. He diverted his attention to Kayan, who was above him and had used his throw to power himself down toward Zul.

A barrier of wind enshrouded Kayan's body. "Take this, Zul. It'll be tough to puncture my barrier."

"We'll see about that." Zul tilted his head and smirked. He aimed his gun at Kayan and fired.

"No!" Nezha balled her hands into fists and made a punching motion. Balls of fire rushed at Zul, but they unraveled and sputtered into the air.

Thunderbolt pointed a finger, lightning bolts shot at Zul, but Lexa's masses of darkness and shadow consumed the tangled electricity.

Zul's blast was trying its best to rupture the wind's front, but there was only pressure pinching on both sides of the blast.

Lexa took advantage of this moment and knocked Sapphire down with her barrage of swords. "Useless creature."

The swords were masses of shadows so thick they'd solidified. Sapphire crashed to the ground. Once the swords had punctured her skin, cold prickled her skin and her heart was pounding. Fear had begun consuming her, but she'd had enough of it. It didn't take her too long until she was on her feet again.

***

Thunderbolt wasn't fast enough to push Lexa or magnetize her in any way, so he pumped his fist into the ground, setting waves of thunder under Lexa's feet. She fell and rolled.

He sent two surges of lightning bolts toward her. As soon as the strikes trembled about her, she leapt out of the way with the grace of a cat and dodged.

"Damn you." Thunderbolt spoke through his teeth.

"Thunderbolt, careful!" Nezha cried.

Flames came in waves and rolled toward Lexa, but Lexa flipped and released a wave of shadow magic toward her.

Thunderbolt clapped and the surge of energy rippled, meeting the wave of shadow magic, and pushing Lexa back.

"Kid, stay out of it. I'll handle her." Thunderbolt's eyebrows furrowed.

Nezha glanced at Kayan.

"Angel, you are good, but not good enough." More shadow magic crept around Lexa, the shadows formed a mist, blocking Thunderbolt's view. Her elbow struck him once in the gut, and he fell to his knees. He stood up as she swung a shadow sword over his head.

Thunderbolt's whole body fizzed with electricity like a bubbling can of soda.

"Oh? How interesting." Lexa smirked. She shot an explosion of shadow toward him. But Thunderbolt's feet were planted to the ground.

Sapphire panted. She ran in front of Thunderbolt and punched Lexa. But Lexa fired an explosion at Sapphire's fist, sending her flying.

"Sapphire, stay there," Thunderbolt urged. Electricity shot from the sky and him. The two bolts collided and then bounced back toward Lexa.

Her eyes widened when the electricity hit her. She formed thick shadows around herself and screamed. Blood dripped from her leg and an arm. There were cuts all over her. "You're diligent."

"I refuse to sit back and watch you all get injured," Sapphire said as she limped toward Lexa. Sapphire's skin glinted. She had become a purple sapphire.

***

Zul Sharr couldn't move under all the pressure. He fired three more blasts.

Nezha shot flames toward Zul, but it took out so much of her energy as Zul formed shields of iron up around him, her fire barely touching him.

She breathed heavily. The shields turned black and caved in, but didn't melt.

I can't get to him. Kayan will just have to hold on. I feel so helpless right now. I can't even protect him.

"No. . ." The wind slowed around Kayan as if time paused.

Zul's eyes widened, his mouth agape.

Lexa shot her swords and various shadow magic. Sapphire was able to easily swat them away. She charged at Lexa. "Go back to hell." Sapphire punched her with such force it sent Lexa flying back. She collided into a wall and crashed through it, only to fall back into another wall behind it.

In midair, Lexa melded with the shadows. Her lips twisted in a sneer, and she blinked out of existence.

"Sis. Nezha and Kayan." Thunderbolt could barely speak.

"I'm aware," Sapphire said. Her eyes glowed.

***

Sapphire was there in a split second, as the pressure collapsed around Kayan and Zul.

Kayan was about to be struck by Zul with another blast when Sapphire smashed her foot into a shield of metal Zul Sharr formed in front of his midsection. As Zul fell to the ground, a crater formed around him from the impact. The blasts just missed Kayan's arms, the pressure knocking him back.

Zul's scythe formed and cut into Sapphire's shoulder. She quickly removed the blade, but Zul jumped up and flipped away, his back pressed to a wall.

"Jinni, we're leaving."

"Oh, no you don't." Sapphire targeted the jinni. Hot, solidified light bursts flew out of her hands and toward the jinni. The jinni covered himself with a shield that looked like a blue blanket. Only one burst managed to cut his thigh.

"Come on," he whined.

"It's time to depart," Zul said and waved. Lexa appeared behind him. Her skin smooth, without a blemish. She blew them a kiss and hooked her arm with Zul's and jumped back with him as they dissolved through the wall.

"You." Sapphire tried to reach Zul but punched the wall. She seared with anger as the rock around her crumpled to her feet.

***

Nezha rushed to Kayan.

"Kayan, are you okay?"

"My arm's hurt, but I'll be fine."

"I felt so helpless seeing you like that," Nezha said and put her face in her hands.

"We all felt that way. Zul's not ordinary. So don't be tough on yourself." He gave her a smile.

"And, Sapphire, she's been so brave." Nezha turned to her.

Sapphire and Thunderbolt ran up to the both of them.

"I'm so sorry we couldn't help you." Sapphire embraced Nezha tightly.

"No, you did so well. Please don't feel bad," Nezha said.

"Are you okay?"

"Yes." Sapphire pulled and fixed Nezha's hijab.

"Kid, you were doing well. An improvement from the first time you had t' fight." Thunderbolt grinned.

"Uh, how could... I was left here?" The jinni with the orb complained.

"Huh? He's still here. That means..." Kayan stood up and turned to the jinni, just as everyone else's gaze fixed on the jinni as well.

"Great, maybe it won't be such a loss then," Thunderbolt said and flexed his muscles.

"Yes. I think you can join me for this one," Sapphire said, her skin still purple.

"Oh, I have to be somewhere." The bull jinni panicked as he started to back away.

"Brother, encircle the light bursts with electricity. Nezha, Kayan, you can both join." Sapphire raised her arm.

Thunderbolt readied himself. "Sure thing, sis."

Sapphire shot the lights out of her hands.

Thunderbolt swirled electricity about them, and Nezha and Kayan's flames and wind twirled as the bursts spiraled toward the jinni and punctured him.

The jinni screamed as the force crushed him and caused a small explosion as he faded away into ashes. In his place, an orb glistened on the ground.

Nezha bent down to pick up the orb, and it melted into her heart. "Let's go home," She said with a sigh.

"Yeah," Thunderbolt said.

"First, I need to heal your wounds." Sapphire looked at Kayan and Nezha.

Nezha's skin welcomed the warmth as the light blurred away the exposed tissue.

"One thing bothers me. What was Zul trying to accomplish? Did he just hand an orb over to us?" Nezha brushed at her top.

"There is a possibility that jinni was working with him and he intentionally left him here. He probably planned to finish us off by luring us with an orb," Sapphire said.

"You saw how he left." Nezha frowned.

"Even so, we have an orb," Kayan reminded them. "We're closer to completing the soul than we were yesterday."

"Yes, that's true." Sapphire smiled.

"That jinni though. Talk about comic relief!" Thunderbolt chuckled.

"Huh?" A smile tugged at Nezha's parted lips.

"He was actually pretty funny. The way he complained, I mean." Thunderbolt grinned.

"We should head back to Equus City, to Tasa's. She must be thinking of us," Sapphire said.

"Good idea," Kayan said. They hopped onto the updraft and were on their way.

CHAPTER 28—CHOCOLATE CHARITY

The next afternoon, Kayan sat by the pond.

"Kayan." Nezha smiled as her eyes met his. "I thought maybe you could use some company. You've been pretty quiet since we got back."

"It's just about Zul. My wind couldn't get him." He leaned in.

Nezha was taken aback as she analyzed his expression, regret and concern washing over his face.

"I know you're worried, Kayan. He's using magic. I was able to graze his shoulder, so there's a way we can get him. Even I've been wondering about how we're supposed to handle Zul. Are we supposed to treat him as our enemy or one who's a victim?"

"All I was thinking about was getting the orb and protecting everyone." His eyes softened.

"It's just like you to not be doubtful."

"It's just like *you* to think of saving someone. I never thought of Zul needing *rescuing*." He chuckled. "I've been thinking of him as an enemy. Someone who took on demonic magic and now wants power." Kayan looked up to the sky and sat back, his hands planted upon the ground.

"Maybe, it's just like how I was before. Running away from what needed to be done. It's that word, *maybe,* that keeps me from going anywhere."

Kayan lowered his head. "Nezha, don't forget that *maybe* is also good. You want to find the good in him, don't you? I don't know why you do."

"It's his words. He once said he didn't want to kill anyone. I know we can't rely on his words alone. It's just, at that time, he really looked like he meant it. His parents want their son back too and in a way I think the angel wants to be merciful to him." Nezha pursed her lips.

"Somehow, we need to weaken Zul. I just feel bad I couldn't do much."

"You're not thinking you're weak, are you? He's not on our level. He's using unlawful ways to gain power. Of course it would be more difficult to weaken him."

"Yeah, I know." Kayan gave a small smile. "Thanks for being by my side."

She searched his eyes and returned the smile. He was opening up to her now.

"Guess what?" Thunderbolt stood behind both of them. Nezha jumped and put a hand to her heart, and Kayan dropped on his back to the grass.

"What the heck is it?" Kayan said, breathing hard.

"Thunderbolt!" Nezha looked at him, annoyed.

"Uh, sorry, I wanted t' tell you good news. Sheesh, I just wanted t' brighten your moods," Thunderbolt mumbled.

Sapphire stood by him. "It's a special day in the city today. I think you're going to have mixed emotions about it though."

"Oh. That sounds… interesting." At first Nezha was enthusiastic and then suspicion stole through her.

Kayan started to walk. "Come on, he said it was a special day. Can't miss it."

"Well, you recover quickly," Nezha said.

"Hey, Saphy, I was going to tell them," Thunderbolt grumbled.

"Sorry, forgive me for spoiling it." Sapphire smiled mischievously.

They arrived in the core of Equus City. It was the city's square where shops lined the sides of the streets in a rainbow of colors.

All sorts of people strolled through. Some whose skin tones were brown, golden, peachy or copper. Some wore djellabas, hooded robes and belghas. It was comforting to see a part of home in a foreign land.

Nezha marveled at a large, rectangular fountain. The sides were painted in cream and a pattern of vermicular. On all sides a mote of water flowed through. Glass walls kept anyone from sticking their fingers in. What flowed within captured Nezha's attention. A waterfall of honey fell into a pool. On one side, there was a hole with a golden hexagon.

Nezha turned to Sapphire.

"Oh, I see you're enamored with our Honey River. You see, there is a nest of bees below ground who produce the honey in abundance. The Angel of Mercy, Mirkhas had been the one to make an agreement for them to supply their beloved food. When you crank the lever beside the hexagonal slit, you must give the bees food in return to taste their honey. Anything sweet, even a flower may suffice."

Nezha immediately went over to the grass and picked a white flower. At the foundation, she dropped her offering through the hexagon and turned the crank. After a few seconds, bees appeared within the glass. Their legs were ornamented with fuzzy yellow balls from the pollen they'd gathered. The thick golden liquid poured out from the hexagon and was coated in bees wax. She held her hand over the slot and was gifted with the hexagon shape in her palms. Nezha took it between her fingertips and placed it into her mouth. The liquid was impeccable, melting into her mouth, coating her tongue in creamy sweetness. Unlike anything she had ever tasted.

"She's speechless," Thunderbolt said as he joined them. "Amazing, right?"

"Uh-huh." Nezha nodded, and a wide smile crossed her face. "Let's—" Her voice faded as she saw her weakness. Chocolate. People around her were carrying boxes, bags and handfuls of chocolate. "It's...There's chocolate everywhere. You said it was a special day, not a punishment." Nezha said, exasperated.

"Well, I did say you'd have mixed emotions. It is tradition. We have a chocolate charity day for the hospitals all across Noorenia. With Wadi Alma having representatives in each country, they are the most influencial country in our world," Sapphire said.

"Oh, well then I guess it's okay. It is for the good of Noorenia." Nezha thought of the festivals they had on earth such as Christmas or Valentine's Day and how some countries had their own ways of celebrating them. Nezha walked over to a shop. "Let's pick out chocolates."

"Whoa, wait a sec. You recover too quickly too." Kayan ran after her.

"Don't you just like it when the kids get giddy?" Thunderbolt laughed.

"I'm happy to see them smile," Sapphire said.

***

Nezha licked her lips as she picked a dozen types of truffles from a glass display case at one small shop. The walls were lined with black stones and the cream and wooden tables all had small leaves and vines snaking up their legs.

"Whoa." Kayan looked at her and then the chocolates she picked out from the display. There were dozens of flavors, from mint chocolate, to the more peculiar white chocolate with passion fruit and roasted orange.

"I'll try not to eat too much, okay?" Nezha smiled as she held a container of twenty truffles.

"You call that a few?" Kayan twirled his index finger, placing many of the truffles back. Only ten truffles remained.

"Why'd you do that? I was going to share, you know." She pouted.

"I know. Hey, we can try other shops," Kayan offered and grinned.

"Oh, all right," Nezha conceded.

He handed money over to the shop keeper as they walked back to the angels.

"So, did you stuff your face?" Thunderbolt teased.

"No, actually, I was sensible and bought just enough to share."

"Yeah, after I intervened." Kayan nudged Thunderbolt and rolled his eyes.

"Thank you," Sapphire bit into one truffle.

"Those were really good." Nezha sighed and looked up at the clear sky. It was such a bright blue it didn't seem to look real at all.

"Sure were," Kayan said.

"Where should we head next?" Nezha leaned in to Kayan, and then looked concerned as she saw his expression. "What are you thinking about?"

Kayan looked up at Nezha and gave her a smile.

"Ah, let's go to that shop. They have brownies." Kayan began walking at a pace to keep up with Nezha.

"J'aime les brownies. You like them too?"

"J... what?"

"Sorry. I said I love brownies! It was French."

"Oh… I don't really like sweet things too much, but a treat once in a while is nice. Come on. Catch me, or I'll eat them all." Kayan grinned and whirled the wind as he sped off to the shop.

"Hey, no fair. You used the wind." Nezha laughed and then ran after him.

The shop was called Madam Marmalade's Bakery. Brightly decorated in blues, oranges and greens, Nezha noticed the patterns along the counter and the chairs. She instantly felt like she had stepped into a part of Morocco.

"Welcome. What would you like, honeysuckle?" The woman at the counter smiled.

The register was at the back of the shop. Along either side, the glass displays were filled with cakes of various sizes and flavors. Some were lemon, strawberry and a curious amalgamation of spices and marmalade. She picked up a small strawberry cake, spiced marmalade cakes and a few other mini chocolate cupcakes.

"Honeysuckle? Pfft." Thunderbolt pressed a hand to his grin. He then plucked a bag from a rack beside the register. He turned to Nezha with his arm stretched out in front of him. "Oh! You need t' try these."

"What are they?" Nezha looked at the small bag. It was blue, with a yellow band in the middle.

"Lightning gummies. Just try one, and you'll know how incredible they are. Remember, sis? We used t' eat these a lot when we were younger."

"Yes, I remember eating many of these at night before bed. Good thing I'm part angel, or I may have lost teeth," Sapphire said.

Nezha raised a brow. "Hmm. All right."

Thunderbolt turned to the counter and paid for the bag of treats. Surprisingly, they were a mere two riatas. He opened the bag and had everyone take one.

Nezha picked a blue one from the bag. It was shaped like a lightning bolt. She chewed the gummy, the treat squishing between her teeth. Her eyes widened at first, her eyebrows furrowed, and then she puckered her lips. "Whoa, there's a whole storm going on… on my tongue."

Thunderbolt laughed. "Yeah, can you tell which flavour?"

"I've tried these before. They're really good. I love that sweet and sour combination." Kayan popped a yellow one into his mouth.

"Yeah, at first you feel a fizz on your tongue, and then you get that sour hit, with some sweetness laced in it. It tastes like blueberry? And there's lemon," Nezha said and tried another one.

"Yeah, it's not blueberries. It's another fruit here. Like a blueberry and cloudberry had a seedling," Thunderbolt said.

"I've never heard of cloudberries before," Nezha said. "Thanks for introducing them to me."

"You're welcome, kid." Thunderbolt put a hand to his heart and grinned.

"Do you have any brownies left?" Nezha asked the woman at the counter.

She had short brown hair and a white blouse dotted in pink flowers. "Ah, yes. We have brownies on a stick. You're in luck. I have one left." The woman winked and handed one to Nezha. It was wrapped up in a blue cloth lined in wax. The stick end was tied with an orange ribbon.

"Thank you." Nezha handed the money over and walked toward the angels.

"Take care, sweets," the woman said.

"Only one huh? Are we sharing it?" Thunderbolt asked.

"Maybe." Nezha then caught Sapphire shaking her head and smiling. "I mean—yes."

Kayan chuckled. "Okay, we got the brownie and a box of cakes. How about we go and sit somewhere? I picked out chocolate ice cream sandwiches too. They'll melt if we don't eat them soon."

Nezha walked beside Thunderbolt as she unwrapped an ice cream sandwich and took a bite of it. Kayan also ate his.

Sapphire carried the rest of the brownies and cakes.

"Shouldn't we visit the elder and Vinci?" Thunderbolt bit into a lemon and white chocolate cupcake topped with ribbons of spiced caramel.

"Yes. It would be a delight to share these treats with them." Even Sapphire's smile showed her joy.

"Yeah, it would be." Nezha tried to take a cupcake from the box, but Sapphire closed the lid and told Nezha they would be sharing with Halim and Vinci.

"Vinci lives here in Equus City, so we can head to his home quite easily." Sapphire turned and took her side by Nezha as they continued to walk through the dirt-paved road, now distant from the hustle and bustle of the urban downtown square they were just in.

They spoke amongst each other, their voices carrying out like a song. It was bliss that led them onward, on a day of sweets.

***

"Welcome. Come right in." Vinci's brown eyes glided over to Nezha as he gave her a polite smile. "I don't think we've met."

"Yes, this is Nezha. She's the one who entered Noorenia from the pond. Our hope." Sapphire sat on the gray futon, as Nezha took a seat beside her.

"Hey, Vinci, my zaan." Thunderbolt patted Vinci's back, embracing him in a swift hold and turned to sit down. At five feet, Vinci was shorter than Thunderbolt.

"Oh? Nice to meet you, Nezha. I'm Vinci the elf, their childhood friend." There was a bold stillness to Vinci, with his square jawline, high cheek bones and clear brown skin. His pointed ears framed a face that was handsome.

"Nice to meet you," Nezha said.

"Are you enjoying the charity event?" Vinci said as he sat down. They were sitting in his living room.

Sapphire placed the box of cupcakes on the glass table.

"You guys came here to share these?" Vinci gestured at the box.

Thunderbolt took a cupcake and bit into it. "Yeah and t' just talk."

"So how is Prince—I mean, Zul Sharr. What about him? Has he been causing trouble?" Vinci picked up a cupcake and took a bite.

"Yeah, he's been one hell of a pain in the hooves." Thunderbolt scowled as his mouth twitched.

"Nezha, you know today's a day of sharing. It's good that you get a chance to sample what Noorenia has to offer."

Nezha took two cupcakes and placed them on a white dish. "I'm really enjoying it too."

"Is the elder with you?" Thunderbolt turned his head to the back of the house.

"He's actually here in the backyard." Vinci gestured for them to follow him.

They walked over the brown carpet and gray hardwood floor into the kitchen. The sunlight fell over a round silver mirror on a blue wall.

Vinci slid the silver glass door open. His yard was quite spacious. He'd kept it neat and clean. There was a small red wooden shed to the right, and farther back was a bed of yellow and blue flowers.

Thunderbolt stepped forward, his shoulder pushing Vinci, and he paused. "Elder..." His lips parted with a smile.

Sapphire stood next to Vinci.

There he was. Their elder, Halim.

The angel siblings rushed over to the elder and reverted to their unicorn forms, their feet into hooves touching the ground, their faces longer, noses soft as velvet and small huffs escaping their breaths. Their horns did not prick the elder as they pressed their cheeks to his.

"Elder, it is so good to see you," Sapphire said.

"Ah, I see you are both well. I missed you too." Halim raised his head.

Nezha and Vinci walked over to him, with Comet walking slowly to the side and then lying on her belly, watching the others.

"Elder Halim, this is Nezha. She's the princess's cousin." Vinci gestured to Nezha as she approached the older unicorn.

"It is a pleasure to meet you, princess," Halim bowed his head.

Nezha smiled. "Likewise."

Vinci sat cross-legged on the grass. Nezha glanced at him and did the same.

Halim spoke, "I had been at the Fire Kingdom mansion when the prince's iron encased the mansion and Sanari. The ceiling had fallen on us and I was not aware of the fates of Princess Sanari or her family. She was still quite young. Both the prince and the princess were twenty-five years old. Too young for their pain." Halim's eyes became glossy with tears.

Tears pricked her eyes too. She closed them momentarily.

"After I escaped the rubble, I followed the prince and witnessed his iron make its way toward Unicorn Valley." He nipped at the grass and chewed it. After he swallowed, he said, "Divine Will has chosen you all to mend the angel's soul. I do hope you will succeed."

"Elder..." Thunderbolt sighed and lowered his head.

Sapphire mirrored him. "It is our duty." She glanced at Thunderbolt, and in unison they said, "Duty before desire."

Halim looked into their eyes. "Do not forget, discarding your desires is not an option." His lips formed a smile. "Speaking of desires, you should know why other humans or jinn may want the angel's broken soul."

"Because it doesn't have the light, right?" Nezha said.

Halim nodded. "Without light, there cannot be good. Our world, Noorenia is named such. A world of light. Within our bodies, light and energy play a role." He lowered his neck. "Princess, please take out the Atlas given to you."

Nezha did so.

"Atlas, show us the Lataif of the heart diagram," Halim said.

At his words, the Atlas glowed, and before their eyes a diagram appeared in the air like a hologram. "Princess Nezha, please align it so the images are right in front of your chest. He turned to the siblings and Kayan. "You three may also participate."

They did as he told.

He continued. "The Lataif, or the six subtleties are energy points, made of swirling electromagnetic energy. The six Lataif are called Qalb, Ruh, Sir Sir, Khafa, Akhfa and Nafs. There is also a seventh called Sultan Al-Azkhar."

The images before Nezha seemed to lay over her chest. There were swirling spheres of color. A yellow sphere under her left breast, red one under her right, a white sphere above her left, a green above her right. In the middle with a black glowing sphere and at her forehead glowed a blue sphere.

"Wow." Kayan sighed out.

"Yes, wow indeed." Halim smiled. "Qalb is heart, for Divine Love." The yellow glowed over Thunderbolt's chest.

"Ruh is soul for the building of the soul." The red sphere glowed over Kayan's chest.

"Sir Sir is the secret of secrets, a point where desires could burn a fire of anger or change to fire of Divine love." The white glowed brighter before Nezha's chest.

"Khafa is hidden mystery or knowledge, for intuition and resurrection, leaving the physicality.

Nafs is the ego and the aim to remove negative thinking, and Akhfa is most hidden and for divinely presence." The black orb in the center pulsed at Sapphire's chest.

"These six points focus on the highest part of the self, the heart and soul. When all are filled with Divine light, the soul is purified and does good." Halim turned his head to Nezha. "The soul can be a great power, and those with ill intent can abuse it. Do you understand?"

"Yes, I understand about that. The names and areas on the chest though, not so much," Nezha said.

"Well, I know I'm confused," Thunderbolt messed with his hair.

Kayan shrugged.

"Yes, I believe I did." Sapphire smiled.

"Of course *you* did." Thunderbolt grinned.

"It was so nice to meet you, Halim. Thank you." Nezha raised her hand toward him.

"Yeah, it was a pleasure to meet you," Kayan said.

Halim's dark gray nose pressed into Nezha's palm and then Kayan's. "It was truly a blessing. May you be resilient. May the Creator smile upon you, children."

"Thank you." Nezha petted his nose and smiled.

***

After they finished their treats, bellies full of sweets, they stood at the front door.

"Ah, that tickles," Vinci said. Comet was licking his hand. "Does Comet belong to you?"

"Yeah. Wait, how did you know her name?" Nezha asked.

"I can speak cat. Well, not too fluently. Right now, she either said she's hungry or that I smell like something tasty."

Nezha smiled.

"It was great to meet you. You all need to visit my jewelry shop some time. I have quite a few rare things there. You'd be amazed by the way they all shine," Vinci said at the door.

"Yes, we should." Sapphire took a step outside, and the others followed.

"Yeah, I'll be looking forward to it." Nezha waved as they all made their way back to the park.

***

A man walked into the shop they had left earlier. His face was wrapped in a black cloth, only his eyes visible.

"Ma'am, do you have any more brownies?" he asked.

"Ah, I'm sorry sweets, I sold the last one," The woman replied.

"Hmm, it's okay."

"Take care!" the woman called out to him and smiled.

"Same to you." The man turned around and as he walked away, he saw Nezha with the brownie in her hand in the distance.

"That's the one," he muttered under his breath and followed behind them.

***

"Too bad I can't get a treat for Comet." Nezha scratched Comet behind the ear as she bent down.

"Maybe buy her something else, after Saphy and I are done with our ice cream sandwiches," Thunderbolt said, the ice cream dripping down his wrist.

Nezha poked Thunderbolt's arm. "I told you to eat them before they melt."

"Yeah, you could get her fish, or even rabbit." Kayan smiled as Comet's ears pricked up.

"Good idea, Kayan. You know, she actually loves rabbit."

The cloaked man was behind them as he walked. But when Nezha had bent down, Sapphire had turned with her wings open and sent him splashing into the water.

"Hmm, did I just hit something?" Sapphire asked as she turned around. Sapphire stopped for a few seconds and then fell into step with the others.

The man was out of the water now and up in a tree.

"Okay, that was close. A little too close. I need to be careful."

***

"This spot looks good," Kayan said and sat as Nezha sat beside him.

"Here." Nezha handed an ice cream sandwich to the siblings.

Comet looked up at Nezha and sniffed the bag. She turned her head up at Nezha, her ears pricked up.

"Sorry Comet. I'll get you some rabbit later, all right?" Nezha winked at her and pet her head.

Comet meowed and then sat by Nezha's legs, curling up.

"Mmm. These brownies are really good," Kayan said and smiled. They had bought more than enough for themselves. They'd planned on giving more to Tasa.

"I thought you didn't like sweet things." Nezha grinned.

"I don't usually. Well, I'm used to you." Kayan bit the ice cream sandwich again. He met her gaze and gave her a lopsided grin.

"Good." Nezha's cheeks heated. *When did he get so playful?*

"You know, today's been really nice. I like just sitting here enjoying it all. The weather is great and the company." Kayan turned to Nezha and caught her eye.

Nezha's lips parted. *This boy...*

"Do you want to head to the shop we used to frequent?" Sapphire asked.

"Do you mean that small bakery with the honey cakes and marbled fudge?" Thunderbolt said.

"Yes." Sapphire smiled.

"Yes," Nezha echoed and walked beside Sapphire.

"So, how long are you going t'—Thunderbolt turned around, alarming the others around him, and threw a ball of lightning toward a wall. "—follow us."

"Well, you're as impulsive as usual." A man with a cloth around his face turned to them from the wall.

"That voice... Ansam?" Thunderbolt stared at the man.

The man unwrapped the cloth from his face. "Yep. Hey, how are you all?"

Thunderbolt rushed over to him. "Seven hells, Ansam! I almost killed you!"

"Huh? Is he a friend of yours?" Kayan asked.

"Yep. He's an angel. He was also the guardian of the feather I now own," Nezha explained.

"Oh, I see," Kayan said.

"Sorry. I had to stay on the down low." Ansam brushed the back of his neck as Thunderbolt scolded him.

"Are you okay? Don't ever do that again."

"Hey, Ansam. Surprise seeing you here," Nezha said.

Ansam blushed. "Ah, it's a pleasure to see you again, Lady Nezha."

"Can you explain to us why you were disguised?" Sapphire asked.

"Uh, well, since Lady Nezha has the feather, I've been given a new role. I'm the guard at the Iron Kingdom. There was a special item I had to retrieve and it's in that brownie."

"In the brownie?" Nezha said.

"Yes. It's a long story. There may be some jinn who would love to have the item, so we need to speak somewhere else. By the way, how are you all liking the charity event? Sweet, right? Oh, pun intended." Ansam smiled wide again.

"Yes, it's been really good. Oh, you haven't met Kayan yet." Nezha introduced them.

"Nice to meet you, Kayan," Ansam said and held out his hand.

"You too." Kayan smiled politely and patted his back. "I'm a wind jawhar. I joined them to search for a flower that would heal my father and now to find the angel's soul and to kick Zul's snarky butt."

"That's a noble cause. And someone definitely has to." Ansam said and shone with a hearty smile as they wrapped an arm around each other's shoulders.

"Aw, you guys are so energetic. Ansam, where can you explain the brownie to us?" Nezha asked.

His stomach growled, and he hunched over a bit, rubbing his stomach.

"Hungry?" Thunderbolt asked.

"Not even." Ansam blushed again. "I had to eat a ton of brownies to keep the item safe."

They all stared at him and then Kayan started to laugh, along with Thunderbolt.

"Aw, guys, don't be like that," Nezha said.

"It's okay." Ansam laughed a bit.

"Sorry. Now I really want t' know what's so special about this brownie." Thunderbolt put his arm around Ansam as they walked out from the other side of the bridge.

"We were going to head to a small bakery, but we could go somewhere else to speak about this situation," Sapphire said.

"Oh, I really don't want to have to bother you all." Ansam shrugged.

"No, there's no turning back. I'm curious. I really want to know what's in this brownie," Nezha said.

"We'll have to head to the Iron Kingdom. It's the only place that's safe," Ansam said.

"I don't mind, as long you guys don't," Nezha said.

"Yeah, let's go." Kayan swirled the air with his fingers.

"You need ginger soda," Thunderbolt said, concerned.

"Yes, we'll make you some ginger soda as soon as we get to the kingdom," Sapphire said and smiled at Ansam.

"You always know how to take care of me. You're the best." Ansam walked with them as they headed to the Iron Kingdom.

"Oh, wait... I kind of promised Comet she'd get to eat rabbit today." Nezha looked down at Comet who walked along her side.

"Yes, that's right. We'll pick some up along the way."
Sapphire smiled.

***

At the Iron Kingdom's mansion, Ansam sipped his ginger soda, and Comet was by the table, chomping down on raw rabbit.

"Lady Nezha, you can break the brownie, and you'll see what's inside."

Nezha nodded and broke the brownie in half. Inside was a small silver key. She broke off the pieces and crumbs into a bowl.

"This?" She held it in her fingertips.

"Yes, it safeguards an important item," Queen Laiqa said.

Laiqa turned to Ansam. "Ansam, I am relieved that you found the key. Good job."

"You're welcome, Queen." He sipped his drink and placed the glass down.

"So, do we get t' know how a key was baked into a brownie?" Thunderbolt asked.

"Yes, there's no harm in telling you. It's my fault we misplaced the key," the Queen said.

Everyone looked at her silently with wide eyes.

She continued. "Every year we bake brownies on a stick for the Chocolate Charity day. Today I was in the kitchen while our chefs made the brownies." The queen paused and laughed demurely. "I had bumped into someone. That may have been when the key fell into the batter. Poor, silly Ansam had to go to the bakery when we realized what happened. He actually ate each brownie until he found the key."

"Ansam. For the sake of As-Sabur, you know you could have just told the bakery there was a mishap with the brownies and just found them that way," Thunderbolt said as the queen laughed and embarrassed Ansam.

"Yeah, but it was fun being mysterious. I was actually planning on finding you and having you detect the key with your magnetism, but, I was really hungry..." He looked down.

"At least it ended well." Nezha smiled.

"Yes, we're fortunate that it was you, Nezha, who had the key," the king said.

"As for the item, we can't say too much. All I will say is that the key opens a box. Ansam is now protector over it," the queen said.

"Ah, so that's how it is now," Thunderbolt said and grinned at Ansam.

"I'm glad you have the honor of being a guardian again," Sapphire said.

"Thank you." Ansam smiled softly.

Zul's heart throbbed. The pain ached in his chest as he recalled Sanari. The one whom he cared for so much. Her warm glowing smile, the kindness of her eyes that he thrived on each day. *Oh Creator, why? Why did it happen?*

"Sire," Lexa whispered.

Zul flinched. His painful memories withdrew from him once again. He stood at the window looking down at the forest stretching out. The homes were colorful dots in the distance. He placed his hand against the cold glass, and grimaced at the touch. His eyes softened. His jaw relaxed as his expression became bereft of emotion.

Lexa was in her black leopard form. She jumped down from the white stool, her sleek black tail whipping to the side while she rubbed her head against his arm.

"Your expression is delightful." She transformed to her human form. Her arms coiled around his shoulders.

"Do you let my looks deceive you? How ironic, shape shifter." Zul's voice was harsh, but low as he turned to her and plucked her arms from him.

"Of course, not." She turned to the black recliner and stretched as she sat down. "Why are you so neutral all of a sudden?"

Zul stepped over to her. "Why is this such a surprise to you? Aren't you accustomed to changes?"

"Again, with the shape shifting references, are we?"

"Stop asking questions," Zul said, his voice meek as he turned away.

"I miss the wild, dark expression you carry so well. And, dare I say, empathy."

Zul whipped his head back. "Must you banter with me so?" He lowered his head and turned his back to Lexa. "Be aware of me jinni. Pain and numbness are feelings that come naturally to me. The darkness envelopes me in comfort. I don't have to see the true monsters… people and their ever-changing whims, and no one can see me. I can enter my own world, where no one can get there, can't find me there, or hurt me. It engorges on my fears until they become the very abyss of darkness itself." His head fell.

Momentarily he hid his pain-stricken expression. He raised his head and revealed his glowing orange eyes.

"Welcome back." She chuckled, and licked her lips. "I'm famished."

"What do you crave? Flesh?" Zul's tone signaled a hint of mockery.

"Yeah, chicken." She was a leopard once again. Her long pink tongue slipped out like a snake and rested against one of her incisors as her ears twitched.

"Help yourself. I'm not your servant, nor your king... yet." Zul flashed his eyes to her.

"Forgive my insolence. I am unnerved by what I can smell. I sense a sickness too warm and light wafting in the air."

Zul grinned. The iron from the wall across the room snapped. Like water, it dripped down and darted to Zul's hand and formed a long slender rod. "Shall we go?"

Lexa walked over to a cooler and opened it with her mouth. She held a chicken wing in her jaws. She snapped the bone and swallowed the slippery flesh. She tore another piece of the wing, swallowing ravenously. When she licked her paw, a splotch of blood stained her dark fur.

***

"Nezha, try to catch me!" Kayan jumped up and glided on his updraft. It was the next day in the afternoon. He and Nezha were in the field practicing their control while the siblings were a few feet farther. Nezha grinned and lowered her head.

"You're quick, but not enough. Let the *wind* catch on fire," He mused, and gave a sharp turn, hovering before Nezha.

"I think the wind is already on fire." Nezha slipped behind Kayan hopping onto the updraft. When she stood on the board, it was as if she were surfing the sea.

"Try to feel like you're really surfing." Kayan looked back to her and flashed her a shining smile.

Her heart boomed like thunder. The euphoria of flying through the air was scaring her, yet his stunning smile made her heart animate with delight. She couldn't tell if it was fear that pounded her heart or not.

"What if I fall?" Nezha gripped his sleeve tighter.

"Then, I'll catch you. You knew I'd say that, didn't you? What if I crash and burn if you hold onto me?" Kayan laughed.

"I don't know about you crashing, but burning could be a possibility." Nezha laughed, then slowly straightened her arms and let the wind sway her. "I'm not holding onto you. I don't touch strange men."

"Hey, I am not some weirdo." Kayan laughed.

"Other than close family, there's no contact."

"I get it now. So, that's why you didn't hold on to me just now."

"Yup. I'm glad you understand," Nezha said and her grip on his sleeve tightened.

"Why wouldn't I? You're still strange to me though."

Nezha snickered. "Yeah, hopefully that'll change."

"What do you mean by that, huh?" He grinned.

"You won't think I'm some kind of fire hazard," Nezha said and tilted to the left.

"Ah, we'll just have to see, flamethrower." Kayan chuckled and balanced his feet. In that form, he looked just like a surfer at a beach, catching a wave, flying atop a froth of sea water.

***

The air pricked at Nezha's skin.

Kayan yearned for moments like this where he could feel free and happy. The warmth of her smile and her enchanting laugh spun through his mind.

He soared up again, escalating higher until they reached the tops of the clouds. There they hovered.

"Kayan? What are you doing?" Nezha held on tighter to his sleeve.

He turned to her. "I thought you would enjoy the scenery." His eyes shifted from hers to the gaping field below.

"It's beautiful but shouldn't we..." Nezha searched his eyes. "I wish we didn't have to fight, but we have to find the orbs."

Kayan smiled pleasantly. "We've all been through a lot, and who knows when we'll get another day of peace. One more thing..." He stretched his arms and with the wind he swept her off her feet, free-falling through the air with Nezha right by his side.

Nezha let out a small yelp. "Kayan!"

His voice swooshed with the air. "Don't worry, I just want you to feel what I feel when I'm one with the wind. It's not exact, but it's close. I won't let you get hurt."

"I trust you!" Nezha closed her eyes.

Kayan turned to her, admiring how the wind lifted her so gently. The wind ached with emotion. Only he could feel it, being a wind jawhar. The wind sensed his emotions and showed it in the way it brought Nezha close to him. He wanted to understand her. In those few moments, time seemed to let them believe it was still and Kayan believed it.

"So light," Nezha whispered.

"Yeah," Kayan spoke as in a reverie. Their eyes locked in midair. Nezha's eyes turned crimson as fire spiraled out from her palms embodying her like a flowing dress. When they neared the ground, the wind pulled them and they were hovering above the ground.

***

"I told you I wouldn't let you get hurt." Kayan whispered. His eyes were a wild glistening green.

"We should test our powers." Nezha spoke softly and stepped onto the grass. The fire around her flickered relentlessly. She morphed a few flames into petals, moving her arms as if she too were a flickering flame.

"Definitely." He stood in front of her and spun his right finger, never averting his eyes. The wind spun into a small ball that grew, spinning faster and rising into a cyclone.

The flaming petals spun in the center. He widened his eyes, causing the tornado to tear. Wind rushed out, showering them with red petals.

He was breathless. "Wow, I'm already wiped out. I need more practice."

"Maybe, but I think it was my fault."

Kayan looked at her with his eyebrows raised.

"Well, you were concentrating on me. You think I didn't notice your gaze?" She grinned.

Kayan blushed. "In real combat, you need to anticipate your opponent's moves," His gaze shifted to the ground and he combed his fingers through his hair.

"Sure." Nezha laughed.

Kayan walked in a circle around Nezha as he spun her with wind.

This was the first time she didn't hold her breath to kill the fire. She inhaled and breathed out. She kicked forward, raised her knees and punched. It was as if she were in a dance. She slid her foot in a circle, turned her body, and kicked. The movements were powerful. Dynamic.

Kayan remained in a defensive stance, shielding, his arms swinging in circles.

Flames burst from her hands and feet, following her as if they were a dancing partner. In the end, they encased her in a flower made of fire. Her emotions came undone and the flames reacted to how she felt, forming shapes she never thought the fire could take. It was strange, but so liberating.

He stepped back from her. "Well, this is new."

The flower of fire opened up and sent the wind back.

"Wow." Kayan brushed ashes off his clothes as the wind whisked by him.

"I just went with the flow." Nezha stared at her hands.

***

"How do you think the siblings are doing?" he asked.

"They're probably doing more than we are right now." She sat down. Close to the nearby forest.

"Are we allowed here?"

"Yeah. Sapphire told me it was pretty safe here but to stay out of the forest and to make sure we stay together." He sat down in the grass beside her. "I don't know if I feel safer though."

"That's good, and come on. I'm not going to willingly burn you. I can't anyway." Nezha took a deep breath in.

"Yeah, it's been pretty quiet all day, so at least today we have some time." Kayan turned to look at the trees. The wind swept through the leaves. He could taste sweetness in the energy of the wind. He turned to see Nezha looking up at the birds flying by and singing in the trees.

"Kayan?" Nezha asked. Had she noticed him looking at her?

"Yeah?"

"Something up?"

393

"Nah, it's just that I can also taste the energy in the air."

"Really? What's it like?" Nezha leaned in.

He smiled. "No one's ever asked me how it's felt to me. It's salty like the ocean, with a hint of sweetness."

"It's amazing how intuitive our powers can be."

"Yeah, it really is." Kayan grinned. "You know, maybe you're growing on me."

"Yeah? That's good to know. I'm not scary," Nezha said and chuckled.

That's when Kayan turned to the grass. The wind carried a certain sound of movement. He stood, and Nezha mirrored him.

From behind the trees a scorpion dashed toward them through the grass, the sound like rice being sifted. It was around seven feet long. The sharp end of its stinger raised in the air.

Nezha aimed at the scorpion with her flame arrow but it slipped by them.

Kayan's fist glistened with ice. The scorpion grew and towered above them before their eyes.

"Oh damn." His hand whipped to his sword, Ali.

The flames singed its side, but it swiftly moved toward Nezha. She jumped out of the way, and its stinger struck the ground.

Kayan slashed the creature with his blade but its tail slapped him, throwing him deeper into the forest.

"No!" A burst of flames rushed toward the scorpion. "Get out of my way!" Nezha struck it with a burst of fire petals.

The scorpion's tail whipped the air scattering the flames. It grew small and fled.

Her breathing was staggered. *I have to find Kayan.*

***

Kayan's back ached. "Ugh…stupid scorpion." He hissed as he placed his hand to his back. His skin burned over his back. He made his way down the tree with the wind, but his midsection was throbbing. He landed with a thud to his side. Kayan groaned and winced. "Seven hells. It… was that thing after me, or Nezha? Just when I was getting used to her too…" He slid toward the tree and softly pressed his back against its trunk.

The scorpion weaved through the grass in its small form and jumped toward him. Kayan yelled as it appeared before him, its stinger stretched out. His pulse quickened and sweat beaded his forehead. It was swift as the stinger punctured his left arm. He groaned and kicked his feet at the creature and grabbed it by the tail. His attempts were too late. The scorpion had already injected him with its poison. With a grunt, he threw it to the ground. With choppy breaths, he pressed his hand to his arm.

The scorpion turned to face him as if it was glad and disappeared into the grass.

Awkwardly, he wrapped his sash around his arm to constrict the blood flow. Grabbing one end with his teeth as he tied the knot. The simple action tired him. He slumped his shoulders and breathed heavily as his vision started to spin. Kayan attempted to stand and fell to his knees, his energy drained. Breathless, he squinted in pain.

"Nezha…" His hand lifted up and then hit the ground as he blacked out.

***

She brushed through the leaves of trees, frantically searching for him.

"Kayan! Where are you?" Her expression dulled with anguish. She continued to run again.

I don't want to think like this, but, Kayan could be in danger. He's usually so quick. He would have found me by now.

Momentarily, she stopped. Fire roiled about her arms. The wind surrounded her, as if Kayan drew a breath. Her eyes widened. *I feel the wind. The flames are obeying them. It's pulling me.*

She followed the wind tugging her flames through lush forest. Her red tunic cut like blades through the leaves and branches. Once the air pulled her another direction, she continued further. Her heart boomed inside her rib cage. *Kayan, please be okay.*

The wind jerked her forward. "Kayan!" Hands beating at the thick foliage and arms flying carelessly, she urged herself onward until she turned her head to the right and saw him.

She skidded to a stop in front of him onto her knees. Nezha lifted Kayan's head. Tears streamed down her face. She was panting as her hand quivered. His sash was wrapped around his arm.

"I'm here. Don't worry. But, what do I do?" Tears sprung from her eyes.

A warm light appeared and mingled with the flames in her palm. She lifted her hand and hovered it above his arm. "Maybe… The Angel of Mercy is helping me?" She concentrated. Blood was flowing from the sting.

Her flames were hot at first. She gulped and winced as they touched Kayan's skin. "Please, don't let it hurt him. Please let the poison leave his body. Oh Creator, please heal him." She whispered. *He's unconscious, yet the wind is desperate.*

In seconds, a bright white light surrounded them. "Kayan, please don't leave," she cried.

The wind mingled with the flames, creating a fragile pulse. Amidst the display, the blood seeped into the grass. She smiled, pleading to the Creator for the flames from her hand to keep warm. The fire leveled, then it disappeared into smoke. "Thank you."

Kayan opened his eyes and gasped for breath.

"Kayan." Nezha laughed as tears of joy flowed down her face. Relief washed over her.

He sat up straight.

Their eyes met. She smiled at him, her eyes shining with gratitude.

"Nezha, how did you find me?" His voice was soft and delicate like the caress of the wind.

"It was the wind. I felt it call out to me. It pulled me to you."

His eyes widened. "You saved me. I remember being dizzy. It stung me, Nezha. I thought I was a goner."

"Somehow, I was able to extract the poison from your blood with the warm light." She looked down at her hands and then up at him. "I think it was the Divine's mercy through the angel Mirkhas."

"Thank you. You know how I said you're growing on me? You really are. You risked getting hurt by the scorpion though. So, that was stupid."

"Stupid? It threw you into the forest. I had to find you."

"But why, Nezha? Why didn't you go get the siblings? What if it bit you too?" Kayan said a bit harshly.

"I care, okay? And I couldn't leave you all alone. Every second counts in an emergency." Nezha confessed.

"It's just... I'm not used to strangers caring about me this much." Kayan searched her eyes. It was only him and her, her peripheral vision absent. All she could take in was his soft warm eyes, his sweet smile and the wind's velvet touch across her cheeks.

He lifted his hand. He leaned toward her. His body so close, his breath a gentle kiss. Nezha was rooted to the spot. A wisp of air gently wiped her tears away. The wind caressed her cheek like a cupped hand.

"Your smile, your concern, the wind expresses our connection so beautifully."

Nezha's eyes widened. His smile had taken her breath away as if it were on his command. The flames around her were petals again. Their gazes lingered. The lulling warmth enveloped her, closing the gap between them. Her lips parted from astonishment. "Kayan..." she said softly.

"Now, come on, we're both a mess." He grinned and stood.

She smiled, and her shoulders slumped from exhaustion. She couldn't believe how smoothly he was able to switch the conversation. Just like the wind and its direction. Kayan had the wind lift her up off the ground and face him.

He was flushing brightly as she faced him. "Nezha, let's go back to Tasa's."

Nezha agreed.

"Oh, how sweet. You're both flushed in pink, but he's not paralyzed." Zul stood behind them.

A shiver went down Nezha's back as they both turned to him in horror.

"Zul, you!" Kayan grimaced and stood in front of her.

"Yes. Did you like the growing scorpion? Lexa was supposed to paralyze you, but oh well." Zul glared at Nezha. "If I were you, I wouldn't call the angels."

Nezha balled her hands into fists. She tried to throw flames his way, but he threw iron into the air. The slick shower of metal pattered to the ground.

A jinni appeared beside Zul in smoke, and before they could react, it zipped straight to Kayan and crept into his mouth, possessing him.

Kayan grunted and collapsed to his knees. His breath was unsteadied and his fingers gripped the earth. His body trembled. It opposed the entity's abduction of control until it could no longer protest, and he lay still.

"What are you doing?" The words felt choked out of her. Her eyes filled with tears. *We were so careless.*

"Oh, don't be sad, Nezha. It's just a little entertainment." Zul Sharr grinned.

CHAPTER 30—ALL IS FAIR IN LOVE AND WAR?

Kayan stood up and grinned.

"Ah, welcome, *Kayan*," Zul said.

Nezha formed her fire arrows and launched them at Zul. His scythe spun and sliced through each.

"Hmmpf. Fire girl, you should be wary of the wind jawhar, not of me."

"What do you really want?" Nezha demanded and sent a wave of flames.

Zul cocked his head, and with his scythe the iron melted away.

He backed up as Kayan turned to him.

"What does everyone want, Nezha? To belong. I can't belong without love. Sanari's love." Zul turned his attention to Kayan. "Savan, if you have control, do what you want, but I want her alive." His eyes glowed orange as he turned and formed a barrier around himself.

Nezha groaned in anger. "Hurting others won't make you strong! It only shows you the damage that it's done to you." She dragged her finger over her lower lip and exhaled. Her breath fanned out fire. The flames only bounced off the barrier.

Zul Sharr winced when the flames dissipated over the wall of iron. The force of the flames mirrored Nezha's words. He understood what pain was. How its debilitation encompassed your whole being. "I won't let you give the angel its soul!"

***

Nezha flinched when Kayan stood closer to her.

"Fire girl, what a lovely offering to inflict my wrath." It was the jinni, Savan who spoke through Kayan. "This young man has immense power." Savan spoke, flexing Kayan's arms.

"That voice..." Nezha's legs tensed and she stumbled forward. "You're the jinni I saw back at home."

Her nerves sparked. Everything flashed back into her mind. The shadowy jinni who she had glimpses of, leading to her encounter with him in the maze. *He must have been the one.*

"Mm. So you remember me. It's a pleasure to see you again, Nezha. I see you're still wearing kohl. How beautiful you must be when framed in darkness." His lips were in a devilish grin.

"So, it was you. What do you know about us? You're the one who…"

"Who? Who what?" His eyebrows widened as he gestured for her to continue speaking.

Nezha's mind spun as it conflicted with what she saw and who she heard. The face of the boy she barely knew, his strong love for his family, his jovial demeanor, and the voice of a creature, a vengeful darkness. A killer. Her heart constricted, the flames a snake, readying itself for the final bite. "You're zalim. You're the one who did that to Aunt Lamis." Nezha's words stretched out of her voice, and anger lead her actions.

"Cruel? Lamis should have known it would happen. Don't worry, I didn't see pain in her eyes when I appeared before her car. It was the seductive scent of terror."

The tears from her eyes spilled over. "No... No." Nezha's pupils contracted. Heat waves and flames lashed around her body.

When Lamis said she loved her. When Lamis embraced her. The sweetness of eating milk bastilla with her. When

Lamis was in the hospital, enshrouded in white. Lamis's skin so cold, her body lifeless. Not being able to hear her or hug her ever again.

"You killed her. You monster!"

Nezha fell back as the jinni raised his hand. Spirals of wind tore past her, and clawed at the trees behind her. She stood, and one smacked her shoulder, but only cut some of the cloth of her hijab away. She stumbled, but kept her stance.

The wind gripped her, her arms tight against her body. Her body went limp, and her eyes grew wild in her rage.

"Tsk tsk. Poor girl. You never asked to be in this mess. Don't worry. Your pain will be quick. I'll end your agony." Savan's voice gushed with a sickening delight.

"I said don't kill her." Zul Sharr's voice rumbled.

Savan's gaze slid to Zul Sharr, and he showcased a smug smile. "Mm, I love to play with my prey, Zul Sharr."

Frantic flames formed a dress, as it cascaded into a veil around her hijab. "You're going to pay! I will avenge her death. Damn you! Damn you to hell!" *Lamis, I finally found your murderer. You'll find peace, Aunt Lamis.*

"It's foolish to tease a snake whose fangs are bared." Her lips formed a terrible smile.

Savan snarled. "Your hateful gaze is stunning. It suits you."

"Shut up!" Nezha spat. You won't be able to smile when I'm done with you!"

"Nezha, would you really hurt me?" He spoke in Kayan's voice and tightened the wind around her arms.

"Kayan." Her lower lip twitched as she battled with her emotions.

"Ah, you two share an emotional attachment. I can see it in your eyes. Two souls bound by love." He grinned at her, meeting her face to face. "It must be torment to see him hurt you. How sad."

"I know it's not him. Kayan is kind and strong. He'll regain his control." She smiled without warmth. "You're a coward. If you really wanted to face me, you would do so in your true form."

"Doesn't it pain you to see him so harsh and cruel?"

"You can't hurt me, jinni." Nezha lashed out. Her right hand was free. She swept fire across his arm and swung him to the ground. When he hit the ground, a crater formed around him. She freed her other arm, and flames danced about her. Her eyes were like lava. "Leave Kayan's body."

"I admire your persistence, girl." The jinni grunted. He lifted himself off the ground and formed a fist of ice. He swung his fist, but the fire pushed him back. Nezha's shoes dug into the earth as she pushed him further and used the power to lift herself off the ground, now behind him. She used a whirlwind of fire to throw him back.

Savan whisked the air backwards to stop his descent. He sent a burst of air as Nezha tried to hold her ground, the wind lashing her body, and was thrown back.

"Only a slip of strength, huh?" Savan seemed to weaken. "Ah, this boy he's. . . He's pushing me." Savan and Kayan's voices mingled. He gripped his head, and then Kayan regained consciousness.

***

Kayan was on his knees, grimacing in pain. His hands trembled. Nezha was about to collide with a tree. His mouth was agape, as his head turned to her direction. His fingers sunk into the soil as he raised his right hand and gestured it up.

A wall of wind came between her and the tree, forcefully stopping her motion toward injury. Her back curled as the wind placed her back on the ground. Her eyes returned to their original color. She gasped and slowly stood up.

"Kayan," she breathed out. She started to walk toward him. Tears dripped down her face, but she was unrelenting in her determination.

***

Zul directed spikes of iron toward her. She waved her hand as if swatting a fly. The fire spiraled and melted the spikes. Zul drew the iron back to himself and winced. Zul couldn't help it. His heart ached when he heard her speak of Lamis and when her tears slipped across her face. The part of him that was Eisen didn't want to see her in pain. The jinn aura pulsed inside him, coaxing him into the darkness again. *No... I hate hurting her. No one deserves this pain.*

"*She is your enemy,*" *The demonic aura said.*

She's not my enemy.

***

Her face was carved in anger and slowly melted into empathy. "Either welcome redemption, or I have no choice but to cause your destruction, Zul."

"Hmmpf, cause my destruction. You have no will to destroy me." Zul turned his attention to Kayan. "You want to be with Nezha, don't you? Your heart must be breaking with its yearning. I won't be so cruel. Go," He turned to

Nezha, seeing her horrified face. "Savan, let the wind wipe out the fire."

Kayan lifted himself off his knees and ran toward her. His eyes glazed over. He couldn't loosen the grip of the jinni who possessed him. A gust of wind sent Nezha flying up again, and she hit the ground hard. Savan walked over to her.

"Your pain, your delectable agony... treat me to your hatred. Burn me fire girl."

Nezha sucked in air and stood. "Hang in there Kayan." She formed a ring of fire around him. It was seconds, but for Nezha it felt like hours as their eyes met atop the flames.

Savan flicked his wrist and the fire died with a hiss. A ring of ice replaced it.

Nezha tried to jolt his memory. "Kayan, please remember. Remember me. We've been through so much together. Remember the unicorns? Sapphire? Thunderbolt? Kayan, you were searching for the Alstroemeria flower to cure your father's ailment." Her eyes pleaded with him. She had to remind him of himself. The arm he raised above her stood still and trembled.

She continued, "Kayan, remember what you said to me, The wind expresses our connection beautifully?"

"What are you saying?" Kayan's voice struggled. "Nezha?"

"Yes. It's me."

The shine returned to Kayan's eyes once more. The jinni finally let go of him.

Nezha brought the feather to her lips and blew it. The sword's blue flames licked the ground.

The jinni screeched as she loomed over it.

"Return to where you came from, lest I pierce you with this light."

"Ugh. Do you believe you'll really avenge your aunt?"

"What are you saying? You killed her. You admitted it," Nezha said between clenched teeth. She couldn't keep her composure. Now that Savan was in his true form, his gray cast skin, those red eyes and that poisonous sneer boiled her blood. She wanted to sear it off. "You will pay."

He dashed toward the trees. The untameable creature, the fire, roiled toward Savan as Nezha followed him.

Kayan's eyes widened.

"Of course. But you won't ever defeat the ones who are behind it." Savan bent a tree as Nezha sped toward him. Her palms made contact with the trunk, reducing it to ashes. The thick smoke accompanied the flecks of ashes as if they were a swarm of bugs.

"Oh, I'll find out." Nezha's voice shook.

"Yes, feel the joy in killing me." Savan lurched toward Kayan, and she had no choice. She brought the sword to the jinni's face and he moaned in agony.

Nezha breathed deeply. "I want you to suffer as much as I did. Pay for tormenting me and my aunt."

"Don't do it, Nezha. Remember that poisonous wind jinni? You stopped me that time. It'll harden your heart, Nezha," Kayan said.

"It's burning me," the jinni moaned.

"My aunt was everything to me." Nezha's hand trembled as tears pushed at her eyes.

There was something Nezha had said before. Zul Sharr turned to her. "Hurting others just shows the damage it's done to you. You're a hypocrite, fire girl."

"That's right. I said that…" Lamis had said fire was a light too. Her shoulders sagged a touch. "She believed in me. She wanted me to be a light, not a force of destruction. To set the sky on fire. Wear the light like a crown." She turned to Savan. "Repent for forgiveness. Don't interact with any *human* ever again." Nezha's heart still boomed inside her chest. Tears slipped over her cheeks. It was a struggle to keep calm.

"Never. I won't." Savan cackled and his body trembled.

411

She brought the sword's tip to his throat. Her eyes lit like embers. "Tell me who's behind this."

"I can't betray my lady. I won't betray her. I'd rather die than do that," he moaned from the death throes.

"Your lady?" Nezha narrowed her eyes. "Tell me who she is."

"I... Fallen drunk to her wine lips," the jinni rambled. He screeched, and Nezha flinched. "My lady's wrath. My... lady."

"Is she a shadow jinni? Tell me, damn you." Nezha grazed the edge of the sweltering blue flames over his chest.

"I can't betray... my beloved."

She couldn't get him to admit, despite his deplorable condition. "Don't harm another human again. Do you agree?" She wanted him to give in, so she didn't have to kill him. She repeated herself, and her voice cracked.

Savan cackled and then screamed.

She couldn't take it anymore. The sound of his screams filled her eyes with tears. Her heart was aching with both the heat of fear and anger. *This was Lamis's killer.* "I... " Nezha lowered the blade and backed away. Seeing the way he was, so close to death, her anger abated. She closed her eyes for a moment.

Savan gave her a look of confusion and rasped, "Why did you stop?"

"How can I take someone else's beloved? I can't. I see what you are now. An obedient slave to your lady. Someone who doesn't value other's lives unless they're useful to her, and a coward. I was taught to show kindness in the face of hostility, trust in God and love and mercy instead of hatred."

Savan's lips parted, and he lay there, his eyes wide in surprise and confusion. "You're sparing me? Why do that, strange girl?"

"I still hate you, but my love is stronger." Savan sat on his knees. Nezha turned around.

"I am in your debt, fire jawhar. The tribe of the shadow jinn prize their honor. I will not harm another human, unless they harm my lady." He placed a hand to his chest, as if it were a promise.

Nezha turned around at his voice, and then he turned to smoke and shot up into the air, vanishing.

"Nezha..." Kayan stood before her.

"I love her so much." She took in a shaky breath. Her trembling hand sheathed the sword back into her bracelet. She couldn't believe it. She'd found the jinni that had plagued them. She sobbed and fell to her knees.

Kayan walked up to her and knelt beside her. "Here. The warmth of the wind might not be much, but it might help."

He held his hands up, commanding the wind to wrap around her like a warm embrace.

"Thank you." Nezha wiped her tears. Her heart was still beating hard, and her throat tightened. She appreciated what he was doing. His soft voice and the comforting wind didn't match Lamis's hugs, but it was still enough to stop her crying.

"I'm proud of you, Nezha. We'll find who his so-called *lady* is."

"Kayan, I'm so glad you're back to normal again. Thank you for bringing me to my senses." She breathed in. "I know we've fought jinn before. This time it was different. A part of me wanted to kill him... and I was actually enjoying it. But, it felt so wrong."

Zul appeared from thick smoke."Don't make me gag."

Zul was about to grab his gun, when Nezha grimaced. She formed a rope with her fire and lassoed it around him.

The lines of flame squeezed.

Zul groaned in pain. Lashes formed around his body and blood dripped down as his skin singed.

"You're not going to escape. Repent and let me purify you." Nezha's eyes shone in the pulse of light around her, assistance from the angel Mirkhas.

"Repent? I have my own reasons to fight you," He said between choppy breaths. Zul's iron spiked at the rope of fire, melting and then disintegrating.

Kayan unsheathed the sword Ali, but a mass of shadows tumbled before them, with Lexa stepping out, taking them by surprise. A dark glowing matter formed in her hand and pulsated until it exploded and caused Nezha to roll violently against the grass. She passed out.

***

"No!" Kayan's eyes widened. He was about to cause a tornado to whisk them away when Lexa shielded Zul. She grinned at him and disappeared, along with the demonic prince.

It had to be a nightmare. Kayan took in a deep breath and then looked down. He grabbed his head in disbelief, and turned to Nezha who was unconscious in the grass. He ran to her and fell to his knees beside her.

"We were getting along before—" Kayan's voice cracked. He looked at her silently for a moment and stood.

"I'm sorry, Nezha. You saved me and this time, I couldn't help you."

Tears welled up in his eyes. Like a cupped hand, the wind lifted Nezha off the ground. Shame heated his cheeks. He didn't want to touch her, even if it was for carrying her back to the angels. They vanished into the night.

CHAPTER 31—NURTURE AND NATURE

Sapphire placed her hand over Nezha's forehead. The light pulsed. She withdrew her hand not seeing any change in Nezha's condition.

"It is likely she's been cursed. There must have been magic in the explosion you told us about, Kayan."

Nezha was in her bed recovering. Sapphire was doing her best to heal her with various methods of herbs, healing light, flowers and oils. Nothing seemed to wake her.

"I feel useless. I couldn't protect her when she needed it most." Sitting on a brown chair by Nezha's bed, Kayan placed his face in his palms.

"You can't keep beating yourself up about this. We can't change what happened, but we can help her rest and heal." Thunderbolt had walked into the bedroom and had a bowl with lotus petals drifting on the water. The water was infused with a healing light by Sapphire.

"She took you both by surprise." Sapphire wrung a cloth from the water and placed it on Nezha's forehead. "She's warmer than usual right now, but this should keep her comfortable. It may take her some time to heal since the magic induced her into a coma."

"How long?" Kayan asked softly.

"I can't say for sure. Perhaps a week. A regular human would be in bed for around a month. Since she is a jawhar and has the angel's light in her, her recovery should be quick." Sapphire took a deep breath in.

"Nezha's pretty resilient. She's fought off a bunch of creeps since being here, so she's going t' be just fine." Thunderbolt gave him a reassuring smile.

"I know she is. Even when she took on that jinni pretending to be a girl. She's strong." Kayan paused for a few seconds and looked at Nezha again. "Sapphire, I want to help you in treating her."

"You may need to stay up a few nights." Sapphire changed the cloth on Nezha's forehead, and sat back on the chairs around the bed.

"I want to see her recover. I'll do it for her." Kayan stood.

"You really do care about her, huh?" Thunderbolt grinned at Kayan.

Kayan's cheeks betrayed him as they flushed. "Have you found a way to see Zul's mansion?"

"Zul has most likely put a barrier around it. Angels can see them, but it is difficult to pinpoint. He might sidetrack us with false barriers," Sapphire explained and then gestured to the cloth for Kayan.

Kayan lifted the cloth out of the water, wrung it and handed it over to Sapphire. "Okay. You'll have to keep searching then."

"Yes. For now, our priority is to take care of Nezha." Sapphire sat back down on the chair.

"Well, maybe we should take turns taking care of her," Thunderbolt said.

"Wait, do angels even sleep?" Kayan asked.

"Well as part unicorns, we nap when we've done any strenuous activity. Tonight, I will be by Nezha's side," Sapphire said and smiled at Kayan.

"Oh, well I'm still staying by Nezha's side too." Kayan's eyes pleaded.

"All right." Sapphire smiled and continued to use the light to wake her.

Kayan gave a faint smile as Thunderbolt smiled at him and sat down on a chair. *Nezha, I'm going to be by your side. We'll get through this.*

***

"Heh, sire you look like a wounded lamb." Lexa sat on the edge of the bed. Zul hissed when she wrapped bandages around his chest and glared at her.

"Forgive me?" Lexa smirked and continued to wrap up his chest. She leaned close to him and then applied more ointment to his shoulders.

"Lexa, how long am I going to be bed ridden?" Zul spoke angrily and then nervously tried to sit up.

"No moving sire! The fire jawhar had the angel helping her, so it could take you a few weeks. Sire, you're fortunate that you have the jinn aura in your veins. It will cut your recovery time." Lexa sat back up and snickered when he panicked at her movements.

"The fire jawhar is getting on my nerves." Zul rolled his eyes.

"Sire, we'll just have to give you a bit more jinn aura." Lexa proposed.

"Then do so. I'll need to strengthen myself against her light."

"Yes, sire. I will have to embrace you again." Lexa pursed her lips.

"Just get on with it."

Lexa's body became lustrous as jinni aura coursed through Zul's body.

"Hope there's no pain sire, unless you want more."

"No, actually, I feel somewhat better," Zul said. He momentarily closed his eyes.

A voice flashed in his mind. A softer voice. *Stop. This isn't right.*

"Are you going to sleep, Sire?" Lexa whispered into his ear.

"What? Why are you so close? You almost made my heart skip a beat." Zul Sharr ignored the voice in his head. His own voice. The part of him that was him and not demonic. Not the one which was soaked in anger and jinni energy.

"Ooh, sire." Lexa laughed.

"Stop taunting me."

"Ahem. Zaroor, Sire." Lexa jumped off the bed, transformed into a black leopard and sat on the cushion next to the bed table. She quietly chuckled.

"I can hear you!" Zul turned his head to her.

"I can't help it, Sire. You need your rest. No need to waste your breath on complaining."

"Lexa, your tongue is getting as sharp as your teeth. I don't like it."

She raised her eyebrows and smirked. "Mmm." She agreed and then closed her eyes to take a nap.

"Finally, some peace," Zul mumbled.

Lexa's ears twitched, and then she had fallen asleep.

Zul winced again as the ointment tingled over his skin. Lexa had spent most of the night bandaging him. He was relieved and grateful for the care, but the pain had triggered his memories.

His mother always mentally and physically abused him. The times she punched him in the back when he'd simply taken a longer break after training. But, now he knew, because he wasn't being an obedient slave. She would scream at him and spew horrible words. He used to be so alone and numb.

The wetness of his tears clung to the side of his head as he wept in bed every night. He mourned the thought of him having to muffle his cries. *I wasn't even able to cry when I needed to get all that pressure out! That monster. The stupid words, her loud voice. I was smothered. Sanari...*

Sanari's smile gave him peace. The way she would look at him, blushing and smiling at him.

She's beautiful in every way. Her blush, her toughness. And her shyness is so beautiful. Sanari's kindness and smiles were my light. It's all gone now. The tears pushed at Zul's eyes. He let the tears flow. They ran a passage through his hair and wet the sides of his pillow. He frowned and closed his eyes again. Zul had fallen asleep.

***

It was nearly midnight. Kayan sat on the chair at Nezha's right. He looked at her with softened eyes.

"Kayan, please hand that cream to me," Sapphire said and turned to him.

"Oh, of course." He handed it to her.

"Don't let your worry eat away at you like a disease. Hope for the best." She scooped the cream out of the tin and applied it on Nezha's chest.

Kayan turned away from her exposed skin and looked down. "Nezha, we're going to take care of you, and I know I shouldn't worry so much, so I'll be more positive like I am usually."

"Your bashfulness is refreshing. Now, would you please get another bowl of water for me?" Sapphire gave a gentle smile.

Kayan nodded and stood. When he returned with a bowl of water, Sapphire spun her fingers in it. Light churned through it.

"Be a remedy for this girl. By the Divine's will, accept my message of healing and love. Nourish and heal her," Sapphire whispered over the bowl. Kayan could swear he saw the water ripple on its own a few times like a pulse.

She dipped the cloth in the water again and spread it over Nezha's face.

"Is that a supplication? It's amazing how one can change your life," Kayan said.

"Yes. It all starts with your intention. Soldiers of energy. Once that energy becomes a thought, a word, or an action, they have the power to bring change."

Sapphire poured the remaining water over the cloth, which seeped into the fibers.

Kayan smiled as the air around him was warm, bathed in the sun's radiance.

Sapphire removed the cloth and then sat back on the chair.

They were hoping her eyes would slowly open, but she was still.

"She looks like she's sleeping, doesn't she?" Kayan said.

"Yes. This curse is very strong, but nothing will stop me from aiding her." Sapphire stood.

"Is there anything you need? I can get it for you." Kayan was halfway up from his seat.

"Oh, no need to get up. I was going to ask you if you wanted anything to eat or drink. I'm somewhat hungry."

"Oh. No, thank you I'm fine. I can still get it for you," Kayan insisted.

"It's fine, young man. Stay with her." She walked out of the room.

The air blanketed around Nezha, tousling her hijab.

He stood next to her. "You're resilient. I know you can get over this, Nezha. We'll be here by your side. *I'll* be here by your side," Kayan whispered. He stood for a few moments and sighed. He wasn't even sure that she could hear him. He wanted to think that maybe she could, and it would encourage her.

In a way, he envied her. He was ashamed that the thought crept into his mind. He couldn't help it. She had people who took care of her needs. Both parents.

No, I can't think like that. I love my parents, I still have my dad. Kayan sat down. He just wished he could let someone into his heart again without it hurting. *I love others so much. I forget I need it too.* A yawn escaped his mouth.

Sapphire returned from the kitchen with a plate of various fruits.

"Welcome back," Kayan said tiredly.

"How is she? Any movement?" Sapphire checked Nezha's forehead.

"She's still unconscious." Kayan brushed his hair back and sat upright in his chair.

Sapphire opened her palm. "Do you see this small pearl-like object?"

"Yes, what is that?" Kayan leaned forward.

"Have you heard of the Omari fruit? It doesn't grow everywhere, so it's very high in demand. It has all the nutrients a body needs. It usually melts in one's mouth. Since Nezha cannot eat, I can place this under her tongue and it will provide her nourishment."

"I've heard of them, but never seen one. That's amazing."

Sapphire placed the fruit under Nezha's tongue and a pouch filled with herbs on her forehead. She turned around and stood in front of Kayan, her hand outstretched and her palm opened.

"You should eat one as well. If you aren't hungry, it'll give you strength."

"Thank you." Kayan picked up the fruit and ate it. It melted on his tongue. It had a mellow taste, with only a hint of sweetness.

"Do you have any more for Nezha?" Kayan asked.

"Yes, I have enough to last a month. If Nezha doesn't need anymore, I plan on giving them out to those in need." Sapphire gave a gentle smile and continued to tend to Nezha.

They really are angels. Kayan turned to Nezha and helped Sapphire as the night continued onward.

***

For a week, Nezha had been unconscious, and Kayan finally had to go to the market to buy more food and supplies.

"How is Nezha?" Tasa had been over at her mother's house.

"She hasn't woken up yet," Sapphire said.

"Yeah, but we're all trying our best." Kayan gave a smile toward Tasa.

"Good, I was scared for her when you told me the news. I'm just thankful she's being well taken care of. I didn't expect any less." Tasa turned to the kitchen as Kayan placed the bags on the counter. The afternoon sun peered inside through the parted white curtain.

"I got everything except the cabbage. Let's just say I had a mishap with the cart." Kayan laughed hesitantly and fiddled with his hair.

"Thank you. I appreciate your help." Tasa smiled politely.

Sapphire was at the stairs. "I'm going upstairs to check on Nezha."

Kayan followed her up. When they reached the room, Kayan leaned on the doorframe.

"Her fever has gone," Sapphire turned to him after she placed an Omari fruit under Nezha's tongue.

Kayan flinched and then lit up with joy. "Oh, thank the Divine."

"She may not be conscious, but I'm relieved that her fever is gone. We need to be diligent in our care." Sapphire sat down beside Nezha and checked her breathing.

"I've been thinking. Zul's been injured by Nezha too. I have a feeling we're going to face a lot more troubles." Kayan looked out the window.

"Yes, she did. He must also be recovering. I'm only hoping we can protect the soul." Sapphire placed her hand on Nezha's head again.

"How many more orbs are left?"

"We can't tell how many orbs the soul became. To my understanding, Nezha will feel it become whole. I think the angel will be able to speak through her much more easily once the soul is whole."

"I want to do my best to help Nezha. I wanted to ask both you and Thunderbolt something." Kayan turned to Sapphire.

"All right. Do you want to speak about it right now?" Sapphire asked.

"Yeah, if it's not a problem."

Sapphire gave a smile. "Stay here and I will bring him."

After a few minutes, Thunderbolt walked into the room. "So, what's on your mind Kayan?"

"I know supplications are powerful, so can we all supplicate together again for Nezha?"

"That's all?" Thunderbolt nudged Kayan and smiled at him. They'd done supplications for her throughout the week and together once before.

"I agree. Let me go and bring Tasa," Sapphire said.

"Water can pick up on the positive vibrations, so we will also use this," When everyone was in the room, they started the supplication they chose together.

Sapphire poured a glass of water and mingled light within it as they all spoke.

"Please heal Nezha of the afflictions upon her. Bring her strength and shower her with mercy and healing. May this water imbued with our love and prayers be a medicine for her heart and soul."

"Ameen," whispered Tasa and the siblings.

Sapphire let a few drops fall into Nezha's mouth and poured the remaining water onto a cloth and placed it on Nezha's head.

Kayan leaned in. He and the others were focused on her. But, there was nothing.

"I thought it would work." Kayan sighed.

Sapphire smiled. "Let the medicine and our supplications do their job."

It had been twenty minutes when Nezha turned her head to the side and her eyes fluttered open.

"She's awake! A gasp escaped Tasa's lips. She stood next to Nezha's bed.

"What happened?" Nezha's voice was raspy and quiet.

"You're okay." Tasa embraced her.

"Thank the Creator." Sapphire was at the door and rushed in to join the embrace.

Comet, who had never left Nezha's bedside, had also jumped into her lap and was purring.

Kayan's eyes gleamed. He was overjoyed and wanted so badly to embrace her, but he held himself back. "Nezha," he said, his voice high and soft. "I'm so happy you're awake."

"Sapphire, Tasa, you're both crushing me," Nezha said. They stood.

"I'm just so happy you're better. Forgive me for that." Sapphire smiled apologetically, and handed her a glass of water, which she eagerly took and drank.

Thunderbolt stood next to her and bent down to mess up her hair. "I'm glad you're awake too. I missed your voice."

"Thunderbolt. I missed all of you," Nezha said.

"How are you feeling?" Kayan asked.

"I'm much better. What happened to me? The last thing I remember is… I was glad Kayan was back to normal. Then, everything blacked out."

"Lexa cursed you," Sapphire said.

"You've been out for a week," Thunderbolt said.

Nezha slowly stood. "I don't feel weak, so we can get back to finding the orbs again."

Kayan's eyes widened. "What? You just recovered."

"Even though that is true, I'm afraid Nezha's right. As long as she indeed feels up to it," Sapphire said.

"Yeah, don't worry about me." Nezha smiled.

Kayan sighed. "Well, you're right. And throughout the whole week, Thunderbolt and I went out looking for barriers. We found two, but they didn't lead anywhere."

"You've been productive," Nezha said, impressed.

"Yes, the boys have been very helpful, actually," Sapphire said and flashed Thunderbolt a smile.

"Sapphire, have you been taking care of me all this time?" Nezha asked.

"I'm always here for you, dear." Sapphire patted her head.

Nezha pulled her into a hug. "Thank you." Her voice muffled against Sapphire's shoulder.

Sapphire tightened her grip and returned the embrace. "Of course, Nezha. I love you."

Nezha's eyes softened. *Aunt Lamis. That's right. She's in peace. I know she is.* She tightened her grip around Sapphire. "I need to tell you all something."

Sapphire sat back and listened.

"Before I was cursed, a jinni possessed Kayan. I recognized its voice. I'd seen it back in Morocco. My aunt... My Aunt Lamis passed away in an accident and a jinni appeared before her car. The jinni was the same one who was responsible for her death. That day, I didn't kill him. When I wanted to, I'd felt delight... and killing him would have made me as cruel as he was." As Nezha spoke, her voice animated in her emotions.

Sapphire simply held Nezha's hand and kissed her forehead. "She must be proud of you."

Thunderbolt placed a hand on Nezha's head.

Once Sapphire gave Nezha a hearty meal that Thunderbolt insisted he make, she and Thunderbolt left. After them, Tasa left too.

***

Kayan stood at the door with Nezha. The air around them was joyous and buoyant.

"Kayan. Uh, a little help?" The wind had flipped her and made her twirl and float in the air.

"Oh. Sorry, my emotions are showing again." He laughed as he calmed the wind.

She chuckled. "Kayan, I'm glad you took care of me." Nezha's feet touched the floor.

"Wait, how did you know?" He blushed. "I mean, it was three days. The rest I was looking for a barrier."

"I didn't for sure. I guessed. But thank you."

His expression was tender, his eyes soft, lips barely parted. "Nezha," He began, and the wind pushed him close to her. She was against the door. He faced her. His hand was on the door right by her shoulder. "I was worried about you."

"Kayan," she said meekly.

His warm smile caused the wind to fluctuate, rustling over her tunic. "I know you're strong, but I still want to make sure you're okay. We're companions, and we should be there for each other. Just know that I'm here to support you. I'll protect you."

Nezha smiled. "Don't worry, Kayan. Thank you, I really am okay."

He stepped back. "I'm happy to hear that."

"Now, let's head downstairs." She walked past him, her heart pounding in her chest.

Kayan followed behind.

CHAPTER 32—IN ONE'S GRASP

"Lexa, hand me that whistle." Zul sat on his purple throne, the black wooden frame was bejeweled in lapis lazuli and amethyst.

Lexa walked over to the table and handed him the whistle. "Sire, are you planning on summoning one of the dog jinn for a job?" Lexa asked.

"You'll see."

Lexa blocked her ears.

Zul looked over at her.

"Ugh, you know how sensitive my ears are."

Zul blew the whistle and a dog jinni appeared before him.

"Yes, sire, you called?" The jinni said in a smooth tone. His long white hair fell over his back, two pointed ears on his head.

"Any news for me?"

"Yes. We have heard of an item which can bestow great power. It's an item rightfully yours by bloodline."

"Oh? Where is it?"

"Sire, it's in the Iron Kingdom's mansion."

Zul had a disgusted look on his face. He rolled his eyes. "So I'm being lured back there again." Zul waved at the jinni to leave. "Until next time, Yusha."

"I'll take my leave," The jinni said as he pressed his hand to his forehead with a curt nod of his head and disappeared.

Zul stood. "Let's go Lexa. We're going to do some dirty work."

"Mmm, I'm up for it." Lexa gave a smug smile. "Sire, are you?"

"Of course I am! Oh, the look on their faces when they see me." Zul sneered. "Now, Lexa."

"Yes Sire!" Lexa formed a door with her shadow magic and they both stepped in.

***

Zul smirked at his parents as Lexa's shadows held them down.

"Eisen?" his mother said in a hushed voice.

"He's not Eisen anymore. He's Zul Sharr," the Iron King Hariz said.

"Hello, mom and dad." He snickered at them.

"How dare you! You sided with a jinni and brought shame to the kingdom! Shame on you!" King Hariz said.

"You kept a secret from me, your own son. Isn't that a shame?" Zul raised an eyebrow and looked down on his father. "Look, I'm only here to pick up what is rightfully mine by birth. Just hand it over and I won't destroy anything in the mansion."

Bile had risen to his throat. His mother's screams that tore through his ears and crushed his soul, the cursing his mother spewed in his face. All those memories wrapped around him like a tornado of images. The kind motherly act was reserved as a show for outsiders. She was a monster, plain and simple. All they'd done to him was lie, as if he had no thought of his own. Did they consider him a stupid boy, rather than a naive one? He'd rather have truths that would break him free, not the sweet lies that further imprisoned his heart.

He knelt beside them. "Mother if you would be so kind, if you even know how, tell me. Where is it?"

"Eisen... you shouldn't do this! Bastard. I should never have given birth to you," she cried.

Zul stood up, looked to the side and rolled his eyes. "I asked you a question. Tell me, and I'll be on my way."

"You don't deserve it, you monster. You should have died. You're insane." Laiqa screeched and scowled.

"It's just like you to degrade me. It won't work. Don't you see your position? You're stuck. Just give it to me and don't act stupid." Zul walked over to Lexa.

"Look around with your jinn. Keep the mess low; I hate dirty things." He looked over his shoulder and turned to his parents as he spoke.

"You still have time to tell me where it is. Do you really want me to lose my temper?"

The Iron Queen started to scowl and stare daggers at him. "What are you? You can't compare to me, or my name isn't Laiqa Queen of the Iron Kingdom."

"You can do whatever you want, but I won't let you have the item," his father shouted.

"That's funny. You're my parents, so you know I wouldn't hurt you. Sit back and watch the show, you hypocrite." Zul whispered to his father and then walked over to Lexa.

"Sire, I think we found something." Lexa smirked.

"Perfect. See, I didn't need you. I never needed you. You tormented me and now, you'll pay for it."

There was a look of horror on their faces when the box was opened.

"I'll be on my leave, sire." Lexa bowed. A grin played on her lips as she blended into the shadows.

With an aloof expression, Zul looked into the box. "So, this is what you were hiding from me. I was right. You are a hypocrite."

***

Tasa and Thunderbolt had laid out a table of food for dinner.

"Now eat your fill, kid. You need it. I won't have you fainting on my watch." Thunderbolt smiled as he handed Nezha a plate.

She grinned.

As everyone reached their seats, their eyes fixed on Nezha. She had many things on her plate and was eating many mouthfuls.

"Pace yourself, dear," Sapphire said.

Kayan chuckled.

"Uh, sorry, I'm just really hungry." Nezha swallowed the food and took a sip of water.

"We don't blame you. We just don't want you to choke," Tasa said and took a seat.

"You look like Kayan every morning when he inhales his food." Thunderbolt nudged Kayan who exhaled air through his nose with a smile.

When dinner was done, Sapphire and Thunderbolt stood up.

"We need to go out on an errand," Sapphire said as she and her brother walked to the door.

"Do you need any company?" Nezha asked.

"Don't worry, kid. We won't be too long." Thunderbolt assured and waved as he and Sapphire walked out the door.

"Bye," Nezha called out.

"See you later," Sapphire said and closed the door behind her.

***

"Well, I'm full," Nezha said as she walked over to Kayan.

He searched her eyes and then turned to the living room.

"Hey, you two, I'm going to be here if you need me, okay?" Tasa said as she sat on one of the chairs and opened up a book.

"Okay," Nezha said.

"Nezha, where do we need to head to next?" Kayan asked.

"You mean to find the orbs?"

"Yeah. You said you wanted to."

"There's nothing close by yet."

"Oh. Hmm. We need to be aware of Zul. He might have healed."

"Wait, what do you mean?" Nezha asked.

"You don't remember injuring Zul?" Kayan looked concerned.

"Zul… Wait, I think I remember. He had lashes on his body." Nezha tensed.

"Yeah, he definitely was wounded by you. I think the Angel of Mercy was helping you."

"So, we don't know what his next move is then."

"I think we'll be ready for whatever he tries to do."

"You're right. We can't let him have all the orbs. Who knows what he'll do if he has that power."

Kayan nodded as concern washed over Nezha's face.

***

"Sis, this is the last house." Thunderbolt looked back at Sapphire.

They had gone to many houses in the city to give Omari fruits to sick children.

"Yes. Let's hope she recovers." A five-year-old girl had a very high fever and had been bed ridden for a few days. After Sapphire supplicated over a glass of water imbued with her healing light, the girl had been cured of her illness.

***

Lexa had been following Sapphire and Thunderbolt ever since they had left their home.

She had been waiting outside where Sapphire was inside a room.

"I'll have to make sure they can't sense me." It was a good thing she had doused herself in flowers and disgusting salt. Fortunate for her, that the girl was ill. It would make everything easier for her. She'd be undetectable. Lexa crept into the house in her shadow form and slinked underneath the window and stood in the corner of the room just beside Sapphire. She kept herself as a small dot of shadow.

Sapphire gave the girl a glass of water.

Lexa sneered. She'd gone over to the lamp and made it come crashing down.

The girl gasped, and the glass slipped from her hands. It shattered right in front of Sapphire.

After Lexa caused the distraction, she waited for Sapphire or Thunderbolt to cut themselves on the glass.

Fortunate for her, Sapphire cut her finger. Lexa picked up the blood that had spilled on the ground with a tube, which sucked up the liquid.

"Oh, we'll see each other soon." Lexa shifted through the walls. She had to make haste, since the flowers and salt were starting to burn her. Outside, she materialized her body and shook off the irritants. Lexa cocked her head as she held the vial with Sapphire's blood. She bit her finger and snickered.

***

Zul lifted the gauntlet out of the box.

His father's expression dulled and his mother looked in disgust at her son.

"A gauntlet huh? Tell me what it does." He turned to his father.

His father looked him in the eye and was silent for a few moments. "We won't disclose such a thing."

"Stubborn, I see." Zul gave a mocking smile. He turned his back to them for a second and then whirled back around. He grabbed the queen by her collar.

"No! What are you doing?"

"Tell me, dear mother."

Her eyes seemed to pop out of her head. Her heart beat hard against her rib cage like a panicked bird. She squirmed. "Just try to loosen me and I'll beat you. You bastard, you think you can do this to me?"

"Showing your true colors. Spare me the show and just speak." Zul shifted to one knee as he knelt, his face reddened.

She bared her teeth. "Try to find the grip. Try to you monster! You see this Hariz? Your son is going to kill me. You're crazy. Crazy!"

Zul gave a smug smile, yet his jaw was rigid as he spoke. "I won't kill you. I want information." His gaze shifted to his father and then back to his mother again. He grabbed her shoulders, his fingers sunk in.

She cried out with crocodile tears and made incoherent noises.

Zul's mouth contorted. He pulled her to her feet as he stood up. "Stop crying. Just shut up. Stop this show and tell me what it is."

His mother gasped and screamed at him. "You're dead to me!"

"Stop!" His father squirmed.

"Stay out of it." Zul glared at his mother, huffed and then pushed her aside. She sat down, farther from her husband this time.

Zul rubbed his forehead with both hands and then sat next to her. "All right, listen. Tell me about the grip. Then, I won't push you around."

His mother gasped for air. After a few seconds of silence, in a harsh voice she spoke. "It's our heirloom. It has power and wisdom from each generation."

The king slumped. He looked painfully at his wife and turned to Zul. "You won't get away with this!"

"Oh, Dad. Come on. Of course, I won't get away with this," Zul said and grinned.

His father's eyes widened, as Zul sat next to him face to face.

"I'll be getting closer to what I want with this."

Lexa appeared from the shadows. "Sire, I'm back," she said cheerfully and stood by his side.

"Ah, Lexa. Where were you?"

"Oh, it's a secret." She put a finger over her coy smile.

***

"Zul!" It was Ansam. He stood at the living room door. He had been out and just returned.

"Oh, I haven't seen you in a long time. How's it been?" Zul opened his arms and then cocked his head to Lexa.

"King? Queen? The iron grip." Ansam's eyes widened. Before he could move another muscle, Lexa wrapped him in a shadow. It tightened his arms against his body.

"Iron Grip," Zul said mostly to himself and delight flashed in his eyes.

"This aura. It can't be," Ansam said.

"You need light in order to cast a shadow. Shh. Good night." Lexa sneered as she walked up to him and squeezed the shadow further around him. He went limp.

Stars appeared in Ansam's vision and then everything turned black.

***

"Sapphire," the queen said loudly. Help us it's—"

Zul glanced at Laiqa and took the device from her pocket. He ended the call and tapped the Tome against his cheek.

"Thanks, mother. You just made it easier for me." He placed the Tome back in her pocket and grinned.

She stared at him, wide-eyed.

CHAPTER 33—DEBUT

"Hey, I have good and bad news," Thunderbolt said as he walked into the room, where Nezha and Kayan were in deep discussion.

Nezha looked alarmed and slowly stood up, Kayan following her movement.

"What? Tell me the bad news," Nezha said, hushed. She could tell Thunderbolt didn't want to stress Tasa. She didn't need to be brought into matters involving Zul and their pursuit for the orbs.

"Sapphire received an urgent call from Queen Laiqa. She's in some kind of trouble. We suspect Zul's the cause." Thunderbolt looked very serious. It shocked Nezha to see him this way and knew how dire the situation must be.

"Let's get going. Pack up anything you think you need," Thunderbolt said and turned to walk to Tasa.

Nezha and Kayan exchanged glances. Tasa smiled at Thunderbolt and then approached them when they were at the door.

Nezha looked down at Comet. She didn't want to endanger her. She had already lost her aunt and losing Comet would make her pain even worse.

"Tasa, can you please look after Comet while I'm away?"

"Nezha..." Tasa's eyebrows furrowed and her lips tugged to the side.

"She's got tons of energy. She's a handful, so you'll have to keep her entertained." Nezha leaned down and picked up Comet. She tickled her chin. Comet rubbed Nezha's head with hers and licked her cheek. "Comet, I'll be back soon for you. Stay here with Tasa. Be good for her, okay? Don't break too many things." She handed Comet over to Tasa.

Tasa nodded. "I'll take great care of her. I'll keep her busy, don't you worry. Stay safe." Tasa smiled at them as they opened the door.

Nezha whispered a prayer. "There's no might or power except with God."

***

Sapphire and Thunderbolt knocked at the door to the Iron mansion.

"Hello, Queen?" Sapphire said.

A few minutes passed and the tension in their voices grew.

"You don't think…" Thunderbolt started, his eyes wide as he looked at his sister.

"Don't expect the worst." Her voice was hoarse as she pounded the door again.

"If another minute goes by, I think we should break the door down," Kayan said, making fists.

The door opened slowly.

"Are you two okay?" Thunderbolt said as he and Sapphire rushed in.

"Sorry, but please let us in." Sapphire held the queen's shoulders and looked into her eyes. "I know you might be afraid to speak against him, but we are here to help."

The queen's jaw was rigid as she spoke. "It's that disgusting bastard, Eisen. He was in the mansion!"

"I knew it. That…" Thunderbolt gritted his teeth.

The king placed a hand on his shoulder and then leaned. "Also, Ansam has gone missing."

Nezha flinched at the queen's callous words, and her heart sank as she heard the king speak. Nezha looked around at the dim room.

"You need to help us. Get him. Get that crazy Eisen and stop him." The queen's voice shook. Her knees buckled and she sobbed.

Sapphire caught her before she fell. The queen shook with each cry.

Thunderbolt's eyes darted around the room. He held up a fist, which flashed with electricity. In a gruff voice, he asked, "Where is Zul?"

"He might be in the courtyard." The king's voice was hushed.

"Let's go." Thunderbolt glanced at Kayan.

Kayan nodded and walked, as Nezha followed his lead.

With sympathy in her eyes, Sapphire left the queen in the arms of the king and followed the others.

***

The queen's eyes followed them as they left her. Her lips pulled to one side in a spiteful smile. A combination of satisfaction and fear enveloped her. *My son deserves his pain. For disobeying me. It's all his fault. It's all his damn fault. Everything is the bastard's fault. I should never have given birth to him.*

***

"I feel like this is some trap," Nezha whispered to Kayan.

"If it is, we have no choice but to face him."

Thunderbolt opened the door to the courtyard. He readied himself, his hands up in the air.

Kayan looked around and placed his hand on Ali, his sword. "I feel like any moment now, Zul is going to jump out to scare us."

"Come on, Kayan, don't build on the anxiety." Nezha stepped beside Sapphire.

The courtyard had a large gazebo with overhead vines. It was built of Moorish bricks and wrought-iron accents.

"That jinni came here for the item Ansam was telling us about. I should have known," Sapphire said, her shoulders slumping.

"Welcome, guests." Zul's voice echoed through the garden. Thunderbolt turned around, followed by everyone else.

Zul held a cast iron pan, tracing the edge with his finger. His head was tilted. He regarded them out of the corner of his eye and gave a smug smile. He faced them and walked toward them.

Thunderbolt's nostrils flared.

"Where's Ansam?" Nezha pressed her lips into a thin line.

"Oh, Ansam, you say? Don't worry, he's safe. I wouldn't hurt a dear old friend." Zul was now a foot away from them.

"Shut your mouth." Thunderbolt snorted.

"Thunderbolt. Why, have you forgotten something?" Zul turned to Nezha and then to Kayan. He looked at Thunderbolt and then started to laugh.

Nezha and Kayan looked at the angels, unsure of what was going on. Nezha formed a shield of fire and kept a vigilant eye on Zul.

"Oh Thunderbolt, your powers aren't the only thing of value to me. Your undying loyalty will be tested today," Zul said.

"What? What is he talking about?" Nezha asked as she turned to Thunderbolt.

"Hey, what's going on between you two?" Kayan asked.

Thunderbolt exhaled through his teeth. "Look, he's just bluffing. I'm no longer anything to him."

"No... longer?" Nezha's lips parted and she frowned.

"Thunderbolt, tell them what you once were. Pity, that we are in such a state of enmity. Listen well when I say the command. Today's the day you will be free of the duty once and for all. Doesn't that sound liberating?" An amusing smile lifted his lips.

"I told you t' shut up." Thunderbolt sent a bolt of lightning Zul's way.

Zul flipped out his gun and shot at Thunderbolt.

Sapphire raised her arm, sweeping her hand over Thunderbolt with a blanket of light. The wave cascaded down the layer and burned to the ground.

"Brother." Sapphire shot a glance at him.

Thunderbolt sighed. He looked at Nezha.

"I was once a guard for Zul back when he was a prince. I had left after serving many years. A guard's duty isn't fulfilled until—"

"Until the final command." Zul tapped the pan, and it morphed into a mallet.

"So you were his guard," Nezha said.

"You're kidding. A final command? Thunderbolt wouldn't listen to you. You're not his prince anymore." Kayan yelled, the wind picking up around him.

"Oh, it's the law. He wouldn't tolerate broken laws. Would you, Thunderbolt?"

Sapphire glared at Zul. She formed whips of light, which swiftly glided toward Zul, until Ansam materialized in front of him. Ansam was engulfed by shadow, which kept him unconscious. Lexa materialized behind him.

Sapphire gasped and pulled the whips of light back as they faded. Her eyes widened as her hand cupped her mouth.

"Ansam! You monster, what have you done?" Nezha screamed.

"We won't harm him, unless you provoke us." Lexa smirked and ruffled Ansam's hair.

"Keep your hand off of him!" Sapphire's eyes glowed bright. The light vibrated and sent frequencies to Lexa.

Lexa attempted to knock Sapphire down with her shadow magic, but Zul lifted his arm in front of her.

"Lexa, follow the plan."

"Yes, sire." Her teeth gritted, but then she harshly sighed. She plopped herself down onto a chair. Her fingers drummed the arm rest.

Zul sat down on a chair beside her and faced Thunderbolt.

Thunderbolt's lungs constricted. The blood pulsed in his ears, the thrumming mimicking his heart.

"Heed," Zul started.

"You," Thunderbolt whispered, his eyes now slits, his face reddening and his hands trembled.

"… the royal command," Zul finished and grinned.

"Thunderbolt, you wouldn't listen to him, would you?" Nezha asked. "I know you wouldn't."

Thunderbolt stayed silent. He wasn't one to break the law. He always hated those who went against the very laws that would protect and guide others.

"Zaan, what are you thinking? We need to keep Zul from getting stronger." Kayan faced Thunderbolt in astonishment.

"Damn it. Damn it. Damn it." Thunderbolt pounded his fist into the ground.

"Oh, you're in trouble now." Lexa derided him.

Thunderbolt stood up and squared his shoulders. "Yes, I was a guard of Prince Eisen. I served as a guard for the prince. After the years' end, it is tradition and law that the contract ends when a royal command is fulfilled. It lasts until sunset, after which my duty is served."

"So, which do you choose?" Kayan said.

Thunderbolt met Sapphire's gaze. His gaze was soft and his eyebrows furrowed as their gazes locked.

"Brother." Sapphire's voice was quiet.

"You and Sapphire would always be there, to support me. To support us," Nezha said.

Thunderbolt walked toward Sapphire. What was he thinking? If he did obey Zul's command, then that meant he would have to protect him. Protecting him would mean he would have to fight his sister, his friend and Nezha. Could he really abandon them? *Coward.* The word haunted him. If he didn't agree, Zul might harm Ansam. But would he really? Eisen was kind. He'd get beaten up in his training and yet he smiled. Was he missing something? Did Eisen's smiles hide his torment? Thunderbolt gulped and looked toward Zul.

Thunderbolt was silent as moments went by. "The past has caught up t' me."

Nezha's eyes widened.

Kayan shook his head.

Thunderbolt glanced at Ansam. He walked over to Zul and stood beside him.

Sapphire and Nezha stared at Thunderbolt.

Nezha's eyebrows turned downward and she put a hand to her mouth.

Sapphire's eyes widened. She shook her head.

"Ma Sha Allah. Good decision, my friend. I knew you would honor the command," Zul said.

It was calm, until the fizzing of electricity slashed the silence. Thunderbolt was electrocuting Ansam. The shocks danced as Lexa jumped back.

Zul spun his mallet around, but it was useless, only striking the air.

"You really think I would forsake my companions? You are *not* my prince anymore. You forfeited the command. I've broken my bonds to you." Thunderbolt yelled as Ansam opened his eyes. The shadows around him had dispersed, and a light shone brightly.

Lexa recoiled and placed her body between her and the light in front of Zul. She screamed as the light singed her. She then held up a shadow wall in front of herself as she protected Zul Sharr.

***

"Lexa. . ." Zul's lips parted. His limbs were like pillars, supporting his body but unable to move. "No, you can't. Thunderbolt..." *He was my guard. He was my confidante. Why... Why would he do this to me?* "Sanari was the only one I trusted besides you and you stabbed me in the back!"

"Forgive me, Eisen. I'm going to kill that part of you. I'm going to kill Zul Sharr." Thunderbolt snorted. "He'll suffer for his transgression."

"I am Zul Sharr—it's who I am." His voice mingled

457

with pain.

"No, you're not. Stop believing the lies! You're way more than the poison you're slowly feeding. You were a good person."

"How did you know who I am? Did you ever ask me why I was quiet after being around my mother? Did you ever wonder why I didn't speak to you some days? Why I stayed in my room for hours? Didn't you know what she did—" Zul's voice faded. "To me... Sometimes opposites don't attract. They just react." Zul Sharr was thinking of his so-called mother.

Thunderbolt stared. "The queen... I wasn't just your guard. I was your friend."

Zul's eyes widened. The heat of fear and shock scattered in his chest.

Sapphire spilled out light, and it formed into spirals, twisting toward Lexa.

Lexa snickered, her eyes meeting with Zul's, and then turned around to face the angels.

She brought out a vial which held Sapphire's blood. She cracked the vial with her teeth and the blood spilled into her palms, mixing with hardened shadows. She stretched the material like a silken spider web. It enrobed the angels, just as the light spirals reached her, but the spirals of light

shattered like glass. The siblings were numbed and fell
unconscious.

A lopsided smile teased Zul Sharr's lips.

She's done it.

Kayan's sword was an arm's length away from Zul
Sharr's abdomen. Lexa engulfed herself, the siblings and
Ansam, in the rolling and dense darkness and disappeared.

Zul twirled his mallet and kicked Kayan's sword. He
jumped back, just as Nezha fell.

Kayan's arm swung up as he backed up in alarm.

"Thunderbolt, Sapphire... They're... " Nezha's lip
quivered. Tears pushed at her eyes.

Kayan stood protectively in front of her. His teeth
clenched. He looked up at Zul from under his eyebrows and
the wind violently spun around his hands and around
Nezha's. "I'll be the storm to her silence."

Zul Sharr dropped the mallet and aimed his gun right at
Kayan.

CHAPTER 34—COMPLACENT

Ha, I can't believe it." Zul's mouth was open as he swept his fingers through his hair. His eyes darted from side to side. "They're mine. Their powers are mine. They're really mine."

The loss that trembled in Nezha's body reminded her of Lamis's death.

No. No. This can't be. I can't let Zul steal their powers.

Zul aimed his gun and shot at Kayan, who dodged and rolled as the wind spiraled about. For a few minutes, they were at it, until Zul groaned, his left shoulder struck by Kayan's sword.

Zul grabbed his shoulder and smirked. "Now, I'd prefer if you leave quietly. If not, I won't hesitate to make you!" Zul's eyes were glowing, golden like embers. The gash began closing up as he spoke.

I'm not going to sit here and just cry. I need to get them back. Nezha grimaced. The fire's heat fueled her as she balled her hands into fists, her teeth gritting. She stood. Flames illuminated the metal as it melted.

The fire didn't let up as Zul frowned and backed away at Nezha raising her flaming hand.

Kayan's eyes widened. The rapid wind mingled with the flames like waves in the sea.

Nezha's pulse quickened, and her heart fluttered, her soul now engulfed in the chaos. Fire, wind and metal caught in a dance.

Zul's lips curled into a smirk. His head tilted to the side as he shot his gun.

Nezha moved aside as the wind pushed back the blasts. She glanced at Kayan, who now ran toward Zul. A shield of wind formed around him, the blasts forming shockwaves around him. He was very close to Zul. Kayan took to the air and his right leg spun and hurled toward him.

It happened so fast, that Nezha felt like time had stopped.

Zul found a space where there was no wind and had blasted Kayan's arm.

Kayan only managed a murmur as the blast punched his arm. He flew through the air and landed with a thud to the ground.

Her arm broke out in goose-bumps. Her chest tightened, and she let out a yell, her voice raw. Nezha looked back at Kayan and then faced Zul. The veins in her neck pulsed.

Zul's eyes were wide. The impact had pushed him back to the ground. He stood, and his arms were limp by his sides. He simply stared and frowned.

Nezha ran to where Kayan lay. Her breaths were ragged as she looked at his arm. "Kayan." The words only slipped past her breath. Her hands were held up. She wanted to wake him up and hold him close, but she was unsure if she would hurt him further. There was no blood, but his arm was bent in a painful position. *It could be broken.* She grimaced and then looked away.

Fire lapped around her as if her emotions caused an effect on the earth. Flames rippled over the ground as she stood. Her eyes were fixed on Zul as she stalked toward him. "I can't lose anyone again..."

Zul took a deep breath in. "He was getting in the way. You need to understand that much, fire girl." He shrugged and held his palms up.

"First you took away Sapphire and Thunderbolt, and now you hurt Kayan. I won't let you get the upper hand."

"Oh." Zul sounded intrigued. He looked at the iron gauntlet on his right hand and then back to Nezha. "That's where you're wrong. This gauntlet is my upper hand." The gauntlet glinted as metal sparked.

Arrows flashed by Zul's head. Nezha's irritation was making her lose her concentration.

"You missed your mark." Zul sent more metal and sparks her way.

Nezha leaned, and shot flames toward him. She staggered to the right and ducked. Heat was all that she could feel, tingling her skin. Fire was her and she was on fire. Waves of flames swayed at her arms, as she sent them lapping away at Zul's sparks. She attempted another shot of arrows. One arrow almost hit Zul's left leg. Sparks and pieces of metal surrounded her as the fire engorged. She was growing weary. Her movements were starting to slow. She slipped up once and backed away. Zul rubbed his hands, metal and friction birthing sparks. They grew and fizzed like electricity.

Nezha's eyes narrowed, and her cheeks heated. Their memories, her love for Lamis and her own need to never lose anyone fueled the ignition. She spun her hands, and the fire swayed. It became a cyclone of swathing flames.

Zul sent the fizzing metal her way as the cyclone engulfed him.

He was singed by the flames but formed a shield with the fluid metal. His clothes were charred and cuts marred his cheek and hands. "Hey, we're evenly matched."

The sparked metal around Nezha oozed, but then the sparks mingled with the fire around her. Zul cried out but was able to push the fire tornado away from himself and send more metal toward Nezha.

She gasped. The current shocked her all over. She screamed. After a few painful moments, the fizzing popped and discharged.

Zul Sharr pulled the metal back from her and winced. Sparks of light filled her vision, as her head started to feel light. *It can't be. The angels, Kayan...* Her eyes rolled back in her head. There was a blur of silver. *Comet?*

No. It was the metal escaping from her legs. Nezha collapsed.

Her breathing was minimal, and she could hear Zul walking toward her, his breath heavy from exhaustion, his footfalls faint.

He stood over her and looked down. She could make out the image of his lips drawn in a frown. Then her sight began to fog.

"Oh shoot, I went too far. I'm sorry. I...I'm sorry." His voice had softened, and then he groaned. The iron gauntlet was over her. Metal oozed around her surrounding her in a pool of silver. Nezha struggled to keep her eyes open.

Then her eyelids fell.

***

Nezha. A gentle voice spoke to her.

"Who is it?"

Mirkhas. The Angel of Mercy. You have been a brave heart. Have a moment's rest.

The angel's life force, its Divine light seemed to attend to her every sense. It tasted like warm honey, it smelled like wildflowers, it sounded low and soft as silk. As it embodied her with its essence, it lulled her into a peaceful slumber.

CHAPTER 35—PASSAGE

Ansam's eyes shook open like a pair of trembling blinds.
He took a breath in and turned his head. The shadows that
latched onto him disintegrated. He could see now as the
veil of darkness lifted from his eyes. He placed his palm to
his forehead.

"That's right. Thunderbolt. He electrocuted me to help
my heart." He was still dazed.

His mind wandered to Sanari, the princess he had
promised to, that he would keep the feather safe. Then the
Iron Queen, who he promised he'd safeguard the iron grip.
He'd made promise after promise. His whole life had been
full of promise. The type which was both in feeling and in
bond.

Ansam had not always been the arch angel of the Fire
Kingdom. He had once been among one of many in the

heavens, whose purpose was to praise the Creator and pray for the well-being of all life. Created of promise. Created from light and gifted in all of its attributes.

He had no will of his own. He'd been told to do all that was good. To help those in need he was told to help. He never once complained. His orders had never been cruel in nature. They were just. They were always for the good.

Some things had changed ever since the War of Jahalia. He had been sent down as a healer.

Ansam did not own a will, not even now. His heart wasn't empty. Instead, there was a security. *Did humans, who had their own free choice ever feel lost?* He wasn't created to feel lost, just guide the ones who did feel that pull of doubt. Even though he had no will of his own, he had the inclination that led his actions. He had a mind that was curious, a heart that was airy, and a soul which was a compass. It always knew which direction to go.

Ansam stood up from the ground. Voices climbed about the walls.

What is that? It's coming from the courtyard.

As soon as his legs regained their use, Ansam ran.

***

Zul clenched his fist. "It's a shame, really. I wanted you out of the way. Not to die."

A bright light started to grow around Nezha, pushing him back.

"What the...?" His eyes widened as he was thrown back. Zul struggled to take in a breath.

The light around Nezha pulsed like the glow of a firefly.

Zul Sharr breathed out and stood onto his feet. He held his head low. *That girl...*

He lifted his head and rolled his right shoulder as he walked toward her. The iron gauntlet was dripping with melted iron again. He flinched as he got closer and stopped dead in his tracks.

Any closer, and that light is going to affect me again. Sickening. It didn't used to be like that. The light beckoned him as if to say it was a door to reach. An end to his suffering, but also a beginning to something good.

There was shuffling near the entryway of the courtyard. "Hmm?" He turned back.

Ansam had his hand on the door, looking at Nezha. His eyes widened. "Zul Sharr."

"You're conscious huh? It's not what it looks like." Zul turned his body toward Ansam and lifted his gloved hand up.

"You're using the gauntlet. Zul, I will not let you go on this path." Ansam ran toward him.

"I'm at your mercy, Ansam." Zul punched toward him, the iron and sparks colliding with the energy that burst from Ansam's hand.

Zul backed to the side, and with his scythe, he jabbed toward Ansam's stomach.

Ansam spun in the air and landed behind Zul.

Zul spun around, just as Ansam grabbed his gloved hand. Light emanated from Ansam's hand and pulsed around the gauntlet. Zul's eyebrows flitted.

"You're correct. You *are* at my mercy." Ansam tightened his grip.

Right before Zul's eyes, the gauntlet turned inside out and fit itself around Ansam's right hand.

"No." Zul's lower lip quivered. His eyes burned orange as he landed a kick to Ansam's side.

Ansam went flying back but stopped his fall, as his left hand slid against the ground. He tumbled onto his side and then looked up at Zul.

"Ansam, I'd love to catch up, but that's what you need to do." Zul brushed his shoulder and fled.

***

Ansam stood and walked toward Nezha, falling at her side. "Lady Nezha." His voice was soft. "I'll help you. You need to wake up." He put his arms out around her, a blue light appearing around her head.

**

Nezha gasped and opened her eyes. "Where's Zul?" She blinked a few more times and then faced Ansam. She smiled at him and then stood. "You're okay."

"Lady Nezha, Zul has run off."

"I see. Wait, Kayan." Nezha turned and ran to were Kayan was.

Ansam followed and stood by Kayan's side.

"Ansam, his arm..." Nezha's voice trembled. She placed her fingers to her lips and her eyebrows furrowed.

"I can heal him." Ansam placed a hand on Kayan's arm. "I can feel that the bone is broken. Don't worry, he will be all right." He smiled at her and then concentrated on Kayan's arm.

Nezha teared up. She nodded and then looked toward the warm light that wrapped around Kayan's arm like a tourniquet.

"Mm." Kayan's hand moved. He sat up and Nezha looked straight into his eyes.

"Kayan!" Tears dripped from her eyes, and her head fell.

"Please, don't cry. I'm fine." Kayan's voice brushed against her hijab. He lifted his hand as the wind feathered across her cheek.

Nezha felt the warmth and the smell that was always clean, refreshing like the quenching of a glass of water. *I never need his touch. Only the feelings I get when he smiles at me. That warmth is an embrace.*

Kayan turned to Ansam. "Hey, you're here. Did you help me?"

"Yes." Ansam smiled bashfully.

"Thank you." Kayan stood up, as did Nezha, her eyes narrowing. "Hey, what's that on your arm?"

Ansam tilted his head and raised his arm. "Another promise." His voice softened. "I'm afraid Zul is running, and if we don't catch up to him..." Ansam turned back.

"I understand." Kayan turned to Nezha.

"He can't get away from us that easily." Nezha's lips curled as she juggled the flames between her fingers.

***

Kayan formed his updraft. Minutes later, Kayan swerved toward the field where they spotted Zul.

"I hope I'm not being reckless, but... the hell with it!" Nezha jumped off the updraft, the wind carrying her.

"What are you doing?" Kayan lowered the updraft and then swiped his arms up, helping Nezha as she landed in front of Zul.

"Lady!" Ansam landed beside her.

"Hi. Bye." Zul ran right past her.

Nezha's eyes widened. She turned to see him running and then stopping.

"What the seventh hell?" Kayan leaned back and then turned to Nezha.

Zul smirked as he continued to run.

Kayan and Ansam followed after Nezha.

The forest appeared from the clearing. Trees loomed over the grass and hills as if they were waving them in.

"We should use the updraft Nezha. There's no need to run and get exhausted." Kayan noticed the shine in Nezha's eyes.

"Yeah, you're right." She breathed out.

"Lady Nezha." Concerned, Ansam opened his right palm where a light washed over Nezha.

"Ansam, what's this?" Nezha looked around at the light that was like glittering dust.

"It'll help you. That much is all you need to know." Ansam blushed.

Nezha smiled. "Thank you." She turned to Kayan.

Zul shaped iron sheets underneath his feet and slid toward the forest.

Zul looked back to see them in the air, following him. *Good. Follow me, yearn for your friends Nezha.*

"Do you see that? He's sliding." Kayan dived closer.

Nezha squinted. "Well then…"

Through trees, Zul removed the iron sheets and sped into the thickness of foliage.

Nezha nearly crashed as Kayan lifted the draft up higher, above the trees.

"I can't see him that well. We're going to have to go on foot from here." Kayan landed on the soil as Ansam and Nezha followed him, running toward Zul who was far ahead of them. Nezha's breath was heavy, her eyes strained as she followed Zul's back.

Between two trees, Zul vanished as if he were made of smoke.

Ansam and Nezha slipped through the barrier, but Kayan jounced back from it as if it was a trampoline and fell to the ground.

Nezha gasped and turned around. "We… did we just go through something?"

"A barrier. So this is why finding Zul was difficult." Ansam rubbed his chin.

Nezha looked back and saw a large white mansion.

"Ansam... Look."

Ahead of them lay a small garden to the side of the mansion, dotted in yellow and purple flowers. In front of the home was a small cement pathway.

"It must be Zul's mansion," Ansam said.

"So this is where he was all along." Nezha stood motionless.

CHAPTER 36—LEAP ALL BOUNDARIES

Ansam looked around. "Where's Kayan?"

"Hey! Where are you?" Kayan called back.

"Kayan? Oh my God! He's outside the barrier." Nezha approached it but couldn't see him, only hear his voice.

"We went through it!"

"I think your voices are fading!" Kayan said.

"You're right." Nezha leaned toward the wall of energy.

"Looks like Zul kept humans out. Since you have the light of the angel, we were able to get through it." Ansam looked around.

"It's okay. You should be the one to face him," Kayan said. "Just know that you have my support."

"Kayan, I'll return with everyone," She said. "I'll make sure of it."

"See you later." His voice was hardly there.

"See you later."

Kayan barely heard what Nezha had said. All he could decipher was the word *later*.

***

Zul leaned on the door to the room where Sapphire and Thunderbolt were held. "Lexa, are they still alive?"

"Zaroor, sire. Why the doubt?"

"I don't know, maybe because you're a jinni? I'd have thought you hated angels."

Her lips tightened into a thin line. She gave a coy smile. "They're subdued. You can do as you want with them." She walked past him.

"Perfect. Oh, Lexa, when the fire girl and Ansam arrive, keep your eye on them, will you?"

"Yes, sire. I'm of the shadows remember?" She disappeared among the walls.

***

Damn, that always creeps me out, how she just fades away. Zul took in a deep breath and walked toward the angels. When he entered the room, he stood still. Right before him were the siblings, their bodies shackled by shadows.

"Here we are, Thunderbolt, Sapphire. You thought you could escape me." He circled them as he spoke.

He stared for a few moments. "I can't believe it even now. If I can have your powers, it has to work."

His gaze fell on Thunderbolt.

"And you... How could you betray me? Why did you do it? You didn't want to protect me. It's because of Lexa, isn't it? You really think I would forgive you for that?"

His voice squeaked.

He placed a hand on his eyes and then walked over to the futon and slumped down. He raised his head again, his eyes scribbled in orange.

"I can't waste time. I have to do it."

His palms weighed down on the futon as he stood up in one swift movement.

Zul Sharr took a deep breath, and his hands trembled. He raised his right hand, now closer to the siblings. He remembered the incantation Lexa had taught him, the one that would transfer their power to him.

He went over to a shelf. There, he found the vial filled with their blood. He opened the vial and started his incantation. As he spoke, the blood from the vial flowed into the air and around his fingers, swirling and then dotting each of his fingertips in red. As he continued the incantation, his fingertips rippled.

"It's time." His eyes burned orange, as he placed his hands on their bodies.

Electricity and light vibrated around his body.

He breathed heavily as his veins tingled. It was a quick infusion. His breath was forced, as he gasped and backed away.

It was done.

The power he needed was inside him.

He grinned and looked at his hands. He laughed and placed his palms on the table.

"I can fix it." He stumbled as he left the room, to go where he always visited.

Day and night, he would go to a special room in this manor.

Lexa, you can hear me, can't you? Come here. He brushed hair back from his eyes.

Sire. I'll be right there. Lexa's voice echoed in his head.

She appeared before him in thick smoke.

"Take me there." Zul stood straight, his eyes shining from the tears welling up.

"Understood." She pursed her lips and then with a wave of her arm, they both faded into the shadows and reappeared outside a room.

"I'll see you later." Lexa winked and was gone.

***

Zul sighed. His head was light with the energy. He bumped into the wall as if drunk.

"Sweet… my sweet." He shook his head. "This power, it's so strong. I'll have to hurry, before it does something."

He headed to the corner of the room, where the light spilled over the rim of a vase, glinting, inviting life to the iron-cased body of Sanari. The princess who held his heart for many years. The woman he wished to marry. The woman who gave breath to love and peace when all he knew was abuse and pain from his own mother.

Zul fell to his knees, his hand reaching, twisting like the petals of a flower yearning for sunlight.

He forced himself to breathe.

Time stood still. Even now, nothing had changed.

His beloved was still encased in iron. "I'm so sorry."

He could still picture Sanari as she used to be. The way she would walk so gracefully, commanding the room. Her pillowy lips, a touch of pink with she spoke so gently and smiled so honey-sweetly. It was the most beautiful thing he'd seen. She was the most beautiful when she smiled and her green eyes would envelop him in her grace.

He smiled. She would always wear a circlet of small pink and white flowers atop her curly brown hair. How delighted she was when he told her it suited her.

Once, he had smiled widely at her and she had noticed it. They were having a dinner party at the Iron Kingdom. Sanari had walked to him, spoke to him and blushed as she walked away.

His heart spilled over with love and drummed inside his chest.

He spoke again, another incantation to use the power now coursing through him like blood.

***

The manor in front of them was much larger than any others Nezha had seen before in Noorenia. The white paint, the blue door, all seemed so contradicting to the one who lived there.

"Lady Nezha, let us head to the door," Ansam said as he gestured to the pathway.

Nezha was looking back at the barrier and then faced him. "Yeah, let's go."

As they walked onto the cement, Nezha's pulse lept up, like a rabbit that sensed danger.

She swallowed, a lump in her throat. The walk felt stretched out in time as she stared ahead at the mansion. *Sapphire, Thunderbolt, I don't want to lose them.*

Ansam glanced at her. He spoke in a gentle voice and leaned to her. "I'll be right by your side. I can't fight for you, but I can help you."

Nezha's lips turned, a gentle smile on her face. "Thank you. I don't doubt myself. It's just what's around me that I'm not sure about. But I won't let it stop me."

"That's good to hear. You're brave." Ansam smiled wide.

They looked at each other and then at the door. Nezha placed her hand on the knob and turned it.

***

Zul slammed the room's door and then broke down. He fell to his hands and knees while tears streamed from his eyes. His body was racked with the sobbing as he slammed his fist to the ground over and over again. Clenching his teeth, he hugged his body.

"No. No!" A hiss escaped his lips as he breathed out. He stood up, his hands clenched into fists.

It had not worked.

He couldn't awaken Sanari from her slumber.

He thought for sure that the unicorns' powers would break the curse his iron had inflicted on Sanari. If it had worked, he would have even gone to the Valley to release the unicorns also under the iron's grip. *Why Divine? Why?*

Lexa. Take me back.

"Sire?" Lexa materialized behind him. She placed a hand on his shoulder.

Zul shrugged her off. He looked into her eyes. "Let's finish our business."

Lexa's eyebrows rose and then she bit her lower lip. She waved her arms, sending them both back to the door where Sapphire and Thunderbolt were.

"Return to keeping vigilance on the fire girl."

"All right." Lexa melted with the shadows on the wall.

Zul slammed the door open. "Your powers... they forsake me, just like you, Thunderbolt." His lips contorted into a grin. "If I can't use your powers, I have more options at my disposal."

His breath quickened. The energy's escape slammed his chest. The energy flooded over him and toward his hands. The powers he stole from the siblings were trying to escape him. He grunted as the energy rushed out. Light and electricity flowing to their bodies.

His mouth was agape as he placed a hand on his thigh and leaned over. Chills tingled across the back of his head. He rubbed his lips with his hand and exhaled, uncertain of what to do at the moment. *The Angel of Mercy would never let mercy even touch me... I can't forget the look on his face.*

The day Zul—as Eisen—had been invited to the Fire Kingdom mansion, his mother had been in a bad temper. Sword fighting was true hell. He had been beaten and verbally abused. She had told him to die, only the Divine knew how many times.

Eisen had been in a turmoil. He was going to propose to Sanari. A day which should have been joyous had his nerves wrecked. When Sanari's parents spoke to him with affection and kindness, he could not reciprocate their touch nor their voices.

Before they could tell him anything, iron had unearthed under the mansion like large beasts, his own element betraying him and running rampant. He had no control and no idea how it happened. He tried to stop it but couldn't.

The Fire King and Queen were not dead. They presently resided in the same room in the same condition as Sanari. He couldn't forget the look on the Angel of Mercy's face. He had been there. There was just silence.

Zul's demeanor shifted. His lips a thin line, his jaw rigid as he stood up straight. "I'll have the power. I will fight on."

His lips parted, his eyes flickering with hunger. The jinni aura inside him tumbled through his body and surged a warmth through his veins. It was consuming him. *Get stronger,* it growled. *Find more power, more magic, or else you will remain weak, alone, numb.*

The magic isn't working! It's not right. The light is strong and I want that... Zul Sharr argued back.

When you carry so much self-hate, where is the light? Fight, get power.

Zul Sharr's heart ached. But there was a shard of light inside him. His hope and his love for Sanari.

The jinni aura took over.

He walked up another flight of stairs and crossed a hall to another room. He went over to the hanging egg-shaped chair. He nestled inside it and turned it to face the shelf behind him. His forefinger rested over his lower lip. Power. That's what he needed in order to save his beloved.

*** *** ***

Lexa's eyes widened. Lexa was a shadow on the corner of the wall, across from the front door. She could sense Nezha and Ansam on the other side.

Disgraceful humans. Pitiful angels... She rubbed the scar on her shoulder. "This scar is my mark and mark my scar, we jinn will have our way." Disgust twisted her face. She rolled her eyes and looked up at the stairs. *Zul must be waiting for the fire girl...* The knob creaked as it was twisted. Lexa turned her head.

***

Nezha and Ansam stepped inside the mansion.

The grandiose manner caught Nezha off guard.

She held the Atlas in her hands. The colors and patterns reminded her of the tapestry and buildings back in Morocco. The Atlas was glowing and the map told her to move upstairs. Her own chest filled with heat, her heart dancing. "Ansam..."

Ansam looked up toward the stairs. "I feel it. The orbs are here."

"Why couldn't I feel them? Is it because of the barrier? It was capable of blocking off their aura?"

"I believe so, Lady."

"The orbs are here." Nezha bolted toward the stairs, with Ansam by her side.

CHAPTER 37—RECLAIMED

Nezha's muscles burned, and her head was light. The adrenaline shot her with a dizzied urgency as her feet led her up the stairs.

Ansam's face washed over with concern for the girl.

Nezha felt a pull, a magnetism of the orbs wanting to reunite. Like the moon beckoning the shores to rise and fall, the angel's remaining soul was eager for the embrace.

Nezha opened the door.

Ansam stood in front of her and the chair where Zul sat. Zul Sharr spun around.

"It was about time you got here. The orbs sent you running." He stood as he spoke.

A glass bottle containing the orbs was glowing and shaking. It was sealed on the top with a cork, so the soul couldn't escape.

"Zul... you." Nezha's words barely slipped from her lips as Zul sent his scythe flying toward her.

The flames melted around him and his scythe.

Ansam ran toward Zul and they collided, crashing to the ground.

The room quaked as their bodies tumbled across the floor.

The orbs amalgamated with one another, forming one large pearl within the bottle. It shook, the glass clinking against the shelf.

Nezha ran to the bottle, her hands sweating, but she still managed to keep her grip and with all her force, she slammed the bottle to the floor. The glass shattered into shards glinting like tiny pearls. The orb rushed toward her, engulfing her in a colorful aura. They looked like a flock of birds moving in one formation that rushed toward her, right into her chest.

Zul sat up. He stared at her, mouth agape and then jumped up and pushed Ansam out of the way, pointing a gun at Nezha.

Nezha lifted her hand and pictured the flames like waves of the sea. The fire popped like fireworks, bursting toward Zul.

The gun and the metal pieces he panicked to throw her way, melted out of his hands as he skipped and teetered. Zul hissed from the pain.

She gasped. A steady pulse hummed in her neck. She clenched her chest with one hand. Her mouth opened, but she couldn't find her voice. Her tongue was stuck to the roof of her mouth like she was frozen in fear.

"Lady Nezha!" Ansam turned back to her.

She lost all feeling in her limbs. Dark chains coiled around her body.

Ansam jumped to her after he shot a light at Zul.

Zul fell to the ground on his knees. There was no need for him to run after Ansam or from him.

Ansam spilled a warm light over Nezha, as feathers slipped around the chains twisting around Nezha's body. She was mobilized once again when the chains shattered.

Nezha shivered as the cells in her body reanimated. *What just happened? Why couldn't I move? Did Zul do something to the orbs?*

Zul found his composure. The iron gun formed in his hands from the melted metal.

"Ansam." His voice was bitter and threatening.

"You need to go find the angels," Ansam told her, not facing her as a shield of light rose in front of them like a mirror.

"But, Ansam, what about you?" she cried.

"I'll catch up to you. Now, go!" His eyes glowed white when he looked back at her.

Zul snorted. "Good luck with controlling yourself, fire girl... Nezha."

***

Nezha was reluctant to go, but she ran down the stairs anyway. *What is he talking about?* Flames erupted around her and flew from her hands. She had lost control. The stairs around her were collapsing and being eaten away by the fire. She fell through the steps and screamed as she hit the bottom. She coughed and struggled to stand up. Her bruises stung and her body cried out to her to remain still.

I have to find them. She had to keep moving, no matter how much her body protested. Her fingers clawed the ground as she crawled. She slowly stood up when her fingers began aching, and leaned on a wall.

Nezha yelped as a wall collapsed in front of her. *I can't control it...* She stumbled back. Finding her footing again, she ran toward the end of the hall. She was on the second floor, but whatever door she opened she couldn't find Thunderbolt or Sapphire. She pressed her hand against one door, and the fire consumed it. Nezha took in a shaky breath.

All there was, was heat. Heat from the fire, heat from her pain, heat from her fear and heat from her anger. Her eyes filled with tears, and she clenched her hands into fists. She groaned as the flames intensified around her. *I... can't lose myself.*

Nezha stood up straight. Her tears once touching her face, turned to mist.

***

"You're protective as ever, Ansam." Zul's jaw relaxed, and he smiled.

Ansam cracked a gentle smile. "I know what you want. This wasn't the way to help."

Zul scoffed, "Don't start. I'll see you real soon."

He disappeared as Lexa pulled him away with a curtain of shadows.

Ansam's eyes scanned the shattered glass. "I have to get to Lady Nezha." He tried to sense where she was. He picked up a faint energy field and followed it. Ansam reached up to the place where she had fallen through the stairs.

Flames licked around him. They didn't affect him, but they were engorging on everything they touched, throwing up ashes and smoke wherever the flames distended.

"She must have fallen through."

He went through the hole and spotted her at the end of the hall.

"Lady Nezha," Ansam called out to her. He ran up to her and stood behind her.

"Ansam?" She turned to him, and flames slipped by his head.

"Are you okay?" He lifted his hand.

"Stay back," Nezha pleaded with him, her hand spewing fire.

Flames erupted under his feet, the floor behind him crashing down to the next one under it.

"I can't control the fire." Nezha backed up, her face dull, her eyes heavy.

"Don't lose hope. We need to find Lady Sapphire and Thunderbolt."

"I don't want to hurt you."

"Don't fear. As an angel, I'm made of light. Your fire won't harm me." He smiled gently.

Nezha gulped and then nodded. "I'll try. Ansam? Can you sense them?"

Ansam closed his eyes momentarily. "Yes. They're not here. It's the bottom floor."

"Yeah, I checked every door here."

"Lady, do you want me to carry you?" Ansam asked, his hands up, inviting her.

She looked at him for a few moments. "No, Ansam. There's a lot of struggles ahead of me, I know it. No one can carry me. I have to carry myself there."

A glint of hope grew in her eyes.

"You're right, you are wise."

"I don't know about that." A hesitant chuckle escaped her breath.

The flames danced as they reached the next floor down. Each foot fall brought up ashes and lifted up smoke. Nezha carried destruction with each step.

Ansam raised his arm as part of the ceiling swung toward them.

She touched the ceiling, and it crumpled, ashes dancing by her head.

"Thank you, Ansam." She continued to walk as Ansam followed her.

"I can sense them stronger now."

"That's good. I can't wait to see their smiles again." It was the last flight of stairs. Nezha wanted to run down them, but she knew she had to keep whatever energy she had left.

"Good, Lady Nezha, you need to keep thinking positive. It'll strengthen the fortitude of your soul."

Nezha looked up at the ceiling and then forward, the end of the stairwell staring her down.

"Sapphire and Thunderbolt were the ones I first met when I arrived in Noorenia. Sapphire is like a sister to me and Thunderbolt is like an older brother. They're like my family, Ansam. No, they *are* family."

Ansam smiled, his cheeks flushing.

"I'm glad to know that you think of them as family. We're here for you, to support you," Ansam said.

"Finally, you smiled," Nezha said, looking at him.

"Hmm? Lady, I've smiled before today."

"No, you were only forcing it. This is your real smile." Nezha was at the last step now.

Ansam turned, and his eyes widened, his pace now quickening. He pointed to the second door from them. "They're behind this door."

Nezha ran toward the door, swinging it open.

***

There they were. Sapphire and Thunderbolt lying on the floor, shadows slathered across them like paint.

Nezha's lips parted. She walked toward them.

Ansam reached the door, and his shoulders rose. He was beside Nezha.

"Sapphire, Thunderbolt, I'm here," she said.

Fire spouted around her. She backed up, just as Zul appeared behind the angels.

"Ah, fire girl," he said. I see you've taken destruction wherever you've gone."

"Don't get too close, Zul, or I'll burn you, not like I can control where it goes." A mocking smile placed itself on her face, as she gave a slight shrug.

"We've got time for jokes." Ansam grinned and stood by her.

"Really?" Exasperated, Zul's palm flew to his eyes and slipped down his face.

The ceiling behind them collapsed, blocking their escape route.

While Nezha and Ansam had gone through the barrier, Kayan had tried to bypass it. At one point, he realized the whole forest was blocked off. Zul's hideout had been behind a forest all this time and there was no way for him to get through. The barrier just didn't allow him in.

Kayan formed a cyclone with his hands and it started to drill into the barrier.

***

"You'll only get in the way." Lexa appeared behind Ansam, her shadow hands wrapping around him. She shifted him toward Zul. She now stood beside Zul within a barrier, with Ansam by her side.

"Ansam!" Nezha couldn't divert her fire toward anyone anymore.

"The orbs... you did something to them..." Nezha's knees buckled, her voice cracking.

"Oh, how disgraceful. Fires are hungry. They're eager to claim everything in their path, turning them into lovely ash." Lexa bit her lower lip.

"You should appreciate being free of anyone's control. Fire is free." Zul's eyes gleamed.

Nezha forced herself to take even breaths. Her eyes pleaded, gazing at the two siblings. The words Lamis had said flickered in her mind.

Set the sky on fire.

Nezha had set everything on fire.

Lexa licked her lips. A sinister expression crept up her face.

Nezha's eyes widened.

"No," Ansam said, his voice barely audible.

"Shh. Don't ruin the moment." Lexa turned to him, widening her fingers. In one swift movement, she clenched her hand into a fist. The shadows around his neck tightened, roped around him and constricted his breathing. She turned to Nezha.

"Control your magic, Lexa. I don't want her to destroy the siblings." Zul hissed.

Lexa's eyes narrowed, and her green eyes darkened. She balled her hands into fists. Before Zul could turn to her, she closed her eyes and forced herself to relax her body. "Of course, sire. I'm just enjoying the undulating agony in the room."

Zul looked up and air escaped his nostrils. "Face it, fire girl, we're all on our own. You can't rely on others to make you happy."

"You're wrong, Zul. The ones I love make me happy." She'd once let her eating control her, and her cravings for sweets drown out her sadness. *I miss Lamis so much. But Thunderbolt and Sapphire need my help.*

She stood.

Ansam kept his eyes on Nezha, so intently it was as if he was willing her to do something. But what?

Zul sent a shock-wave of metal toward Nezha. The flames around her ripped away the walls. She was knocked down by a stray piece of metal. Her arms trembled as she struggled to push herself up. She refused to stay down.

"Nezha, just give up. You'll only continue to get hurt." Zul's voice was a whisper.

"No." Her voice was small, but defiant. Nezha held her head low when she fell to her knees.

"Lady Nezha. Please… have… hope." Ansam's voice was enough for Nezha to hear.

"Ansam…" The room was smothered in smoke. Her fingers clawed the ground as she pulled herself toward Sapphire and Thunderbolt.

"I'm so sorry. Oh Creator, please, please help me. I don't want to lose them. I can't give up." She coughed and squinted. Her heart's thrum slowed and the side of her head started to pulse.

Ansam's eyes started to glow. A light shone from him and Lexa stumbled to Zul.

"Seven hells." Zul lunged at Ansam, but the purity of the light made him recoil. "Ugh. The light. I can't get close to him."

"I am hope materialized. Do not let your hope dwindle." Ansam's voice echoed in Nezha's mind.

"My hope?" Nezha lifted her hands closer to Sapphire and Thunderbolt.

"Girl of bravery and redemption, don't fight control. Instead, find reason."

"Reason. Reasons of what?" Nezha asked.

"Don't give up."

"But when I keep trying, I get angry, and those stupid emotions make this fire go wild and then I lost Lamis." Her eyes welled up with tears. "My emotions, I'd try to suppress them—"

Nezha widened her eyes. "My emotions aren't meant to be controlled. They're meant to be expressed."

She thought back to the time when she was with Kayan and her last fight with Zul Sharr. She had felt her emotions freely and the fire hadn't been running wild.

It was flowing. Dancing.

It was like when Lamis showed her the flames in her hands.

She had to fight it. What Zul said was right, that she couldn't rely on others to make her happy. This was all her right now. *I can't ask anyone to do it for me. I suffered by keeping all I feel inside. I only made it worse. He's right.*

She looked over toward Ansam and saw the most radiant smile cross his face.

The fire around her started to diminish. She went through a psyche twist, her heart learning flight. She was the phoenix conquering her fate. It could be changed and she would rise.

White light glowed around her as she embraced the siblings. "If I don't take care of myself, who will? I need to. For my sake, for others. I don't care. I'll get angry. I'll love, I'll be sad, I'll…I'll express it all! Lamis, I won't suppress myself. You'd be proud of me!" her voice tore through the room.

The shadows around them crackled and fizzed, then swelled into smoke.

The light pierced through Lexa's shadow barrier, fracturing through it like cracking ice.

"No! How could they..." Lexa retreated to the shadows.

Zul could hardly move his body. He stared at them, his hands trembling.

Sapphire and Thunderbolt both opened their eyes.

Nezha's face lit up with a smile as she took in the details of their faces.

"Nezha." Sapphire sat up.

"Ow, my head. Whoever hit me, it wasn't funny." Thunderbolt sat up and turned to her.

She chuckled and hugged them, tears dripping down her face.

"Kid. Please don't cry. And, what's going on? Why's there smoke?" Thunderbolt looked over to his sister and then at Ansam who was now behind them.

"There's no time to explain. It's Zul we must deal with," Ansam said.

Nezha and Ansam helped them up. They stood side by side and looked over at Zul.

"Lexa!" Zul turned to look back at her, but she had already disappeared.

"Zul, you have a lot of explaining to do, you bastard." Thunderbolt stood in front of Nezha, his fists electrified.

"Oh, I could say the same."

Nezha pushed Thunderbolt's arms down. She nodded at him as she walked past.

"Hey, kid?" He stood up straight and blinked at her.

A warm yellow light encased her body.

"Eisen..." Nezha's voice was melodic and sounded masculine. Mirkhas. The Angel of Mercy had taken over.

"No. Don't call me that." His voice shook. Zul pressed his hands over his ears.

"My Lord wants you to reach for him. If you walk to him, he will run to you. Ask."

Nezha stood before him. It was as if she were an audience as the angel spoke through her. Zul Sharr looked up at her, and their eyes met. His hands fell to his sides, expression shifting. It was peaceful.

"I want to love. Help me," Eisen said.

Nezha's eyes widened. *That must be Eisen's true need...* She raised her hand to him, becoming conscious again. *There's still time.*

She smiled at him. Not one of happiness, but of warmth.

Even a smile was charity.

Lexa appeared before him, breaking their eye contact.

Sapphire sent light spinning toward her, and Thunderbolt spun into action, as lightning sparked where the jinni stood.

Lexa leaned to the side as the lightning missed her and twirled to Zul, grabbing his hand.

Nezha backed up and bumped into Sapphire. She shook her head.

"Nezha, I'm so sorry." Sapphire held Nezha's shoulders and rubbed them.

Zul's eyes started to burn orange as his helpless demeanor changed into a frown. Before Nezha could even try again to get close enough, he formed a shield of iron around him. "Don't you dare get close to me. Stop getting in my way, fire girl."

"Zul, there's still time to start over," she said. Don't be scared."

"That's what I'm trying to do. Fear is a deceitful leader. It demands subordination. It kept me from finding love. I don't fear others anymore. I'm only scared of myself," Zul said bitterly. The image of Lexa and Zul crumbled away, and they vanished.

The room they were in started to deteriorate as the fire engulfed it.

Thunderbolt kicked away a part of the door that fell in. "We have t' get outta here, before we're buried in all this."

They ran through the door. Charred wood, and pieces of burned stone littered the hall.

Sapphire and Thunderbolt started to cough.

"Hey, are you going to be okay?" Nezha placed a hand on Sapphire's back.

"Yes. We are still weak is all."

"Can anyone see the door?" Ansam asked as he stepped over a fallen beam.

"I can't." Nezha looked around, only fire and ashes scattered about them.

***

Kayan hit the ground. He was breathless. His hands started to cramp and his back was aching. "I think I felt something tear, but it won't let me through." He stood. "No way am I giving up!" Kayan grinned. He rolled up his sleeves. "All right, let's get down to this!"

The wind formed spirals in both of his hands. He yelled as he slammed both of his palms to the barrier. The pressure pushed back at Kayan's arms. His heels dug into the ground as he was being pushed back and it pinched at his palms. "Come on... come on... Let me through!" That's when a crack snaked over it. He gasped. This time the barrier threw him back harder.

Kayan's eyes began glowing like shining emeralds.

***

Flames ate away at the wall as it came crashing down behind them.

Nezha took a step forward. "A breeze." It flew by her hands and then she heard the voice.

"Nezha? Can you hear me?"

"Kayan," she breathed out.

"What? Where is he?" Thunderbolt asked.

"I hear him. He couldn't go through the barrier. I think he found a way in. Are you here, Kayan?" Nezha called out.

"No. I was able to find an opening. Follow my voice and the wind."

"What is he saying, Nezha?" Sapphire asked.

"He said to follow the wind. I can feel it. Let's go."

The others followed her.

"I see the door." Nezha turned a corner.

"Good. I smell something burning." Kayan called out.

"Yeah, I'll explain later." Nezha cracked a smile.

A door burned to ashes at her touch.

They all ran out. The wood creaked, and the fire crackled and hissed as it turned in on itself.

They were now walking on the cemented pathway.

"It's straight ahead. Kayan, stand back," Nezha warned.

CHAPTER 39—WHOLEHEARTED

Nezha first emerged from the barrier, followed by the siblings and Ansam.

"Kayan!" She fell to her knees right in front of him.

"You're all back." Kayan nearly jumped. His arms flew up to embrace her, but then he swept his fingers through his hair. His cheeks flushed. "Ow."

Nezha brushed the dirt off her knees.

Thunderbolt grinned. Kayan's eyes met his and widened at him like two beacons.

Thunderbolt winked back at him.

"Thank you for helping us out back there." Ansam smiled as he grabbed Kayan's hand and embraced him.

"No problem." Kayan smiled.

"Ansam. I am so glad you are okay," Sapphire said as she smiled at him.

Ansam smiled, his cheeks reddening.

"Yeah, I was worried sick." Thunderbolt grabbed Ansam into a hug.

"Well, your shock helped me wake up." Ansam looked at Thunderbolt and then at Sapphire.

"You all look so exhausted. How about we catch a ride on the updraft?" Kayan smiled at them.

"Good idea." Nezha tilted her head and relaxed her shoulders.

***

"You know, there's something different about you, Nezha." Kayan turned to her on the updraft.

"Well, I'll tell you when we're not eight feet in the air."

"Aww, zaan. Okay."

Nezha laughed.

"It's good to have you back." Kayan looked forward.

"Yeah, it's good to be out of there." Nezha could see the city ahead of her.

***

The evening rolled in as they stood at the door to Tasa's place. They rang the door bell.

"Welcome home." Tasa answered the door, her smile warm and inviting.

507

"Thank you." Nezha walked toward her and embraced her. "It's good to see a happy face."

"Thank you, Tasa. Hope you were doing well." Sapphire was next to hug her.

At Tasa's feet, Comet ran through her legs and meowed up at Nezha.

"Comet!" Nezha went to her knees, as Comet raised her tail and started to purr. Nezha held her in her arms, fingers running through Comet's silken fur. Comet nudged Nezha's palms and then went to her hind legs and rubbed her head against Nezha's, licking her cheek.

"Wow, well, Comet missed you." Kayan grinned and gave a gentle swipe behind Comet's ears.

"Yes, she's been a good cat. She meowed for a while after you left, but then accompanied me wherever I was in the house." Tasa took a longer look at them and gasped. "You're all beat up. Okay, go sit down."

"All right, *mom*." Thunderbolt grinned and sat on the couch as the others followed.

"Ouch." Kayan cringed as he sat down and rubbed his side.

Nezha sighed, and sat beside Sapphire and then glanced at Kayan with a worried look.

"How much pain are you feeling?" Tasa asked as she stood before him.

"It's okay. I'm just feeling achy all over. Mostly my arms and back."

"I'll make sure I prepare some medicine for you. You'll have to apply a paste and take some internally." Tasa walked over to a shelf and grabbed a pen and a sheet that looked like gray glass. She was writing notes.

"Wow, you're a great doctor too." Thunderbolt grinned at her and turned to Kayan. "If you don't want Tasa t' help, you can ask Nezha t' nurture you."

Kayan's face flushed.

Nezha raised a brow and smacked Thunderbolt's shoulder.

"I didn't mean it." He shrugged and pouted. "I still feel a little dizzy."

"Sure, that's what it is." Nezha shook her head and smiled.

"Nah, really. I think it was from that stupid stuff that made sis and I faint." Thunderbolt rubbed the side of his head.

"Oh. Yeah." Nezha rubbed his shoulder. "Sorry for hitting you."

"What happened t' us anyway?" Thunderbolt pushed his back into the couch.

Nezha recounted what had happened to them and her eyebrows furrowed. She closed her eyes for a few moments.

"For the sake of the Divine, I can't believe it. He just took us captive that easily?" Thunderbolt raked his fingers through his hair.

"At least we were able to get you two out of there," Kayan said and blew out a sigh.

"Yeah, and if it wasn't for your wind, I don't think we would have made it out in time." Nezha turned to Kayan.

"That's correct. You said you could hear him," Sapphire said in a quiet voice.

"It's really strange. Nezha's fire doesn't hurt me, but Zul Sharr's iron is able to hurt us. And I was able to talk to her through the crack in the barrier." Kayan glanced at Nezha.

Thunderbolt sighed loudly and changed the air in the room. Electricity sparked around his fingers. "I'm still dizzy, hungry and my wings are aching."

Tasa left the room and after a few minutes she returned with two small boxes filled with dried herbs, tinctures in amber glasses, bottles of liquid medicines in oranges and reds, pastes in steel containers and bandages.

"I know most of you act tough, but it's time for treating your aches and pains." Tasa smiled warmly at the group. "Don't worry, you can cry if you want to," she said as she walked toward Thunderbolt.

"Me, cry? Pfft."

Tasa applied a paste on his shoulder, and he yelped.

Nezha and Kayan chuckled.

After everyone was treated, Tasa stretched and walked toward the kitchen. "I'll make dinner."

"About time." Thunderbolt smirked.

"Lady Tasa, allow me to help you." Ansam offered.

"Oh, well…" Tasa stammered, an embarrassed smile appearing on her face.

Ansam smiled as he walked with her to the kitchen.

"Thank you,"

"Ansam's such a gentleman." Nezha chimed. "And I have good news."

Sapphire leaned in a touch. She was sitting on Nezha's right.

"The soul is whole." Nezha looked over at everyone, their mouths agape in astonishment and their eyes gleaming with joy.

"No way! That's amazing." Kayan placed his hands on the table and then cringed. It seemed his hands still ached.

"Nezha, that's great news. I'm so proud of you."
Sapphire pulled Nezha close to her and hugged her.

"That explains the light from you earlier. I second what
Sapphire said. You did great, Nezha." Thunderbolt patted
her shoulder.

"Huh? You didn't call me kid," Nezha teased.

"Yeah, you're tough." Thunderbolt glanced at the table.

She poked his shoulder and grinned. "Well, it wasn't all
me. Ansam helped. He had me realize I shouldn't give up.
It kept me from losing hope. All this time I've been
wanting to control my emotion, suppress them. Even when
I was scared, I'd just hide it. When, in reality they've been
the fuel for my powers. I just need to express myself,
without letting my anger get out of control." Nezha looked
down at Comet, who sat in her lap and rested.

"Oh, Lady Nezha, it was all you. All I did was grow
your hope, and you acted on it," Ansam said.

Thunderbolt smiled. "You've really grown. Ah, zaan,
they grow up so fast." Then he tensed. "That means we
need t' find the angel's body."

The room quieted for a few moments.

"You're right. Do we even have a lead on where it could
be?" Nezha faced Sapphire. "I have the whole angel's soul
inside me, but it doesn't belong to me."

It still comforted Nezha's soul somewhat, but she could feel it wanted to leave her heart.

"I'm afraid I don't know. Zul Sharr cursed the angel." Sapphire shook her head.

"We should stay positive," Kayan said.

"Speaking of Zul, what happened between you and him?" Thunderbolt's eyes softened.

"Yeah, I remember I smelled something burning." Kayan recalled.

"Zul had the remaining collection of orbs," Nezha said. I'm fortunate that I found the strength to accept my aunt's passing."

Sapphire placed a hand on her shoulder.

"May the Creator smile upon her and upon her peace." Thunderbolt's voice was soft as he looked at the table.

"Ameen. It still hurts to know she's passed on. But I know her memories, her love and my love for her, won't ever be gone. I need to move forward." Nezha played with Comet's ears and then felt Kayan's gaze on her. She looked up.

"And we'll be here to support you through it."

"Thank you. Sapphire, Thunderbolt, you have family waiting for you in Unicorn Valley. I don't want you to lose your hope either."

Thunderbolt turned to her, his expression full of longing. "You're right. One day."

"I want to check on the state of the unicorns in the valley again and see them one more time. Zul Sharr tried to take our powers, so perhaps he was trying to use them for Sanari, since he loves her and he has been talking about wanting her back. There is a possibility that Sanari is alive and that may mean our family and friends in the valley are also alive."

Thunderbolt raised his brows at Sapphire. "Yeah, I want to know too, sis." He clenched his right hand into a fist. "It's Eisen that loves her. When I was a guard, he didn't tell me too much, but I remember one day he told me he wanted to marry the Princess Sanari. He was such a nice kid. He was so kind to others, even the servants."

"Brother, why didn't you tell us before?" Sapphire turned to him.

"I didn't want you t' worry about me, okay? You had enough responsibilities as a guardian and mom and dad and our friends relying on you."

Sapphire's lips quirked.

"I don't want us to be so serious. We've been through too much and need to celebrate. We achieved something. I know there's still more to do, but before we get caught up in another mess, let's try to enjoy ourselves." Kayan tipped his head and tapped Thunderbolt's back.

Thunderbolt gave a slow blink and smiled. "You're right zaan. I'm supposed t' be the life of the party. When we have one."

Nezha placed a hand out and hugged Sapphire. They shared a look, and Sapphire smiled softly in return.

"Dinner is ready." Tasa held a plate as she placed it in the center.

"Enjoy, everyone." Ansam's face lit up with an inviting smile as he held two plates in his hands.

"Oh wow, you have outdone yourself, Ansam." Sapphire smiled at him.

"Thank you." He blushed as he served everyone their meals.

"Come on, Ansam, sit with us, and let's all eat together." Kayan grinned at him.

Ansam nodded energetically and sat beside Kayan.

"C'est magnifique. You're both great cooks." Nezha took a bite of the food, the flavor blossoming in every mouthful.

"Hey, I'm a great cook too ya know. If I wasn't in pain, I would have cooked something amazing too." Thunderbolt rolled his eyes.

"Stop pouting, you big baby." Nezha chuckled.

"Say many…what?" Kayan raised his brows at her.

"Oh." Nezha chuckled. "It's French. I'm pretty much saying it's great. When I get really excited, my mind sort of shifts to it."

He grinned at her.

Comet jumped out of Nezha's lap and headed to a dish where Tasa placed her meal.

"Nezha told me you liked rabbit, so here it is. Enjoy it." Tasa returned to the table and took a seat.

Everyone ate their meals. They smiled, laughed and were actually enjoying themselves. Everyone sounded so happy. Nezha could see the glow on their faces. She could tell they never wanted it to change. *She* never wanted it to change.

***

They headed outside to the pond out back.

"The sun is setting soon." Tasa walked beside Nezha.

"Yeah, it's nice to be outside to enjoy the scenery." She held Comet in her arms. The sky was cast in a dusty blue.

"Let's put it here." Kayan and Thunderbolt placed a blue blanket on the grass.

Ansam sat down as everyone found their place.

Nezha let Comet down. She meowed at her and then lay on her belly beside her.

"Nezha, how are you doing?" Kayan sat next to her, facing his shoulders toward her.

"I'm well now." Nezha smiled. Their gazes lingered.

Kayan mirrored her. "Good. I didn't want to see you like a ghul."

"A ghul, really?"

"Yeah, you know, all…ugh, so tired. Nezha want rest or I burn you." Kayan put his hands up, trying his best to speak in a creepy voice.

Nezha lifted her palms and swayed them at him, flames rising up. "Careful, now."

They both shared a laugh.

The sun lowered on the horizon, and shades of red and pink tinted the sky and dappled the clouds in a deep purple.

"It's nice, isn't it?" Thunderbolt sighed.

"Sure is." Kayan reclined, leaning back on his hands.

"Beautiful." Sapphire breathed out.

Nezha turned to the others and smiled. "So, who's up for sleep? I'm exhausted."

Sapphire turned to her. "Nezha, my girl, try not to be hard on yourself, or I will be hearing it from Thunderbolt."

"Oh yeah, can't forget Mr. Grumpy."

"I heard that." Thunderbolt's head flocked with countless pops of electricity.

"Sleep's right. I'm exhausted." Kayan stretched.

"Yes, and I will have to head back to the Iron Kingdom. The queen and king must be worried," Ansam said.

"Yeah, I almost forgot. Do you need an escort?" Thunderbolt walked over to Ansam and rested a hand on his shoulder.

"Don't worry. I can manage it."

"Give us a call when you get back, all right?"

Ansam smiled. "Of course, I will. Good night."

"Good night, Ansam, and thanks again." Nezha waved to him.

"No problem, Lady Nezha. Sleep well."

***

Morning light poured through the windows as Nezha slipped into her clothes and packed up her belongings.

"Good morning." Sapphire entered her room and then smiled.

"Oh. Good morning." Nezha turned to her as she zipped her bag.

"Have you packed up all your belongings?"

"Yeah, I have everything I need."

She and Sapphire walked down the stairs, where the others waited for her in the living room.

Kayan stood as soon as he saw her. "Nezha." His voice was soft as he walked up to her side and stuffed his hands in his pockets.

"Hey, Kayan." Nezha flashed him a coy smile.

"Nezha, you all ready?" Thunderbolt stood as Tasa walked into the living room.

"Yeah." She nodded.

"Aww, Nezha, do you really need to go back now?" Tasa asked as she hugged her.

"I need to catch up with school and I need to see family and friends. When I get back, we can find the angel's body."

"I suppose you're right. I sound selfish..." Tasa lowered her head.

"No, it's okay. I know how you feel." Nezha gave a gentle squeeze to Tasa's shoulder.

"Yes. We will remain vigilant. If we can find a lead about the angel's body or Zul Sharr's next moves, you will know the details," Sapphire said.

"So, I just need to wait then?" Nezha asked.

"That's gonna be tough." Thunderbolt grinned, and Nezha elbowed him. "Hey. I know how you feel too you know. Waiting doesn't help. But if you keep busy, you'll be fine."

"I..." Nezha sighed. "Yeah. I *am* going to be busy with school and family. It's going to be Eid in a few months too."

"The angel's soul is safe with you. Like Sapphire said, we'll try to find a lead on where his body is. And keep an eye on Lexa," Kayan said.

"Yeah. Lexa's the one who cursed the orbs. It made me sick the way she looked at me. She was too excited about it." Nezha cringed.

"She'll be our problem. You better take care of yourself and enjoy your time." Thunderbolt grinned and patted her head.

"Don't tell me what to do," Nezha said with a playful tone and messed up Thunderbolt's hair.

"Since the soul will not be in Noorenia, the jinni activity might not increase," Sapphire said.

"The Angel of Mercy is your link to the Divine, right? So, is it really good for me to return home with it?"

"Noorenia has my brother, Ansam and myself to safeguard it. We are guardians, after all. Although, the angel would have helped us in bringing the heartbeat of Noorenia back to its normal pulse. I don't want to burden you, Nezha. You have a life in your dimension, and we can't steal that from you."

"Saphy's right. Besides, we plan on keeping a connection with the other countries. We'll make sure the Iron Kingdom has contact with the mayors of each city and the royalty of each country. Sis thought of everything." Thunderbolt winked.

Sapphire's eyes welled up with tears.

"Sapphire…" Nezha opened her arms and Sapphire embraced her.

"If you ever need to talk about something, I will be a call away," Sapphire said.

"Yeah. Same goes for you." Nezha held on a bit longer.

Soon, Sapphire stood beside Thunderbolt.

"Nezha, don't stress about us." Kayan and Nezha stood apart from the others.

"Okay, but you're always worrying, so try not to, huh?" Nezha tilted her head.

"I can't promise it." His expression softened and a look of concern washed over him. After a few moments, he grinned. "Nezha, we'll be here when you get back."

She beamed at him. "Of course, you think anything could stop me?" Flames spun around her freely, the glow glittering in her eyes like embers as she walked over to the pond.

***

Nezha stood before everyone. They were huddled at the door. Thunderbolt elbowed Kayan, and Kayan pushed him back. Typical.

It made her grin.

Nezha waved at them and they waved back. She whispered her intention to go back home. Comet's head was nestled under her chin as she dove deep into the pond.

For the next few months, she'd be going to university, tending to the flower shop and living as a somewhat normal girl. What a journey. It was different now. She had a stronger bond with her parents and a better grasp on her fire wielding.

She'd miss them. All of them.

Kayan's joy. Sapphire's wisdom. Thunderbolt's stubbornness. Tasa's compassion. Ansam's hope. Even though Nezha knew she'd return again, it was a bittersweet moment. She wanted to change the world. She'd do it. They'd do it. She'd hold onto courage and her smile. She wasn't afraid when she'd be with them. She was going to be true to herself.

522

Noorenian Alphabet

A = 1 M = 3ɹ Y = ρ

B = 3 N = ⊓ Z = ⅄

C = ⑤ O = 9

D = ⅅ P = ♭

E = E Q = ℈

F = ℙ R = ५

G = ⑤ S = ℈

H = ⊞ T = ℉

I = ḻ U = ℧

J = ₹ V = ⑤

K = ⅄ W = ℘

L = ⅊ X = ℗

Acknowledgements

Thank you to Allah SWT, for all you've done for me and all the people you've brought into my life. Thank you to the community of WriteOn. When I was ready to share my story with the outside world, I went in search for an online community and found a place of encouragement and growth in a field of kindness. We were like a small village. Even if the site is gone, your support will always remain. I won't ever forget you all. R.C. Fletcher, thank you for being my cheerleader, my friend, for finding me on WriteOn. Thank you for helping create what we all lovingly now call Bearwood Forest. Thank you, K.V. Wilson, for reading and helping to polish all the versions of my story. Thank you for all your overwhelming kindness. Thank you Staci Hudson, I won't forget your love for my story and your encouragement. Thank you Xanxa Raggatt for always supporting me and uplifting me. If it wasn't for all of you and your loving support and encouragement, I wouldn't have the story I've written today. That leap was a wonderful one. I grew wings. Thank you all so much. It happened. It's a book now. Let's always keep a path open to Bearwood Forest.

Thank you to my editors: Mariam, Jeni Chappelle and Rachel Wollaston, who gave me hope and support. Thank you so much for believing in me and my story.

Thank you to my little brothers who told me they were proud of me. I love you.

A big thank you to Karuna Riazi, whose tweets led me to the amazing people I know now on Twitter. Your words were inspiring, they were bold and they were asking the right questions to answers I'd been hoping to see one day. Not just about the world of books and getting published, but about humanity, about the rights and needs of those who are marginalized, invisible, or taken to a stage in the media to be villainized.

Thank you to my wonderful supporters, beta readers and friends on book twitter. I couldn't have done it without all your encouragement and kindness. You gave me hope. Thank you, Maria, you're like a sister to me and I can't wait for your book to be out there. You are a light and so sweet. Thank you, Priyanka Tasleem, for all the love. Thank you dear Angel K. Thank you Mariam, I swear you're like my long-lost sister. Thank you sweet behena for everything. Thank you Adiba. Thank you Shoohada Janiya, sis, for being there for me. Thank you, Eliza Benerjee, for your encouragement and kindness. Thank you Eshana Ranasinghe, for all the fan art and tolerating all my random DMs, and loving Lexa and the villain squad so much. Thank you, Laura Weymouth, for believing in me. Thank you Merve Karan for reading the story and your support. Thank you, Mary E Roach you gave me hope and made me so happy for believing in me. Thank you, Kiara Zuri, for helping make the world of Noorenia make more sense. Thank you for being one of my beta readers, ERK @er_reads, Eram Rizwan and Alwia Al Hassan. Thank you for your love, kindness and support Erin Kinsella. Thank you, Ryan Ramkelawan, for always being so supportive and your uplifting encouragement. Thank you Naley Gonzalez, I hope you love those InuYasha easter eggs.

Thank you Sumaiyah Tasneem, you encouraged me so much. Thank you Christine E. Schulz for all your kindness. Thank you Umairah for all your help, your support and push. Thank you Anum Rajput, your excitement, your love and overwhelming kindness and gifs always made my day. Thank you to Kosta at The Hero Program, I wouldn't have had the courage if it wasn't for you and the wonderful heroes!

Thank you to those who looked over my book for critiques: Loretta Chefchaoni, Erin J Cotter.

Thank you to my sweet cousin Sana Shaheen Sikander, who gave me translations for Pashto.

And most of all, thank you to all the readers. I hope my story gives you hope and you find great things inside your heart. I'm blessed to have you all.

About The Author

SAHIRA JAVAID is a YA fantasy writer and poetess from Ottawa who shares her poems on her Twitter page and her website. Fond of animals, nature and learning, she passes time reading about the world around her, nature's healing ways, chatting with friends and making others smile and laugh every chance she gets. You can find her on Twitter as Bittersweetbook. *Crowning Soul* is Sahira's debut novel.